*Dan Moren*

# THE NOVA INCIDENT

## THE GALACTIC COLD WAR, BOOK III

ANGRY
ROBOT

ANGRY ROBOT
An imprint of Watkins Media Ltd

Unit 11, Shepperton House
89-93 Shepperton Road
London N1 3DF
UK

*angryrobotbooks.com*
*twitter.com/angryrobotbooks*
Bombtastic

An Angry Robot paperback original, 2022

Cover by Tom Shone
Set in Meridien

ISBN 978 0 85766 945 2
Ebook ISBN 978 0 85766 946 9

Printed and bound in the United Kingdom by TJ Books Limited

9 8 7 6 5 4 3 2 1

MIX
Paper from responsible sources
FSC
www.fsc.org   FSC® C013056

*To those who keep the lights on and the mind fed:*
*librarians everywhere.*

# CHAPTER 1

Simon Kovalic was halfway through his grocery shopping when the explosion hit.

He'd been picking up some bread from a stand at the Salaam farmer's market on Oluo Plaza when there had been a brilliant flash of light; his head jerked up just in time for the deafening thunderclap that had followed.

Even unconsciously braced against the shockwave that his instincts knew was coming, he felt the loaf knocked from his hand. Debris littered the pavement all around him with a sizzling pitter-patter. Through the ringing in his ears he could just make out raised voices, but he could clearly feel the vibration of footsteps pounding away from the crowded market.

He leaned on the farmstand and wiped a sleeve across his eyes. The bread and pastries, pristine and mouthwatering just a moment ago, were now dusted with a fine layer of grit; more drifted through the air like ashen snow.

Behind the table, the vendor was on his backside, eyes widened to their whites in a face streaked with grime. A trickle of blood worked its way down the side of his head – nothing serious, Kovalic's battlefield intuition immediately told him, but the man was in shock.

Reaching out a hand, he opened his mouth to say

something encouraging, then immediately started coughing as he took in a lungful of the same grit. He spat onto the ground, dark against the fine dust.

Then something automatic took over and he was in motion. It took him a second to realize where his instincts were pushing him, but his peripheral vision had already registered the cloud of black smoke roiling from the upper stories of a nearby building.

Dimly, he felt his sleeve buzz, glanced down at the smart fabric display in time to see EMERGENCY ALERT splashed across it in red, then wiped it away with a palm. No shit.

A steadily increasing number of sirens filled the air and Kovalic looked up to see fast-response drones with flashing red lights swarming the building, spraying flame-retardant foam at the source of the fire.

People rippled past him like a wave, stumbling or running away from the source of the explosion as he threaded his way upstream through them.

Some still cowered behind stalls, and Kovalic did his best to check on them as he made his way past. Most were uninjured, more shocked and scared than anything else. A few had lacerations or minor cuts like the baker's, but none seemed to require more serious intervention. They'd keep until emergency services arrived.

The building hadn't been so lucky. As he stepped out past the last of the stalls and into the open plaza, he got his first good look at the explosion site.

A mid-height office building, around fifteen stories, mainly constructed of dark burnished metal, interspersed with panels of tinted glass. Unremarkable in any other way – he wouldn't have looked twice at it, had it not been for the thick smoke pouring from a floor about halfway up. By its look it was mostly offices; his breath caught before he remembered with relief that it was early Saturday morning, which hopefully meant there hadn't been too many people inside.

Movement caught his eye: a red groundtruck with flashing lights pulled up at the base of the building, offloading fire personnel in heavy insulated suits, masks, and helmets. Damn fast response, Kovalic thought in appreciation as they formed up and headed into the building. They'd even beat the security forces to the punch.

He approached the fire brigade, waiting for them to notice him, but they had mostly disappeared into the building, leaving only a couple of figures behind, anonymous in their emergency gear.

"Whoa, whoa, whoa," said one of them, a man with dark eyes whose voice was muffled through his mask, as he stepped in front of Kovalic. "Where do you think you're going, pal?"

"Came to see if I could help," he rasped, then coughed again. "I'm Commonwealth military. I've got field medic training."

He thought he saw the man's brow furrow behind the transparent face shield.

"I'm going to need you to step back, sir," said the firefighter, putting a hand on Kovalic's chest. "The structure is unsafe, and there may be another explosive device."

Kovalic blinked as he stepped backwards. Explosive device? He looked up at the black cloud which had begun to filter throughout the blue sky, obscuring the sun with a fine haze. Salaam was the safest place he'd ever lived. Even when the conflict with the Illyrican Empire had been a shooting war, the fighting had never reached Terra Nova – it had been largely insulated ever since the Commonwealth had declared the planet its capital, almost two decades ago.

He started to open his mouth to ask how they knew it was a bomb, but at that moment several of the fire brigade came out of the building, escorting a handful of civilians in suits. Their clothes were ragged and torn and many of them had blood dripping down their stunned faces as they stumbled into the light.

A handful of security vehicles and three ambulances pulled up in the plaza, the latter disgorging blue-suited EMTs with military efficiency; they quickly took charge of the injured from the fire brigade. An additional pair of fire engines pulled up, producing their own water cannons and some drones. The security officers quickly started setting up a cordon, pushing the crowds back.

Kovalic stared up at the fire, something in the back of his head still rolling back and forth like one of those puzzles where you had to get a little metal ball into a hole. This seemed *wrong*. Like reality was askew on its axis.

He looked back at the initial team of firefighters, but they were loading up on their truck, their work of evacuating the building apparently complete. One of them, a tall slender man by his silhouette, hung back, still looking up at the building with an uncertain air, but as he turned, he made eye contact with Kovalic through his faceplate.

The dark eyes were cool and collected, not betraying anything, but Kovalic thought he detected a quirk of the eyebrows, almost in recognition.

His breath drew in deep. No, it couldn't be. His brain was still muddled, playing tricks on him. He squeezed his eyes shut for a moment, then opened them for a closer look, but the firefighter was gone, the truck already starting to pull away from the scene.

Kovalic looked around the plaza, at all the people rushing to and fro – the uniformed personnel, the walking wounded, the weeping, the shocked – and his mind flashed through all the battlefields he'd stood on in the past twenty-odd years.

He found himself sinking to a nearby bench, his head in his hands. This shouldn't be happening. Not here. The firefighter must have been wrong – it couldn't have been a bomb. Must have been an accident. A power overload. Unstable fuel cells. Who would bomb an office building in the downtown district on a weekend morning?

His sleeve vibrated again. He thought he'd silenced it after the first emergency alert, but when he glanced down he saw the display was garbled, pixelated with visual artifacts, as though it were a glass screen that had shattered after being dropped on the floor.

After a moment, the pixels started to reorganize themselves, unscrambling into a series of irregular letters, like someone had cut them out of an old magazine. And as each word became clear Kovalic's stomach sank deeper and deeper, the conviction that this wasn't some unfortunate accident solidified into cold hard fact.

He stared at the screen, the three words written there, and with them his entire reality tilted, in ways that seemed almost imperceptible, but irrevocable. And as he glanced about, he saw the same look on faces all around him, as others looked down at their own buzzing sleeves.

Out of the corner of his eye, he caught sight of scrolling video signs attached to nearby buildings, the kind usually reserved for weather reports or headline news or ads. But now they were also repeating the same three words as the ones on his sleeve, over and over, a never-ending chorus.

SIC SEMPER TYRANNIS.

# CHAPTER 2

"Whoa," said Eli Brody as the acceleration from even the slight tap to the throttle pushed him back into the pilot's seat. "This thing is *moving*."

Beside him, in the co-pilot's seat, Cassie Engel's smile was all kinds of smug. "Boosted the lift/mass ratio." Not for the first time, Eli silently thanked whatever quirk of fate had assigned her as the team's resident mechanic; the performance she'd managed to eke out of the *Cavalier* had pushed it way past its baseline specs. And, given how critical the ship was when the team was in the field, even a hairline improvement could end up saving their lives.

"By almost a factor of five," chimed in another voice from behind them. If it weren't for the g-forces keeping all of them in their chairs, Cary Maldonado would have no doubt been poking their head up in between the two of them, eager as a puppy. After Mal had helped Eli and Sergeant Tapper escape the *Queen Amina* six months ago, the sergeant's endorsement had gotten them hired as the team's resident technical expert, a role that they'd taken on with a gusto only matched by their genuine enthusiasm for their colleague's work. "I don't know where she found more headroom in the intermix, but she did it!"

Cassie waved a hand. "There's always room if you know where to look."

Eli eased off the throttle, watching the white blurs in front of them resolve once again into clouds. The weather over Terra Nova's northern continent was often stormy, but today the skies were blue as his sister Meghann's eyes, with nothing but fluffy white pillows of cumulus.

"Gotta admit, the *Cav* has never flown better," he said. "She's come a long way since that seized patrol ship they requisitioned for me almost a year ago." *Jesus, has it been that long?* Sometimes it seemed like just yesterday that he'd been dragooned into the Special Projects Team, other days it felt more like a lifetime – and with everything he'd been through since joining the SPT, it more or less was.

"We've made a few other modifications," said Mal. "I mean, Cassie did most of the hard work, replacing some burned out waveguides and retuning the central reactor."

"Mal's just being modest," said Cassie. "They spent almost as much time rewiring the cockpit systems as I did with grease on my hands."

"I *did* upgrade the core OS to the latest version to patch some nasty firmware bugs. And installed some encrypted communications gear that will probably come in handy. But!" Mal just avoided clapping their hands together in glee. "My *favorite* is the new transponder system. Check this out." They spun around and tapped a few commands on the flight engineer's console. "Usually transponder codes are burned in, to make them harder to fake. That's why every time you need a new cover for a mission, you have to swap out the chips. But I managed to replicate that with a software-programmable unit. So, now you can broadcast a clone of any transponder the *Cav* has seen." With a flourish, they punched the execute button.

In front of Eli, a holographic window popped up, alerting him to the change, and noting that the ship was now broadcasting as a Commonwealth bulk freighter.

Eli choked back a cough. *That's like a half-dozen class five Intersystem Traffic violations there. Probably ten years of jail time, easy.* Then again, the punishment for espionage was probably way, way worse.

"Pretty cool, right? Man, the transponder system is so old. You totally shouldn't be able to hack it this easy." Mal shook their head.

The tech's enthusiasm was so genuine that it couldn't help but be infectious, and a grin threatened to split Eli's face, but he just managed to hold it back. *Technically, I think I'm supposed to be the responsible one here.*

"With this system, I could make it look like the secretary-general of the Commonwealth's personal transport. I'm telling you: nobody would know the difference. Oh! And I cracked the Illyrican IFF system too – check this out." Mal slid their fingers over the controls and the holo display switched to the familiar image of an L-37 fighter, the backbone of the Imperial Navy. Eli's heart ached as he looked over the ship's angular lines, tracing the familiar pattern of its weaponry. More than six years – or, again, depending on how you counted, a lifetime – since he'd flown one, and he could still remember every inch of the cockpit like it was his childhood bedroom.

"Attention, unidentified fighter!" blared the radio suddenly. "This is Yamanaka Base Tower. Emergency lockdown protocols are now in place. Transmit a clearance code immediately or our automated systems will open fire."

*Lockdown protocols?* That was weird. Had Eli missed

a scheduled drill? He sure as hell didn't have any sort of clearance code for this.

"A little too real, I guess," he said under his breath. "Okay, Mal. You've scared the poor flight controllers enough for today. Turn that thing off."

"Oh, sure. Sorry. One sec." Mal swung back to the controls and tapped a few buttons.

Nothing happened.

"Huh," said the tech, frowning at the panel. "Getting an error thrown back here. Hold on."

"Unidentified fighter, this is your final warning," said the flight controller. "Transmit a clearance code immediately. Our systems are acquiring now."

A red TARGET LOCK warning appeared on Eli's display, along with a steady, high-pitched tone. If this *was* a drill, they were taking it to the extremes. And Eli didn't want to wait and see exactly how far the verisimilitude went.

"Mal, turn that thing off *now.*" He flipped the transmit switch. "Yamanaka Base Tower, this is ST321. We're having a malfunction with our transponder system, but we are definitely authorized to be here. Disengage target lock!"

"ST321, Tower. Lockdown protocols require clearance code. You have ten seconds."

"Shit," swore Eli, slapping the cutoff switch. *"Mal."*

The tech's fingers interlaced in their short, dark hair, tugging at it in frustration. "It's not responding! I'll need to reboot the entire transponder system."

"Will that take longer than ten seconds?"

"Uh… probably?"

Eli gritted his teeth. "In that case, don't bother. Everybody's strapped in, right?" *Looks like we're about to find out exactly what these upgrades can do.*

MISSILE LAUNCH the console blared at him in stark, bright red letters.

"Cassie, get me a read on those inbound!"

Wide-eyed, the mechanic looked down at the display in front of her. "What? I don't know–"

"Middle toggle, right side."

Cassie found the button and hit it, producing a holodisplay just in time for Eli to see two missiles closing fast from below. *Ground launch*, he had just enough time to think as he opened the *Cav*'s throttle, throwing all three of them back into their seats.

At least the response time on the *Cavalier*'s upgraded engines was better than the missiles' ability to make a sharp turn. Blue sky blurred above them as the ship punched through a cloud. They'd bought some time, but only a little. At least the tower hadn't scrambled interceptors yet. The *Cav*'s performance might be good for a patrol ship, but if they had to go up against armed fighters, even drones, this was going to be over faster than every chess game Eli had ever tried to play.

"Cass? Where are they?"

"Coming about. Trailing us aft."

"Tell me this new engine tuning means we can outrun them."

Her gulp was audible. "I think so."

*Not the ringing endorsement I was looking for.* "Mal? How's it going?" He risked a glance over his shoulder to see that the tech had the engineering panel flipped open and was buried up to their elbows in wiring. "Working on it! I need a minute."

"I don't know if we have a minute!"

"Eli!" said Cassie, stabbing a finger at the display, where

the two blips were moving rapidly from the aft. "They're almost on top of us!"

"Jamming countermeasures. Top left."

Mal looked up from their panel. "Uh, is this a bad time to mention that the jamming package piggybacks on the transponder system?"

Eli stared at the tech. "Are you fucking *kidding me*?"

"So it is a bad time."

Without a second thought, Eli slammed the yoke forward, putting the *Cavalier* into a steep dive; there was a split second of weightlessness, a calm before the storm, and then they were slammed back against their restraints. *See if you can follow that one, you automated buckets of bolts.*

"Tell me there's a system on this boat that *does* work," he said through gritted teeth.

Cassie exchanged a glance with Mal. "Well, we did put in an escape pod. But it's not designed to work in atmo."

*And we're not abandoning the damn ship.*

*Although…*

"Mal, can you just power down the entire transponder system?"

"But if we do that, we'll be flying blind–"

"Yes or no?"

"Well, yes."

"Get ready to do it on my mark. Cassie, when I tell you, launch the escape pod."

The mechanic opened her mouth to respond, then closed it with a nod.

The ship punched through another cloud and the equatorial content of Terra Nova lay before them, all mottled greens and browns. As it grew closer, Eli could start to see the black ribbons of roads, the glimmer of the sun off lakes and ponds, and the occasional carefully squared-off field of crops; on the horizon gleamed the skyscrapers of Salaam, the planet's capital.

All of it growing steadily larger.

WARNING blinked on the screen. RAPID ALTITUDE LOSS.

*Kind of the point.* He'd known Cassie long enough to trust that she didn't oversell her work. But this was going to be tight.

He watched the altimeter tick down, feeling the g-forces pressing at him even through the ship's inertial compensators. Casting his eyes about, he saw a likely target: a shining lake abutting one of those fields.

"Missiles are still with us!" said Cassie.

"Here goes nothing." Eli throttled up and the ground rushed to meet them. Five thousand meters. Four thousand. Three. Two. The field grew so close he thought he could see individual stalks of corn.

"Mal, *mark.*"

The tech unplugged something and there was an electronic whine as several displays on Eli's console went abruptly black.

"Cassie!"

There was a loud *bang* and the ship shook as the escape pod fired its explosive bolts and detached. Eli hauled back on the yoke, flattening the ship out and hit the throttle to maximum, skimming so close to the field that they may have brushed the tops of the crops. *No higher than an elephant's eye.*

The *Cav* rocketed forward, careening drunkenly from side to side, and suddenly there was nothing but water in front of them.

"Missiles still incom – wait, they're tracking the escape pod."
*Well, that plan worked.* "Hard shutdown!"

"*Now?*" chorused Cassie and Mal in disbelief.

"Now, goddamnit!"

Eli slapped the control for the landing repulsors and the ship hit the lake, skipping like a stone. Cassie flipped up the cover on the emergency cutoff switch and hesitated, but Eli reached over and slapped the button, turning everything dark even as they continued to slide across the lake.

Without sensors, they were flying blind, so when the shockwave from the missiles hitting the escape pod reached the *Cav,* it sent them bouncing like they were surfing a wave.

Hard shutdown, as it turned out, included the compensators, so they were suddenly heaved side to side against their harnesses, teeth rattling in their heads. Eli let go of the yoke – with no power, it wasn't doing anything anyway – and grabbed the safety webbing across his chest, closing his eyes. He'd have crossed his fingers if he weren't worried that would break them.

Water splashed up against the canopy and the ship finally slowed to a stop, bobbing gently atop the lake. Everything was aggressively quiet.

Next to him, Cassie let one eye crack open. "Are we alive?"

Eli let out a breath. "Close enough."

"How the hell did you know that would work?"

"Redundant targeting systems – when the missile lost our transponder signal, it tried to fall back to its sensors. Fortunately, the mass profile of an escape pod is way closer to an Illyrican fighter than the *Cavalier* actually is." He leaned his head back against his seat, trying to will his heart rate to come back down to something like normal.

"Ha," said Mal, from behind them. "Silly me. Turns out I put this jumper block on the E4 pins instead of the E5 pins." They held up a small plastic clip.

Eli put his head down on the console, resisting the urge to bang it repeatedly. "Okay, let's just all agree to never tell anyone about this." He hit the release button on his harness and struggled out of it. "Come on, we've got about fifteen minutes before the shit hits the fan."

Cassie looked up at him. "What happens in fifteen minutes?"

"Two things," said Eli, ticking them off on his fingers. "First, traffic control scrambles fighters to figure out what the hell just happened. Second, I'm going to be late for lunch." *And I know which one I'm more worried about.*

"So let's get to work. And remember," he added, leveling a finger in their direction. "This. Stays. Between. Us."

# CHAPTER 3

"So, I hear you almost died this morning," said Addy Sayers as the sandy-haired pilot dropped far too casually into the seat across from her. She'd been reading the news on her tablet, sitting and enjoying the cool late morning breeze on the cafe's patio and trying to restrain her irritation at her lunch partner's tardiness.

Brody's cocksure smile, already plastered across his face, froze. "How the hell – ?"

"Cassie is terrible at keeping secrets. You should know that by now. She sent me a picture of your 'landing' site half an hour ago."

"How is she still cleared to work with a covert operations team?" said Brody with a sigh.

The mechanic's cheery personality had wormed its way past Addy's defenses with the offer of a glass of whisky and a gravball match projected in their hangar, and Cassie had subsequently decided that she and Addy were now the best of friends. Addy hadn't had the heart to refuse and, if she was being terribly honest, she kind of missed having friends. After six months with the Special Projects Team, she'd started to finally feel at ease with her teammates, but she still couldn't quite imagine kicking back for a drink with Kovalic, or Commander Taylor, or even Tapper.

And Brody was... well, Brody.

The server, a young pink-haired woman, appeared at the table and handed them a pair of flimsies. "Sorry about the hard-copy menus. Our network is down, so we have to do things the old fashioned way today." Her expression was apologetic but distracted.

"No problem," said Brody. "I'm an old-fashioned kind of guy."

Addy rolled her eyes. "I'll take a coffee refill when you have a chance," she said, raising her cup.

"Sure thing. Be right back." She disappeared into the café.

"Can't believe the communications network is still down," said Addy, glancing at her tablet where a video showing a gaping hole in a Salaam office building played on mute. A big LIVE banner was splashed across it. "Crazy morning."

"You're telling me," said Brody. "I can see the logic of a lockdown triggering automated defense systems, but I really did *not* want to be on that end of it. At least we managed to convince traffic control that it was just a transponder glitch." He jutted his chin at Addy's tablet. "I caught a little bit of the news, but I still don't know what the hell is going on."

"There was an explosion in downtown Salaam – 1342 Oluo Plaza. Turned out it was a major ConComm hub, and it knocked out the entire civilian communications network for the capital region."

Brody's eyebrows went up and he let out a low whistle. "Do they know what caused it?"

Addy tapped her tablet's screen and turned it towards Brody. A replay of footage from the morning's events showed every display, news ticker, and device in the vicinity of Oluo Plaza splashed with the same three accusatory words: SIC SEMPER TYRANNIS. "What do you think?"

In the six months that she'd known Eli Brody, she'd only seen him struck wordless maybe a couple times. When the server reappeared and put down Addy's coffee, Brody mutely pointed at something on the menu and gave the woman a shaky smile.

"Christ," said Brody, when they were alone again. "Somebody *bombed* a building? In Salaam?"

Addy's stomach roiled. She'd grown up on the streets of Salaam, knew every inch of the Commonwealth capital city. It wasn't as though it were all gleaming buildings and clean sidewalks, but Oluo Plaza had always been amongst the nicest, brightest, and, well, *safest* places in the city. Seeing it scarred and violated in this way felt intimately personal.

"Any idea who did it?" Brody's voice lowered, and he glanced around. "The Illyricans?" The ongoing conflict with the rival superpower might have largely stayed cold in the two decades since the Imperium had occupied Earth and its colonies, but flare-ups had been known to happen.

Addy couldn't believe that the Illyricans would have the guts to set off a bomb in the Commonwealth capital, though. Especially like this. "The talking heads have been on all morning, but it's just speculation right now. I've heard a bunch of people talking about the Nova First movement."

"Those kooks who want Nova to leave the Commonwealth? They always seemed... extreme, but not exactly bomb-a-building extreme."

The server reappeared, placing a plate of eggs and toast in front of Brody and asked if they needed anything else. At the pilot's request, she produced a bottle of hot sauce, before going back into the café to sit at the mostly empty bar and watch the vidscreen there.

Brody was right about one thing: Nova First was a fringe

group. The central thrust of their message was that Terra Nova's membership in the Commonwealth of Independent Systems was tantamount to the occupation of Earth and its colonies by the Illyrican Empire. They claimed they'd been dragged into an endless war against the Imperium without a voice or a vote – which was *technically* true, since the Commonwealth had been formed by Earth refugees fleeing the planet's occupation by the Imperium. Nova had already been a settled colony at the time, albeit with a relatively small population. But the group's message had always had a pacifistic bent which seemed somewhat undercut by blowing up a building.

And why *that* building? Consolidated Communications ran the planet's communication infrastructure – with the blessing of the Commonwealth Executive, to be sure, which had granted it a near monopolistic status, since it connected everybody on the planet and off. But despite its close ties to the government, it was a civilian corporation. Not a military target, or even an official government entity.

"Addy?"

She blinked and found Brody looking at her curiously. "Sorry, drifted off there. What?"

A more familiar, and more genuine smile crossed his lips. "I can tell when you're focused on something."

She bristled, more out of instinct than anything; somehow, he always seemed to pick up on what she was thinking. Her self-control must be slipping.

In which case, this couldn't come too soon.

"Look, there's something I wanted to talk to you about," she said.

Brody stabbed a chunk of eggs, smeared it in the hot sauce, and popped it in his mouth. "Sure, what's up?"

Addy had always been the type to rip the bandage off, and this was no exception. "I think maybe it's time I found my own place." There. Done.

Brody paused mid-chew, before forcing a swallow with a swig of water. "Oh," he said. "Yeah. I mean, you know you can stay as long as you *want*, it's not like I'm hurting for space or any–"

Something plucked inside of her, a heartstring she didn't even know she'd had. Guilt, probably. "I mean, I've been having *fun* and everything. But maybe it's best if we, you know, cool it?" Her eyes went to her coffee because it was someplace to look that wasn't at him. "I just think the longer this goes on, the more likely the rest of the team is to find out." The second the words were out of her mouth, she wished she could reel them back in, like a fish on a line.

Hurt glinted in Brody's blue eyes, but only for a moment. "Well," he said, half-heartedly spearing another piece of egg, "we could always solve that problem by just *telling* them."

Addy flinched. "Why the hell would we do that?"

The pilot's eyes snapped back up to her, and they had hardened into flint. "Because keeping secrets doesn't end well, Addy. Not for this team. Better that we just be honest with everyone now, instead of hurting them later when they invariably find out anyway."

She bit back a bitter laugh. "That's easy for you to say, flyboy."

Brody opened his mouth, but she leaned forward before he could speak. "It's *different*, Eli. They need you. What happens when *this*," she waved her hands at the space between them, "ends? When it gets awkward, or when it affects our jobs? Who do you think they'll keep around: the expert pilot or the expendable grunt?" She had no illusions:

she'd been tossed back out on the street, no home, no job.

Never again.

They sat in silence for a moment, enough time for regret to creep its way into Addy's mind. Was this really what she wanted? Or was she just making excuses to protect herself? She shoved it down into a crevice somewhere, out of sight, if not out of mind. It needed to be done: sometimes you had to amputate before the infection spread.

Another server – a tall man with nondescript features – appeared and placed a paper check in between the two of them, murmuring apologies for the network being down, and then disappeared again, clearly sensing the vibe.

"I get it," said Brody quietly. "If that's what you want, okay. I just – I'd really like you to stay. That's all." He took the check from the table and was just digging into his pocket for some cash when he froze.

The hairs on Addy's neck went up at his expression and her vision widened, hyperaware of the few other people on the café patio: the older man sitting two tables away, the family of four on the other side, the servers coming in and out. "What is it?"

Brody looked up sharply, his fingers splayed on the paper. "The server. Where'd she go?"

"It was a different one," said Addy, playing the exchange back in her mind. "A tall man, light brown skin." She peered into the dark interior of the café, her eyes taking a moment to adjust from the bright sunlight. "I don't see him. Why?"

Brody pushed back from the table, crumpling the paper. "Uh. Nothing. Just a mistake on the check."

Addy snorted. "Bull*shit*." He could read her? She could return the favor – something had spooked him, and it hadn't been a double charge for a cup of coffee.

"Leave it, Addy." His voice was hard, harder than she'd ever heard it before, clenched no less tightly than his fist. "This doesn't concern you."

"Oh? What were you just saying about secrets?"

For a moment she thought he was going to snap at her, but his face softened and he gave a reluctant laugh. "Touché." His fingers relaxed and he held the paper out to her.

She took it, smoothed it out on the table: eggs, coffee, tax, everything normal. At the bottom, someone had scrawled a handwritten "Thanks!" with a smiley face. And then, below it, just one word, in a different hand: BERWICK.

"What the hell is Berwick?"

His lips pressed together. "I think it's a threat."

"Pretty weird threat."

"It's… a place on Caledonia. Where my sister lives."

Addy blinked. "You have a sister?" *So much for no secrets.*

"Look, I'll explain everything later. Right now, we need to find that server." He dug into his pocket, tossed some cash on the table, and started towards the café, Addy following closely behind.

If the patio had been quiet, it was dead inside the café, probably in no small part because of this morning's attack in Salaam. What there was of the staff were sitting at the bar, watching the vidscreens behind it, all of which were playing news reports from the capital, mostly of the same footage she'd seen on her tablet: firefighting and surveillance drones swarming around the smoldering building.

Brody made a beeline for their original server. "Pardon me?"

"Yes – oh, is everything all right?"

"Fine, thanks. I'm just looking for one of your colleagues." He relayed Addy's description, but the woman's brow just furrowed in confusion.

"Julia and I are the only servers today," she said, nodding at another woman with spiked blond hair, who was serving the family on the patio. "Manager told everybody else not to come in."

Addy's pulse quickened. Part of her had thought Brody had been making a mountain out of a molehill, she had to admit, but she'd seen the server, even if she hadn't been playing close attention – she cursed herself for that; letting her guard down wasn't like her, but that conversation had been... distracting.

"Is there any other way out of here?" Brody asked. "Besides the front door?"

The server looked even more puzzled, but she nodded to the kitchen. "There's a backdoor into the alley, for the trash. Some of us take our breaks out there too."

Brody nodded his thanks and pushed through the kitchen door over the protests of the server. Addy waved her off. "Sorry, he just... doesn't like crowds." *Well, that's a terrible cover story.* Nothing to be done about it: she followed Brody out through the empty kitchen. Addy quickened her pace to catch up before the pilot could open the back door.

"Damn it, Brody, hold up. You don't know who's out there."

Brody paused, hand on the door. "You're not armed, are you?"

Addy shook her head. Kovalic had made it clear that though the Special Projects Team members might be outside the normal hierarchy, they were technically intelligence personnel, and thus banned from operating domestically. So carrying weapons on a Commonwealth planet – especially the capital – was a big no-no.

"Who else knows about your sister?"

"Kovalic, obviously. Tapper. Probably Commander Taylor, assuming the boss read her in. And the general."

Addy still hadn't met Kovalic's boss, but the rest of the team spoke of him with respect – and perhaps a bit of trepidation too. "So basically everybody."

With a grunt, the pilot started to push the door open, but Addy caught his wrist. "Jesus, Brody, slow your roll. Let me go first."

"This is my *family* we're talking about, Addy." And with that, he stepped out into the alley.

Addy let out a string of muttered curses and followed him.

The alley seemed, at first glance, to be empty. A few trash containers were pushed up against the rear wall of the café; to the left it dead-ended in a blank wall; to the right it hooked around the corner of the building, back toward the street.

She was still checking the angles when the man emerged from the shadows around the corner. He'd ditched the white apron of the servers, leaving a black button-down shirt and matching trousers. Dark hair had been buzzed close to his light brown skin, and he had a face that could have easily gotten lost in a crowd – no wonder she hadn't noticed him. But he carried himself with the loose confidence of a seasoned fighter, and that set all her alarm bells ringing. *This can't be good.*

Her muscles tensed and she stepped in front of Brody, putting herself between the two even as she heard him sharply suck in a breath.

The man tilted his head toward the pilot and, when he spoke, it was in precise, almost gentle tones. "Hello, Brody. It's been a while."

"Holy shit," said Brody, and Addy glanced back to see his jaw hanging open, eyes wide with shock. *"Page?"*

# CHAPTER 4

By the time Kovalic arrived in mid-afternoon the security presence around the Commonwealth Executive building had been beefed up considerably in light of the morning's now-confirmed bombing. He presented his military ID to the rifle-toting, heavily armored guard at the gate. Arrayed around the building's perimeter were half-a-dozen Commonwealth marines in full combat gear, as well as a pair of hover tanks bristling with weaponry. There was always some security at government buildings, but this brazen show of force curdled Kovalic's stomach; it was out of place here, in the usually peaceful capital. Wrong. Like weeds in his carefully cultivated flower bed.

After a few moments, the gate guard cleared him with the central office and he was granted entry, albeit with an armed marine as an escort. The freckled young woman, brown hair shorn to regs, didn't utter a word as they wound up the pathway to the Executive building, gravel crunching beneath their feet.

It had been a long time since Kovalic had visited the general in his official digs: Hasan al-Adaj was a man who didn't like to spend too much time in any one place, lest his well-armed past catch up with him. But the secretary-general of the Executive had made it clear that, in the wake of the Oluo Plaza attack, this was an all-hands on deck situation, and the general's presence was requested at the highest level.

Kovalic had risked a short detour to check his signals. Especially, given what he'd seen – or thought he'd seen – this morning, the dead-drop for NOMAD. But after months of receiving no response over that channel, he hadn't gotten his hopes up, and sure enough, the dead-drop remained empty.

Inside the Executive building it was cool, a bracing respite from the heat of the Novan day. They passed a number of uniformed personnel from all three branches of the Commonwealth military, all moving with the quiet and efficient bustle of important work.

Five minutes of being led through twisty corridors and Kovalic was deposited by his escort at an unremarkable door bearing a small plaque that read "Office of the Special Adviser on Strategic Intelligence." The marine took up a post at the door – evidently he couldn't be trusted to see himself out – as he stepped inside.

The small antechamber contained little more than a desk, behind which sat another young woman, this one a far more familiar sight. She greeted him with a broad, genuine smile. "Hello, major."

"Rance. Good to see you."

"I wish it were under better circumstances."

"I'd say this is about par for the course. How are you holding up?"

"It's been busy, as you'd expect. He's been in and out, going from meeting to meeting, and when he's not in one, he's on a call. And you know how he hates calls."

"Almost as much as he hates meetings."

Rance laughed, dropping her voice to a conspiratorial level. "Especially with politicians. How are you? Commander Taylor still on leave?"

Kovalic tried to ignore the way his breath caught at the mention of his executive officer, who also happened to be his not quite ex-wife. When it came to their relationship, 'it's complicated' was an understatement.

"Yes, she's due back in a few days. Had some personal matters to attend to." And some personal matters to get away from. He shook it off. "Is he ready for me?"

"One moment." Rance touched her earpiece, listening intently, then gave him a nod. "Sounds like he's off his call. I can tell by the swearing." She grinned. "Go right in." At a wave from her, the door in the wall behind her slid aside.

Most of the general's sanctums had a distinctly different feel to them. Some were sleek and modern, others felt like cramped studies pulled from eras long past. This one was devoid of almost any personality: a small, windowless room with a flat metal desk, flanked by empty bookshelves. A painting of a landscape, generic and, even to Kovalic's untutored eye, not particularly good, hung on one wall.

And sitting at the desk in a standard-issue office chair sat Hasan al-Adaj. As usual, he wore a civilian outfit in a military cut: high-collared black shirt, black trousers, spit-shined shoes. His white, van dyke beard was carefully groomed, echoing the fringe of white hair around his head. As Kovalic entered, he was rubbing his forehead with one hand, a pained expression on his face.

"Afternoon, sir."

"Simon. Do you know what I miss *least* about running a large intelligence organization?"

"Well, at a guess, it's either dealing with politicians' inflated egos or the cafeteria food."

The general made a sour face. "I was going to say meetings, but now I'm revising my list." He sighed. "Retirement looks more attractive by the day. Perhaps I should have just stepped down from leading the Imperial Intelligence Service instead of defecting."

"Sure would have saved us both a lot of trouble."

"Indeed. Please, sit down," he said, gesturing to the plain wood chair opposite him. "I'd offer you a drink, but apparently the Commonwealth imposes strict rules on liquor in government buildings. Then again, if I end up needing to be here more than once every few months, I may have Rance smuggle something in."

Kovalic lowered himself into the chair with slightly more of an *oof* than he was proud of. His PT regimen had fallen by the wayside in recent weeks, and it was starting to show.

The general leaned back in his chair. "How are you doing, Simon?"

"Well enough. Mainly just missing the field – this is the longest stretch the team has gone without being deployed in… well, probably ever."

"I am sorry about that, but it was a necessary precaution. That assassin on your last job on Anselm IV came too close for comfort. I had hoped that the threat would blow over, but it appears Ofeibia Xi didn't get to where she is today by not holding a grudge."

True: heads of galaxy-spanning criminal syndicates weren't exactly known for their forgiving natures, especially when it came to people who stole from them. Never mind that it had been Xi who had first stolen the Aleph Tablet from someone else, or that the tablet itself had been destroyed in their escape from the *Queen Amina*. Clearly, she was still pissed.

"What's the bounty at?"

"Five hundred thousand for you and Specialist Sayers apiece. One hundred thousand for Sergeant Tapper and Lieutenant Brody. Even your technician friend, Maldonado, is at twenty-five thousand. But still nothing for Commander Taylor – she seems to have escaped notice."

Kovalic huffed a laugh. Nat had a way of flying beneath the radar, and that was why she'd been the only one on the team to get a green light to travel offworld in the last six weeks. "I don't relish putting the team in harm's way, but it *is* part of the job. And, frankly, the team is getting antsy. More than a little rusty, too. We're still a valuable strategic asset – I hate to see us go to waste."

The general's slender fingers drummed on the desktop and, after a moment, he inclined his head. "Agreed. Which is why you're here. There's something I'd like you to look into. It's somewhat more... sensitive than your usual operations."

"Oh?"

"This morning's bombing. It's caused substantial havoc: transport on and off world has been suspended, final activation of the retrofitted orbital station has been put on hold, and communication networks in the capital area are still seeing significant disruption. Moreover, there is of course the concern that another attack may be imminent."

"Do you think the Illyricans are behind the bombing?" Not directly, of course. Attacking the Commonwealth on its own soil would have been grounds for thrusting them once again into open war, which he doubted the Imperium was ready to risk even after six years of detente, but Kovalic certainly wouldn't rule out the Imperium having used a proxy of some sort.

Hesitation bloomed across the old man's face. "While I can't dismiss the theory, I have no evidence pointing in that direction, even from my... best-placed sources."

Which meant CARDINAL, the general's secretive asset inside the Imperium. Kovalic still wasn't sure of the exact nature of the source but, despite how uncomfortable it made him not to know the provenance of the intelligence they received from it, he'd resisted pressing. The general remained protective of both the source's identity and its existence – as far as Kovalic knew, he was the only one with whom the general had shared its information thus far.

"That lack of intelligence is our biggest weakness," the general continued, "which is why I'd like you to investigate."

Kovalic couldn't say he was surprised. It's not as though there was anything more pressing than an attack on the Commonwealth's capital. Even at the height of hostilities with the Illyrican Empire, Nova had never been directly attacked. "So, where are we headed? Bayern again? If the Illyricans did fund the attack, I imagine any money transfer would go through there."

"Ah," said the general, his fingers forming a steeple. "Here is where we reach the particularly sensitive part of this operation. I'd like you to take a look at the bomb site."

"I'm sorry?" said Kovalic, his eyebrows climbing. "Oluo Plaza?"

"You know of another?"

"General, with all due respect, the Commonwealth charter expressly prohibits intelligence operations on member worlds. Domestic investigation is a matter for the Commonwealth Security Bureau." As the government's main law enforcement agency, the Bureau's remit covered criminal matters, counter-intelligence, and, most relevantly, terrorism.

The old man's eyes narrowed. "No need to quote me chapter and verse, major. I'm well aware of the restrictions on military and intelligence operations. But since my office – and by extension, the Special Projects Team – is attached directly to the Commonwealth Executive, technically we are classified as neither."

"That's a hell of a loophole, sir."

"Perhaps. But, in this case it's both useful and necessary."

"How so?"

The general combed his fingers through his beard. Something was troubling him. "Following the bombing, a message was sent to the Commonwealth Executive, claiming responsibility."

"There wasn't anything on the news about that."

"The Executive has kept it under wraps for the moment, for reasons that will become apparent." The general reached over and pressed a control on his desk. A holoscreen sprang into life between them, floating over the surface and showing the shadowy silhouette of a figure. The voice that issued forth was heavily modulated, distorted so as to be unrecognizable, but even and almost calm in its delivery.

"Too long the Commonwealth oppressors have taken advantage of native-born Novans, imposing their will on those who want an end to this eternal conflict. And now it goes further, abusing the very liberties of its citizens. Now is the time for resistance. Now is the time to rise up. You have seen what we can do. If the Commonwealth Executive does not put forth a proposal for Terra Nova to exit the Commonwealth in the next seventy-two hours, your treachery will be revealed for all to see. Sic semper tyrannis!"

The message blinked out of existence, leaving Kovalic eye-to-eye with the general.

"Well," said Kovalic. "That was theatrical." The three-word sign-off had sent a prickle down his spine. 'Thus always to tyrants.' A phrase with a loaded history, to be sure. "I know that the Nova First movement has taken some pot shots from time to time, but this seems more aggressive than their usual behavior."

There had always been a low simmering frustration with the Commonwealth from Terra Nova's original settlers, who'd spent close to a hundred years on the planet before Earthers fleeing the Illyrican invasion of humanity's homeworld had chosen it as the location for their government in exile. Not long thereafter, it had evolved into the Commonwealth of Independent Systems and things had never really gone back to the way they'd been. Kovalic could, admittedly, understand the objections of those native-born Novans who felt like they'd been shoved aside, but all you had to do was look at Earth's two decades of Illyrican rule to conclude that things could have been much, much worse.

"Our perpetrators seem to be a militant offshoot of the movement," said the general. "The Novan Liberation Front, formally, though they go predominantly by 'Nova Front.' And this seems to constitute their introductory remarks."

"Hell of an opening number. What's this bit about 'your treachery will be revealed'?"

"That *is* an enigma," said the general, his eyes glinting. "I've had Rance and some of my other contacts digging around, but so far we've encountered nothing but a series of brick walls."

"Did you ask the Executive?"

"They were unsurprisingly mum on the subject – the old 'neither confirm nor deny' line. But I do believe that Oluo Plaza was not a target of happenstance. If there's a connection, it's there. Which is why I want you to investigate."

Kovalic pushed down the upset in his stomach. It wasn't as though he hadn't taken advantage of loopholes or evaded regulations in the past, but there were some lines one didn't cross. Potentially investigating Commonwealth citizens was outside of the purview of the intelligence apparatus for good reason – it was the first step on the slippery slope to a surveillance state, and that first step was a doozy.

"Sir, I'm not sure how comfortable I am with this. Shouldn't we leave it to the Bureau? They're surely better equipped to investigate this incident." He frowned. "Unless there's some reason you don't think they can handle it?"

"Quite the opposite, major. I have nothing but respect and admiration for the Bureau – if anything, I worry they may be *too* effective."

"I'm… not sure I follow."

Teeth raking his upper lip, the general let out a sigh. "I understand your concerns and, under normal circumstances, I wouldn't ask this of you. But the situation is anything but normal. I'm afraid the stakes are rather personal."

"Personal?"

"The chief of communications analysis at Naval Intelligence Command owes me a favor; she sent me a preliminary de-obfuscated copy of the message before it goes into wide circulation. And it's not good news." At another tap of his fingers, the holoscreen reappeared, showing the same silhouetted figure. The general keyed in a sequence and the shadow resolved into a face: a young man with a light brown complexion, and dark, hard eyes.

All the air was squeezed from Kovalic's lungs. "No. It can't be."

For the second time today, he found himself face-to-face with a pair of familiar looking eyes; this time, though, they weren't obscured by a respirator mask. Aaron Page stared back at him, stolid and impassive as ever.

"I was just as surprised as you," said the general, staring down his hawk nose at Kovalic. "Perhaps more so, since you personally assured me at the conclusion of the Bayern operation that Lieutenant Page had met his fate."

Kovalic straightened. Page had been a member of his team, right up until that job on Bayern, when Kovalic had discovered the lieutenant had been funneling information to Aidan Kester, the Commonwealth Intelligence Directorate's deputy director of operations – and, more importantly, the general's chief rival in the intelligence community. According to Page, the betrayal had been born out of concern that the general might be harboring ulterior motives that were not in the Commonwealth's best interests.

"I thought he had." If perhaps not exactly in the way that the general, who had quite the ruthless streak, had understood.

At times the old man could remind one of a kindly grandfather, but now his mien took on a distinctly haughty look, reminding Kovalic that, once upon a time, he had been not only the feared spymaster of the Illyrican Empire, but also a member of its high nobility. "I'm… disappointed, Simon. I left this matter up to your discretion," he gestured to the screen, "and this is exactly the kind of outcome I had hoped to avoid."

Kovalic shook his head. "This isn't right. I can't see Page doing something like this." Even as he said it, his heart sank.

He wouldn't have believed it from the message alone, but after being convinced that he'd seen Page at Oluo Plaza with his own eyes? It didn't look good. "I don't know what his motivation would be."

A speculative grunt issued from the general. "To be honest, major, I'm not sure it matters. Given the explicit threat in the message, the Commonwealth Security Bureau and every other law enforcement and security agency onworld is already hunting Nova Front." A frown creased his face. "More to the point, it's only a matter of time before Deputy Director Kester sees *this* version of the video, and he will no doubt be most motivated to talk to Lieutenant Page once he's been apprehended." His blue eyes went to Kovalic. "Which is why I would like you to find him before the Bureau, or anybody else, can bring him in."

"You're worried this could blow back on us?" Kovalic's jaw set. It wasn't what he would have prioritized, given an attack on the Commonwealth capital and another one potentially in the offing, but being cold and calculating had gotten the general this far.

The old man's eyes glittered. "I consider all the angles, major. We've ruled nothing out. But you see why it is imperative that we get to the bottom of this. Something is afoot here, and if there is a loaded gun on the stage, I would like to be certain it's not going to be pointed at us."

*There was an exhalation from Page, as though all his secrets had been squeezed out of him like a tube of toothpaste. "So now what? Back to Nova for a court martial?"*

*"No," Kovalic said at last. "There won't be a trial, lieutenant." He reached into his jacket and drew out the pistol, which he turned*

*over slowly in both hands. "But I can't have someone on my team that I don't trust." Looking up, he forced himself to meet Page's eyes.*

*"You were a good officer and I hate to lose you. I'm sorry, Aaron."*

*"Yeah," said Page slowly. "Me too, sir."*

Kovalic's eyes blinked open and he stared blearily out the window of the autocab as the skyline zipped by. The same scene had played over and over again in his mind during the last nine months – seemingly every time he'd closed his eyes.

The park bench in Bergfestung on Bayern. The cold grip of the pistol in his hand. The stoic expression on Aaron Page's face. What should have been a moment of triumph, having undermined the Illyrican plot to annex the banking hub, had instead turned to ashes in his mouth.

Betrayal cut both ways. Page had made his choice in providing information to Kester, and Kovalic had made his. The doubt had crept up on him in quieter moments, insisting that there must have been another option, but at the time, he'd only seen one path forward.

He'd trusted Page implicitly. Plucked him from the elite operative training program at the School and deployed with him on a score of missions over five years, from Jericho Station to Caledonia to Sevastapol. The man had been cool under fire and competent in the extreme, and Kovalic had never once worried that Page might not have his back.

But now that doubt had returned, and it had brought reinforcements. It made him wonder whether he'd ever really known the mind of the man behind that ever-dispassionate exterior.

Thoughts rolled around in Kovalic's head like the rattling of dice. Working with Novan terrorists? Page had been born on Terra Nova, sure, but he'd never expressed any sympathies for the kind of radical views Nova Front espoused. On the other hand, the lieutenant's choice to spy for Kester had been rooted in his distrust of the general's motives, combined with secret bank accounts and a mysterious code name – LOOKING GLASS – which he'd heavily implied that Kovalic should ask the general about.

But Kovalic's discreet poking into LOOKING GLASS had found very little. There was no official record of the code name in any of the databases he had access to. He'd started to wonder if Page had been delusional, had somehow concocted this mysterious and sinister operation out of whole cloth.

After he'd told Nat about, well, everything, she'd dug around and gotten wind of a hush-hush project under that code name, run out of the military's Research & Development branch. But they'd found nothing more than that, much less any connection with the general.

He rubbed his eyes, a weariness emanating from his very core. Faking Page's death had been necessary at the time. Or at least so he'd believed. But it had gnawed at him ever since, especially having to keep the truth from the rest of the team.

The rest of the team, whose help he was surely about to need. Which meant coming clean about everything that had happened since Bayern.

He let out a long sigh as the autocab slowed to a stop, depositing him in front of the Yamanaka Base entrance. The gate guard knew him by sight and waved him in – no calling in to the central office here – and he made his way to the hangar complex that the SPT had been calling home while onworld.

Breaking it to them would be rough; glad as he was to have told Nat, the results hadn't been exactly what he'd hoped. She'd stepped back from team operations, then been all too happy to take some leave when a priority flag had gone up on Centauri. And, if anything, Tapper and Brody had taken Page's disappearance much harder.

Stepping into the conference room attached to the hangar, he was surprised to see not only Tapper, but also Brody and Sayers. The four of them generally only met a couple times a week, and there was nothing scheduled for today.

Brody was pacing back and forth, clearly agitated.

"Settle down, kid," Tapper was saying. "Look, the boss is here, you can ask him yourself."

The pilot looked up as Kovalic entered, his blue eyes flashing with unbottled anger. He pushed his way past Tapper and strode to Kovalic, his fists clenched.

"You absolute son of a *bitch*," said Brody, and then, to Kovalic's complete and utter surprise, the pilot punched him squarely in the jaw.

# CHAPTER 5

There had been no shortage of surprising incidents in Eli Brody's relatively young life. The time the Sabaeans had destroyed their own wormhole gate after the Illyrican fleet that he had been a part of had attempted to invade that planet. Finding out his brother was the leader of a terrorist organization on his homeworld. Discovering that someone he'd counted as a friend was trying to kill the crown prince of the Illyrican Empire.

But the moment Page stepped out of the shadows, Eli almost lost it. The world spun on its axis, and he felt pretty sure that if he didn't sit down in the next thirty seconds, he'd be flat on his back anyway. *Maybe my brains are still rattled from that rough landing.*

Addy put herself between the two of them, casting a worried glance at Eli while still sizing up Page as a potential threat. "Brody... you know this guy?"

Eli put a hand on her shoulder – more to steady himself than to stop her.

"We were colleagues," said Page, with the same carefully maintained neutral expression he'd always worn.

"You're supposed to be... I thought you were... Kovalic said..." Eli struggled to sort through the thoughts that flurried at him like dead leaves in a gust. Something pinged in his brain, as though some long-running background process had finally finished its arduous search, and he realized that not once had Kovalic ever actually *said* Page was dead. He'd always just talked around it. "What the *fuck*, Page?"

"I'm sorry, I don't have time to explain."

"You *don't have time*?" Eli repeated dumbly. "Page, you've been dead for nine months."

"He looks pretty good for a dead guy," said Addy. Eli could tell she was still prepared for a fight, coiled and ready to spring, prepared to interpose herself at a moment's notice. Not ten minutes after she'd told him they should cool their... whatever was going on between them. *Aw, maybe she does care.*

Page's calculating glance flitted to her, as though summing her up in a single look, then came back to Eli. "I need you to relay a message to Captain Kovalic."

"Major," Eli corrected him absently. *Like that's important right now.*

Page blinked, apparently incorporating this new information into his databanks. "Indeed. Well, then. Tell Kovalic to stay away from Nova Front and Oluo Plaza."

Eli's head spun. "Oluo Plaza? The what? What the hell is this all about?" He felt like his brain was still playing catch up. *Goddamned cloak and dagger theatrics.* "Does this have something to do with the explosion?"

"If Kovalic insists on getting involved, I cannot guarantee his safety. Somebody will get hurt."

Addy's grip tightened on Eli's shoulder but her eyes were still on Page. "What do you mean, get hurt?" she said.

The dispassionate gaze went to her, then back to Eli. "You have my message." He nodded to them and turned to walk out of the alley, then paused for a moment, looking back over his shoulder. "It's good to see you, Brody."

And with that, he disappeared, leaving Eli just as speechless as he'd been at the man's first appearance. "Wait, hold on," he said weakly.

With a look to make sure he was all right, Addy jogged to the corner, then looked down the alley's exit to the street. "Where the fuck did he go?"

"He does that," said Eli, leaning against the wall and rubbing his temples. "Jesus." *Damn it, Kovalic, why didn't you tell me? All this time I spent worrying that I'd put my trust in the wrong person, in somebody who* killed *his teammate.*

"Brody, hey," said Addy, who was suddenly standing in front of him again, snapping her fingers. "You still with me?" Her expression was surprisingly concerned – he didn't think he'd seen that particular look before.

"Yeah. I'm okay."

"You want to explain to me what that was all about?"

Eli's mouth set in a grim line. "You're not the only one who wants answers. And I know where to get them."


Punching someone in the face hurt Eli's hand way more than he'd thought it would. Either that or Kovalic had reinforced cheek bones. His knuckles screamed at him and he shook his hand out and flexed them, trying to keep his cool while jolts of pain shot up his arm. Only the faint sound of Tapper sucking in a breath broke the quiet.

For his part, the major seemed startled, but not particularly hurt by the punch. He'd probably taken much, much worse than one limp sock from a pilot's noodle arms. Rubbing at the red spot on his cheek, he raised an eyebrow at Eli. "Something on your mind, lieutenant?"

The anger already at a simmer boiled over. "Am I part of this team or not?"

"Easy, kid." Tapper had come up behind him and put a hand on his shoulder.

Eli shrugged it off. "I can't *believe* you would all keep something like this from me."

Kovalic's expression turned bland, but there was a glint in his eye that seemed puzzled... or maybe curious? "I'm not sure what you're talking about, lieutenant."

Something about that only irked Eli further. "How the hell could you not tell me that Page is *alive*?"

An eerie silence descended over the room, like everyone had been flash frozen in place.

"Christ, Brody, you've lost the plot," said Tapper. "Page is gone. You know that. Sorry, boss, I knew this was eating at him, but I thought we'd put it to bed."

Eli tried not to let the pain show on his face; Kovalic lying to him was one thing, but Tapper? That stabbed deep.

"Downtime is making us all antsy," said the sergeant, "but I don't know where he's getting this cockamamie story."

And then the knife slipped deeper into Eli's gut as horrified realization dawned. *Oh my god, Tapper wasn't gaslighting me – he doesn't know either.* "Tell him, Kovalic."

Kovalic's face had remained remarkably impassive throughout, but at this, something in it seemed to crumple, and he let out a long sigh. "I think maybe we'd better all sit down."

Eli felt more than heard Tapper go still. "What's he talking about, boss?"

Kovalic gestured to the table in the middle of the room. Addy pushed a chair back against the wall and sat down and, after a moment, Eli stalked to a seat and joined her.

*This better be a hell of a story. Like, five stars, ten out of ten.*

"Tap?" said Kovalic.

"I'll stand, thanks."

The major rested his hands on the back of a chair, almost as if leaning for support. "I don't know where to start, other than to say that I'm sorry I had to keep this from you. Maybe there was another way, or I could have made a better decision. But, yes, Page is alive."

In the corner, Tapper seemed to falter, and for the first time since he'd met the man, Eli thought he saw a glint in the weathered sergeant's eyes. *Must be a trick of the light.*

"I'd be interested to know how exactly you came by this information, lieutenant."

Suddenly, Eli felt tired all the way down to his bones. The anger should have been fueling him – there was so much anger in him – but it was as if a vacuum had opened up and sucked out everything except fatigue. "He made contact with me."

Both Kovalic and Tapper's eyes were on him now, and he tried to avoid squirming beneath their respective gazes.

"When?" said Kovalic.

"A couple hours ago. At a café. Addy was there too."

He sensed her shift in the chair next to him, the slight discomfort, and his mind went back to the conversation they'd had. *Can't think about that now.* "We're getting away from the point here. Why didn't you tell us Page was still alive?" All these months, Eli had done his best to push down the doubt, but it had lingered in the back of his mind: the little voice that would, in quiet moments, murmur that he'd signed up to work with a cadre of cold-blooded murderers.

Equal parts regret and determination stole across Kovalic's face. "It was the safest option."

"Safest?" Eli scoffed. "For you, maybe."

"For Page. And for the rest of you. You can't tell what you don't know."

It wasn't the whole story. Not by a long shot. But before Eli could press for something more substantive, Kovalic had shifted the conversation back to his line of questioning. "So, he reached out to you. Why? What did he want?"

He wanted to push back, but from experience he knew parting Kovalic from his secrets would be like prying apart two powerful magnets and right now he just didn't have the energy. "He wanted me to tell you to stay away from Oluo Plaza. And Nova Front, whatever that is. If you don't... well, he didn't mince words. Somebody's going to get hurt – I think he might have meant you."

"I see."

"So what's Nova Front?" said Addy.

"The Novan Liberation Front," said Kovalic. "Radical splinter group of the Nova First movement. And the most likely suspects behind the Oluo Plaza bombing."

"How the hell is Page connected to a group of terrorists?" said Tapper.

The major hesitated for a moment, and Eli's frustration spiked. *Just something else he's holding back?*

"The Commonwealth Executive received a message this morning, taking responsibility for the attack and threatening further repercussions if it did not authorize a vote on Nova's withdrawal from the Commonwealth. When we reversed the obfuscation protocols on the message, it yielded, well, this." He tapped a few buttons on his sleeve and waved it over the table's controls. A holographic screen appeared, framing a still image of Aaron Page.

Eli's jaw dropped. "Whoa, whoa, *whoa*. Are you saying Page was behind the Oluo Plaza explosion?"

Kovalic spread his hands. "I can't say *anything* for sure right now, Brody. Wish that I could. But I can tell you that I was at Oluo Plaza this morning when the bomb went off and I'm pretty sure that Page was too."

Once again, a heavy silence draped the room, and Eli slowly took in the rest of his team: Kovalic, staring off into space while still rubbing at his mouth in thought, Addy studying the image of Page with interest, and Tapper looking down at his shoes.

"Oh, come *on*," said Eli, shooting to his feet. "You can't tell me that you think that Page – *our* Page – would set off a bomb right in the middle of the city. People got *hurt*. You think he's capable of that?"

"I don't know," said Kovalic. "But what I *do* know is that seconds after that bomb went off, a widespread hack covered the entire area with a message that was clearly from Nova Front." At another tap, the screen changed to show the scene at Oluo Plaza, the building still smoking, while screens across the area all showed the same three words, rendered in blood red: SIC SEMPER TYRANNIS. "That's not easy to pull off, but if anyone could do it, it's Page."

"But why?" said Eli. "What possible reason could he have?"

"He *is* Novan," said Tapper, not looking up from his shoes. "Maybe he had enough."

"You don't believe that."

The sergeant's face had turned grim. "I don't know what to believe. Page was a good soldier, but he didn't exactly spend a lot of time talking about his feelings."

Memories of the lieutenant whirled through Eli's mind. The first time they had met, when Page had saved him from a mugging in Caledonia's capital city. The lieutenant, unruffled, as they tried to seize control of the Illyrican's experimental jump ship while under fire. Eli rescuing him and the rest of the team from their mission gone sideways on Sevastapol. He hadn't known Page long, but he'd always seemed solid. Even-keeled. *Maybe I'm not the best judge of character*. His eyes drifted to Addy.

"Look, it doesn't matter what we believe," said Kovalic. "Page is our responsibility, and we're the only ones who can deal with him."

Tapper looked up, his eyes sharp. "Boss, we're talking about something that happened here, on Commonwealth soil. It's out of our hands."

"Our focus isn't Nova Front, sergeant. It's on finding and containing Page. We're not going to be the only ones looking for him. If he did do this, well, then we should be the ones to bring him in. And if he didn't, it's better that we find him first. We're threading the needle on this one, I know." Kovalic's gaze swept over each of them. "I won't begrudge you if you don't want any part of this. I was Page's CO, I made the call to cut him loose."

A deep snort escaped from Tapper. "No need to fall on your sword, boss. Not like I'm going to let you do this on your own."

Eli shifted in his chair. *There's the door*, part of his brain told him. All he had to do was walk through it and maybe he could stop worrying about lies and counter-lies and wheels within wheels. But Page had been... well, if not a friend then perhaps a potential friend? It was no exaggeration to say that without him, Eli wouldn't be sitting here today. He owed him that much. "Count me in."

Three pairs of eyes turned to Addy. "Don't look at me. I didn't know the guy." Resignation settled over her face.

"Look, I don't like anybody blowing up my city. If your pal there is involved, then we bring his ass in and he gets what's coming to him. If not then maybe he helps us figure out who *did* set that bomb, and we find *them*." She brushed a lock of hair out of her eyes. "And turn them over to the appropriate authorities. Of course."

Kovalic tilted his head. "Of course."

"So," said Tapper. "Where do we start?"

"Well," said Kovalic, "they say criminals always return to the scene of the crime, so I figured no better place to start than Oluo Plaza."

"It's going to be crawling with cops," Tapper pointed out. "Plus they'll have it locked down to authorized personnel only, and last I checked, that's not us."

Kovalic relaxed back into his chair and smiled. "I was sort of thinking we might avoid regular business hours, sergeant."

Eli swallowed. *Here we go again.*

# CHAPTER 6

At night, 1342 Oluo Plaza took on a decidedly sepulchral tone, a dark black monolith rising into the sky amongst the illuminated spires of Salaam. A cloud of drones still hovered around the building like gnats: news organizations capturing B-roll footage for the feeds; law enforcement patrolling and collecting forensic data and detailed scans from the explosion site; probably even a few private thrill-seekers, darting around the perimeter while trying to keep clear of the authorities.

Kovalic could just make out the gaping hole about halfway up the building, where the bomb had blown out the floor-to-ceiling plexisteel windows. In his memory, the explosion echoed and he tasted grit. An icy finger dug into his chest.

But looking back never helped anybody.

"How's it looking up there, Birdseye?"

He could almost hear the *tch* of dissatisfaction from Sayers at the callsign, but she swallowed it down.

"Everything seems clear. I've got eyes on the twelfth floor, and it looks quiet. Only one person on duty."

Brody piped up from his position in the car across the street. "You've got a couple at the entrance though."

Shaking off his unease, Kovalic strolled up to the front of

the building. As Brody had said, two officers in the uniforms of Salaam's public safety department stood watch at the perimeter, knockout guns holstered at their hips. They eyed him as approached, but as soon as he produced an official ID – not his actual one, of course – they waved him through with only a cursory look. Who else would be bold enough to walk right up to the scene of a crime? Sloppy. If it weren't to his advantage, he'd have dropped a note to their superior. Maybe when he was done.

Inside, the lobby of marble and glass was dimly illuminated, but completely devoid of any personnel. A holoscreen floating nearby noted that the building had been switched over to an independent backup circuit – the main power was still disconnected as a precaution. But the lift was functioning so Kovalic rode to the twelfth floor and stepped out into a nondescript hallway.

Just opposite the elevator, a pair of large glass doors were emblazoned with the radiating globe logo of Consolidated Communications. To either side, the hallway continued for a few yards or so, punctuated by plain doors.

He keyed his comm. "Brawler, can you pull up schematics for this floor? Any other firms have offices up here?"

After a brief pause, during which Kovalic could hear Tapper cursing under his breath, the sergeant seemed to wrestle the information into submission. "Copy that, Trailblazer. Records suggest that there are a few other small companies leasing space on the floor: a clerical firm, a small manufacturing concern, and a chartered accountant. But ConComm accounts for upwards of eighty-five percent of the space."

About as dominant as their market position. ConComm wasn't the only communications company in the Commonwealth but it was by far the largest, and a series of acquisitions and mergers had ensured that it owned most of the infrastructure for onworld data traffic. More crucially, its satellite constellation was the primary jumping off point for communications to the rest of the galaxy. The company had recently won a government contract to install upgraded communications infrastructure on Station Zero, the aging space station at the top of Nova's space elevator, and they were supposed to significantly improve communications throughput. You couldn't do much about speed when your message was subject to the limitations of physics, but there were other places for optimization: for example, the drones that jumped back and forth through the wormholes to transmit and receive messages from the systems on either side could benefit from increased capacity, more efficient batching, and updated software.

The Oluo Plaza location was one of the major data communication hubs for Salaam. As far as targets went, it would be a tempting one: the impact of the bombing had severely disrupted communications throughout the capital region. The primary networks still weren't back online and the backup networks weren't designed to handle the full load for this long, leading to sporadic smaller outages and communication interruptions.

Of course, Oluo Plaza's soft target status made it easier to hit than, say, a military installation. But it was also a predominantly civilian target, which puzzled Kovalic. The Commonwealth military did use ConComm infrastructure at times, but it had its own private networks too. Taking down the Oluo Plaza hub did far more to hurt the average citizen of Salaam than the so-called 'occupying government' itself. For a group that purported to have Novans' best interests at heart, it was a mixed message at best.

"Going in," he murmured.

Kovalic stepped up to the glass doors; another uniformed officer stood just inside. She frowned and beckoned him to press his ID against the glass so she could scrutinize it. Kovalic held up the card – which declared him to be an inspector from the Commonwealth Security Bureau – and she punched in an access code and cracked the door.

"I'm sorry, sir. Orders are nobody inside until the forensic team has done their sweep."

He'd been ready with an excuse for the late hour, but that gave him pause. The forensic team hadn't been in yet? It had been more than twelve hours – what the hell were they waiting for?

But at least it gave him an opening. "Right, right. It's just that I'm supposed to do the preliminary setup for them. Lay some groundwork."

She frowned. "Nobody told me."

"Well, shit," said Kovalic, rubbing his face. "It *is* a new procedure, which means of course there's a communication foul-up. Damn it, I'm *already* on thin ice with the chief. Forensics is supposed to be here first thing in the morning, and if this setup isn't done, *my* next assignment is going to be parking hovercars in the Bureau garage." He summoned a heavy sigh. "Well, nothing to do but to get this all settled. He really hates it when people call him at home." He raised his sleeve, preparing to punch in Tapper's number. The sergeant did an excellent 'grumpy boss roused in the middle of the night,' probably because it wasn't a huge stretch for him.

The expression on the officer's face shifted into a kind of reluctant resignation. "How long does this setup take?"

He paused, sleeve still raised, allowed a flicker of hope to show. "Five minutes. Ten tops."

She seemed to think it over and then relented, picking up a slim package from a nearby table and handing it to him: a disposable bunny suit to put over his clothes, so as to avoid contaminating the crime scene, complete with a filtration mask. "You've got ten minutes. A second more and I'm coming back there and dragging you out myself."

"Thanks, I really appreciate it. You won't even know I'm here."

She nodded, albeit stiffly, and re-locked the door as he donned the get-up. It reminded him of the hazmat emergency suits that they'd been issued in the marines and the endless drills to don them properly and expeditiously. Those, however, were far more robust, designed to withstand hazards from getting in rather than parts of him getting out.

Once suited up, he made his way back into the office. Locating the source of the explosion wasn't difficult: the shockwave had shifted the furniture, shattered some of the windows of the offices, and knocked loose items from desks to the floor. The authorities had at least performed some initial engineering scans to make sure the building was in no danger of collapsing or damaging the surrounding environments; fortunately, it had been hardened and reinforced against anything short of an aerial bombardment and the blast hadn't done any significant structural damage.

He followed the pattern of disruption back to the explosion's origin site, which appeared to be a small corridor that had once ended in an external-facing window. The window had been totally destroyed; a temporary plastic barrier had been hastily erected in its place, though it did little to stop the wind from whistling in. Glass crunched under the forensic booties on his feet as he surveyed the site.

If this was the origin, then the direction and pattern of the explosion clearly indicated that it had come from *outside* the building. Probably, based on the building's height and the external-facing window, a drone. He hadn't seen that in any of the early reports, but if the forensic team really hadn't been allowed in yet, perhaps that wasn't surprising.

Kovalic cast his mind back, trying to remember if he'd noticed anything in the moments before the explosion, but there was always a fair amount of drone traffic in the air around Salaam and he'd had no reason to be curious.

Moreover, the damage suggested that the charge had been shaped – set to explode in a specific direction rather than just outwards. That meant the attack had been targeted to do damage in this particular spot, probably because it was the external wall closest to the data hub's server equipment. So not just your garden-variety grenade; he was sure Tapper and his encyclopedic knowledge of explosives would be able to narrow it down once he'd collected some details.

Retracing his steps, Kovalic located the server room, about ten meters or so from the explosion site. The door had been knocked askew on its hinges, the side that had faced inward pitted with damage from debris. It had at one point been secured by a card swipe, but the reader was hanging out of the wall by a wire. The open doorway had yellow caution tape strung across it from a few different angles.

Kovalic poked his head through a gap in the tape and peered into the room. The red emergency lighting did little to illuminate it, but from what Kovalic could tell it was roughly twenty feet by twenty feet and packed to the gills with equipment. Or at least it had been. Servers and networking equipment lay askew, knocked loose from their racks, and frayed wires poked here and there out of boxes the size of industrial refrigeration units. Even through the face mask, the smell of burned plastic and acrid smoke hung thick in the air.

Unzipping his suit, he pulled out the microdrone he'd brought and activated it before tossing it up in the air. Its repulsors hummed to life and it began to float around the room, dutifully capturing three-dimensional scans in all available spectrums, while its other sensors sampled residue and particulates in the air. If Nat were here, she'd no doubt have programmed a more thorough forensic package. But she wasn't due back until later this week, if she were even willing to help out. For now, they'd have to make do with his more modest skills.

While the drone worked, Kovalic made a visual sweep of his own. Scientific instruments and high-resolution scans were all well and good, but sometimes there was no substitute for the human brain and its penchant for finding connections.

He wasn't sure he knew exactly what a communications hub should look like, but if he'd had to imagine it, this was basically what he would have pictured: a room full of esoteric hardware. Tech had never been his strong suit: these days, he trusted Nat with that part of the job. And, before that, Page. Which, he supposed, meant his former officer would have a pretty good idea of exactly where to place such an explosion to inflict maximum damage.

He'd been avoiding presuming Page guilty, despite the preponderance of evidence: the message to the Executive, spotting Page at the bombing site, and, of course, the betrayal to Kester. Keeping an open mind was important, because sometimes when everything told you that the world was one way, you got stuck into thinking that was the only way it could be. But the growing knot in his stomach was starting to make him question whether he wasn't letting his own relationship with Page overrule his common sense. You couldn't ignore the facts, no matter how inconvenient they might be.

He reeled his brain back to the here and now. Draw conclusions from the evidence, don't fit the evidence to your theories, he reminded himself.

There was something of a contradiction in the attack's methodology: the drone delivery felt convenient, but the shaped charge felt purposeful. If Nova Front had just wanted to make a statement by targeting ConComm, they could have planted the explosive anywhere in the office. Hell, they could probably have had it delivered in a package. But no, they'd picked the place most likely to do damage to this room full of equipment. Why?

Shifting for a better viewpoint, he noticed that the equipment rack on the far wall was no longer sitting flush against it, but rather had been shoved aside. Which wouldn't have been weird except for the fact that it seemed to have been shifted inward, as though someone had pulled it *away* from the wall.

Tapping a command into his sleeve – the forensic suit thoughtfully offered passthrough connectivity via a smart fabric patch – the drone hissed its way over and played a spotlight over that section. Kovalic watched the live telemetry on his sleeve's display and angled the drone's camera to see behind the rack – where it found a very neat square hole about two feet by two feet. But it was the edges of the hole that really piqued his interest: they weren't ragged as though from explosive damage, but smooth and slightly singed.

Cut. Probably with some sort of torch.

Kovalic raised his eyebrows and told the drone to continue its scan through the hole. He was about to squeeze through the caution tape and into the room, do a little more directed poking around, when there was a crunch of glass underfoot from behind him.

His training reactions would have had him whirling quickly, moving into a defensive posture, but his brain overrode the impulse; his cover was that he was *supposed* to be here. Instead, he forced himself to turn slowly to face the figure behind him.

There wasn't much he could tell about them, other than that they were of a height with him and broad-shouldered: like Kovalic, they wore a white forensic suit, covered from head to toe, with a respirator mask and a pair of safety glasses obscuring most of their face.

"Evening," said the figure, their voice a deep, rich bass. "Can I help you?"

"Hi there." Kovalic pulled his ID out of a pocket on the suit. "Commonwealth Security Bureau."

"Funny," said the figure, producing a similar-looking folio. "Mine says the same thing." Their posture was relaxed, but to Kovalic it was a little *too* relaxed – the kind of looseness you got when you knew you might have to fight at any minute.

Damn it. Tapper, or Sayers, or *someone* – even Brody – should have alerted him that somebody else had come through the perimeter.

"Looks like they double-booked us," said Kovalic with a hapless smile that he realized they wouldn't be able to see. With the glasses and tightly drawn hood he had no facial expressions to read, so he had to go on body language. "Isn't that just like the office?" He wondered exactly how they'd talked their way past that officer on duty – she'd barely bought his excuse.

"Uh huh. Why don't you and I take a walk outside and we can call the duty supervisor and clear this all up, Inspector…?"

"Kaplan," said Kovalic. It was the name on the ID, anyway. "I work with Inspector Fayerweather." That was stretching the truth – he'd helped her out on one case a long time ago, but they'd been amicable. Mostly.

The man's head cocked to one side, as if taken aback. "Ronnie? How's she doing?"

"Oh, well enough, you know. Same old, same old."

"Yeah," said the man, and suddenly there was a KO gun pointed at Kovalic. He mentally kicked himself for not realizing that the officer's lack of tension had more to do with the fact that he'd already had his weapon at the ready. "Only she's my partner, and she's been on parental leave for the last three months. Let's take that walk, shall we? Hands where I can see them."

Kovalic held up his hands, finally getting a moment to spare a glance at his sleeve. The drone was almost done with its scan – just needed another minute. "Okay, this looks bad, I get it. But I *do* know Inspector Faverweather, and I'm sure if you gave her a call, she'd be happy to vouch for me." Well, 'happy' might be overstating it. Especially if she heard he'd been impersonating a Commonwealth Security officer. Again.

"Well, we've already established that you're not who you say you are. And you're trespassing on an active crime scene," said the officer. "I'm not about to–"

Whatever he'd been about to do, Kovalic might never

know; he was cut off by a distinctive high-pitched whine from the front of the office, followed quickly by a yelp and the thump of something heavy hitting the floor.

The officer seemed split on whether to turn towards this new threat or keep an eye on Kovalic. "What the hell was that?"

Kovalic's senses had sharpened at the telltale sound of a knockout gun's stun field, his pulse elevating. Even through the muffling effect of the bunny suit, he heard footsteps coming from down the hall. More than one pair, moving with a quick efficiency. "Sounds like we have company."

"Friends of yours?"

"Not going to lie: I don't have that many friends." And the ones he *did* have had missed more than one party crasher in the last five minutes, which was making him increasingly worried. But he didn't want to tip his hand to either the officer or these new interlopers by calling in the cavalry just yet.

The officer's grip tightened on the weapon he was holding, but its aim at Kovalic had wavered. "Give me one good reason that I shouldn't stun you out of hand, just so I don't have to deal with you."

"I'll give you two. First, something weird is going on here, and if you care about getting to the bottom of it, you're going to need my help. And second, you stun me, it's one of you against however many there are out there." He nodded to the corridor.

The footsteps had gotten louder and were now incontrovertibly moving in their direction. After a moment's indecision, the officer shifted his grip on the weapon and pointed it towards the incoming threat. "We're not done here, but I guess it can wait. I don't suppose you're armed?"

"Not yet." Kovalic pulled up his sleeve even as the drone finished making its scan. With a quick sequence of taps, he bundled and encrypted the data and dumped it into his sleeve. He was preparing to upload it to a remote server when he noticed the red circle with a slash through it – no connection. Ironic as it would be to have the headquarters of the planet's largest communications company in a dead spot, it seemed more likely that something was blocking the local signals.

Which was definitely not good.

Having retrieved the drone's data, he hardwiped its memory banks, then, after a moment's thought, punched in a sequence of commands to transfer the encrypted file on his sleeve to the nearest location he could think of. No such thing as being too careful. "Come on."

They stepped out into the corridor, as flashlight beams bounced down the hallway like rubber balls.

"You there!" shouted a voice. "Stand where you are!" Kovalic had just enough time to glimpse a pair of individuals in black tactical gear holding knockout guns at the ready, with less friendly-looking weapons slung over their backs.

Well, *that* wasn't going to happen. Kovalic shoved the officer through the doorway opposite the server room even as the blue ripple of a stun field filled the corridor, just narrowly catching his foot as he dove through. His heel went numb and it was only the loud *thump* that told him he'd also banged it hard on the doorframe.

The officer had rolled over onto his back, KO gun pointed at the doorway. "This isn't exactly going to slow them down."

He wasn't wrong. Kovalic could hear them approaching, double-time. The more analytical part of his mind was cataloging their gear, their tactics, trying to figure out who the hell they were, but the reactive part muscled that aside in favor of sheer survival.

Raising his sleeve, he punched in a command. "Get ready to move."

"What?"

Rising into a crouch, Kovalic stabbed the execute button. For a moment, nothing happened. Then a silver streak zipped out of the server room, hurtling down the hallway towards the approaching force. Kovalic heard a cry of alarm, followed by the whine of KO guns. But they had no effect on the target and a split second later, the micro-drone exploded into a flash of blindingly brilliant light.

"Now!" said Kovalic, pushing off with his non-numb foot. Pins and needles dogged his other heel with every step, but he half-ran half-hobbled out the door and down the corridor to where the armed assailants were still recovering from the drone attack, shaking their heads and rubbing at their goggled eyes.

Kovalic plowed into the nearest one, slamming them to the ground with a satisfying grunt. He seized their hand, attempting to wrest the KO gun from their grip. Their partner tried to raise their own weapon and stun Kovalic but were interrupted by the officer colliding with them – the stun field rippled harmlessly into the ceiling.

After slamming the attacker's hand into the ground a few times, Kovalic pried the KO gun loose, then rolled to his feet, pointing the gun down at them.

Next to him, the Commonwealth Security officer had put the other assailant into an armlock, holding them in front of him like a human shield. "Well, *you're* under arrest. Trespassing on an active crime scene, assaulting a law enforcement officer, and we're definitely going to have to see some weapons permits for these." The officer unclipped the carbine slung over the back of their captive and slid it onto a nearby desk.

Kovalic hauled his own catch to their feet and followed suit, removing their carbine. He kept the KO gun he'd taken from them trained on their back as he pushed them forward. "Move."

They led the two out to the front of the ConComm office where they found the uniformed officer who'd been on duty lying on the ground. Kovalic covered both of the armored goons while the Security officer knelt and checked on her.

"Just stunned. She'll be fine in a little while." Standing, he faced the assailants. "But let's find out who these two are, shall we?"

"I wouldn't do that," said one of them suddenly, the first words that they'd spoken since that initial adjuration.

"Oh?" said the officer. "Do tell."

Barely perceptibly, one of them jutted their chin towards the glass main doors. A second later the lift there chimed and out poured another four figures dressed in the same black tactical gear. But these weren't carrying knockout guns – they had real, live-fire weapons pointed through the doors at them.

Kovalic glanced at the officer, then down at the KO gun he held. "Looks like we came to the party underdressed." He let the weapon fall as he slowly raised his hands. "On the upside, you may get your wish."

"Yeah?" said the officer, as they put their own hands in the air.

"You wanted to know who they were. I think we're about to find out."

# CHAPTER 7

It was cold up on the rooftop, the wind whistling through Addy's hair. Salaam's hot and humid air didn't dissipate when night came down, but ride thirty stories to the top of a skyscraper and you were bound to feel a little bit chillier. Even more so when you were lying as still as possible with your eye pressed to a scope.

She could have just used her sleeve to view telemetry from the rifle – or from the half dozen stealth recon micro-drones she'd deployed to give her alternative angles – but her sniper school training had drilled that even the slightest bit of lag from the connection could make a significant difference when trying to take a shot. More to the point, there was just something about having that direct connection to the weapon that made it all seem weightier – not a bad feeling to have when someone's life might be on the other end of that trigger squeeze.

Kovalic had walked into the ConComm office a moment ago, talking his way past the uniformed officer that Addy could just make out from her vantage point, and was now poking around in a room that she couldn't see. She'd locked his biometrics into the recon drones, so they'd shifted automatically to try and get the best angle possible, but that turned out to be only a sliver of him, standing in a doorway.

She still wasn't sure exactly what Kovalic hoped to gain from this, and something in the back of her mind was bothering her about this whole operation. An operation on a Commonwealth planet for one thing – and her home on top of that. It felt weird, skulking around on rooftops that she'd stared up at as a kid. At least she had the homefield advantage for once.

Then there was the whole matter of this Page guy. She'd only had a moment to take him in, back in the alley, but even that brief impression had told her that the man was capable and self-assured. His words might have sounded threatening, but they'd been delivered with a flat, matter-of-fact tone that promised inevitability, if not maliciousness. Poking into Nova Front was going to get them hurt, he'd been certain, but he hadn't said he'd be the one to do the hurting.

"Birdseye, Freefall, I've got movement, possibly headed for 1342," came Tapper's voice over their encrypted channel. "One individual. Male. Mid-30s. About 1.8 meters tall. Dark skin, dark hair. By his bearing, I'd say cop."

Addy's index finger twitched – there was no angle for her to see the street below without re-tasking one of her drones. But that wasn't her job: Tapper and Brody were on the ground, keeping an eye on building access while she watched up top. Teamwork, she reminded herself.

*Do your part, trust them to do the rest.*

"Oh, he's going in all right," said Brody. "Heading for the elevator. Somebody want to let Trailblazer know?"

"Copying him in now," said Tapper. "Or trying to… my connection's going nowhere. Birdseye, you got anything?"

Rolling away from the rifle scope, Addy raised her sleeve

and tried to connect Kovalic to their comm line. The major had insisted that, given the sensitive nature of this mission, they rely on civilian comm networks instead of the military ones they'd usually use. Which meant they were subject to all the unreliability and disruptions that customers experienced. Even, potentially, surveillance, though civilian communications were still securely encrypted. *Maybe it's just an outage – the network's been flaky since the bombing.* An outage at the exact time that they were conducting a covert operation. Sure. "Uh, no dice here either. But *we're* still talking…"

"So it can't be broad-spectrum jamming," said Brody, finishing her thought.

"What, then? Did he step into some sort of black hole?" Her eyes went to the building in front of them, half-expecting it to have vanished from the street. But it still stood, a black slab punctuated with a few lights, against what passed for the dark of night in the city. She pressed her eye back to the scope, trying to track Kovalic.

"Eyes on," she said as she picked him up, still standing in the doorway where she'd last seen him. But he wasn't the only one – one of her drones had an angle on the front of the ConComm office, where an individual matching the description Tapper had given was pulling on a forensic suit. "And he's about to have company."

"Shit," said Tapper. "What are we supposed to do, shoot a signal flare?"

"Actually…" muttered Addy. "Not the worst idea. Hold on." She called up the drone controls and directed one of the constellation towards the window nearest Kovalic's position. "I'm going to try and see if I can get his attention." The drone was equipped with a variety of tools, including a bright spotlight, but that would raise a lot of attention from other parties, including the other drones buzzing around the building. If the team blew its cover, Kovalic wasn't going to be the only one in trouble.

Fumbling her way through the drone's remote control interface, Addy cursed herself once again for not spending more time on her tech skills. Commander Taylor probably could have had the entire set of drones doing choreographed dance routines, whereas she was struggling just trying to get it to relay a microburst transmission to Kovalic.

*But Taylor's not here.* She didn't know where the commander had gone; Kovalic had said something about a personal matter, and when she'd done a little of her own snooping, all she could find was that Taylor had left the planet. If anybody had accused her of missing the commander, she'd deny it, but it was hard not to admit that the lack of her steady presence changed the team's dynamic, maybe even knocked it off-axis.

"Okay, got it," she said, as she tapped the last command in. *I think, anyway.* "Transmitting now." But Kovalic had disappeared from view, stepping into the apparently windowless room that he'd been hovering outside of. The drone emitted a high-frequency burst of data, but she couldn't see any indication that it had been received. *That room could be shielded. Or, hell, maybe the whole building.* She glanced back down at the telemetry on her sleeve and her heart sunk as she saw the man in the forensic suit approaching Kovalic's last location.

"Shit," she said, pressing her eye back to the scope. Her finger flipped the safety on the rifle, and she double-checked that she had shock-gel rounds dialed in. Nothing lethal on this operation; Kovalic had made that much clear. "I think we're too late. Brawler, permission to engage?" Technically Brody was the ranking officer, but he hadn't argued with Kovalic putting the sergeant in operational control. *He knows when he's out of his depth. Usually.*

"Wait one, Birdseye," said Tapper. "Rules of engagement are no firing unless a team member is in serious jeopardy."

"Uh, guys," said Brody.

"Brawler, Trailblazer is about to be potentially apprehended by suspected law enforcement personnel, which constitutes a threat to mission completion," said Addy, squinting as she leveled her crosshairs on what she could see of the man in the forensic suit. The rangefinder automatically adjusted the smart round's built-in programming based on distance: it would punch through the temporary plastic window, then shed the hard casing around its gel payload in the split-second before it hit the target. "I'm not going to have a shot for long. I can disable only. Permission to engage?"

Tapper's voice was sharp. "Negative, Birdseye. Do not fire."

Addy's finger caressed the trigger. One squeeze was all it would take; the shock-gel round would incapacitate the man long enough for Kovalic to exfil.

"*Guys.*"

"Jesus, Brody," said Addy, her frustration boiling over. "*What?*"

"We've got a vehicle on scene discharging multiple armed bogeys heading for the building and, uh, I think they made me." Brody's voice had gone up an octave.

There was a catch in Addy's breath as she tried to swing the rifle down to Brody's position, but the angle of the building didn't allow for it. "Get out. *Now!* Brawler, have you got him?"

Nothing came back on the channel but silence. "Brawler? Freefall?" Her sleeve chirped and she glanced down to see a bright red circle with a slash through it over her data connection indicator, as though the whole local comm network had gone down. That included her encrypted comm channel with the team and even the telemetry from her drones. *The fuck?* The only way that should happen is if all the power in the city had gone out, but as she cast a glance around the rooftop the lights of Salaam were still glowing in the darkness.

Goosebumps rose on her arms that had nothing to do with the wind whipping around her.

*They're coming for me next.* The thought popped in her head from some reflex deep in her brain, by which point she was already moving, pulling her rifle from where it lay, and bringing it to her shoulder as she rolled to her feet.

Access to the roof was via a single door at the top of a stairwell, and she had the rifle aimed in that direction by instinct alone. It was only about fifteen meters away, but her scope was dialed to a much farther range, so she ignored it, sighting along the rifle's barrel instead.

*Who*, exactly, was coming for her was still an open question, but one that she didn't have time to explore right now. Getting out of this situation was priority one. Then she had time for the bigger issues.

As if on cue, the door cracked open. Addy moved quickly and quietly, ducking behind an air handler and bracing her weapon on its corner, keeping the entryway in her line of sight while reducing her profile. Her finger twitched toward the trigger, but she held her fire, waiting to assess the strength and position of the enemy. Boxing them up in the doorway was a tempting option, but it also cut off her escape route.

Patience was a virtue. Or so she'd been told. Repeatedly.

They deployed in efficient silence, a fireteam of three, moving in almost elegant synchrony, nearly invisible matte-black lancer carbines evincing a deadly seriousness. Whoever they were, they meant business. These weren't knockout guns they were carrying, and they were in full assault gear: black helmets, balaclavas, and body armor that would all too adequately protect them from the shock-gel rounds she still had loaded.

Addy gave them a moment to clear the doorway and begin sweeping the roof, waiting to make sure that was all of them. There could be more down the stairs – no way to know – but she felt relatively confident that only the trio had deployed to the roof.

*Fine. Three I can deal with.*

Putting up her rifle, she slid behind the air handler, positioning it between her and the assault team. Path of least resistance would be to circle around behind them and try to get to the door while they continued their search for her. Then she could find Tapper and – her heart twinged – Brody and they could go get Kovalic together. Regroup, figure out what the hell was going on.

She crept to the other end of the metal frame and peered around it. The vantage was clear, so she snuck across to another large piece of the environmental control system – a heat pump maybe? It's not like she was an HVAC specialist – and then around that until she was within sight of the doorway. A quick sprint and she'd be home free.

But she'd lost sight of her adversaries too, which made it a risky move. What she needed was a distraction, to draw them further away from the door and give her a chance at making a run for it. One of her drones would have been ideal, but a glance down at her sleeve showed her that the local network was still registering as offline, so there was no way to control them. She'd have to do it herself.

Taking an inventory, she came up short. She'd divested herself of most of her possessions before they'd deployed: less risk of losing things, or making her easy to identify. All she had was her sleeve and the rifle. She might be able to use the shock-gel round to take down a low-flying drone or short out the electrical system, but she didn't see any likely targets.

*The old ways are the best.* One of Kovalic and Tapper's favorite operational maxims, which was to say, don't overcomplicate things.

It was the work of a moment to unlatch the scope and slide it off the rifle's rails. Not like it was doing her any good anyway. Putting her back to the environmental unit, she risked a peek over it and aimed at a spot across the roof from where she stood, then turned and lobbed the heavy scope in that direction and braced herself.

The scope hit the roof with a clatter, but no hue and cry was raised. Not that she could afford to wait – she was already headed towards the access door, moving as fast as she could without drawing attention. She counted down the feet as she ran: thirty… twenty… ten… and then she was at the door, pulling it open and starting down the steps.

Only to find herself staring directly down the barrel of a bouncer – a non-lethal crowd dispersal weapon – held by a fourth black-suited individual positioned on the first stair landing.

*Well, shit.*

The assailant fired in her direction, but she was already swinging herself over the railing to the next flight down;

she felt the concussive wave just ruffle her hair as she fell, hitting the stairs at an awkward angle that sent her sprawling down the rest of the flight, one bruise at a time, to the landing below. She landed in a heap at the bottom, entangled with her rifle.

This individual clearly wasn't as well trained as their associates, as she heard them let loose a muffled curse through their balaclava as they quickly adjusted their aim down towards her.

She had just enough time to roll over and bring her rifle up, firing a shock-gel round that took them square in the chest. The armor would absorb most of the electric shock, but the rifle had been set to fire a high velocity round to the building next door – the force alone threw them back against the wall, knocking the bouncer's muzzle upward, where the next concussion wave rippled harmlessly against the ceiling.

Climbing to her feet, she got her rifle strap loose and wasted no time in heading for the next flight of stairs, and she didn't stop until she'd descended all thirty stories, heart pounding, breath heaving. Reaching the bottom, she slammed the crash bar on the emergency exit and pushed out into the sultry Salaam night.

Bright spotlights flared around her, blurring her darkness-adjusted vision, and instinctively she threw up an arm to shield her eyes, even as she was cursing her mistake. Not that it would have mattered, as a dozen personnel in the same tactical assault gear trained weapons of assorted degrees of lethality on her.

Off to one side she glimpsed two men, one short and one tall, standing against the side of a ground truck, hands cuffed behind their backs. There was a grimace on Brody's face, no doubt mirrored on her own as the rifle was pulled from her hands and a pair of plasticuffs slapped on her own wrists.

*This was not how I saw this night going,* she had just enough time to think before somebody yanked a black hood down over her head.

# CHAPTER 8

When he looked back at his life, Kovalic calculated that he'd spent a disproportionate amount of time in windowless rooms. A lot of them had been in the basements of embassies, hunched over a terminal or sipping on stale coffee, or tucked away in otherwise abandoned warehouses.

A few had been like this: plasticrete walls, a single metal table with a few unremarkable chairs, a long mirror stretching opposite him.

They'd put cuffs on him – real metal cuffs, looped through a bar bolted to the table, not the plastic quick cuffs that he could break if he needed to – and he knew that even if he couldn't see the cameras or the people behind the mirror, he was being watched.

Where exactly this particular windowless room was, well, that was more of a mystery. The armed personnel who'd shown up at Oluo Plaza had thrown a noise-canceling hood over his head before tossing him in the back of a gravtruck and driven him in what felt like slowly widening circles until he'd had to give up tracking where they were headed.

That had been the last that he'd seen of the Commonwealth Security officer too. They'd gotten the hood treatment a moment before Kovalic, and, he had to assume, been subjected to the same tactics.

Then, an hour or so later, he'd been escorted into this room, the hood yanked off, and abandoned by his captors before his eyes even had the chance to adapt to the bright light.

Interrogation, then. Well, that was just fine. The process was an old friend. First they'd try to disorient him, then they'd pepper him with questions until he slipped up. Or they'd start with the harder stuff. Exactly what their methodology would be depended on one big question:

Who the hell were these guys?

As if in response to his unvoiced query, the door whisked open and in walked a middle-aged woman, her dark hair flecked with silver. She tapped a small card against the fingernails of one hand. Her eyes were dark, impassive with the knowledge of how this was going to go. She'd done this before.

As she took the seat opposite Kovalic, he leaned back in his own chair. Her suit was black over a white shirt, devoid of any identifying information. Standard issue, no personality.

She was studying him just as intently, arms crossed over her chest. Kovalic gave her his most disarming smile, a sympathetic 'I know you're just doing your job, so let's get this over with, shall we?'

She broke the silence first. "Your name is Kaplan."

Kovalic kept his smile up, offered a roll of his shoulders. "You say so."

She tossed what she'd been holding onto the table. An ID card from the Commonwealth Security Bureau, his own picture staring back at him.

"Handsome fellow."

"It's a good fake. Right down to the cryptographic seals. But it *is* a fake. There's no Kaplan in the counterterrorism division."

"Bureaucracy. Such a pain."

"What were you doing at Oluo Plaza?"

"Who's asking?"

She didn't seem to be in a sharing mood.

"Well, the truth is that I'm just a curious guy," said Kovalic, spreading his hands, at least as far as the cuffs would allow him. "My mother always said it would get me into trouble one day, and here we are."

"Okay, 'Kaplan', let's cut the bullshit here." The firm line of her mouth brooked no argument. "You were poking your head where it doesn't belong, and if you don't tell me why, I'm going to throw you in a hole so deep and dark that you'll think you're back in the womb."

"Really? That actually sounds kind of relaxing. The world these days, it's just so *stressful*, you know–"

There was a click and from loudspeakers that Kovalic couldn't see a voice – oddly familiar, though distorted and hard to place – blared. "Cut him loose."

His interrogator looked up, her stoic countenance broken for the first time. "What? I was just getting started."

"Now."

Her lip curling in frustration, she kicked back her chair and stalked to the door, which slid open at her approach. She gave a curt wave, one step short of a rude gesture. "You're free to go."

"I'd say it was a pleasure, but I don't like to lie about small things." He proffered his cuffed hands in her direction.

She tapped her sleeve and the cuffs popped open. "Today's your lucky day."

Doubtful: whatever luck he might have once possessed had started to run out years ago, as was more or less confirmed when he stepped out into the hallway and found himself confronted by a pale-skinned man, glancing down at his sleeve with all the impatience of someone who hopes he has someplace more important to be.

"Major," said Aidan Kester, running a hand through waves of brown hair, impeccably coiffed as always. "Walk with me. Thank you, Agent Lee. That will be all."

Kovalic fell into step with Kester. The Deputy Director of Operations for the Commonwealth Intelligence Directorate was, as per usual for him, wearing an elegantly cut suit, a far cry from the bland number that Agent Lee had sported. His sole concession to the late hour was forgoing a tie, but if they'd woken him up to come down to talk to Kovalic, it didn't show.

Kester led the way down the empty corridor, lined with doors no doubt leading to rooms similar to the one Kovalic had so recently had the pleasure of occupying, and stopped at a lift. The deputy director said nothing, just tapped his foot impatiently until it arrived.

The lift rose smoothly for several levels until it slowed to a stop at what appeared to be the top floor. Kester stepped out, walking through an open reception area where a young blond man, looking a little ragged around the edges, sat at a desk. He straightened as Kester appeared and wordlessly handed him a folded piece of paper.

The director glanced at it, looked back at his assistant and held up a finger, then ushered Kovalic into the office beyond, closing the door behind them.

Kovalic could instantly feel the pressure change in his ears; the whole room was baffled against eavesdropping.

It was a sleek and elegant office, one wall entirely taken up by a wide window, though it was currently frosted to near-opacity. An abstract painting of muddled yellows and blues hung over a black leather sofa, and tall potted plants stood in two of the corners. Nice, yes, but lacking in personality. If he had to sum up the decor in a word, he'd probably have said 'calculated.'

Kester took a seat behind a large waterfall desk of dark brown wood and gestured for Kovalic to take the one opposite.

"So," he said, folding his hands and leaning his elbows on the desk. "Why were you at Oluo Plaza?"

Round two, then. At least he knew who he was dealing with now. "Was I?"

"Don't fuck with me, Kovalic. I'm not some junior interrogator. We've got you and three members of your team, all in a restricted area in the middle of the night."

His first instinct was that Kester was bluffing, trying to use the team as leverage to convince him to talk. But the calm assurance with which he'd thrown out the number of his colleagues made his heart sink. He'd hoped Tapper, Sayers, and Brody might have been able to escape the dragnet that had caught him up, but apparently luck hadn't been on their side either.

When in doubt, answer a question with a question. "Why don't you tell *me* why armed CID commandos have been deployed on Commonwealth soil?" Surprisingly well armed for a *civilian* intelligence agency, to boot; Kovalic was well aware that the directorate maintained its own paramilitary force – including its black-bag Activities division, alongside whom he'd worked several times in the past – but the troops they'd encountered tonight hadn't seemed like standard issue.

Kester adjusted the cuffs on his suit, but Kovalic caught the slightest hint of unease in the gesture, as if he was trying to reassure himself by maintaining his veneer. "First of all, major, I don't have to explain anything to you. Your boss might go toe-to-toe with me, but the key word there is *boss*. Allow me to be the one to inform you that that, as a result of the terrorist bombing on Oluo Plaza and the atmosphere of imminent threat, the Commonwealth Executive asked Director Özkul to coordinate a task force to track down the perpetrators before they can launch whatever subsequent attack they're planning – and, given that I'm the deputy director of operations, she put me in charge of that effort. That mandate includes the temporary suspension of the executive order barring CID from operating domestically, as well as the use of assets from other agencies. Within the remit of these exigent circumstances, naturally." He met Kovalic's eyes again. "Satisfied?"

"Rarely." At least that tacitly answered the question about how Kester had mobilized assault teams on short notice: they were probably critical response personnel from the Bureau or local law enforcement.

But the thought of CID coordinating action on a Commonwealth planet still burned like cheap whisky. The proviso against domestic intelligence operations was there for a reason: to prevent the abuses of power that were all too easy to slide into when those in charge had a force with little to no accountability at their beck and call. Intelligence agencies were not law enforcement; they were intended to investigate external threats, not those within – a line he himself was already toeing by snooping around Oluo Plaza, but one he was doing his best not to cross. CID's brass didn't seem to have the same concerns.

"Well, I don't really care," said Kester, leveling a hawk-like stare at Kovalic. "You're here because not only were you poking your nose in where it doesn't belong, but your – and Adaj's – close ties to this case have already raised some eyebrows." He touched a control on his desk and a holoscreen sprang to life above it, a familiar face shimmering in three dimensions. "Tell me about Aaron Page."

Kovalic shouldn't have been surprised: as the general had said, it was inevitable that CID and Kester would have gotten ahold of the de-obfuscated version of the message. But he'd hoped for a little more time to nail down exactly what Page was up to before he had to run interference.

"Tall. Quiet. He liked books."

Kester's lip twisted into a sneer. "That's what you're going to go with? Books? I read his file, Kovalic. You handpicked him from the School and he served on your team for three years, up until his tragic 'death' nine months ago. Condolences, by the way."

A subterfuge that had ultimately stemmed from the fact that the man in front of him right now had convinced Page to provide intelligence on Kovalic's team, taking advantage of the lieutenant's suspicions that the general was running his own agenda behind the Commonwealth's back. The irony wasn't lost on Kovalic. "It seems those reports were greatly exaggerated. Happens more than you think."

Kester's fingers drummed across the table, rapid-fire. "Apparently he's back. And he seems to have quite the axe to grind. Any idea why?"

"Hard to say. Lieutenant Page was a very private man."

"Well, now he's a very wanted man. Do you know where he is?"

A question he could answer truthfully, at least. "No idea."

"When was the last time you saw him?"

"Classified, I'm afraid," said Kovalic, with a helpless shrug.

"Oh, I assure you, I've got clearance. I know all about Operation LOCKBOX. You know, that time you jeopardized our relationship with the Bayern Corporation and almost thrust us into open war with the Illyricans. Right after which Lieutenant Page suffered a sudden and convenient hovercar accident. Only it seems he didn't. And I want to know why."

"You'd have to ask him."

"I would very much like to. Because not only do I think it would be enlightening, but I imagine he might have quite a bit to say about your little outfit."

Kovalic still didn't know exactly what information Page had funneled to Kester, beyond the mission on Bayern; there hadn't been time for a full debrief at their last meeting on that park bench in Bergfestung. Regardless, it was probably more than he or the general would have liked. The truth was the team's operations had crossed lines in the past, though Kovalic flattered himself that it was out of the best intentions for the galaxy. But Kester would have no hesitation using that information to his advantage if it put him in a better position with the Commonwealth Executive – especially if it tarnished the general's reputation in the bargain.

"I imagine he might."

Even voicing agreement wasn't enough to lighten Kester's mood. "Let's be clear about one thing, Kovalic. I'm in direct operational command here. There's an imminent threat against the Commonwealth – Nova Front's ultimatum gives us only two days. If you have any intelligence about a clear and present danger to the Commonwealth, I'm ordering you to tell me now. If I find out later that you withheld information that might have saved lives, it will go harshly for you. And your boss."

It was probably the authoritative tone Kester used when talking to underlings and politicians, the kind of forceful oratory that no doubt convinced them to fear him and provide him with funding, respectively. Once upon a time, even Kovalic might have been browbeaten into capitulating, but he was too goddamned old and too tired for this shit.

"Understood. Was there anything else?"

The deputy director looked to be contemplating throwing Kovalic back into a room with Agent Lee, but eventually he flicked his hand in a dismissive gesture. "That will be all, major. For now."

Kovalic rose from the chair with a tilt of his head. "And my team?"

Kester's eyes bored lasers into him. "They'll be released. This time. But if you insist on continuing to interfere with this investigation, then I won't be so generous when we cross paths again. Count on it."

# CHAPTER 9

It wasn't the first time that Eli Brody had found himself hooded, restrained, and interrogated. Come to think of it, it wasn't even the second time in as many years.

*This is a weird lifestyle I've gotten myself into.*

The good – good? – news was that he felt like he'd come up in the world. For one thing, the hood they slung over his head, though it dampened sound like he was in a vacuum, didn't smell like a towel used to clean up after a vomiting pet.

For another, any tactic – even if it was still off-putting and nerve-wracking – lost some of its shock value after you'd seen the same playbook a couple times. So when they whisked the hood off in an interrogation room, full of bright lights and a one-way mirror, all he could think was *Ah. This again.*

The interrogation part didn't even last long. After an hour of questions that he deflected, redirected, and ignored, he was cut loose and deposited in the nondescript foyer of the building; Tapper and Addy arrived within minutes of him, and all three stood around as though not sure what to do next.

"Uh," said Eli, "fancy meeting you here?"

As usual the other two members of his team were smarter than him, holding their tongues until Kovalic stepped from the nearby lift and walked out the door, without even a gesture to them. They filed out afterwards, Eli having little option but to trail behind the others.

A waiting hovercar, far nicer than the truck that they'd been thrown into earlier in the evening, ferried them back to Salaam, where they were deposited with no fanfare in the middle of a darkened downtown square. A fountain burbled away happily in its center, surrounded by trees.

*What the hell time is it, anyway?* Eli instinctively glanced at his sleeve, which the interrogator had returned when he was released, but before he even registered the number, Kovalic had reached over and pulled it from his arm, wadding it up with his own and stuffing them into a nearby trash receptacle. "Hey..." protested Eli.

But Kovalic had already walked over to the fountain and taken a seat on the stone wall around it, letting his hand trail in the water. Addy and Tapper followed the major's lead, disposing of their own sleeves, and joining him near the water feature.

Kovalic's eyes drifted around the plaza with an almost lazy disposition, but Eli was close enough to see the sharpness in it: looking for surveillance, tails, cameras.

Tapper spoke first. "What's going on, boss?"

Kovalic removed his hand, flicking water droplets from it. "The situation just got more complicated. Those goons were Kester's – he wants Page."

Beside Eli, he could sense Addy shifting.

"Something on your mind, specialist?" said Kovalic.

"It's just... are you sure Page is worth all this trouble? Maybe we'd be better off just letting Kester have him."

Tapper grunted. "Not a chance. Page is still family. We look out for him like he was one of us. Same as we would for you or Commander Taylor. Or even Brody." He jerked a thumb in Eli's direction.

Eli resisted the urge to roll his eyes. "Thanks."

Tension had gathered around the corners of Addy's mouth, but the specialist just nodded. The team had proved in the past that they had her back, and Eli knew how much that meant to her. Even if she wasn't always willing to admit it.

"So, what's the plan?" said Eli, looking to Kovalic. "You do have a plan, right?"

"It's in progress. Currently, we have two questions that need addressing. First, where's Page?"

Tapper let out a whoosh of air. "Finding him isn't going to be easy. He was always careful as a cat on a cactus, and that was *before* he was on the top of the most wanted list. Hell, I think you were the only person who ever knew where he lived."

"Well, we need to find a way to reach out and make contact. Convince him to come in from the cold."

"You're the one who knew he was still alive," said Tapper. "You're telling me you don't have a contact protocol in place?"

The major's lips pressed together in a thin line, and Eli could tell that the sergeant had hit a nerve. "If I had a way to contact him, I'd like to think we wouldn't be in this position right now."

Which made perfect sense to Eli, but something poked at his brain, telling him that Kovalic *still* wasn't being forthcoming with all the details.

"This dovetails into the second question," Kovalic

continued. "We know Page was connected to what happened at Oluo Plaza. Which means we need to figure out what the hell was going on there."

"They already kicked you out once," said Eli. "I think they're going to frown on you going back."

"Us, yes. But I think I know somebody who isn't likely to be deterred by that *and* who might have a better shot than we do. Anyway, that's for me to work on."

The gentle night breeze fluffed Eli's hair as he glanced at Tapper and Addy. "What about the rest of us?"

"Divide and conquer. Tapper, I need you to dig up every old friend, contact, and drinking buddy in the Commonwealth's intelligence apparatus and see if any of them knows anything about Oluo Plaza."

Tapper scratched at the gray bristles on his chin. "I think I know a few people who know a few people."

"Good. Sayers, I'll give you the access codes for Commander Taylor's terminal – she's got sniffer programs that can tap into local surveillance networks. I need you to search for any sign of Page, see if we can't track him down."

"Uh, data crunching isn't really my thing."

Kovalic rubbed at his forehead. "I know, but we're a little shorthanded, so we're all going to have to stretch ourselves a bit."

Addy nodded, though her reluctance was plain.

Eli looked around. "What about me?"

"Brody, I need you on operational readiness."

*Operational readiness?* "What's that in normal person speak?"

"When we find Page, we're going to need to move fast, and I want to ensure that we're not caught flat-footed. We don't know when, much less where, so just make sure the

*Cavalier* is fueled and ready to go, then coordinate with Sayers and Tapper so any gear they need is onboard."

*Soooo, basically packing.* "Uh, sure."

Kovalic looked around at each of them in turn. "We've all got our assignments – I suggest we get some sleep. We'll reconvene tomorrow afternoon, 1300, at Yamanaka." With a nod, he walked away, no doubt to the comfort of an apartment in which there wasn't somebody who had just this morning thrown their entire relationship up in the air. *And where it lands, nobody knows.*

Eli studiously avoided looking at Addy; the specialist hovered uncertainly for a moment before turning on her heel and heading towards the street, where autocabs and other vehicles still zipped by, even at this late an hour. *Yeah, I guess it's best if we aren't seen leaving together. Also, that would be a fun ride home.*

As he steeled his courage to follow, Eli felt a heavy hand descend on his shoulder.

"Why don't you and me go have a drink before we call it a night?" said Tapper.

"A drink? It's like…" He made to glance at his sleeve before remembering it was in the trash, so he just stared at his actual jacket sleeve blankly before looking back up at Tapper. "…very late. Or very early."

"Humor an old man." The grip on Eli's shoulder tightened a bit, and he got the idea that this was something more than a polite suggestion.

Without their sleeves, Eli wasn't sure how they were going to find a bar, much less pay for drinks, but Tapper steered them directly to an establishment that was not only within a five-minute walk, but also still doing a brisk business. To its credit, it was also clean and not overwhelmingly raucous, and within a few moments they were seated at a booth, each with a pint of beer that Tapper had somehow managed to convince one of the bar's denizens to put on their tab. *Probably from swapping war stories.*

"Cheers," said the sergeant, raising his glass.

Eli clinked his own against the sergeant's, then took a swig. It was good beer: dark and malty, with a pleasant hint of spice, and against all odds he felt some of the tension ebb away. The constant murmur of the bar's other patrons was, if not quite soporific, at least soothing, and he felt himself drifting into a warm lull. He raised his ale and took a long pull.

"So," said Tapper, "you and Sayers, huh?"

One element of pilot training was being able to keep your stomach under control, and it was only by dint of that experience that the sergeant didn't end up wearing Eli's drink. Instead, he managed to force the liquid down, then sputtered for air.

*"What?"*

Tapper raised a hand. "Not making any judgments. Small unit like this, high pressure situations, bonds develop. I get it."

"I didn't – she's just – I mean – look, she needed a place to crash. Housing in the city isn't cheap." *Oh, yes, the old 'housing is expensive' argument. Very smooth.*

"Sure. Just saying that I know things can get complicated. And if you need to talk… well, there's probably someone out there in the wide world who would listen."

"Oh, thanks."

"Don't mention it." The sergeant leaned back against the banquette, resting his arms across the top and letting his eyes close for a moment. "What I'm saying is we all keep secrets, kid."

Eli's hand closed around the glass, feeling his body heat

leach away. "Oh come *on*. It's not the same. We're talking about my personal life not…" he hesitated, glancing around, but it didn't seem like anybody was overly interested in their conversation, "…life or death. You can't tell me you're okay with this."

He could see the sergeant's arms tense, but when his eyes opened, they were steady and clear. "Brody, I know it's easy to forget sometimes, because the boss, he doesn't mind keeping things casual. We play outside the box. We improvise. But there's still a chain of command here, and he's the one making the decisions. It doesn't matter if we *like* them. We follow them. End of story."

"Blind loyalty." It left a sour taste in Eli's stomach that wasn't entirely from drinking a pint of beer after not having eaten anything all night.

Almost seven years ago, he'd sat behind the stick of a fighter and watched his squadron-mates blown to kingdom come as they fought a battle they couldn't possibly win, all because of that same obedience to the chain of command. "That's not what I signed up for."

The sergeant let out a long sigh. "I get it. There's a fine line between blind loyalty and trust. I've known the major for a long time, and I trust him. With my life and, to be honest, with my soul. He's saved both more times than I can count. That trust doesn't come easy, and it doesn't come cheap. And maybe you're not there yet – maybe you never will be. That's okay."

"And what about Page?"

A slight twitch in the brow of that lined face. "What about him?"

"You trusted him, right? And now we're what, hunting him down? It doesn't seem right, sarge."

Tapper didn't say anything for a moment, just took a swallow of beer.

*Uh oh. Maybe I broke him.*

"No," he said finally. "It doesn't seem right. That's what my gut's saying, anyway. But it's the mission. We find Page, we bring him in. Then we figure out what the hell is going on." Tapper drained the last of his drink and set the glass back down. "The major gets paid to make the hard decisions, Brody. I'm just a grunt."

*Uh huh, sure.* As much as the sergeant liked playing that card, Eli had spent enough time with him to know it for the convenient fiction it was. He'd seen the way Kovalic leaned on Tapper, relied on him as a sounding board and, yes, even as a conscience. But he'd take even the sergeant's tacit admission that something was wrong about this whole situation as a win of sorts.

Tapper stood without the slightest waver. "If you want my advice, and lord help me, I don't know why you would, go home, get some sleep, and come back tomorrow ready to work." He turned to go, then paused and looked over his shoulder. "Oh, and maybe talk things out with your *roommate*. Before it gets either of you into trouble." And with that, he was gone into the night, leaving Eli alone in the bar to nurse his thoughts and the remainder of his drink.

*I don't know, sarge. Somehow talking things out only ever seems to get me into* more *trouble.*

# CHAPTER 10

The car was waiting for Addy when she stepped out of the apartment.

She'd tried to sleep in after last night's excursion, but had just ended up tossing and turning; the eventual invasion of morning sunlight had found her unrested, so she'd risen before her usual hour with the hope of getting a jump on the day.

Despite her early start, a note on the kitchen display suggested Brody hadn't slept much better: he'd gone into the hangar early, supposedly to check in on the *Cavalier*'s status, but she knew it was mainly so he wouldn't be there when she got up.

It wasn't fair to say they'd been avoiding each other ever since their awkward conversation the previous day – they really hadn't had time to avoid each other, what with old comrades coming back from the dead, terrorist attacks, and covert missions in the Commonwealth's capital. But eventually they'd had to go back to the three-room efficiency apartment, and it was hard to stay out from under foot of each other. In some misplaced fit of chivalry, Brody had elected to sleep on the couch in the living area, leaving Addy the loft bedroom to herself. The bed had been too big and, much as she hated to admit it, too cold. *I'm getting soft. Used to sleep in any corner where I could pile a grubby blanket, and now I'm complaining that it's a bit chilly?*

She'd grabbed a quick shower to slough off the rest of her sleep-addled funk, gotten dressed, and snagged a food bar from the pantry before stepping out into the marginally cooler morning.

*Time to start apartment hunting, I guess.* Making sure the door was closed behind her, she had just unwrapped the food bar and taken a bite when she turned and saw the car.

Long and sleek, the vehicle was all black with tinted windows, which wasn't ominous at all. Her reflexes flared as she immediately began checking her surroundings for other threats. Only yesterday morning a bomb had gone off in downtown Salaam, so an attack in broad daylight in a peaceful suburb was hardly out of the question.

The front door to the car cracked open and a young woman around Addy's own age stepped out. Pinkish complexion with brown hair in a pixie cut, a light dusting of freckles coating the bridge of her nose. She wore the same kind of casual attire favored by off-duty military officers, which ended up being about as reliable a way to identify them as if they were in full uniform.

The processed food bar went even drier in Addy's mouth, but she choked the lump down and stuffed the remainder in her pocket, walking slowly towards the street.

"Whatever it is you're selling, I'm not interested," said Addy, keeping her hands by her sides, fingers lightly curled, but not yet fists.

The woman reached over to the car's rear door and pulled it open. From within an old man slowly emerged, knees creaking with effort as he leaned heavily on a wooden stick.

It may not have been the most impressive entrance Addy had ever seen, but what it lacked in grace it more than made up for in dignity.

When the man drew himself up, Addy found herself looking into a pair of pale blue eyes that already seemed to know everything about her.

"I assure you, Specialist Sayers, that I am not selling anything. I am merely asking for a moment of your time." His voice was smooth, cultured, with just the hint of an accent.

Addy stayed loose, pushing down the combat instincts that wanted to bubble to the surface. "My time's valuable. Why should I spend it talking to you?"

If she expected someone this imposing to look insulted, she was surprised again. A smile cracked the old man's face, followed by a throaty chuckle. "Simon did not misrepresent you. I'm only sorry it's taken us this long to meet face-to-face."

*What the hell is he on ab – oh, crap.* Old man? Fancy hovercar? Dropping Kovalic's first name?

"You're the gen–"

He offered a slight, stiff bow. "At your service. May I offer you a ride to work?"

Addy's food bar was threatening to reverse course, but she forced it back down with a gulp. Throwing up on the boss's boss was one way to make an impression, but probably not the kind you made if you wanted to stay employed.

"Uh, sure. Thanks." *What, am I going to say no?*

He stood to the side, gesturing to the open door, and she slid into the darkened interior. The old man followed her after a moment, with what almost sounded like a mechanical whir, then the door was shut from the outside.

Addy's ears popped almost immediately as the noise of the street vanished. *Of course he's got the car baffled – he's the head of a secret intelligence unit.* A moment later, she saw the back of the young woman's head appear in the front compartment.

"Yamanaka Base, if you please, Rance," said the general, and the car pulled smoothly away from the curb.

"It's a nice neighborhood," he said in appraisal, watching the houses and apartment buildings stream past through the darkened window. "Very kind of Lieutenant Brody to put you up while you're looking for a more permanent place to stay."

Now the food bar had turned into a knot in the pit of her stomach. The general's expression hadn't changed in the least at the comment – not a suggestive glance, nor so much as a knowing glint in his eyes. He'd made the comment seemingly entirely without guile.

But he'd made it nonetheless. And he didn't seem like the kind of person who made a habit of idle chit-chat.

*Easy, Addy.* "He's got a comfortable couch," she said, cool as you like.

The general nodded absently, as though he hadn't cared in the slightest about where Addy might be sleeping. "I am sorry to show up without any notice," he said, resting his stick against the door. "But I prefer not to pre-announce my plans – old habits die hard."

Addy wasn't quite sure what he meant by that, but apparently it was a rhetorical comment, as he continued without a pause.

"As I said, I did think it was time for us to meet face-to-face. Simon does a very capable job of handling the day-to-day operations of the SPT, but I do like to at least have a face to put with a name. And I'd like to say that your performance thus far has been impressive, Specialist Sayers. I know we threw you into the deep end on the *Queen Amina* operation, but you acquitted yourself well."

Kovalic hadn't shown her the report of the mission to retrieve the Aleph Tablet, but if the general was impressed with her performance, then clearly her CO had taken some liberties with his assessment. *I almost botched the whole thing at least three or four times.* But she knew how to seize a compliment when it was offered. "Thank you, sir."

The car accelerated as it merged onto the highway, and Addy could feel the slightest of jolts as control relinquished to the automated traffic systems.

The old man glanced out the window again, and Addy's focus sharpened. *He's buttering me up for something.* This whole thing was carefully constructed – knocking her off-kilter, praising her performance… there was a hook coming somewhere at the end of all of this, just like the short cons she used to run. Play the person, not the game.

The catch came soon enough, as the general continued gazing out the window. "I need your help, specialist."

Addy allowed herself a moment of feeling smug before worry descended anew. "What kind of help?"

"I'm sure Major Kovalic has read you in on the situation with the Novan Liberation Front and Lieutenant Page."

*How polite of him to call it 'a situation' and not 'a clusterfuck.'*
"Yes, sir."

"This is a thorny matter, as I'm sure you'll agree. Having one of our own – a former member of the Special Projects Team – engaged in a terrorist attack on Novan soil not only poses a significant threat to the Commonwealth, but also potentially compromises the other members of the team."

His fingers drummed rapidly against his thigh. "My concern is that Major Kovalic, Sergeant Tapper, and Lieutenant Brody are too close to this matter and will be unable to remain… objective."

A grimace stole over Addy's face as she remembered Brody decking Kovalic, not to mention the resulting argument amongst the team. Loss of objectivity was one way to put it. She would have said they'd lost their goddamn minds. "I see."

"May I ask your assessment?"

She kept her mouth shut for a moment. Was she being asked to inform on her team? She hesitated – the general was Kovalic's boss, and if there was one thing Kovalic and Taylor had drilled into her, it was to give authority its due.

Which didn't mean she couldn't do it her way. "I don't disagree with you, sir."

The general gave a short, sharp nod, as though she had just confirmed his expectations. "My priority, Specialist Sayers, is the safety of the SPT. In this matter I think they could be the Commonwealth's most valuable asset – nobody else has as good an understanding of how Lieutenant Page thinks, what he might do, and, most importantly, how he might do it. But the same connection that lends them that insight also makes them particularly vulnerable."

"And I assume you're coming to me because I have no connection with Page."

"Very astute. Yes, I trust that you can remain… detached from this matter, in a way that the rest of the team cannot. And so I need to ask you to do something that will potentially be difficult."

The food bar had migrated upward, a lump in her throat that she couldn't swallow down.

"I won't spy on them."

"I'm sorry?"

"If you're looking for someone to report back to you on what's going on within the team, that's not me." Informants always got what was coming to them in her experience, and she had no intention of betraying anybody.

"Nor would I ask you to," he said, his voice almost gentle. "As I said, this is about keeping them safe." Leaning closer, the old man's blue eyes had gone suddenly warmer, sympathetic even. "I would not ask you to do this if it weren't of the utmost importance, Specialist Sayers. I know how hard the adjustment has been for you, and I don't wish you to put your standing in the team at risk, but you're the only one I can turn to."

"Spit it out. Sir."

Probably brusquer than she should have been, but he didn't blink. "I need you to watch Major Kovalic's back. Aaron Page is a most resourceful young man, possibly the greatest threat the SPT has ever had to contend with. If it seems like Simon is behaving… irrationally, then I would like you to intervene."

Addy's heart kicked into overdrive, thumping in her chest. "To be clear, sir, when you say 'intervene', what exactly do you mean?"

"I've read your jacket, specialist. You're fully qualified by the Commonwealth's sniper school. High marks in tactical training. Plus, a knack for reading people. I trust you to use your instincts and whatever means seem… necessary."

*But you're still not going to say it out loud. That you want me to kill Page if it comes to it.* Plausible deniability and all that. But if he'd read her file, then he knew *all* the numbers.

"Adelaide," said the general, and she felt her eyes snap to him, drawn almost gravitationally. "I am sorry to put this burden on you. But I need you to protect Major Kovalic and the rest of your team. I believe you're up to the task."

The hovercar slowed, and Addy glanced out the window to see the low-slung buildings of Yamanaka Base stretching out from behind gleaming security barriers. Somewhere in there were her team, her friends, her – though the word almost made her break out in hives – *family*. And they were in danger from somebody who knew them even better than she did, somebody who'd been part of that family, and might use that very fact against them. Addy's teeth raked over her bottom lip, but finally, she ducked her head. "I understand."

Relief washed over the general's face. "Good. If you need anything at all, do not hesitate to get in touch. Rance will provide you with the necessary details."

As if summoned by her name, the young woman opened the car door, admitting the blinding sunlight, and Addy took her cue to step out into the Novan morning that was already turning hot and humid.

"Specialist?" called the general from inside the car, and Addy had to bend over to look inside.

"Sir?"

One corner of the old man's mouth twitched upwards. "Thank you."

Then Rance closed the door and waved her sleeve over Addy's. "Encrypted comm channel," she said. "Direct line, any time, day or night. Good luck." And with that she ducked back into the car, which zipped away leaving only a wisp of dust in its wake.

Dazed, Addy turned towards the base, and tried not to let the crushing weight of expectations fold her into a puddle on the pavement.

*Oh well. Wouldn't be the first time.*

# CHAPTER 11

Unlike the highly secretive, cordoned-off headquarters of CID or Yamanaka Base's imposing perimeter fencing, the main building of the Commonwealth Security Bureau was a stately edifice smack in the center of downtown Salaam. Glass and steel, it reflected the city back at itself, which Kovalic had once heard Tapper – noted architecture enthusiast – say was the intent of the designer. "It's supposed to remind everybody, citizen and employee alike, that they're all part of the same populace."

Kovalic couldn't help but note that the sheen on the glass also made it impossible to see *into*, thus making the law enforcement agency not only functionally opaque, but also turning them into the kind of one-way glass used in interrogation windows. Mixed metaphor, that.

The sun glinted off the building as he walked into the lobby and up to the main reception desk. Automated kiosks spread throughout the room allowed citizens to enter complaints or make appointments, but Kovalic always preferred the human touch.

The young man behind the desk was carefully groomed, in a dark suit and tie, and looked up with a trained pleasantry as he approached. "Good morning. How can I help you?"

"Good morning. I'd like to see Inspector Laurent of the counterterrorism division, please."

"May I ask what this is in regards to?"

"Tell him that Mr Kaplan would like a word."

Without so much as batting an eye at the potential oddness of the request, the young man tapped his earpiece and murmured the message into it. He waited for a moment, then nodded and looked back up at Kovalic. "I'll just need your sleeve, sir."

Kovalic waved his brand new sleeve – pulled out of his not insignificant reserve collection – over the contact terminal indicated, and an icon appeared on the smart fabric display, indicating that he had been granted visitor access for two hours.

"You can go right up, sir. Swipe in through the gates over there, which will take you to the lifts. Inspector Laurent's office is on the seventh floor. He'll meet you there."

Nodding his thanks, Kovalic followed the instructions and minutes later was stepping out into a foyer that was clearly the public-facing side of the operation: it looked like nothing so much as the waiting room of a doctor's office, except for the much better views through the tinted glass windows. Before Kovalic had a chance to take a seat, a nondescript door in the opposite wall buzzed open to discharge the man he presumed was Inspector Rashad Laurent.

It hadn't been too hard to track him down: Kovalic had poked around after their brief detention in the wee hours of the morning and pulled Laurent's name from some contacts. The inspector was as tall and broad-shouldered as Kovalic had expected, but, now free of last night's forensic suit, his sharp, skeptical eyes brooked no nonsense. His carefully trimmed black beard was thick and full over his dark brown skin.

"So you're Kaplan," he said, in that same basso profundo from last night, tilting his head to one side.

"Nice to see you again, Inspector Laurent. Especially under better circumstances."

"You here to turn yourself in?"

"What, is there a reward for assisting the authorities?"

Laurent raised an eyebrow. "As I recall, we both ended up at gunpoint before being detained. All of which I was perfectly capable of doing on my own."

"Fair point. Well, then, let me give it a second try. I've got information about the Oluo Plaza bombing that might be of interest to you."

The skepticism had never left Laurent's eyes. If anything, it only seemed to intensify. "Oh? And can I ask where you acquired this information?"

"You were there."

"From the scene?" The doubt was commingled with interest – Kovalic suspected that Kester had been no more forthcoming with Laurent, despite the inspector's actual jurisdiction over the crime scene. And Laurent didn't seem like the kind of person who was willing to let those sorts of things slide.

"Got it in one."

"And why exactly are you willing to share it with me? I assume it's not out of the goodness of your heart."

"You wound me," said Kovalic, putting a hand to his chest. "I'm just a citizen trying to do his part."

"Uh huh. A citizen who was impersonating a law enforcement officer."

"I'm not sure you have any hard evidence of that." Kester's goons had taken his fake Commonwealth Security identification – not that he couldn't get another if he needed to, but without that as proof, all Laurent had was a person whose face he had never seen.

"Touché. I don't suppose you want anything in return for sharing this information?"

"Well, now that you mention it…"

"There's always a catch with you spooks." He rubbed his chin. "You dropped Ronnie Faverweather's name last night, so I called her up. Asked about some cloak-and-dagger type butting into Bureau business and she didn't need three guesses to know who I meant."

"Oh?" Kovalic tried not to hold his breath. "She had only good things to say, I take it?"

"She said you were an arrogant son of a bitch and if she never saw you again, it would be too soon."

"Ah."

"But she also said you were a man of your word and that you could be… resourceful." Laurent's lips flickered in an almost smile as he reached behind himself, waving his sleeve over the access panel, which glowed green as the door clicked open. He pulled it wide and jerked his head. "Coming?"

Beyond the door lay a bustling bullpen surrounded on all sides by partitioned offices. The susurration of officers hard at it had been inaudible from the other side, and while Kovalic caught a few sidelong glances of curiosity about the visitor in their midst, their discipline mainly kept them glued to their work. Holoscreens and large wall-mounted displays showed images of the Oluo Plaza bomb site, analysis that was too dense for Kovalic to read – much less understand – and even some images of people, though he noticed one very specific face missing.

Kester may have known of Page's involvement, but it

seemed as though he was keeping that information close to the vest. Self-interest or the usual interagency politics?

Laurent led him into one of the offices, then toggled the privacy shield, the glass turning opaque behind them. As offices went, it was utilitarian: a desk, flanked by two chairs, and topped by a terminal. One photo sat on the shelf behind, a pair of young kids with a resemblance to Laurent, mugging for the camera.

They took their seats and Laurent leaned back, crossing his arms. "All right, so, where's this intel?"

"Ah, well, that's a bit awkward. You have your sleeve?"

Laurent looked puzzled, but raised his arm, where the smart fabric display glowed to life.

"I took a bit of a calculated risk last night," said Kovalic. "I figured that whoever those armed goons were, they would be less likely to injure, interrogate, or otherwise interfere with a legitimate Commonwealth Security officer doing his job." He nodded to Laurent. "No such compunction with me, you see. So I guessed that the data would be safer with you."

"What are you – wait, you put the data on *my* sleeve?"

"Heavily encrypted microburst transmission, hidden on a low-level partition. Nobody's going to find it unless they know where to look." Kester and his team had doubtless picked apart Kovalic's own sleeve with a fine-tooth comb, and while he was reasonably confident in his skills to keep data hidden, he was glad that his instinct that Laurent would be subject to less scrutiny seemed to have paid off.

Laurent's brow furrowed, partly in annoyance and partly in genuine curiosity. "But I didn't accept any connections."

Kovalic gave him an embarrassed smile. "So many unknown security flaws in these things – you've got to be careful." He sent a mental thanks to Nat for making sure that the team was still well equipped with the right tools in her absence, though it came with a pang; she would have been invaluable on this one.

"You hacked my sleeve."

"I preemptively provided you with critical information about a case you were investigating."

The expression on Laurent's face was one that Kovalic was all too familiar with, that of an impending headache. "I'm starting to understand the 'son of a bitch' part. All of this better be worth it."

"I understand that your forensic team hasn't gotten access to the site yet," said Kovalic, ignoring the comment.

The inspector's lips pressed together in a flat line. After a moment, he relaxed slightly, huffing a breath. "They're not the only ones. Deputy Director Kester's joint task force has Oluo Plaza locked down. Even I couldn't get *official* clearance, and counterterrorism is my goddamn department."

"Didn't seem to stop you."

"Well, I just happened to be perusing the duty logs and noticed that Officer Miyaki was assigned to Oluo Plaza last night. She owed me one." He eyed Kovalic with a faint note of suspicion. "Though she was cagey about exactly why she let you in."

"I can be charming. When the need calls for it."

Laurent laughed for the first time, a short, sharp *hah*. "So, what did you find that was so important you had to compromise my sleeve's security?"

"Before you interrupted my poking around, my micro-drone was performing a thorough scan of the scene. It discovered a hole in the wall behind one of the server racks."

"*Behind* the server rack?" That had gotten a rise out of

Laurent. Or his eyebrows, at least. "Okay, I'll bite. What's in the hole?"

Kovalic gestured to the inspector's sleeve. "Great question. Let's find out."

"Hm," said Laurent, leaning back in his chair. "So, if I have the data on my sleeve, what do I need you for?"

"Like I said, it's encrypted. I'm happy to decrypt it for you, but there is a condition."

"I suspected there might be."

"I know I'm not involved in this investigation in an official capacity, but I think I could be of some help to you. I'd like to be kept apprised of any developments."

"You want me to – against all rules and regulations, I might add – read you in on a top priority, extremely sensitive law enforcement operation?"

"I can't help if I don't know what's going on." And having all the information he could get meant a better chance of finding Page before either the Bureau *or* Kester did.

"And I want your help?"

"I have resources that you don't – especially if you're on the outside on this one. And, while I don't want to break any laws, I don't mind giving them a bend once in a while. Just to make sure they're working, naturally."

In another situation, Laurent's expression might have been a half-smile. "So I suppose the more important question is: why would you trust *me*?"

Kovalic didn't relax entirely, but he did let himself sink back into the chair a bit more; this was a formality – Laurent was in. "I did some digging on you, too. You've been Inspector Faverweather's partner for three years. If you've lasted that long working side-by-side with her, then it tells me that you're somebody who can be trusted."

The twitch about Laurent's eyes didn't betray much, but Kovalic could tell that he was pleased. "Sounds like we understand each other then. Mind decrypting this?" He raised his sleeve.

A few taps on his own device and Kovalic sent the key to Laurent. The inspector pulled up the drone scans on a holoscreen and scrubbed forward to the point where it had passed through the hole in the wall... and into another small room.

A very empty room.

"I have to admit: somewhat less exciting than I'd hoped," said Laurent.

"I'm more interested in what that room is doing there," said Kovalic. "Is it part of the ConComm office?"

Laurent frowned and pulled up the blueprints for 1342 Oluo Plaza, then started flipping through the floors. "Let's see. Looks like... well, that's weird. There's nothing there."

"So, what, it's just empty office space?"

The inspector shook his head and gestured at the plans, zooming in. "No, I mean *nothing*. The blueprints don't show a room there at all – just a maintenance shaft that runs the height of the building, and some structural beams."

Kovalic looked back at the drone scan. It was hard to make out the detail of the hidden room: it had been dark inside and there were clearly no windows, so they were limited to the infrared, low-light, and thermal scans, none of which had the highest resolution. But there was something in the far wall that could be a door or hatch – possibly into the maintenance shaft Laurent had mentioned?

Otherwise, all the video showed were patchy areas on the wall it shared with the server room. Though surprisingly *regular* patches: large, rectangular, sharp edged. Almost as if there had been something there, and the wall around it had accumulated a layer of dust.

"Something was removed," said Laurent, almost at the same time that Kovalic came to the identical conclusion. "Quite a few things, by the look of it." He ran back the drone's sweep, replayed it.

Peering more closely at the image, Kovalic noticed something else: within the patches, there were some small sections that also registered as lighter against the dark, but it was difficult to see in the low-contrast image. "Do you mind if I…?" he asked, gesturing to the terminal.

Laurent flicked the holoscreen in his direction. "Be my guest."

Kovalic reached up and adjusted the exposure controls, upping the contrast and overlaying the different scan layers. Those sections *were* lighter. Moreover, they seemed to have a slightly different composition than the rest of the wall. "Those were holes," he said. "They were patched up. Recently."

"So something was removed and then *literally* covered up," said Laurent.

"Which leaves three big questions: what was it, who put it there, and who removed it?"

"And was it all the same people?"

Kovalic bit his lip. It was a good point: he'd been assuming one party was responsible, but he also knew that Page had been on scene as part of the emergency response team that had showed up directly after the explosion. Which meant they had access to the building before the genuine authorities had arrived and could have easily removed… well, whatever had been there.

"How much do you know about Nova Front? Were they on your radar?"

"Not as such," said Laurent. "We'd heard whispers of a more militant offshoot of the Nova First movement, but this kind of came out of nowhere. Bold opening statement, for sure."

"I'm guessing it's not the last you're going to be hearing from them, either. Especially if we don't meet their deadline."

The inspector looked like he'd sucked a lemon. "I wish I could disagree with you. I've got several officers looking into Nova Front, but we haven't turned up anything yet."

Kovalic turned back to the screen and idly panned the drone footage around again. There had to be something here that would shed light on the room's former contents, and whoever had removed what had been there.

He flipped to the mass spectrometer readings the drone had collected and scanned through the footage again. Maybe there was something that they just couldn't see.

There was a chirp as the readout highlighted an anomalous patch on the floor – something that didn't match the readings from the rest of the room – and spat out a chemical formula, then helpfully annotated it.

"Looks like there's some trace residue," said Kovalic. "Seems to be the same paint that was used to clean up the walls." Easy to miss at a glance: the dingy off-white shade blended in all too well with the grime on the floor. He keyed in a command and had the terminal start enhancing the image.

Laurent peered at the picture as the drone sharpened and added contrast. "That sure looks like…"

"…a footprint." Kovalic peered closer.

It wasn't the whole print, just a slightly smudged section, but that was enough to tell them a few important things. He glanced over at the inspector, only to see Laurent had already reached the same conclusion.

"Looks like whoever was doing the cover-up work got sloppy," Laurent said. He reached out and grabbed the picture, then flicked it out into its own holoscreen. "Well, it's not much, but it's somewhere to start, at least. I'll let you know what I find."

The dismissal was implicit, but Kovalic didn't take it personally – he had his own work to do. He straightened his jacket as he stood. "Appreciate it, inspector. In the meantime, I need to check in with my own people."

"Then we've got an understanding," said Laurent, his gaze fixing on Kovalic as he leaned back in his chair. "Free flow of information – two ways."

"Two ways. What, you think I won't share?"

"Let's just say it hasn't been my experience with your sort," said Laurent, looking back down at his terminal and giving Kovalic an offhand wave.

An officer escorted Kovalic back out through the bullpen, which didn't give him a chance to snoop on any of the rest of the work going on there, and then back down to the lobby, where his visitor badge was politely but firmly rescinded as he swiped out of the gates.

Out in the street, he just had time to draw a deep breath before his sleeve chimed. He glanced down: Tapper.

"Tap."

"I think I've got something, boss." There was an uncharacteristic air of hesitation in the soldier's voice. "But I'm not exactly sure what."

# CHAPTER 12

The good news was that Mal had already been hard at work when Eli arrived at the Yamanaka Base hangar in the morning. The less-than-good news was that said work seemed to entail disassembling the *Cavalier*'s entire cockpit. Rat's nests of wiring and heaps of circuit boards were strewn about the compartment in what looked like some form of expressionist art.

"Mal, what the hell?" said Eli, when he'd retrieved his jaw from the floor. "Have you gone full saboteur?"

There was a *bang* as the tech whacked their head on the underside of the console, then rolled out from under it, rubbing their brow. "Oh, hey! I know this looks bad."

"Bad?! It looks like someone let a rabid weasel loose with a pair of wire-cutters."

Mal's grease-streaked forehead wrinkled. "I don't think weasels have opposable thum–"

"Not the point, Mal. Where's Cassie?"

The tech jerked a thumb out the cockpit. "Engine crawlspace. Said she thought she could eke another point-zero-five thrust out of the reactor. As long as we were on downtime."

Eli opened his mouth to correct Mal, then remembered

that as far as official business was concerned, the SPT were stood down. So, with a sigh, he left them to their chaos and went to find the mechanic.

*Downtime.* Tell him two years ago that he'd be feeling antsy and on edge without a job to do, and he would have laughed into his flask between cleaning out toilets on a remote arctic military base.

But that had been another life entirely, one that had largely faded into memory after even his relatively short tenure with the team. And, much as he hated to admit it, he'd gotten accustomed to the breakneck pace of this weird world he'd found himself in. So not having something to do just gave him more time to dwell on the things that he couldn't do anything about.

Like Addy.

Part of him felt cruddy for slipping out this morning without so much as a word, but it had been a late night even before Tapper had talked him into that drink, and he wanted to afford her some rest. He couldn't quite shake the feeling that no matter what he chose to do, it would be the wrong decision.

Relationships were not his strong suit, to be sure. He hadn't dated anybody seriously since his time at the naval academy, and most of those had been short affairs that burned out after a few months. Spending a year as a prisoner of war, followed by a lengthy stint as a janitor, hadn't exactly done wonders for his love life either.

So he didn't have a lot of experience to go on. Nor did he have much in the way of examples. His parents must have had a loving relationship at some point, but by the time Eli was old enough to scrutinize it, he'd realized that his father tended to take his mother for granted, and his mother tended to let him. Not exactly a winning combination.

Ironically, the most solid relationship he'd gotten to see up close was Kovalic and Taylor. Who had their own set of challenges, to be sure, but were clearly two people who loved and respected each other nonetheless. Even if things had started to seem strained during the mission on the *Queen Amina* and Taylor had subsequently disappeared on some mysterious operation. *And that's the* best *example I have.*

Anyway, he certainly wasn't going to convince Addy of anything if she was dead set on moving on, but he owed it to himself to at least tell her how he felt before she made a final decision. Seemed like the adult thing to do.

Having reached that conclusion, he promptly tripped over a coil of power cabling that was just inside the door of the *Cav*'s engine room, and narrowly avoided a headfirst dive into the open crawlspace in which the top of Cassie's unruly brown mop was just visible.

"Why is everything *everywhere*?" he growled as he untangled himself, rubbing at his bruised knees.

"Why aren't you watching where you're going?" said Cassie, propping herself up on her elbows. "Distracted by something? Or *someooooone?*" She grinned broadly.

Eli pinched the bridge of his nose. "No. I just didn't expect you to have strategically deployed tripwires in our own engine room."

"Ooh, somebody woke up on the wrong side of the bed today. Or the wrong side of the person in the bed." She looked about one step from making exaggerated kissing noises.

Eli's stomach did a somersault. *Not so much.*

"Is a point-zero-five boost really worth all this?" he asked, gesturing around the compartment.

Cassie blew a dark strand of curls out of her face. "I don't know, do you *want* to get shot down by our own automated defense systems next time?"

The urge to loose a kick on one of the many pieces of equipment sitting in the hold was powerful, but Eli restrained himself, not least of all because with his luck, he'd end up breaking his foot. "Is it too much to ask for *something* here to work right?"

"Throttle down there, chief. SPT's still on standby and we'll have the *Cav* right as rain by the next time you get spun up." She jabbed a finger in his direction. "And don't you dare take this out on Mal. Kid made an honest mistake and they're fixing it. Whatever's crawled up your intake, it's not their fault."

Eli sucked in a deep lungful of air, and then it all whooshed out of him in one go. Unsurprisingly, she was right. "Sorry, Cass." He sat down heavily on a crate and rubbed his forehead. "I just feel kind of useless right now, especially without a ship to fly."

"Hey, I get it. When you all go off on a mission, I have to find some other project to work on, and let me tell you, nothing else on base is nearly as fun as tinkering with this bucket of bolts." She patted the deck fondly. "Everything will be fine, you'll see." There was a brief pause. "You want to talk about what's really bothering you?"

*Nope, not really.* "Thanks, but I've got packing to do."

Her brow scrunched up. "Packing?"

"Uh, logistics stuff. Kovalic's got me on quartermaster duty."

"Sounds like a blast." She slithered back into the crawlspace. "Don't sprain anything from all the... fun."

"Wait, hold on, when's the ship going to be ready?"

But the compartment was once again filled with the sounds of banging interspersed with mild cursing. *Let's hope that means soon.* With a sigh, Eli got to his feet and headed back into the hangar.

A warm wind blew in through the building's wide open doors; while the team had a small conference room and lockers assigned to them, they tended to do most of their work in the hangar, which they had to themselves; working for the general did have its privileges. Off to one side, a handful of tables had been set up with terminals and Addy was sitting at one, a hand at her temple as she stared into the screen.

As Eli approached, she let out a low growl – at the screen, not at him – and rocked back in her seat; in any other circumstance, Eli was certain she would have punched the display in its smug little pixels.

"Going that well, huh?"

She spared him a glance, and if there was any hint of her personal feelings there, it was quickly masked by her usual stoicism, garnished with annoyance at the task at hand. "Might as well be looking for a needle in a haystack, only the needle is made out of a piece of hay."

"He's good at blending in," said Eli, taking a seat on the opposite side of the table. "It's kind of his thing."

Addy ran her fingers through her short, dark hair. "How well did you know him?"

"Not well. When Kovalic recruited me, Page was there to keep an eye on me. Saved my life once or twice. I helped pull him and Kovalic and Tapper off Sevastapol on a mission gone bad… and that was basically the last time I saw him. Before yesterday, anyway. He's smart, and incredibly competent at what he does, which as far as I can tell is spy on people and kick ass when need be."

There was a sound from Addy that might have been a cynical snort. "That's kind of table stakes for this job."

"Oh, I mean, sure, I'm an old pro, too, of course. But some people might be impressed."

The ghost of a smile threatened to crack Addy's demeanor, but all too quickly it was deported. "Anyway, I've been trying to pin him down, but we only have two sightings: the café yesterday and Oluo Plaza around the time of the bombing. The cameras at the former all seem to have conveniently missed him, and the latter were already hacked by the time he showed up."

"Makes sense. If he was involved, he had time to control the scene at the bombing site. And he had plenty of opportunity to appraise the scene at the café before making contact." He still wasn't entirely comfortable that Page had been so easily surveilling him; so much for the hope that any of Kovalic's counterespionage training had worn off on him.

"The guy does seem to work fast," said Addy, a note of admiration reluctantly creeping into her voice. She stopped, frowned, and then glanced at Eli. "Too fast. What time was the bombing?"

"The news reports said 10.30 in the morning or so."

Sitting forward, Addy started plugging something into the terminal. "So he was downtown at 10.30 and then at the café near Yamanaka by around noon. The gravtrain trip from Oluo to the café would take about an hour, and the closest one he could have gotten would have been the 10.37." Her shoulders sagged. "I guess he could have made it with time to spare."

Eli sat up. "No, he couldn't have. There's no way the Oluo Plaza station wasn't shut down because of the explosion –

hell, the whole line should have been stopped. The automatic lockdown procedures went into effect, remember?" He shivered slightly at the memory of almost getting shot down by the Commonwealth's own defenses.

"Shit," said Addy, meeting his eyes. "He couldn't have taken a gravtrain. In order to make it from the Plaza to the café in time, he had to have been in a hovercar or a skimmer."

"Which means—"

"Ring road to the southbound expressway would be the fastest route," said Addy, tapping some commands into the terminal.

"And the most obvious. Wouldn't he have taken something a little more circuitous?"

"The next fastest would have taken him half again as long. He wouldn't make it in time."

"Fair point."

"Commander Taylor's sniffer can scan the traffic networks and help us narrow down which vehicles followed that particular route at that particular time."

Eli shook his head. "There's no way Page would be careless enough to let the automated traffic systems track him. He'd probably have spoofed his vehicle's identification, found some way to remain anonymous." It was the same principle as Mal's transponder hack on the *Cavalier*, though, given Page's legendary efficiency, Eli had no doubt his version would work better.

"Shit," said Addy, her brow furrowed. "Wait, how would that even work? It would probably have to rotate through different IDs as it went, maybe cloning them off vehicles it passes?"

"Seems like that would confuse the system," said Eli. *At least nobody would probably shoot a missile at* them.

"Yeah, it does, doesn't it? So what if I set the commander's sniffer to look for anomalies in the traffic network?" She tapped a few keys, revising the search parameters. "If we can track down all the places where there's an inconsistency along that route at that time – two versions of the same identifier, for example – maybe we can find his vehicle."

"But if two of them have identical identifiers, how are we going to know which one's real? They're just numbers in a log."

A smile blossomed on Addy's face, and Eli felt a tingle run up his spine. "Ah, but the commander, in her infinite annoying wisdom, was ready for that eventuality. Her program doesn't just look at the vehicle's electronic signature – it also looks at video footage to identify and tag vehicles by distinguishing features. Your pal Page might be good, but avoiding or erasing himself from every single camera along his route would be a hell of a lot harder. If we can identify his vehicle we may just get a bead on him."

*And then what?* Tracking down Page might be the mission, but Eli still hadn't come to terms with the idea of the man being a terrorist. Blowing up buildings, injuring people, all to make some political point? It was the kind of thing that the SPT was supposed to be *preventing*, not causing. As long as Page was out there, his guilt remained purely theoretical, but the second they brought him in, it became all too real.

"There are seven anomalies recorded along the most likely route within the time window," said Addy, interrupting his thoughts. "Three of them are cases where vehicles got on the expressway, but then never got off, which could be an identifier error or simply a gap in the automated traffic network. But there are also four cases where vehicles seemingly exited the expressway but *also* apparently continued along the route, which seems more promising."

She flicked a holoscreen into existence between the two of them: three hovercars, one with tinted windows, and one skimmer, with a helmeted individual. Reaching up, she zoomed in on the two hovercars where they could see through the windshield, then shook her head. "An older woman and a middle-aged man with totally different build and complexion. Strike those. Two left."

Eli eyed the two remaining possibilities. "The tinted windows seem a bit, I don't know, conspicuous? The helmet for the skimmer seems like a better guess."

"Well," said Addy, "I guess we should trace them both back using camera footage. I'll take the hovercar." She started scrubbing back through the footage, trying to find the earliest point that it showed up in the surveillance feeds.

Eli shook his head. "Great thinking. Pretty sure even Commander Taylor would be impressed."

A mixture of pleasure and annoyance flickered across the specialist's face. *Still not great at taking compliments.* But she cleared her throat. "Thanks." And then her head was back down over the terminal.

Eli waved up his own holoscreen and accepted the data share from Addy's terminal to start tracking down the skimmer. Settling back in his chair, he started poring over the footage from the cameras.

Exciting work, it was not. He glanced over at Addy, suppressing a smile as he watched her chew her lip and study footage. As recently as a few months ago, she would have probably thrown up her hands at this kind of desk work, but like him, she'd adapted to the demands of the life.

*This job definitely has a way of changing us. I just hope it's for the better.*

# CHAPTER 13

Addy drummed her fingers on the roof of the hovercar as she stepped out. It was a typical Novan afternoon, hot and sunny with a faint breeze in the air that just managed to cut the humidity. Across from her, Brody got out of the driver's seat, the light glinting off his aviator's sunglasses. It was an affectation at which she had tried not to roll her eyes on more than one occasion and, also on more than one occasion, had mightily failed.

*Flyboys gonna be flyboys, I guess.*

Emem, a small neighborhood about a twenty minute drive from downtown Salaam, was quiet and appropriately peaceful. Small houses had been built on decent-sized plots of land here, allowing those of modest income to have access to their own outdoor space. As Addy watched, a handful of kids zipped past on gravscooters, yelling and laughing in the time-honored tradition.

*The ones that didn't have to grow up scavenging on the streets, anyway.* She couldn't remember ever coming to Emem before; it was on the gravtrain line, so it wasn't as if she couldn't have, but it wasn't exactly somewhere that she'd had any reason to visit.

"Well," said Brody, "this couldn't possibly go worse than the last place, right?"

After Addy had managed to trace back the owner of the hovercar with tinted windows, they'd driven downtown to find him at his workplace, a trading firm headquartered in a tall office building in the financial district. Once they'd bulled their way past the receptionist, their quarry had turned out to be an obstreperous older gentleman who hadn't been particularly forthcoming, other than to say that he drove his hovercar every day, yes, down south of the city where he lived, and please get out of his office. They'd verified that the hovercar was in the garage, so short of Page stealing it and then returning it – plausible, certainly, but convoluted – it was probably a swing and a miss.

So they'd turned to the skimmer and its helmeted rider, following a path that led them back to its origin point: this cute little house in Emem. Addy's skim through property records suggested that it was mainly rented out by its owners, though when they pulled up across the street, there was no immediate indication of whether or not it was currently occupied. Nor was the skimmer itself in evidence.

"How do you want to play this?" Brody asked, across the roof of the car. "You cover the front, I cover the back?"

Addy eyed the house. "If Page *is* inside, maybe you'd better take the front – he knows you." Not for the first time, she missed the comforting weight of a sidearm in the small of her back. She hadn't had time to source her own weapon, and drawing one from the SPT's armory without Kovalic's approval seemed unwise, given the scrutiny they'd already attracted. Besides, she wasn't quite ready to come out shooting, despite the general's implications. If it came to that, it came to that. But it wasn't where she was starting. *Self-defense is one thing – preemptive strikes are another.*

"Roger that." Brody stuck his hands in his pockets and

strolled towards the front door as though he were going to visit an old friend. Addy set off towards the gap between the house and its neighboring abode, a green-and-white model built on more or less the same design. She picked her way past trash receptacles and into the backyard.

*Backyard.* She marveled at the concept as she let herself through the gate. Growing up, the city had been her home, and the closest she'd had to a yard was Izumi Park, with its dilapidated playground and scrubby field. But it had been bounded by high rises and skyscrapers, and wasn't really a private space, like this little fenced-off patch of carefully tended green. Along its border, flowers grew: a riot of colorful rocket roses and azaleas.

A low cement stoop led up to the rear door of the house and, as she climbed, she heard the faint sound of the doorbell ring as Brody reached the front. To her surprise, when she tried the door handle, it was unlocked.

*That seems… unwise.* Emem seemed like a safe neighborhood, and she imagined someone like Page didn't have a lot to worry about from your run-of-the-mill crime, but from a security perspective it seemed remarkably casual. Enough that it put her on high alert, her muscles tensing and ready as she stepped inside.

The back hallway opened into a small kitchen, tidy as a pin. In fact, as her eyes cast around the room, there was absolutely no indication that it had been used recently. No lingering cooking smells in the air, no dishes in the sink, not so much as a crumb on the counter.

*Either Page is a neatnik of the highest order, or he's been eating out a lot.*

Step after step, heel to toe, she crept through the kitchen. Brody rang the doorbell again, and the electronic chime echoed throughout the house. It didn't *seem* like anybody was home, but there was something in the air, a certain charge that prompted goosebumps on Addy's arms. She didn't *feel* alone. Her fingers twitched, again missing a weapon; she reached over and slid a knife from the block on the counter. It wasn't exactly balanced for combat, but a blade was a blade.

The entrance to the kitchen opened on a short hall that led to the foyer and the front door. Through a curtain on the door's window, she could just see the shadowy form of Brody, cupping a hand against the glass and peering inside.

Slowly, she continued her creep towards the front door, knife at the ready. On either side of the hall, open doorways led off to other rooms. Opposite the door, stairs led upwards; when the angle presented itself, she leaned over the bannister and up the stairs, but nobody was standing there, ready to pounce on her. So she turned back to the door, running a quick visual check along the edges for any signs of booby traps.

*Can't be too careful.* Especially with the back door already unlocked. If it were her safe house, she would have had a tripwire or some sort of trigger on the door, but aside from the usual sensors, there didn't appear to be anything of note. She unlocked the door, and waved Brody in.

"Anything?" he asked quietly.

"Nothing yet. You sweep the rest of the downstairs, I'll go up."

Brody's throat bobbed, but to his credit, he pushed down whatever nervousness he was feeling. "Got it."

Addy climbed the stairs – amazingly, only one creaked beneath her weight – all the while trying to settle the roiling in her stomach from her body's continued insistence that there was danger here somewhere. On the streets of Salaam, that instinct had kept her alive, but if there was one thing she'd struggled with over the last several months, it was how to distinguish the real threats from the false alarms.

*Easy does it*, she told herself, drawing a deep but quiet breath as she came to the landing at the top of the stairs. Three bedrooms and a bathroom branched off from here and, as she paused, deciding which one to check out first, she heard it – just the barest of sounds, a click that could have been a door latch.

Or the safety on a gun.

Her entire body went on red alert, heartbeat ratcheting up even as her breath quickened. That instinct telling her that they weren't alone was blaring in her ears, drowning out any subsequent noises which, admittedly, made it hard to figure out exactly where the sound had come from. She readjusted her grip on the knife, her palms sweating.

*I don't like this at all. None of it.* From the unlocked door to the too-quiet house, everything seemed wrong, like someone brushing the short hairs at the base of her neck against the grain. The fingernails of her empty hand pressed crescent moons into her palm as she crept into the room that might have been the source of the noise.

The door was open and inside she found a carefully made bed that looked as though it hadn't been disturbed, next to a nightstand with a single fake flower in a vase. One wall contained a closet door and Addy clenched her jaw as she moved towards it, knife hand out in front of her.

Without further preamble, she yanked open the closet door, ready for an attack from whomever was hiding within.

But all she found were spare towels and sheets, and what looked like a small box of body wash and shampoo that had been knocked over. Breath poofed out of her mouth at the anticlimax.

There was a thump and an abbreviated grunt from somewhere below.

*Brody.*

And then she was in motion, dashing out of the room and clattering down the stairs so fast that it was a miracle she didn't slip and impale herself on the kitchen knife. The noise had been from below the room she'd been in, so she wrapped around the stairs to the right, which proved to be the living area. The first thing she noticed were the curtains flapping around the open window at the rear, then Brody, who was pulling himself up from the ground while rubbing at his neck.

"I'm okay," he coughed, waving towards the window. "Go!"

She didn't need further encouragement, letting the knife – now more of a liability than an asset – drop with a clatter before sprinting towards the window and making a headfirst dive through it. Thankfully, her memory of the yard out back proved accurate, and she hit the soft dirt in a forward roll, coming up on her knees just in time to see a dark jacket disappearing over the rear fence. Without a pause, she launched into a run, leaping to grab the top of the fence and hoisting herself over.

*You're making this harder than it needs to be, bucko.* She swung a leg over, then spun around and dropped into the neighboring yard. The figure had already blazed their way through, leaving a scruffy trail through what had once been a pleasant herb garden, and was already busy scaling the next fence and preparing to leap off towards the fire escape bolted to the taller apartment building next door.

*Shit shit shit* thought Addy, realizing that she was going way too fast to slow down. Her body slammed into the fence, jostling her target, who ended up narrowly grabbing the fire escape with one arm and loosing a grunt of pain.

Addy blinked the stars from her vision, shaking her head, and yanked herself up to the top of the fence. With the adrenaline flooding through her system, she barely noticed the strain in her muscles.

But the person she was pursuing had managed to not only get their other hand on the fire escape, but had pulled themselves up until they could wedge their feet on the platform. And then they were off and away, clanging up the stairs at a breakneck pace.

*I don't know if I can make it that fa* – but her body was operating on instinct, well outpacing her brain by this point, and she was already pushing off the top of the fence towards the fire escape. She took the railing in the gut, knocking all the wind out of her, and inelegantly rolled over it and onto the landing as she tried to catch her breath.

*Up!* The voice in her head was insistent and, she was starting to notice, kind of annoying. Staggering to her feet, she reeled towards the stairs and started climbing.

It was three floors to the top of the apartment building and she picked up steam as she went, so that by the time she reached the roof, her target was still making their way across to the other side.

A grim smile crossed Addy's face as she crested the top and saw what her quarry must have figured out too late: all the adjacent buildings were much, much lower than the one that they'd climbed. There was no easy way down.

Well, there was one way, but there wasn't much coming back from that.

Addy laughed, even though it came out as more of a wheeze, and her target wheeled on her. For the first time, she caught sight of their face: to her surprise, she saw that it wasn't Page, but a striking woman with an old scar across one cheek, and dark eyes under brows that were knit in frustration and anger. Teeth gritted as she met Addy's gaze.

"Nowhere to go," said Addy, straightening her spine with an effort and putting her hands up, palms out. "So let's talk."

The woman didn't seem to be interested in talking, instead uttering a growl and launching herself at Addy, lashing out in a series of punches and kicks.

The assault was fast and brutal; Addy stumbled backwards, still winded from the chase, and narrowly avoided taking a fist to the temple. She got her hands up in time to block a kick to her ribs, but before she could even think about making a counterattack, the woman had spun around and come at her from the other side.

*Son of a bitch. Shouldn't have dropped the knife.* The woman's heel caught her in the hip and Addy winced as pain radiated down through her left leg. *Come on, Addy, wake up.* She sucked in a lungful of air and felt some vestige of her combat sense return, dousing her like a cold wave.

When the elbow came whistling over, she was ready, stepping back and circling around the woman to catch her arm in a lock. She jockeyed for position, trying to get a chokehold around her attacker's neck, but the other woman slipped through it with a sinuous grace, ducking into a low sweep kick to knock Addy off her feet.

But the elbow lock had caught the woman off guard and slowed her, enough for Addy to jump back from the kick, then rebound into a flurry of jabs, one of which caught the woman in the shoulder, and sent her reeling.

*You're not such hot shit now, are you?* A feral smile came from somewhere within Addy as she pressed the attack, dealing a kick to the knee that the woman just managed to block. Addy spun, using her other leg to feint a strike that the woman moved to intercept; but the foot never finished its snap and Addy instead punched her in the head.

The woman staggered away, towards the middle of the roof, wiping a trickle of blood from her upper lip, even as it twisted into a sneer.

"We can go another round if you want," said Addy, rolling her neck and settling into a fighting stance. "Or you can tell me who the fuck you are and what you were doing in that house."

The woman eyed her for a moment, as if considering her offer, but said nothing. Then she raised her left arm, a sleeve blinking to life there as though she were about to call someone, but as her right hand hovered over it, the woman's eyes flicked to something behind Addy, back in the direction from which they'd come. *Backup?* Addy resisted looking over her shoulder, just in case it gave the woman an opening.

But it kind of seemed like her attention was on the house where they'd started their merry chase.

*Oh n –*

She didn't have time to finish the thought, much less to whirl around, as the woman tapped her sleeve. A loud explosion ripped through the quiet afternoon and a fireball of blended reds, oranges, and yellows erupted skyward from the vicinity of the house.

Addy's eyes shot wide, her breath catching in her throat. *ELI!*

The woman capitalized on Addy's hesitation, using the

opportunity to make for the edge of the roof, where a flyer had risen on a repulsor field. Its canopy opened, an inviting maw for the woman to make her escape.

An urge pressed Addy forward – she could stop her from getting away, she was sure of it, if she could just *get there*. But even as the thought flashed across her mind, she felt a force more powerful than gravity tugging her back towards the billowing plume of smoke, where her teammate, her friend, her… whatever he was… might be lying, injured. Or unconscious.

Or worse.

And then, before she could even really intentionally make a decision, her body was already turning and sprinting back towards the house, even as the flyer rose into the air and disappeared. A distant symphony of sirens began to crescendo over the neighborhood.

# CHAPTER 14

When Tapper had set the location for their meet, Kovalic had frankly been expecting a neighborhood bar, pitted plastistock counter, maybe some splintering chairs, and quiet but companionable silence occasionally broken by shouts at a gravball match on the holoscreen.

Instead, the word that came to mind was 'plush' – almost sumptuous. Winged armchairs stood in alcoves by tall windows, their upholstery stark bursts of color against the wood paneling. While there was a bar in one corner, it was a beautifully stained mahogany, and waiters traipsed between it and the chairs, delivering crystal tumblers.

He found Tapper sitting in a remote corner of the room, across from a free armchair, into which Kovalic sank immediately. Some of the day's stress drained out of him as its adaptive foam conformed to his body, providing just the right amount of back and leg support. "Not your usual digs, sergeant."

Tapper, who had clearly found time to shave and don some fresh – and surprisingly stylish – attire raised a glass of dark liquor in his direction. "Multitudes, boss. I contain 'em."

Before Kovalic could utter a reply, a waiter appeared at

his elbow, asking in hushed tones if the gentleman would like a drink. Kovalic ordered a mai tai and the waiter made no judgment, just nodding before vanishing again.

"Rarified air," said Kovalic, glancing around the room. "Is that Admiral Mohapi over there? I thought she retired."

"Not until next year. From where I'm sitting, I can see three generals, two agency directors, and the undersecretary for foreign affairs. Plus a smattering of high-ranking civil servants from across the government."

Kovalic made an impressed face, even as the waiter reappeared with his drink on a tray, before promptly slipping away. He raised the cocktail to Tapper, who returned the gesture.

"I assume you didn't call me here just to show off," said Kovalic, once he'd taken a sip of the drink, which was, he could honestly say, one of the best he'd had in a place that wasn't directly next to an ocean. The salt air always added a little extra something, but still, he wasn't complaining.

"Only partially to show off." Tapper leaned back into his chair. "But hold that thought." He reached over to one of the arms and touched a control there. Kovalic felt the pressure in his ears as a baffle field activated, and the noise of the room – already quiet to begin with – faded away. A heat-like shimmer rose around their chairs, just enough visual distortion to make it more challenging for anybody inclined to try lip reading, without the tackiness of a full opacity holo.

"Peer-to-peer," said the sergeant, gesturing between their two chairs. "As you can tell, it's the kind of place where the members value their privacy."

Kovalic raised an eyebrow. "You've never mentioned being a member of a club before."

"Of a place like this? Hardly. But I know a few people who are very generous with their guest invitations."

Of course. The sergeant sometimes seemed to know everybody – or, at least, anybody worth knowing. In another officer, that might have come across as schmoozing one's way up the ladder, but Tapper had never seemed to harbor a particular ambition for promotion, having long ago carved out a comfortable little niche for himself. The man had seen a lot of people come and go, but he'd remained constant throughout, like a feature of the landscape.

"Handy. What have you got?"

"Well, I heard an interesting story. Friend of mine, Gus, works a personal security detail high up in CID. He said that Director Özkul was off-campus on Saturday morning, a fact that even her private personal schedule omitted."

"The head of an intelligence agency has a secret meeting?" said Kovalic dubiously. "Not exactly setting the world on fire. Where'd she go?"

"That's just it – she never got there. Traffic delays from an accident on the expressway. By the time it cleared up, they'd already diverted back to CID headquarters."

"I'm not sure that 'traffic' qualifies as an interesting story, sergeant."

"Ah," said Tapper, raising a finger, "but it does once you add where she was *supposed* to go: 1342 Oluo Plaza."

Kovalic paused, drink halfway to his mouth. All of a sudden, 'interesting' didn't quite do it justice. "What time was this?"

"Around 09.30. Which, had she arrived on time, would have put the CID director at Oluo Plaza…"

"…right around the time Nova Front's bomb went off." Kovalic shifted in his seat as the facts whirled around him.

"So maybe this wasn't just an attack on critical network infrastructure."

Tapper's eyes met his, stolid as ever. "Maybe it was an assassination attempt."

It would be a riskier move, to be sure. Setting off a bomb had gotten Nova Front on the Commonwealth's radar, but had they successfully killed a government official – especially one as prominent as the leader of its main intelligence organization – then there were going to be a lot of people not only out for justice, but also revenge.

Still, there were too many aspects that didn't quite make sense. Why target an administration official, important as they might be, and not, say, a more outward-facing politician, especially when your driving complaint was a matter of policy? Nor did it feel like a particularly efficient assassination attempt: damage from the explosion had been extremely localized, and though it had caused injuries, there had been no fatalities. If the intent had been to kill a specific person, Nova Front would have had to know exactly where that target would be at precisely the right time. Which led to an even bigger question: why was the CID director going to Oluo Plaza in the first place? As Kovalic and Laurent had already discovered, something there was more than it seemed – they just lacked the details.

"I don't like how this is adding up." He briefly spelled out what he and Laurent had discovered: the hidden room *behind* the ConComm server room at Oluo Plaza, and how somebody had tried to cover up that it had ever been there. "Combine that with Kester's goons hauling us in when we poked around, and it sure seems like CID would like us to stay the hell away from Oluo Plaza. We need to figure out what exactly the connection is."

"Not going to be easy," Tapper warned. "Even Gus clammed up after he told me about the director's schedule, like maybe he shouldn't have said anything. Whatever it is, it's off the books."

This whole damn thing was off the books, that was the problem. They were perilously short on actual leads. There was the footprint in the hidden room, which Laurent would probably have better luck running down. But navigating the thorny labyrinth of the Commonwealth's intelligence community and its internecine squabbles, well, that was something better suited to Kovalic and his team.

"Keep digging," said Kovalic. "Carefully. Whatever's going on here, we're just scratching the surface. I'll talk to the general and see if there's anything else he can find out on his end."

Tapper nodded, and it may have been Kovalic's imagination, but the gesture looked a little bit stiff. More than twenty years he'd worked with the man, and he knew the signs when he saw them. "Something on your mind, sergeant?"

Wrinkles spiderwebbed across Tapper's face, like he'd eaten something sour. Two impulses were at war in the man: the one that respected the chain of command, and the one that valued speaking his mind above all else.

"Come on, let's have it."

"It's Page, sir. You let m – us, the whole team, think he was dead. I get it: it was your call, and I'm sure you had your reasons. I don't have to like it, but I'll get over it." The sergeant stared meditatively into his drink. "But if I were you, I'd worry more about Brody. The kid's come a long way, but he's not the type to take it on faith that you had good intentions. He feels betrayed and lied to and, given his history, you can see why that wouldn't sit well with him." He took a sip of his drink, his lips thinning. "Plus, I'm not sure he's entirely wrong."

Something prodded Kovalic, deep in his gut, twisting it into a knot. He counted on the sergeant's frank counsel, and when Tapper had called him out in the past, he was usually right. But Tapper didn't know the whole story here, and as much as Kovalic might want to read him in, it would just muddy the waters at present, distracting them from the more important task at hand.

"I appreciate the sentiment, sergeant. But our priority is finding Page. After that, we'll have time to deal with the fallout."

The older man took the brush-off in stride, as Kovalic had expected he would. "Yes, sir. Of course."

Didn't mean he had to like it.

At a nod from Kovalic, Tapper deactivated the baffle, and the sounds of the room flooded in around them once again. Almost seamlessly, the waiter was at their side, but Kovalic and Tapper turned down a second drink, and the sergeant signed off on the bill, which was apparently on their host's tab as well.

Outside, the afternoon was seasonably warm and Kovalic didn't bother with his jacket, draping it over one forearm. Tapper, as per usual, didn't seem to break a sweat, trotting along next to him as though it were as comfortable as his living room.

Kovalic was about to suggest they grab lunch when his sleeve pinged with an incoming call. Laurent. He slowed and raised a finger at Tapper to wait, then answered the call. "Inspector."

"Kaplan. I assume this line is secure on your end?"

Well. That sounded ominous. Kovalic checked his sleeve, where a small glowing padlock indicated the connection had been encrypted. "Far as I can tell. What have you got?"

"Couldn't shake the feeling that the pattern in that footprint was familiar, somehow. I ran it through a database, and got a match: the Devlin KTRX-3."

"Devlin... they make tactical boots, don't they?"

"Indeed they do. And you'll love this: the KTRX-3 is standard issue for a number of agencies... including the Bureau's own Situation Response Team."

Kovalic couldn't help his eyebrows from rising as he started to see where this was going. "Let me guess: the exact team that was seconded to CID's task force and deployed to Oluo Plaza last night."

"The very same."

"I don't suppose you were able to track down the officer who owned that particular pair?"

Laurent's sigh was heavy, even over the comm channel. "There I ran into a bit of a problem. I tried to get in touch with the team's commander and got immediately bounced up the chain: all inquiries referred to Deputy Director Kester at CID."

Kovalic chewed his lip. So the people responsible for the cover-up had been under Kester's purview. In all fairness, he supposed it could have been someone pretending to be a Commonwealth Security officer – he'd done the exact same thing last night, after all – but given everything else they'd discovered about CID's connections to Oluo Plaza, that seemed an unnecessarily convoluted line of thinking. "I don't suppose you talked to Kester?"

"Couldn't even get through to him. But not fifteen minutes after I hung up, I got a call from my Chief Inspector, who's none too pleased that I'm investigating footwear instead of tracking down the people responsible for blowing up a building." Laurent paused, and Kovalic could picture the officer gritting his teeth. "A counterterrorism investigation is usually the kind of thing that opens all the doors, but right now I feel like they're just getting slammed in my face. I still haven't gotten official access to the scene, and neither has the Bureau's forensic team, so I'm working with both hands tied behind my back. Though from what I hear, CID's brought in its own techs."

Kovalic couldn't even muster surprise at that detail. Every indication pointed to Kester doing his best to control the flow of information out of Oluo Plaza. But he still wasn't sure why. "So, where does this leave us?"

"Nowhere good. It's hard to chase down leads when you don't have access to evidence. Oh," he said, suddenly remembering. "I also pulled all the intel we had on Nova Front. We did turn up something, but it's thin. A name: Kassandra."

"Kassandra? That's it? Not a lot to go on."

"I said it was thin. We think they may be the driving force behind Nova Front, but I don't have a description or anything else to go on. I hope you've got another angle in mind."

The real problem was that there were just too many angles. The general probably had the access to get them whatever information CID was holding back, but that would risk tipping their hand to Kester that they were still investigating, and Kovalic preferred to stay off the man's radar; there was always the chance that it might point him in the direction of Page. The same could be said of any of their contacts within the intelligence agency – too much risk that it would find its way up the chain to the deputy director.

So they couldn't go to any of their Commonwealth sources. Kovalic gave a sideways glance at Tapper, who had taken up a spot leaning against the building, arms crossed. The sergeant raised his shoulders in a shrug, as if to say 'don't look at me.'

"I've got an idea," said Kovalic slowly, "but it may be just as much of a brick wall."

"Doesn't sound very promising."

"Maybe, but I don't mind running headlong into one, as long as I can learn something in the process."

"Like 'don't run headlong into brick walls'? Shit, Kaplan, I could tell you that for free."

"My drill sergeant used to say the same thing. Look, can you dig up a name for me?"

"That depends on the name."

"See if your counterintelligence department can find me someone at the Illyrican embassy."

Silence from the other end of the line. "The Illyricans?" Laurent said finally, and there was no small degree of wariness in his voice. "What do you want to talk to the crims for?"

"You wanted a different angle," said Kovalic. "It looks like CID's up to its neck in whatever was going on at Oluo Plaza, and if we can't go *to* them, we're going to have to go around them. Weird as it might be, the Illyricans seem like the only ones who haven't been implicated so far."

Laurent let out a long breath. "The less I know, the better, I guess. Who are we looking for?"

"Tell them you want the embassy's cultural attaché. They'll know who I mean." He could feel Tapper's eyes boring into him as he ended the call, and he didn't even have to ask the sergeant what he was thinking: this was a dumb, and potentially dangerous idea.

And somehow it was still the best option they had.

# CHAPTER 15

Eli had been poking around the house's living room when the assailant had grabbed him from behind, putting him in a headlock as neatly as if they were opening a bottle of wine. Instinctively, he lashed out with a foot, trying to kick his attacker in the shin, even as his hands struggled to undo the arm around his throat, but the black spots were starting in his vision and his heartbeat was deafening in his ears.

*It's not Page.* That's all he could tell himself in reassurance as he struggled against the grip and tried not to panic. The person's smell was different – a sharp scent of sweat with a hint of something almost floral. Plus, he couldn't bring himself to believe that Page would assault him in this way, no matter the situation.

He was swatting feebly at the arm, trying not to pass out, and then the pressure was gone and he was on the floor, gasping for breath, a fluttering curtain glimpsed out of the corner of his eye the only sign of his assailant's exit.

Addy rounded the corner from the stairs in a dead run. He was still getting to his hands and knees, coughing as the air – sweet, sweet air – filtered back into his lungs. He waved at the window, forestalling her concern. "I'm okay. Go!"

She didn't hesitate, executing a dive through the window

that, under other circumstances, Eli would have judged among the top five most impressive sights of his life.

Eli pulled himself to his feet, leaning on a nearby bookshelf, catching his breath as he stared blankly at the colorful spines in front of him. Page seemed to have made himself a popular fellow: they were looking for him, CID was looking for him, and it seemed somebody else had him in their sights too. Whoever it was had tracked him here somehow, possibly the same way Eli and Addy had. But it appeared Page was one step ahead of all of them.

*How the hell are we going to find him now? Like looking for a ghost in a graveyard.*

He rested his head on his arm, his heartbeat still going Mach three, and then glanced up again – something on the bookshelf had caught his attention.

*Paper books?* Physical books weren't exactly uncommon, but they were a definite choice. Most people read in digital formats, but, despite that, the printed word had never really gone out of style. And there were always some people who bought physical books for nothing more than decoration purposes – heaven forbid they'd ever crack one open.

But a whole floor-to-ceiling bookshelf full? That was unusual.

Their mere presence wasn't what had grabbed Eli, though. It had been something more specific about one of the books. Frowning, he stared at the titles, trying to figure out which one, but they were all over the place. There were potboiler mysteries, a history of the Illyrican Empire, and a colorful guide to Novan birds. He'd heard Tapper and Kovalic joke about the man's voracious reading appetites, but this was like an all-you-could-read buffet.

Still, something had stuck out. His eyes rapidly scanned

the shelves again, zipping over the book titles so fast that he almost went past it. But something lodged in his subconscious like a splinter, and he dragged his eyes back a few volumes.

*Integrated Communications Networks, 2nd Edition.* Eli blinked. Of all the books to have in hard copy, a technical manual seemed especially weird. Surely a digital copy would be a lot easier to keep updated. He slid it from the shelf: the purple cover showed a circuit schematic, and he was just about to flip it open and start leafing through when a hand landed on his shoulder and he almost climbed up the shelves.

"Jesus, Add – Page?!"

Somehow, the man had gotten within a few feet of him without Eli ever hearing a sound.

Page's eyes were darting around the room, on high alert. "Brody, we need to go. Right now."

"What the *hell*? What is going on? Did you *bomb* the goddamn plaza?"

But Page didn't respond to a single question, only grabbed him by the arm and half-led, half-dragged him to the front door. Eli couldn't seem to stop asking questions though; they spat out of him like a starfighter on an attack run.

"Who the hell are these Nova Front people? Why are you attacking the Commonwealth?"

From somewhere, deep in the house, came an ominous beep. Then another. And then the beeping started accelerating.

Page didn't seem surprised at the sound, just increased his pace toward the front door. He kicked it open and pulled Eli down the front steps, even as the beeping reached a fever pitch. Breaking into a run, Page dashed towards the house across the street, and Eli bounced around after him, his arm still tight in the other man's grasp.

"Hey, slow do–"

An enormous ripping boom interrupted him, heat blossoming across his back as his slow jog suddenly accelerated like he'd been launched out of a cannon, and then he was careening across the pavement to the front lawn opposite. He tumbled into a roll that slammed him into the foundation of the house, knocking the wind out of him for the second time in what seemed like as many minutes.

The world spun around him, adrift on its axis, and hot air blew into his face like he was a kid on Caledonia again, feeling the engine wash as he watched the ships take off from the spaceport. When his vision stabilized, he gawped at the house where he'd been standing only a moment ago, now engulfed in flames.

"What the *fuck*." Someone had tried to *blow him up*. It wasn't the first time he'd almost been killed – he'd been a fighter pilot, after all – but somehow this felt... personal? Except, his brain reminded him, as it slowly caught up, this wasn't about him, not really; it was about the person who was supposed to be living in that house.

Rubbing at his head, he looked around groggily for Page, but he was alone on the ground. The street flooded with people who had run from their homes upon hearing the explosion and were now yelling and pointing at the house. Distantly, over the roar that still sounded in his ears, he could hear the high-pitched whine of sirens approaching.

But of Page, there was no sign at all. *Oh my god, he was vaporized,* Eli thought in panic before realizing that it was extremely unlikely that he himself would be sitting here if the bomb had been that powerful.

No, the man had once again vanished, having appeared just

long enough to… save Eli's life? Leaving him with nothing more than a singed back and, Eli realized, looking down, a book still clutched in his arms: *Integrated Communications Networks, 2nd Edition*. Shakily, he climbed to his feet.

Fire suppression drones were already buzzing overhead, analyzing the blaze and deploying the optimal mix of chemicals to douse the flames. Law enforcement drones, blinking red and blue, had also descended, scanning and cataloging the scene in advance of security forces' appearance on the ground. But Eli wasn't really seeing them, just staring blankly at the inferno and holding the book to his chest as though it were his only lifeline.

"Brody!" He heard the call dimly, even recognized it as his name. And then he was being shaken, the blurred and surprisingly concerned face of Addy Sayers in front of him. *I guess she does care.* She said something, but it was distorted, garbled in his ears. He let her take his arm and haul him limply away from the scene, back down the street towards their hovercar, which fortunately had been outside the blast zone.

It wasn't until he was buckled into the passenger seat with Addy firing up the car's engine that sounds started to push their way past the wall of fog swaddling him. The ping of the car's systems, the whine of the repulsors, and suddenly, he could even hear Addy muttering to herself.

"…going to be a trick," she was saying, checking the displays.

Slowly the car started gliding away and Eli found himself glancing out the window, catching the sight of oncoming emergency vehicles. *It's a crime scene. Shouldn't we, like, stay and answer questions?* His gaze slid to Addy, whose face had set in grim determination. *Oh, right. Questions that we can't answer.* No, getting out of here was the right call.

Addy turned the car around a corner and accelerated slowly, so as not to draw undue attention. "Easy does it." Her eyes darted towards him. "Brody? You back with me?"

"Uh… yeah." His head still felt muzzy. "Yeah, sorry." There was something he was supposed to tell her.

"Good. I need you to keep an eye out. Make sure the cops aren't following us."

"Right." He craned his neck: there were lights, but they were far off behind them. "What the hell was that?"

"Incendiary explosive device. Medium yield, by the look of it."

"Medium?! It leveled the house."

"Could have been the whole block."

"But why?"

"Covering her tracks, I assume."

"Huh? Her who?"

Addy pulled onto a main road, heading for the expressway. "She didn't exactly stop and introduce herself before she tried to beat the crap out of me. How's our six look?"

This time, Eli had enough presence to bring up the vehicle's rear camera. "Seems clear. I don't think they've picked us up."

"For now, anyway. But if we found Page by following traffic cams – assuming that really was his house, anyway – I wouldn't put them past being able to do the same. We'll need to wipe and ditch the car."

The mention of Page brought the events of the past half hour rushing back to Eli's mind like he'd been dunked in a cold bath. The chokehold, Page dragging him from the house, the explosion. Involuntary shivers racked him. *I would have been in very small pieces.* There were so many things left to *do*, he'd barely even scratched the surface of lif–

He flinched as fingers snapped inches from his face.

"Hey. Brody. I need you to not freak out right now. This is important. Stay with me." She reached out and put a hand on his shoulder, squeezing it, and the warmth from that simple gesture flooded through him, pushing back the tides of shock that had threatened to overwhelm him. He nodded.

"I'm here. I'm with you." He took a deep breath. "Addy, there's something important I need to tell–"

Her glance darted to him, eyes wary. "Is it going to help us get out of this mess?"

"No, it's about P–"

"Then now's not the time, Brody. See if you can find us a safe route home."

"Uh, sure." Eli brought up the passenger-side holoscreen and started checking their route for possible options. Heading directly back downtown was tempting, but it was also a straight shot on the expressway, making it all too easy for them to get trapped if the authorities were on the lookout. Better to opt for the smaller side streets and try to find somewhere along there to ditch the vehicle. Preferably not far from some other transit options.

"Here," he said, stabbing a finger at the map; a blinking waypoint appeared and the directions overlaid themselves on the windshield in front of Addy. "Parking garage near the gravtrain station. There are autobus options from there too – it'll make it harder for them to narrow down which way we've gone."

"You're not half bad at this."

"I guess I'll take that as a compliment."

"It was intended as one."

Addy took the indicated exit and, a few minutes later,

they pulled into the large concrete edifice of a garage. There were cameras sprinkled throughout but it only took them a few minutes to find a spot outside of their coverage area. Five minutes after that, they'd boarded an autobus on a roundabout route to the city center, paying with untraceable credit chits and careful to keep their heads angled away from the bus's onboard surveillance system. They settled into a pair of seats near the back of the vehicle as it rumbled to life and, for the first time since Eli had been put in that headlock more than half an hour ago, he heaved a sigh of relief.

"So," said Addy. "You want to tell me why you've been lugging that along?" She nodded at the book that he was still carrying, gripped tightly in one hand.

Eli looked down at the volume, as if surprised to see he was still carrying it. "Oh. I think it's a clue?"

"A clue? About…?"

"About Page," he said, as though it were obvious. "It was his house, wasn't it?"

"Are we sure about that? I mean, the fact that somebody blew it up seems like a solid argument in favor. Unless we just stumbled into the middle of a really intense neighborhood feud."

"Well, he did drag me out before it exploded."

"He *what*?"

"Page," Eli repeated. "He pulled me out before the bomb went off."

"You *saw* him?"

"Yeah, I mean, he's sneaky, but he's not *invisible*."

She pressed a hand to her forehead. "Jesus, Brody, why didn't you mention this before?"

"I tried!"

Addy's sidelong look clearly conveyed that she thought

his brains had been scrambled by the explosion. And he couldn't entirely dismiss the possibility that she was right.

But Page *had* been there, had gotten him out of the house, had saved his life. Which, to Eli's mind, wasn't the behavior of somebody bent on havoc and destruction. Something else was going on here, and they were only seeing a tiny piece of it. Like, what was the old expression? The tip of the elephant? He rubbed his head; maybe his brains had been scrambled. Either way, though.

"I'm telling you, Addy. I saw him. He was there." Eli lifted the book. "And this is our best chance of finding him before anybody else does."

# CHAPTER 16

It took them the better part of the afternoon to get back to Yamanaka Base. Even with their roundabout route, Addy kept doubling back to lose any possible active tails and use blindspots to help avoid surveillance. Not until she'd been satisfied that their trail had been thoroughly sanitized was she willing to hail an autocab to take them back to the base.

Kovalic and Tapper weren't back yet from wherever their investigations had taken them, so Addy took the opportunity to give Brody a once-over in the team's conference room. Though her medic training was limited, he mainly seemed to have suffered minor scrapes and bruises – a little antibiotic gel here and there would seem to suffice.

Despite that, the pilot seemed determined to make a production out of it, squirming as she daubed on the gel. "Ow."

"Oh, hold still. This is nothing."

"You weren't the one who was almost blown up!"

Addy rolled her eyes as she turned back to the supply tray. "You're fine, Brody."

"Thanks to Page." He'd stuck to the story that the errant SPT officer had been the one to drag him out of the building, despite any supporting evidence. Clearly *he* believed it.

Then again, he'd also had his bell rung by that detonation, which didn't exactly make him a reliable witness.

Addy chewed her lip. The general had asked her to get eyes on Page and she'd had less than zero luck with that so far. Meanwhile, Brody seemed to have an almost gravitational pull for his former colleague. This was twice now that Page had shown up around him.

She hesitated, her hand hovering over the small plastic packet in front of her. *It might be the only way to keep him safe.* With a grim expression, she ripped it open, then turned back to Brody, plastering a smile on her face. "Almost done."

He gave her a dubious look as she reached behind his ear and applied the small bandage, her fingers drifting almost unconsciously through his impossibly soft hair before she caught herself. "There."

She stepped back and found his blue eyes on her. "Thanks. Addy, I just wanted to say–"

*Not now.* "You should take it easy. I'll go call Kovalic and let him know what we found." Her stomach threatened to upset itself as she quickly stepped out of the conference room. With the door closed behind her, she leaned against it and drew a deep breath.

Then she called Rance.

The car appeared less than ten minutes later, whisking her away to a posh section on the outskirts of Salaam with tree-lined streets, families out walking, and coffee shops on every corner, constructed out of brick to look like an old-fashioned Earth neighborhood.

When the car deposited her, it was at a brownstone that could have been plucked from a history book, crawling with ivy and fronted by an imposing brick and mortar stoop. She walked up the steps to the door and pressed the only button, an unmarked buzzer. After a moment, during which she was sure she was scanned with every sensor at their disposal, the door clicked open.

Rance met her in the hallway, wearing the same pleasant smile she'd had when last they'd met. "Thanks for reaching out."

Addy shrugged, trying to ignore the discomfort that pricked at her neck. Maybe she ought to have looped Kovalic in, but the general's whole concern was that the major might be too close to all of this. And the general was Kovalic's boss, and thus her superior. She was just following orders – isn't that what Kovalic and Taylor had tried to drill into her during the *Amina* operation?

Rather than leading her up the grand staircase in the foyer, Rance instead ushered her down a narrow passage and into a surprisingly bright and cheerful kitchen at the back of the house. The windows looked out on a compact garden, filled to the brim with plants and hedges, obscuring any sign of the neighboring properties. In the kitchen's breakfast nook sat the general, studying a tablet while a stoneware mug with a blue-black ombré design steamed away on the table in front of him.

"Ah, Specialist Sayers," he said, looking up as she entered. His smile was almost grandfatherly and he gestured to the seat opposite him. "Can I get you anything? A cup of tea, perhaps? A sandwich?"

"Uh, sure, a cup of tea." She was more of a coffee drinker, but it seemed impolite to order off-menu.

The general nodded at Rance, who busied herself at the counter with a clattering of dishes.

Addy glanced around, taking in the surroundings. There were a few small paintings on the wall, some of an impressionistic bent, others far more abstract. That was about as far as her art expertise took her. She tried to avoid the appearance of casing the place – the last time she'd set foot in a house this posh, she'd been burgling it. But that had been another life. "Is this your home? It's very… nice."

"Thank you," said the general, his voice grave, as though he were delivering bad news. "It's a place I stay sometimes. I prefer not to remain in any one location for too long."

"I understand that." Addy had never really had a permanent home as a kid – even when Boyland, the old cop who'd done his best to keep her out of trouble, came along, she'd only crashed at his place once or twice a week. No point in getting attached when everybody left eventually.

"So." The general put down his tablet. "You told Rance you had some further information."

Addy straightened her spine out of habit. "Lieutenant Brody and I found what we believe to be Page's safe house, in Emem."

The thin, white eyebrows rose. "Indeed? You are to be commended, specialist. Excellent work." He stroked his pointed white beard. "Emem, you say? I think Rance mentioned a little while ago that she saw notice of an explosion in that neighborhood."

Color seeped into Addy's cheeks. "Yes. Our investigation of the property was interrupted by an encounter with an unknown woman, who appeared to have planted an explosive device on the premises."

"Curiouser and curiouser. An ally of Page's, perhaps, from Nova Front? Covering his tracks?"

"Possibly." But even as Addy said it, she felt like she was stroking a cat's fur in the wrong direction. It just didn't seem to fit. Boyland, police officer to the core, had always made it a point that investigations proceeded from evidence. *'Don't try to make the facts fit your guesses, Adelaide. It's the other way around.'* But he also hadn't been one to discount the strength of intuition.

"Did you get a good look at this interloper?"

"Yes, but no footage or image capture. I'm sure I could identify her if I saw her again, though."

"Hm. That is something, I suppose."

Rance chose that moment to bring over another mug, this one a simple black affair, not nearly as colorful or interesting as the general's. The liquid inside took on some of the darkness of its container, almost as black as coffee. Her charge delivered, Rance took up a stool next to the counter and picked up a tablet of her own.

"There's something else," said Addy. "Brody was in the house right before the explosion. He says Page saved him."

The general leaned back in his chair and interlaced his fingers. "I see. I take it you didn't witness this?"

Addy shook her head. "I was dealing with our mystery woman. By the time I got back to the house, Brody was already outside – a bit worse for wear, but not seriously injured. He said Page dragged him out, then vanished again."

"Most intriguing. Rance?"

The young woman looked up. "Yes, sir?"

"Collect any footage we can find from the emergency response to the Emem fire, as well as, oh, seven days prior. See if we can't find any trace of our former operative in the vicinity. Page is the type to keep a close eye on things, so I would be surprised if he strayed too far from his base of operations – if indeed it was his base of operations to begin with."

Addy raised the steaming mug, cupping it between her

hands; it warmed them pleasantly. "But he was there."

"Oh, of that I have no doubt, specialist. But Aaron Page is the kind of person who believes that there is no such thing as too many precautions. A belt and suspender approach, if you will."

"You think that the house was, what, a decoy?"

"Perhaps. Let us simply say that he may have had a fallback position from which he could observe anything that occurred at that location." He nodded, pleased. "Excellent work, Adelaide. Thank you."

She ventured a sip of the tea – hot, astringent, and not as flavorless as she would have guessed. "This is good."

"My own private stock. I've had to go to great measures to acquire it from back home – the tea they make here is, frankly," he lowered his voice to a conspiratorial level, "abysmal." The old man's eyes twinkled with mischief and Addy laughed despite herself.

They sat in companionable silence for a moment, each sipping their tea, and Addy found her eyes drawn to the garden outside the window, the bright pinks and yellows of the flowers in bloom. As she watched, a shape zipped in, flitting from flower to flower almost impossibly fast – her pulse spiked at what looked like a surveillance drone, before she realized it wasn't artificial at all: it was a hummingbird, its wings beating so quickly that they were nothing more than a blur. She only recognized it from vids; she'd never seen one in real life before, hadn't even been aware that they had them on Nova.

"Ah, yes, my daily visitor," said the general, following her gaze. "They're not native to the planet, of course, but they have adapted quite well from their lives on Earth; one of the best to make the transition, as a matter of fact."

*They work so hard and yet it looks almost effortless.* It darted from a blue-purple flower with the appearance of a cornucopia to an orange-yellow one with a wide, bell-like mouth.

"It's beautiful. So… delicate."

"Indeed. And yet, sometimes the things we feel are the most fragile surprise us with their resiliency."

There was a polite cough from behind them; Rance. "Sir, you should see this."

He put down his tea and took the tablet Rance proffered, studying it for a few moments, before turning it to face Addy. "It looks as though the media has gotten ahold of the story, I suspect in no small part due to Director Kester's task force. They're suggesting it's likely connected somehow to the Oluo Plaza incident, though the explosion itself may have been an accident."

Addy frowned at that. "It definitely wasn't an accident."

"Quite. But despite Page's intervention to save Lieutenant Brody, I don't think we can entirely dismiss our concerns about him. It's entirely possible the explosion was intended to eliminate evidence of the Oluo Plaza attack. I'd ask that you continue to observe the situation, and – though hopefully it won't come to it – if intervention is warranted, you take any necessary steps."

She shifted in her seat. *No reprieve then.* "Yes, sir."

The general's gaze drifted to the garden, where the hummingbird still flitted from flower to flower. "A person may do something terrible and still attempt to make amends on a personal level, but the scales are not quite so easy to balance. One moment of heroism does not excuse all the mistakes of a lifetime."

*But people can be forgiven.* Not that it was easy. And the most difficult part was, as always, forgiving oneself.

With the old man's eyes still on the garden, it seemed almost as though Addy had intruded on a personal moment. Clearing her throat, she rose. "If that's all, sir?"

"Hm? Oh yes, of course. Rance will see you out. Thank you again."

Addy nodded, then let the younger woman lead her to the door. She paused on the threshold, looking back towards the nook where they'd sat. "Is he all right? He seems... sad."

Rance smiled faintly. "Wistful, I should say." She tapped a button on her sleeve and the car that had delivered Addy slid smoothly back into view, its rear door opening. "Consider yourself on standby alert, specialist. We'll be in touch." And with that, she disappeared back inside, the door closing behind her.

Addy slowly walked down the steps to the inviting maw of the vehicle. As she set her foot inside, she glanced back over her shoulder at the building, even though she couldn't see the man within, and found herself wondering exactly what terrible things the general was trying to atone for.

# CHAPTER 17

Kovalic jammed his hands in his pockets. It didn't really get cold anywhere in the Salaam region, but up on the top of this hill, in an empty parking lot with no windbreaks, it definitely felt on the nippy side. Especially at night.

The groundcar sat alone, nestled between two pools of light cast from the tall poles that dotted the lot. Dark grey, with the sleek lines of a shark and tinted windows, the vehicle all but shouted 'danger'. Not the kind of car that you wanted to cut off on the highway, unless you were comfortable with the idea that you might not make it home in time for dinner. Or ever.

As Kovalic approached, the driver's door opened and a man unfolded himself, smoothing out a dark suit as he did so. If he hadn't played gravball, somebody had missed a serious opportunity: towering over Kovalic by almost a foot, the breadth of his shoulders gave the groundcar itself a run for its money. His expression didn't betray an iota of emotion; he might have been an automaton. He opened the rear door to the car and gestured to Kovalic.

If the outside was sleek, the inside was luxurious. Two bench seats faced each other, upholstered in a rich, black material with all the feeling of real leather. When the door closed behind Kovalic with a muted *thump*, it was dead silent in the compartment. The air smelled faintly of rosewater, although that might have been emanating from its occupant.

She sat kitty-corner to Kovalic, comfortably arrayed on the forward-facing seat. Silver hair, trimmed to fall no lower than her cheekbones, framing a brown face that had seen some years without bowing to them. On the lapel of her deep-blue jacket, a silver brooch of a hawk spread its wings in flight.

"Mr Kovalic," she said, tilting her chin up.

Unwelcome, but not surprising. He'd suspected after the incident aboard the *Queen Amina*, where he'd gotten one over on his Illyrican counterpart, that the Imperium's intelligence agents would be taking a stronger interest in him. Roll with the punches. He smiled and returned the nod.

"You have me at a disadvantage."

"You're goddamn right I do. So keep that in mind."

"In that case, the pleasure is all mine."

"Hm." She sniffed. "You may call me… Lakshmi."

Kovalic didn't blink. Goddess of love and beauty, yes, but also wealth and fortune. This conversation was going to be very interesting. "I appreciate you taking the time to meet with me."

"I have to admit, I was intrigued when your request came across my desk. I was supposed to go to a stage production of Arroyo's *Seed of Eden* – the first time it has been performed in the Commonwealth, I might note – but it was canceled due to the… unrest." There was the vaguest hint of amusement about the last word, as though suggesting that what the Commonwealth considered a terrorist attack might have been viewed very differently in the Illyrican Empire.

"Sorry to hear that," said Kovalic. "I saw the Imperial Repertory production in '11, while I was attached to the embassy on Illyrica – Amal Tinubu as Talia Malik? Hell of a performance, especially the soliloquy in the third act."

Lakshmi didn't so much as bat an eyelash. "I assume you didn't call me to compare notes on classical Illyrican theater."

"Not primarily, no, but I'm always happy to make the time." Down to business, then. "I need a favor."

"Seeing as we're just meeting for the first time, I don't believe I owe you anything."

"That's why it's a favor."

She looked skeptical. "Ask, then."

"Oluo Plaza."

"Ah, yes. The attack. Allow me to extend my government's condolences." There wasn't so much as a hitch in her voice.

"I don't suppose you have any idea why someone would target that particular location?"

She tapped a finger on her armrest. "Interesting that you're coming to me, rather than your friends in the Commonwealth Intelligence Directorate." Her eyes widened in feigned surprise. "Unless you don't trust them, for some reason?"

"Let's just say I value an outside perspective."

"I see. And say I do tell you what I've... heard... about that particular location? What might I expect to receive in return?"

"You mean it wouldn't be out of the goodness of your own heart?"

"That would be most unusual," said Lakshmi, her voice baked dry.

It was hardly a surprise that she'd expect something in exchange for information, so Kovalic had given this some thought. Walking the line between something valuable enough that the Illyricans might want it while not giving up anything that was a serious advantage was a tricky proposition. Figuring out what was going on in Oluo Plaza was important – it might help avert another attack from Nova Front – but it wasn't worth jeopardizing the larger galacti-political standings.

"The Aleph Tablet," he said. The Special Projects Team had almost made off with the legendary artifact and its purported secrets from the clutches of Ofeibia Xi.

Key word being 'almost.'

Lakshmi froze for a moment, but just a moment. "Destroyed, I believe."

"We don't think it was the genuine article."

"Oh?" Not a flicker of emotion in her eyes. Kovalic had to hand it to her.

"Let's just say that circumstances of its destruction don't *quite* add up." Tapper had been the one to plant the seed in Kovalic's head, and the more he'd thought about it, the more he was convinced that the tablet he'd seen destroyed was a forgery. The real question was whether or not the real tablet was still out there. But it wasn't the first time in history that it had disappeared, only to surface again someplace completely different.

Her fingers drummed a riff. "I hear the Commonwealth's new communication hub will be up and running soon. They say it'll increase intergalactic message throughput by fifty percent. Very impressive."

The change of topic strained Kovalic's neck. "Oh, Station Zero, yes." There wasn't anything secretive about the project – it was public knowledge. Hell, the Commonwealth government had splashed out on a lavish PR campaign trumpeting the improvements.

She sighed, flicking two fingers in the air. "Shame we won't be able to take advantage of it. Our communications are so slow comparatively – everything is done by diplomatic pouch, hand delivered by couriers. Standard protocol, you know."

Kovalic blinked. Where was this going? "That is too bad," he said, carefully.

"Well, this has been a treat," she said, in the same tone one might use when handing over a child who had started sobbing. "I appreciate your gesture of good faith and if I can be of help, I'll be in touch."

"Of course. I look forward to hearing from you." It was the best he was going to get, under the circumstances, so he had no choice but to take it.

Even though a partition separated the two compartments and Kovalic was relatively certain that it was baffled against eavesdropping even from the bruiser in the front, the door to the back seat was suddenly opened from the outside and he was ushered out into the dark, empty parking lot.

"Oh, and Mr. Kovalic?"

He glanced back to see the window rolled down and Lakshmi looking out at him. Her eyes sparked, even in the dim light. "I heard about your little encounter with Commander Mirza aboard the *Queen Amina* – after they retrieved her from that lifeboat you stranded her in – and I just wanted to say that while I remain *professionally* your sworn enemy, I do have a deep *personal* appreciation for your handiwork." The first smile he'd seen from her curved across her lips. "Ekaterin can be quite... trying." And with that, the window slid back up, the bodyguard compressed himself back into the driver seat, and the car glided silently away into the night.

Not the first time that Kovalic had found himself going to his government's nominal enemies for help and, he strongly suspected, not the last. With Kester holding the reins on the task force *and* CID involved in the cover up, he'd be lucky not to end up back in an interrogation room if he came knocking at their door. Moreover, Lakshmi was right: he didn't trust them, even in the best of times.

Giving up the information he had on the Aleph Tablet was a risky play and something still didn't sit right with him about Lakshmi's reaction. It was almost as though she'd already known. At least a couple of the surviving members of Mirza's team had been there when the tablet had met its end – perhaps one of them had developed similar suspicions. Or perhaps, more worryingly, there was some other explanation as to how the Illyrican Intelligence Service knew that the Aleph Tablet wasn't genuine.

Now there was an idea that didn't sit well with him. Not one bit.

And there had been that weird tangent about the communication hub. What was Lakshmi getting at? She clearly weighed her words carefully, certainly not one for small talk.

But he set it aside. As many plates as he was spinning, the Illyricans were more of a back-burner concern right now. If they could help him untangle this mess, then they were nothing more than a means to an end. It didn't change how he felt about them.

He zipped up his jacket as he walked, a small part of his brain suggesting that he should call an autocab, but for some reason he didn't, just kept walking as his mind examined the pieces that he'd assembled so far: Nova Front. The cover-up. The CID director's trip to Oluo Plaza the morning of the bombing. Kester and his task force. It was starting to resolve into a picture, but an abstract one: all blobs that didn't look like much of anything yet. He needed a way to fill in the gaps, to make the connections that he just didn't have the data for yet.

He needed Page.

Even if his erstwhile operative wasn't at the center of all of this, he probably knew what *was*. But Kovalic's attempts to reach out to the man had gone unheeded and the only contact they'd had was via Brody – and that message had been anything but reassuring. If they could just sit down, face-to-face, for ten minutes, uninterrupted, Kovalic felt confident that the pieces would come together.

But he'd taught Page too well. Not that he could take all the credit; even before the lieutenant had joined his team, he'd displayed a preternatural talent for subterfuge and stealth. Formal training had only honed those skills. If Page didn't want to be found, he wouldn't be. In all their years working together, Kovalic had rarely seen the man make a mistake.

He found himself looking up at the stars overhead. Not the constellations of his youth; the first settlers here had tried to create images and stories around them, but somehow traveling through the stars had robbed them of some of their mystery and none of the names had really stuck. Sure, certain formations stood out, especially those incorporating systems that he'd actually visited. But being real places changed them in his mind; he knew he'd never quite see them the way he'd seen the stars from Earth – the ones he still saw, whenever he closed his eyes, despite the two decades since he'd set foot there.

That's all he was doing now, really. Looking at some dots and trying to draw connections between them, to see the larger image. Maybe it required a little more imagination to see what wasn't explicitly there.

After another minute's walk, he emerged onto a main thoroughfare, the cars whipping by, raising dust and drafts in their wakes. Nobody walked in this area; there really wasn't much of a reason to be here in the first place, clandestine meetings aside. He headed back toward the city proper, turning over the details in his mind.

He'd only been walking for a few minutes when it began to drizzle, a fine mist filling the air and turning the street lights into miniature, glowing suns. The sharp splash from the passing vehicles seemed to resonate more in the fog.

It kept coming back to Page. He still couldn't believe what he'd seen with his own eyes: that Page was somehow involved in the bombing at Oluo Plaza. He knew the man – thought he'd known him, anyway. But, he had to remind himself, that same man had betrayed him and the rest of the team, had funneled information to Kester about their operations, and had alleged that the general was manipulating all of them for some sort of complex endgame.

Which left three options: first, that Page was right, and the general had pulled the wool over all their eyes. Second, that Page was genuinely delusional, had lost the plot somewhere along the way, and was in need of help. Or, third, that there was something else going on here, and they were all being played for fools.

He shivered at that last thought. It was bordering on conspiracy theory, he realized, but the idea that somebody else could set this entire plan into motion, cause this much havoc and disruption, and keep themselves totally hidden at the same time… that scared the shit out of him.

Drawing his jacket tighter around himself, he suddenly noticed that he felt damp and wretched, as though whatever shield had protected him from the elements had suddenly been pierced.

He'd felt briefly as though he'd been about to stumble onto some sort of realization, but now he just felt cold and tired, and a bit silly for having walked all this way in the rain. Now his foot was starting to ache from where he'd banged it on the doorframe at Oluo Plaza… had it really only been last night? Too much had happened in the past day; it was already starting to blur together. Not exactly a good sign for his mental acuity, but there wasn't exactly time to stop and take a nap.

With a sigh, he flagged down a passing autocab and had it take him back to Yamanaka base. Maybe Lakshmi would come through for them, maybe she wouldn't. Either way, they still had work to do.

# CHAPTER 18

For the fifth time Eli cursed as a RESOURCE NOT FOUND message blinked on the screen. He'd been trying to use Commander Taylor's sniffer program to check the video footage from Emem, to see if he could find any trace of Page near the explosion, but once again, the former operative had proved uncannily proficient at not being seen.

As extensive as the camera network in Salaam and its suburbs was, the populace had vociferously pushed back on ubiquitous surveillance, leaving plenty of blind spots and gaps for someone as skilled as Page to exploit. Plus, more than a few of the cameras had been conveniently offline at sporadic times in the past week. For all he knew, the man had figured out a way to hack the network so that he never showed up on video. *Or maybe he's a vampire.*

Eli rubbed his eyes. His brain was still a little addled from earlier and he was clearly getting tired – somehow it had only been a little more than a day since someone had blown up a building downtown and in the meantime he'd almost been shot down, nearly choked to death, and blown up.

Just another day at the office.

At least Page had saved him from dying in a fiery explosion, which seemed awfully thoughtful for someone accused of being an unhinged terrorist. But despite that, he'd been his usual laconic self, even in the face of possible death. *Not so much as a wave goodbye.*

He spared a glance at the table, where the book that he'd taken from Page's house – or what he was concluding was Page's house – sat silently, almost mocking him. *Integrated Communications Networks, 2nd Edition*. He'd thumbed through it briefly, even tried shaking it just in case Page had hidden something inside, but despite the odd nature of it being a physical book, it seemed to be exactly what it purported: a manual about the technology and construction of communication networks.

Eli's eyes had glazed over after about two minutes.

So he'd given up on trying to extract the volume's unknowable secrets and instead had turned his attention to what he *did* know: Page had been at the house. Which led Eli to conclude that they ought to be able to use the same tech that had tracked him down in the first place to figure out where he had gone afterwards.

Except that said attempt had quickly been met with nothing but frustration. Even expanding the search area to the surrounding houses and scanning back through the last several days had yet to yield any results.

Eli's leg had already been jittering rapidly under the table, and that had only intensified with his fruitless search. *Time to change tactics.* Maybe he couldn't find Page, but it was clear that someone *else* had known he was there. And then, apparently, they had blown up his house.

There was a clink as something was put down on the table and he looked up to find a steaming cup of coffee at his right hand.

"Thought you could use a kick," said Cassie, grinning.

She raised her own mug in salute. "Thank god nobody's ever tried to outlaw caffeine."

Eli seized the cup gratefully, warming his hands on it as he leaned back in his chair. "Thanks, Cass. I owe you one."

Cassie dropped into the chair opposite him, bringing one knee up to her chest as she took a sip. "You owe me way more than *one*, lieutenant. Anyway, seems like you're having some trouble." She nodded at the holoscreen.

"Just trying to track someone down. Except I keep hitting dead ends." *Computers, technology, surveillance – not exactly my strong suit.*

"Well, when I'm trying to diagnose an engine fault, I start with what I *do* know. For example, if there's low thrust output, I check to make sure the fuel transfer is clean. If it's running dirty, I start at the exhaust and make my way in from there. Work backward, you know."

*Work backward. Some days it feels like I'm going backward.* But it made a sort of sense. So, what did he actually know? The mystery woman – and he only knew it was a woman from Addy's encounter with her, as he hadn't gotten so much as a glimpse while she had him in a headlock – had been inside Page's house, and would seem to be the prime suspect for planting the bomb. Why? She probably hadn't been gunning for him or Addy – how would she have even known they were coming? So Page was the likely target, which made sense: it seemed like everybody was after him.

Of course, this wasn't the first bomb to go off in the capital over the last two days. Going by modus operandi alone, an explosive device seemed like the handiwork of the Novan Liberation Front.

Eli rubbed his hands over his face. Why would Nova Front target Page? They had assumed he was affiliated with the group in some way: he was in the video threatening the Commonwealth Executive on their behalf, Kovalic had seen him at the bombing site, and Page himself had warned them to stay away from the group.

And yet it ate at Eli. *Something doesn't fit here.* Maybe he was making too many assumptions.

Sliding his fingers over the terminal keyboard, he again brought up the video message sent to the Commonwealth Executive. A sidelong glance at Cassie showed she had gotten caught up reading on her tablet. He wasn't sure how Kovalic would feel about sharing the video of Page outside the team, so best to keep it to himself for now. He popped in his earpieces and rerouted the audio, then played back the message again, looking for any sort of clue.

*"Too long the Commonwealth oppressors have taken advantage of native-born Novans…"*

The message wasn't long, and it was to the point, which was very Page-like. But the demand was rubbish: put forth a proposal for Nova to exit the Commonwealth? Hardly real change, and not something that the government was likely to do because of a terrorist threat. That kind of amorphous political maneuvering didn't seem like the kind of direct action that the Page he knew would favor.

A shadow loomed over Eli's shoulder, and he jumped as his heartbeat skyrocketed. Yanking out an earpiece, he looked up to see Cary Maldonado hovering over the table, staring intently at the video.

"Whatcha watching? Who's that guy?"

"Jesus, Mal. Give a guy a heart attack!"

Mal put up their hands. "Sorry! I was just curious. You seemed really interested in the video, so I figured it was important."

"It is. Which is why I'm trying to concentrate on it."

"Ah," said Mal, nodding knowingly. "I get it. Looking for artifacts and illumination discrepancies."

"Right, lookin – wait, what now?"

It was Mal's turn to look puzzled. "Inconsistencies in the video." At Eli's continued blank expression, they went on. "Like that." They pointed at a spot on the screen that, to Eli, looked indistinguishable from the rest of the image.

"What are you talking about?"

"I mean, it's not a bad effort, I'll be honest, but if you know what to look for, there's always something to spot. A thorough spectral analysis could probably pick out more, but it takes some time."

"Whoa, whoa, whoa, back up. You're saying this video is... what... fake?"

"Well, it's hard to say *exactly*," said Mal, their hands fluttering like they were conducting a symphony. "Some of it could be taken from actual video footage, interpolated into a larger message. But, yeah, pretty sure it's been manipulated."

*Holy shit*. Eli pushed his chair back from the screen and gestured to Mal. "Show me."

The tech swallowed, their eyes widening as though suddenly realizing they'd stuck their nose in too far, but the desire to help seemed to overwhelm any nervousness, and they nodded, bending over the keyboard and typing in a flurry of commands. The image changed color, turning almost schematic, and lines appeared over various portions of Page's face, mapping it to geometric shapes. "Is he real?"

"What?"

"Him." Mal motioned at Page. "If he's a real person, not a totally synthetic generation, I can run a comparison between verified video footage of him and this, which would make it even easier to prove that it's counterfeit."

"Yeah, he is real. I'll see if we can dig something up." He didn't have any video of Page off hand, but surely Kovalic or Tapper did. Page had been in the Commonwealth military for several years before joining the team, so there must be *something* in the archives, no matter how good he was at avoiding cameras now.

Mal punched a key with a flourish and a spool of numbers scrolled across the screen. "This is solid work – they've managed to avoid a lot of the most common pitfalls, like mismatched exposures and errors with hair and eyes. What there is, you might chalk up to compression artifacts, especially if you didn't know what you were looking for." They pointed at a couple of figures that, to Eli, might as well have been random numbers. "This suggests they generated a composite based on the real person, essentially overlaying his features on someone else. His voice patterns too, which is even easier. Turns out you don't need that many phonemes in order to build an entirely synthetic…"

Mal's voice dwindled to a hum in Eli's ears as they continued to rattle off increasingly technical words. *A fake.* Eli swallowed, staring at the screen. If Page wasn't the person in the message, it sure made a lot more sense that he was at odds with Nova Front. But why the hell would a terrorist group have sent a message with Page in it? Had he gotten on their bad side somehow?

One thing was for sure: the attempt to blow up his house was starting to look a lot more like someone covering their tracks. And they had almost gotten away with it too – if it hadn't been for Mal.

"Mal, this is great work." He reached over and patted them on the upper arm.

A beaming smile cut through the tech's unease. "Thanks! It's really not that hard, once you know where to look."

Eli tried not to laugh, worried Mal might take the wrong meaning from it. Somehow, he didn't think he'd ever be able to identify a sophisticated fake video from a moment's glance.

More importantly, this evidence changed everything, which meant he needed to tell Kovalic right away. Not to mention letting the Commonwealth authorities know that they were looking for the wrong suspect.

"Mal, I need you to run a full analysis on this and give me every shred of evidence I need to prove beyond a reasonable doubt that this video is faked and that he," Eli pointed at Page's image, "isn't the one in it."

"Uh, sure. When do you need it?"

Eli rubbed at his face, feeling the bristles of his nascent beard stiff against his fingertips. Doubt roiled his stomach: would it be enough to get CID and everybody else hunting Page to back off? He had to hope so.

"I need it now, Mal. Right the hell now."

# CHAPTER 19

"It's what?" said Kovalic, staring down at a visibly distressed Brody. He'd arrived back at the hangar to find the pilot pacing a rut into the floor, Tapper looking on in bemusement. Before Kovalic had even had a chance to open his mouth, Brody had pulled up a holoscreen of Page's video, and started babbling away about compression artifacts and encoding inconsistencies.

"It's not real – well, it *is* real, but it's not what it claims to be." The pilot was pointing at the holoscreen hovering over the desk, which clearly showed an image of Aaron Page delivering an ultimatum to the Commonwealth government. "That's not Page."

"Kid, I'm *looking* at him," said Tapper, arms crossed. "I know the guy like I know my own grandson."

"Well, then, check on your grandson, sarge, because he might be a computer-generated forgery."

It was late, past midnight, and the three of them were clustered in the small conference room at Yamanaka Base. There was no sign of Sayers, but Kovalic couldn't blame her for having gone home to get some rack time. Hell, he could have used some himself – his whole body had that warm buzzing feeling of having been awake for far too long, which was dangerous. That's when mistakes got made.

He shook his head and focused. "Okay, Brody. Run me through this again."

"All right. So, Mal explained it to me–"

"Mal? You showed *Mal* the video? This is highly sensitive material, Brody, and they aren't cleared for it."

"Uhhh, okay, not so much 'showed' as they saw it over my shoulder."

Kovalic pinched the bridge of his nose. How effective really were security protocols if they could be defeated by someone walking by? Well, the damage was done, and while he certainly couldn't imagine Mal spreading this far and wide, he'd still have to have a talk with them. "Fine. Go on."

"Long story short: somebody used video and audio footage of Page to construct a digital duplicate. They then fed in the words they wanted Page to say and it generated a video that, for all intents and purposes, *is* Page. Just, you know, not actually him."

"Seems like it would take a lot of footage," said Tapper, "otherwise they'd be creating videos of people all the time."

"Apparently they can do some truly frightening things with a fairly limited amount of material," said Brody, "but yeah, for something this realistic, it probably would have required extended direct access to Page. Or, you know, for him to be an extremely prominent figure, like a politician or vid star."

"Why aren't people making fakes of *them* all the time?"

"Well, the short answer is that they do. But what prevents those fakes from being taken as real are cryptographic seals. Most cameras digitally sign their footage and provide proof to any device playing the video; significant alterations will break the signature, and flag that the footage has been changed. But the original video sent to the Executive, where the identity of the speaker was hidden, was sanitized – likely to wipe any other identifying information, like what kind of device it was shot on, or geolocation. Or so Mal tells me. That would make authenticating it trickier."

"Convenient," said Kovalic. Frankly, a little *too* convenient for his tastes: it seemed like the kind of thing that both Naval Intelligence's and CID's analysis teams should have flagged immediately. But right now, they had more important issues to deal with. "So, if this isn't Page, then somebody is setting him up to take the fall. Presumably whoever actually planted the bomb at Oluo Plaza." It still seemed likely that it was Nova Front, though that raised the question of how the Novan militants had gotten enough footage of Page – notoriously camera shy as he was – to build this kind of sophisticated construct. And, of course, how they'd picked him in the first place: he wasn't exactly someone who stood out in a crowd.

"This is giving me a headache," said Tapper, echoing Kovalic's feelings.

"The point is," said Brody, "everybody's chasing the wrong person. We need to clear Page's name."

"But that means finding him," said the sergeant, "and it sure seems like he doesn't want to be found."

"I… might have something on that, too," said Brody.

Kovalic's eyebrows went up. And he thought *he'd* been busy today.

Digging into a satchel hanging over his chair, the pilot pulled out a book and put it down on the table with an authoritative *thud*.

"*Integrated Communications Networks, 2ⁿᵈ Edition,*" muttered

Tapper. "I hope you're not expecting us to read this."

"No, it's Page's. I got it from his house."

"I'm sorry, you got it from his *where*?" said Kovalic.

"Add – Specialist Sayers and I tracked Page to his safe house. I managed to get out with this before the building, uh," his voice lowered to a quieter level, "exploded."

Kovalic exchanged a look with Tapper, seeing the surprise on the sergeant's face and assuming it mirrored that on his own. "*Exploded*?"

"Christ, Brody, you really buried the lead."

And here Kovalic had been out trying to scrounge up any helpful information at all from Laurent and even the Illyricans. Meanwhile, his two junior operatives had basically walked right up to their target's location and apparently waltzed in without so much as an invitation.

Brody frowned. "Addy said she was going to call you and loop you in."

Had she now? Kovalic checked his sleeve, but there was no sign that the specialist had left a message or, indeed, even tried. And here he'd thought she'd started to settle in with regulations and protocol. "Any idea where she is?"

"Uhhh, I think she said she had an errand to run."

As excuses went, it wasn't the most convincing. Brody was covering for her, he knew that much. Probably because of the whole living situation that they'd tried to keep on the down-low. Kovalic had let it slide so far because it hadn't affected their work. The key words being 'so far.'

"We'll track her down shortly. But I think you'd better start at the beginning, lieutenant."

Blue eyes darting between the two of them, Brody took a deep breath and launched into the entire story of locating Page via his movements on the day of the bombing, which led him and Sayers to the Emem suburb, where they were attacked by an unknown woman, who then set off a bomb in the house – but not before Brody grabbed the book in question, and Page briefly showed up to drag him out, before, naturally, disappearing again.

When the pilot was finished, Kovalic let out a breath, like he'd just gone through the whole ordeal himself. "Hell of a day."

"It was... eventful." And that was saying something, given the breakneck pace that seemed to be the only speed at which the situation was unfolding.

"So, this book." Kovalic reached over and picked up the volume. "Why do you think it's the key to finding Page?"

"Two reasons," said Brody, enumerating them on his fingers. "First, he must have gotten it for a reason. Second, who the hell buys paper books anymore? It's not like they're available on every street corner."

They were good reasons, Kovalic had to admit. A textbook on communication networks... "Oluo Plaza was a communications hub. So that might answer your first question."

"I thought we just established he *didn't* set off the bomb there," said Tapper.

"Maybe not, but he *was* there. So he must have had an interest, at the least. As for the second question... books were kind of a hobby for Page." He'd cleaned out the lieutenant's apartment after the mission on Bayern and his "death," and while most of it had been sparsely furnished, the extra bedroom had been piled full of books on every available subject, their margins dotted with notes in Page's precise hand, cross-referencing details and making citations. Putting it all together had been beyond

Kovalic, but he hadn't wanted to simply dispose of all of Page's hard work – whatever it was.

He pushed back his chair. "Come with me."

This time it was Brody and Tapper who were giving each other a look, but they dutifully trailed Kovalic out of the conference room, into the hangar, and then to the secure storage area where they kept their gear. Kovalic punched in his security code and opened the door; beyond stood a handful of small rooms, each secured with their own private codes. Brody, Tapper, Sayers, Nat – the whole team each had their own locked compartment where they could keep gear and any personal belongings.

But down at the end was an extra, unmarked storage locker that Kovalic had annexed for his own personal use. He punched in his code again and opened the door into a small room packed with containers. Dragging one over, he lifted the lid to reveal it was brimming with books.

"These all belonged to Page," he said, pulling out the top volume, which turned out to be a history of the Sabaean monarchy. "The man was – *is* – a bit of a fiend for research."

Brody took the book from Kovalic's hands, almost gingerly, and flipped through the pages. His eyes widened as he saw the scrawls in the margin. "Holy shit, he wrote in all of these? Aren't they, like, antiques?"

Tapper rolled his eyes. "Just paper, kid. Don't go trying to hock 'em." He glanced at Kovalic. "What are you thinking, boss?"

Kovalic gestured to the books. "A man buys this many of *anything*, he must know all the places to do so. This isn't just a casual hobby. And old habits are hard to break, even – or maybe *especially* – for someone as regimented as Page."

"So, you think he went back to one of his old haunts?"

"Good a guess as any." Kovalic hefted the communications textbook. "If we can figure out where he bought this, maybe we can use that to find him. Before Kester or the security forces do, anyway."

"Or Nova Front," added Brody, still thumbing through the history book. "If they did try to blow him up, we have to assume they still want to tie up their loose ends."

Tapper looked almost impressed by Brody's conclusion. "I agree. They would seem to be the most likely culprits for the safe house bomb. Especially if they framed him for Oluo Plaza in the first place."

"So," said Brody, "how do we use these to find him?"

Kovalic reclaimed the history book from Brody, flipped to the inside of the back cover, and held it out. Stamped in patchy black ink there was a logo: three stylized letters on something that looked like a shield.

Brody scratched his head. "TBL?"

"The store where he bought it, I assume." Kovalic checked the inside covers of the communications textbook, but any hope he had was quickly dashed – they were blank.

"How many stores selling books could there even *be*?" said Tapper.

"More than you'd think, even just in Salaam. You'd be surprised how many people still prefer the idea of a physical object. There are dedicated bookshops, general antique stores, private dealers…"

"Oi," said Tapper, rubbing his eyes. "You're doing my head in."

"There are hundreds of books here, and they didn't all come from the same source. Like I said, the man was a collector. Still, if we can narrow it down to the two or three most common, it gives us a place to start."

A dubious look crossed Brody's face as he eyed all the containers. "This is going to take a while."

Tapper slapped the younger man on the shoulder. "Good thing you didn't have any plans for tonight. We start now, we might be done by the time they open in the morning."

"Yeah," said Brody glumly. "That's kind of what I was afraid of." With a groan, he grabbed one of the containers by the handles and dragged it out of the storage locker, leaving Tapper and Kovalic alone in the room.

"Geez," said the sergeant, "I hope you keep this much of my shit when I go."

"Well, I, uh, had a feeling he might be back."

"Yeah," said Tapper quietly. "You did, didn't you."

He tried not to wince at his oldest friend's tone. Keeping Page's fate a secret from the rest of his team had nearly eaten him alive – it's why he'd had to read in Nat when she'd confronted him. Not that he hadn't *wanted* to tell the rest of them too, but at the time, it had seemed the only way to keep everybody safe. Looking back, he wasn't sure how much of a difference it had ended up making.

"Tap, I'm sorry about all of this. I am."

"It's the job, boss. I get it. I won't say I'm happy, but I understand." The sergeant shook his head, his lips thinning. "But right now, let's worry about finding the boy wonder before Kester uses him for target practice." Following Brody's lead, Tapper grabbed another crate, hefted it with a grunt, and disappeared back into the hangar.

Kovalic glanced around the room. He hadn't bothered with most of Page's other belongings; there was a container of the man's clothes in here somewhere, mostly because he couldn't bring himself to throw out his uniform. But it was about ninety percent books because, well, that had been about ninety percent of what Page had owned.

Part of him sure wished the man had collected something lighter. Like pillows.

Grabbing a container, he made his way back towards the conference room, but hitched up when he glanced over at the locked room belonging to Sayers. He wasn't sure exactly why the specialist hadn't checked in – or, for that matter, where she'd gone – but he'd been the one to make the argument to Taylor that Sayers benefited from a long tether.

Still, he thought, as he lugged the container out into the hangar, convenient that she'd managed to avoid the mind-numbing work of poring over a box full of books. If nothing else, she definitely had her timing down.

Now *that* sounded like Sayers.

# CHAPTER 20

The previous night's foggy weather still hadn't dissipated by morning. It hung low over the city like a lid, turning streetlights into lighthouses and cars into stealth fighters, emerging briefly from the mist only to disappear as quickly as they had appeared. The muggy damp clung to Eli's forehead like a fever chill as they approached the bookshop.

It was the second store they'd visited; the first had opened an hour earlier, but the owners, a younger couple who were trying valiantly to prove that a bookstore could still be something that appealed to the masses and not just to eccentric collectors, had stared at them blankly when they'd produced their increasingly worn copy of *Integrated Communications Networks, 2nd Edition*. They didn't carry textbooks, they pointed out, and they weren't sure about anybody matching Page's description, but they'd be happy to make some artisanal cappuccinos for the lot of them and there was a book club that met every Wednesday, if they were interested.

They politely demurred, and then it was on to the next place on their list.

Over the course of the night, Eli had surreptitiously

sent Addy several messages, not a one of which had been returned. He felt a little awkward inventing the story about her running errands, but otherwise, it looked like she'd just disappeared, and he couldn't imagine Kovalic would be too happy about that state of affairs. He wasn't sure why she hadn't told Kovalic about the explosion at the safe house, or where she'd gone, but Eli trusted she had a good reason to be off doing, well, whatever she was up to – he just wished she'd have trusted him enough to let him in. *Also, she's missing out on all the fun of visiting bookstores and being stared at like we're a bunch of weirdos.*

The next store, Bourgoin & Jeune, occupied a small corner of the first story of a residential building in East Salaam. In its front window an assortment of books were assembled, cover out, like mannequins showing off the latest fashions.

At a minute before ten, the front door was unlocked and the smart fabric flag hanging outside rippled from "Closed" to "Open." Within thirty seconds, Eli was following Kovalic and Tapper into the shop.

'Musty' was the first word that came to Eli's mind. He'd been poring over books all night, pulling them from the storage crates, flipping to the front and back covers, then tossing them in a pile. He'd had the smell of old paper and binding glue in his nostrils for hours, and frankly he was amazed that he could still detect mustiness after being immersed in it for so long.

Bourgoin & Jeune seemed to have been among Page's most frequented stores, based on the marks inside the covers, and as the bell chimed after them, Eli thought he could see why. The shop itself was cluttered with books on every available shelf, some with creased spines from long use, others that looked almost new. Shelves reached all the way to the low ceiling, and there were a few places that Eli had to duck, lest he take a three-volume history in the forehead.

The proprietor, an older man with dark skin, a slight paunch, and a neatly trimmed beard gone to white, raised his eyebrows at the unlikely trio of early bird customers. "Good morning. Can I help you?"

"We're looking for one of your regulars," said Kovalic. "He bought this sometime in the last month or two." He laid the purple communications textbook down on the counter, one hand splayed possessively on top.

"Hmmm," said the owner, studying the book. "Might have been one of mine, but can't say I remember. You got a receipt?"

"Afraid not."

"Uh huh. Well, I don't give out customer information. Especially to – what are you, a book-buying gang?"

"He's a young man," Kovalic continued, undaunted. He tapped his sleeve and a holographic image of Page sprung to life, hovering over it. "Doesn't talk much. Buys a lot of books."

The man glanced at the image and his eyes flicked almost imperceptibly toward the back of his shop, but he quickly looked down at his terminal, offering nothing more than a shrug. "Get a lot of customers through here."

*Well, this is going swimmingly.* "Look," said Eli, earning himself sharp glares from both Kovalic and Tapper, "we're friends of his, and we think he may be in trouble. All we want is to find him. Can you help us?"

The owner squinted at Eli, and there was the slightest of cracks in his frosty demeanor. "I really wish I could, I'm sorry."

*So much for the honesty approach.* "Oh, well, thanks, anyw–"

"But you gentlemen seem like serious collectors," he said, looking them up and down. "There are some volumes in the back of the shop that might interest you." He waved a hand at an archway that seemed to be constructed entirely out of more overflowing bookshelves, which almost certainly wasn't up to code.

"Uh, we're not really that–"

"That sounds perfect," Kovalic smoothly interjected. "We'd love to see what you've got."

"Help yourself, then. The real good stuff is in the little room in the back right. Rare volumes, you know. I especially recommend the first-edition Pratchetts." Eli could swear there was a faint glimmer in the man's eyes, but he looked back down at the volume on his desk, dispatching them with a half-hearted wave.

Kovalic ushered a still befuddled Eli towards the back rooms, and Tapper trailed behind them, glancing at the shelves as they went, finger trailing along the spines as though he could absorb everything he needed to know about the books at a mere touch.

"Should we really be wasting our time?" asked Eli. "Seems like there are more useful things we could be doing."

"Unless you've uncovered some new evidence in the last two hours, this is still our best lead."

The number of books lining the walls was staggering. Intellectually, Eli knew that this many existed, but it was daunting to see so many of them gathered in a place this small. He felt the same way about sharks.

Kovalic bobbed and weaved through the labyrinth of bookshelves, narrowly avoiding a few volumes that teetered just over their heads. It seemed to Eli as though the shelves were getting lower and closer together, almost as though they were descending into a series of caves. It was dimmer back here, too, with only the occasional lightstrip to provide illumination. He thought he caught sight of a window at one point, high up, but it could have just been some very gray bindings.

At last, there was another opening to their right, and Kovalic ducked underneath a low-hanging shelf into a small room with a table full of books as its centerpiece. Shelves ringed the edges, the only way in or out the entrance they'd just passed through. Immediately, Tapper and Kovalic set off in opposite directions around the shelves, scanning all the titles there.

*Oooookay*, thought Eli, glancing at the table in the middle. He wasn't entirely sure what he was looking for, but he could appear busy while Tapper and Kovalic did the heavy lifting. The books on the table had their spines up, the easier to peruse them, so Eli started idly scanning through the titles.

"Must be here somewhere," Kovalic muttered.

"Nothing yet, boss," said Tapper, craning his neck to take in the topmost shelves.

*O'Connor… Mahfouz… huh, Pratchett?* Hadn't that been the name that the shopkeeper had mentioned? *Wonder what all the fuss is about.* Reaching over, Eli plucked the book from its place, wedged neatly between two others… only it wouldn't come. It was almost like it was bolted to the table. Frowning, he gave it a harder yank; this time, it moved up an inch, and there was an almost ominous *click*.

Kovalic and Tapper both froze, the sergeant's head swiveling slowly to lock his gaze on Eli. "Brody… what did you *do*?"

With a rumble the table slid a few feet backwards, taking the floor with it, to reveal a ladder descending into the darkness.

"Uh, so, I guess that was what you were looking for?"

"Good work, lieutenant." Kovalic crossed to the opening and peered in.

"And we're totally going down that, aren't we?" said Eli, trying not to sigh. Just once it'd be nice if a trip to a bookshop were just a trip to a bookshop.

"Course," said Tapper. "We didn't come here *not* to go into the spooky tunnel."

Kovalic grinned at the sergeant, then climbed down, his head disappearing from view.

Tapper slapped Eli on the back. "Once more into the breach, like the man said." And with that, he followed in Kovalic's wake, leaving Eli alone in the room full of books.

He stared down into the dark opening, just seeing Tapper's gray hair vanish into the gloom. *It's always something.* With a sigh, he lowered himself into the hole, working his way slowly down the ladder.

As he neared the bottom, he heard a grinding noise and looked up to see a panel rolling back into place over the opening, thrusting them into darkness.

Reaching the bottom of the ladder, Eli's eyes adjusted to find that there was still a dim light being cast, emanating from down the cramped passageway to the left. The walls were a plasticrete foundation, suggesting that this had probably begun as a cellar. Eli had to hunch to avoid whacking his head on the ceiling. *Christ, is everything in this place designed for children? Or short people?*

Kovalic and Tapper had already picked their way carefully down the corridor toward the source of the light – not that there was any other option – so Eli resigned himself to following them.

After a few meters the passageway widened, and a

couple of steps led down into a larger room in which he could actually stand up straight. The place seemed to mainly be used for storage, with lots of crates and boxes neatly stacked around the periphery. On the far side of the room, a shadowed alcove seemed to lead deeper into the basement.

In the room's center was a workbench, atop which were neatly laid out a collection of tools and materials, including thread, scissors, a small brush, and something that looked like a doorknob with a long thin metal needle jutting from it. A wooden contraption sat atop the table, looking almost like a gallows, with metal hooks hanging from it; what its purpose was, Eli couldn't hazard a guess, but probably some sort of torture device for... books?

"Are we sure we're supposed to be down here? It kind of looks like we walked into the laboratory of a mad... uh... bookstore owner."

"Bookbinder, actually," said a familiar voice from the shadowed niche in the opposite wall. "But I understand: It's not precisely a common occupation."

Aaron Page stepped into the room. "I really wish you had listened to me when I told you to stay away from Nova Front," he said, his tone betraying no remorse or regret as he raised a knockout gun in their direction. "Because now we have a problem."

# CHAPTER 21

The blip on the display had stopped in a commercial district, about a quarter kilometer from Addy, just a little outside of her visual range. She pulled the hovercar over, sliding it into a convenient parking space, glad it was early enough that the traffic hadn't picked up yet.

Reaching out, she swiped the blip from the car's display onto her sleeve, confirming that the location hadn't changed. A certain amount of guilt accompanied it, but she pushed it down. *This is the job. No time for feelings.*

Brody had sent her a bunch of messages over the last few hours, and though he was just barely keeping the plaintive note out of them, she could tell that he was worried. She was supposed to have called Kovalic after their run-in at the safe house, but to be honest, by the time she'd finished her meeting with the general, she'd forgotten. Really, she ought to have responded to Brody's messages, but every time she started typing out an answer, she deleted it nearly as quickly.

It was almost a relief to have something else to think about.

Stepping out of the car, she went to the trunk and removed the shopping tote there. It hung heavy on her shoulder, digging a groove into the muscles. Hardly ideal for this kind of work, but with its local supermarket logo on the side, at least it wouldn't raise undue attention. She tucked her earpiece into her left ear, hearing the reassuring constant *ping* from the tracking program that allowed her to monitor her proximity to the target without constantly glancing down at her sleeve.

It was only a few blocks stroll to the target itself, a mid-rise with apartments on the top several levels over a first floor commercial property. The streets were not precisely empty at this hour, but the throngs hadn't descended yet. Or maybe people weren't yet ready to jump back into their normal routines after the Oluo Plaza bombing.

*Lots of sightlines.* She glanced up at the other buildings in the area, all of which climbed higher into the sky than the one she was interested in. There was one across the street from her target that looked like it might provide a particularly good angle. As she walked by the building, she slapped the tiny remote cam she'd palmed onto the wall facing her target. Its feed would be sent directly to her sleeve – normally she'd use a drone constellation, like she had at Oluo Plaza the other night, but daylight hours made it far too conspicuous.

With the camera planted, she slipped into the building itself. It didn't take long to find an emergency stairwell and jimmy the lock, and then she was on the way to the roof.

Sunlight blazed in as she stepped out on top of the building. Making her way to the edge, she crouched by the lip, and reached into her tote to pull out the rifle scope. It wasn't as good as the one she'd thrown away as a distraction the other night – which, to her annoyance, CID hadn't bothered to return – but it'd do.

She'd been right: the vantage here was solid. The beeping in her earpiece had remained constant; her quarry hadn't moved since entering the building. Plenty of time for her to set up.

It was the work of a moment to remove the rifle components from the tote bag. The Krennhauser 17G was lighter and shorter range than the full-size sniper rifles she'd predominantly trained on, but it also had the benefit of being easy to disassemble and store in a shopping bag instead of a bulky and obvious hard case. Plus, its modular mounting system meant she could attach both a laser mic and a targeting package for recon: who wanted to have to choose?

Snapping everything together, she flipped down the bipod and aimed the weapon at the target building, activating the laser mic and switching the scope to thermal mode. Peering through, she spotted one heat signature at the front of the building – probably a store employee.

But the team had gone in. She was sure of it. Unless they'd found the tracker and ditched it, which was possible but unlikely, they were in there somewhere.

That pang of guilt in her stomach again, telling her that she shouldn't be doing this. The whole situation felt wrong. She should be down there with her teammates, not up here with a rifle. Her teeth grated over her lip.

*Come on, Addy. You're doing your job. Following orders.* This *is what you should be doing.*

She pressed her eye against the rubber ring around the scope, as though the action could isolate her from those intrusive thoughts, and swept the scene with the laser mic, bringing it to bear on the shop's window. The sound resonance from inside the building would vibrate the glass, which the laser would then turn back into audio and play into her earpiece.

But the only noise she could make out was a sort of idle humming that seemed to be the owner going about their business.

Maybe it was the wrong shop. What if she'd missed the team coming and going; but no, the tone in her ear had remained regular, indicating a constant distance from the tracker. She flipped the scope over to the view from her sticky cam and played back the footage from the time between planting the camera and getting set up in her perch, just in case she'd missed something.

A few people went back and forth, but none entered the building and nobody came out. Still, she couldn't banish her unease – the feeling that she'd missed something. She switched the camera back to the live view just in time to catch a figure approaching the shop.

Addy's breath caught in her throat. Something about the figure, the way it moved, was familiar. She'd seen them before. They moved with a calm surety, not so much as a hesitation or hitch in their step. But the camera couldn't make out their face, shrouded by the hood of their jacket.

Flipping back to the view from her scope was little better. She was higher up but the angle was still wrong. She needed a view from the shop itself.

Or did she?

She only had a split second to act, so she hunched upwards, pointing the rifle barrel at a hovercar parked in front of the shop. *Sorry about your paint job.* She fired a single low-impact round into the car's side, careful not to hit any place too vital, then quickly rolled flat onto the roof, clutching the rifle to her chest.

*Come on, you're human. Be curious.* She raised her sleeve and ran back the last ten seconds of footage from the sticky cam. The shot from the rifle dinged into the side of the car, leaving a nice little dent that hopefully the owner would chalk up to a parking mishap, but more importantly, the sound of the impact had gotten the figure's attention; instinctively, they'd frozen, one hand on the door to the shop, looking back over their shoulder for the source of the sudden sharp noise. But with Addy out of sight, they'd had nothing to see, so they merely frowned and continued into the building.

But that split second was enough for Addy to recognize the face: the same woman who she'd faced off against at the safe house. Headed into the exact same building where the team had followed Page's trail.

*Coincidence?* No such thing in this line of work. She wasn't sure if the woman and Page were working together or not, but if they were, then the team had walked directly into the exact trap that the general had warned Addy about.

And here she was, stuck on a rooftop.

She crouched at the building's edge again, balancing the rifle on the low wall, and trained the microphone back on the shop.

"– looking for a very specific volume." It was a low woman's voice, and Addy would have put money on it belonging to her mysterious friend.

"Well, I'll help if I can." The shopkeeper, Addy assumed. "Do you know the title? Or the author?"

"Neither, I'm afraid. A friend recommended it to me. Perhaps you know him."

"Oh," said the owner. But the tone of his voice had changed suddenly. Become more trepidatious. She'd missed something – something she couldn't *hear*.

Cursing, she switched back to the thermal scope. The two

heat signatures were standing on opposite sides of a desk from each other, but the image was still too abstract for her to make out what was going on – just large person-shaped blobs of red and yellow.

*Shit.* She flipped back to the camera, but it couldn't see into the shop from its position either. *Not good.* A deep impulse was telling her she needed to get down there as fast as possible; she could feel it practically tugging her down the steps. But the time it would take would just blow any advantage she had, and she risked losing sight of all her targets.

Sometimes she missed just punching things. Too much thinking and overthinking complicated these kinds of missions.

"Uh… the back room," the owner said. "Last on the right. You might find what you're looking for there."

"Why don't you show me?" Her tone said it was less a question than a command.

"Well, I can't exactly leave the counter untended. I mean, a customer might come in."

"There's only one customer you should be worrying about right now." A familiar click punctuated the heartbeat rhythm of the tracker in Addy's earpiece. Of course the woman was armed: she'd had no compunction about blowing up Page's safe house.

*I guess I could just start shooting out the windows.* It didn't seem like a *good* idea, but at least it would be doing something. Otherwise, she'd just be lying here and squirming. Or she could blow it entirely by calling Kovalic or Brody and warning them that they were about to be in hot water. But that would definitely raise some uncomfortable questions that she wasn't sure she'd be able to answer.

Or she could do... nothing. See how it all played out. *They can take care of themselves. They don't* need *me.*

It felt like a cop-out.

She took a deep breath, let her finger whisper over the trigger... then exhaled. Patience, she reminded herself. It wasn't her strong suit, but that didn't mean that it wasn't the right choice sometimes. Running in, guns blazing, might be the way her gut was telling her to act, but a little voice in her brain that sounded suspiciously like Commander Taylor was reminding her that you could always wait to see what happened next.

It wasn't a long wait.

Mere minutes after the mystery woman had entered the shop, Addy noticed that people were filtering out of the streets in the area, almost as though they were being directed to do so. She trained the rifle scope on one of the cross streets just in time to catch a familiar sight: armored troopers – just like the ones that had arrested her and the rest of the team at Oluo Plaza – moving in formation, ushering civilians away. A quick look in the other direction down the street yielded an identical team, this one led by a man in civilian garb with a flak vest over a button-down shirt.

She zoomed in closer. He was clearly in charge of the whole operation and he looked familiar: carefully groomed, slick brown hair, yelling orders she couldn't hear.

Her sleeve chose that exact moment to buzz, and she spared a glance, then did a double take at the bright red security alert splashed across the smart fabric: "WARNING: Wanted. Armed and dangerous." And below it an image of the same taciturn face that she'd seen in the alley behind the café, albeit an unflattering image that she immediately recognized as being pulled from a Commonwealth personnel file. *So much for Page staying under the radar.*

Down below, the troops had moved in a standard security pattern to lock down the intersection, and it wasn't hard to see that their efforts were centered on the exact same building that Addy was watching. The same one that her team was in.

*The same one that I've got an ideal sniper vantage on.*

Addy didn't even think, just moved, slinging the tote bag over her shoulder and hightailing it back to the stairwell door. *Jesus, again?* But this time, hopefully, they weren't expecting her. Which meant she might not get caught up in the net.

But her teammates might not be so lucky.

# CHAPTER 22

The torrent of emotions that flowed through Kovalic jostled him like whitewater rapids: relief at seeing Page alive, remorse at the situation that had brought them to this point, and not a little bit of irritation at having a gun pointed at him. But as his brain was still sorting through them, it was Tapper who cut through the moment with his usual grace of a shaped explosive charge.

"I thought we lost you, kid." Gruff though the sergeant's words were, Kovalic couldn't help but notice the glimmer in his eyes. Tapper stepped towards the man, ignoring the weapon trained on them like it was nothing more than a toy, laid a hand on Page's shoulder and squeezed. "Damn good to see you."

Page seemed adrift for a moment, not sure how to respond, then gave a curt nod and lowered the gun. "Sergeant." He looked around at the rest of them. "We don't have a lot of time."

"Time? Until what?" said Kovalic.

Page opened his mouth to respond but was almost immediately interrupted by the sound of heavy footfalls overhead. "Until that."

"You expecting more visitors?" said Tapper.

"In a manner of speaking. I doubted that this location would remain secure for long, and I assumed I would have to vacate the premises."

"While we're on that subject," said Brody, looking around, "what exactly *is* this pla–"

*Thump.*

All four of them looked up at the noise, which had the unmistakable cadence of a body hitting the floor. It was followed by the click and rumble of the disguised entrance above rolling open.

Kovalic glanced at Page. "Tell me you've got another way out of here."

The lieutenant nodded his head at the shadowy niche from which he had stepped only a moment ago. "In there, for now."

"All of us?!" hissed Brody. "We won't fit."

"We'd better, kid," said Tapper, seizing the pilot by the arm and dragging him towards the opening.

"Major," said Page. He held out the KO gun, butt first, to Kovalic, summoning a memory of nine months past: a bench in a park on Bayern, Page coming clean about his betrayal, Kovalic making a choice. Except then he'd been the one handing over the weapon, and it had started them all inexorably down this path. But this was no time for reminiscences: Kovalic nodded and took the weapon.

The niche proved to be a narrow corridor that led deeper into the basement, lined with plastic containers that Kovalic suspected were full of books and possibly more… controversial items? This all seemed a bit over the top for a bookbinding workshop, and he was starting to suspect that books weren't the store's only business. Not that illicit activities were his primary concern at this exact moment.

Kovalic pressed himself against the wall near the opening, in a spot he hoped was cloaked in shadow. And none too soon: not a moment after they'd squeezed themselves into their hiding spot, a woman entered the workshop, looking around warily. A slugthrower was held tightly in her hands – no knockout gun, this – and as her gaze alit upon Page, the barrel was leveled at him. The lieutenant had both his hands up already, as though he'd expected this greeting.

Kovalic held the knockout gun at the ready; he'd glanced at the power meter to ensure it was charged, but that was just a formality. Page wasn't the type to be unprepared.

"Aaron," said the woman. Her eyes darted around the room, as though looking for something – or someone – she knew was there, even if she couldn't see it. Dark, slender eyebrows divided by a crease in an otherwise smooth forehead. She was shorter than Page by several inches and her black hair was braided close to her head. "You alone?"

"At present. I'm impressed you found me."

A vague shrug. "You're not the only one who's been trained to go to ground. You know why I'm here."

"Do I?"

"The chip. Give it to me."

Kovalic wouldn't exactly call Page's expression 'stony-faced', but as usual, the man gave nothing away for free.

"I don't have it."

"The hell you don't," she said, grip tightening on her weapon. "You were there with the rest of us – only you disappeared for a solid five minutes. Nobody else had the opportunity to take it."

"You misunderstand. I don't have it *on* me."

"Where is it, then?"

"It's safe."

"I hope you don't mean your lovely little house," she said. "Because I'm afraid that's a pile of ash by now."

"So I saw. Was that really necessary?"

"What can I say? It seemed appropriate at the time. Don't worry: I searched it first. Thoroughly. You're not the clumsy type; you'd never leave it someplace so obvious."

"I respect you enough not to make it easy."

"You goddamn asshole." But, to Kovalic's ears, there was no real surprise or anger in the sentiment: just a statement of fact. "I knew I shouldn't have trusted you."

Page's shoulders lifted in a shrug of acknowledgment. "We all make bad calls sometimes."

Her expression had turned thoughtful. "Then again, you might be bluffing."

"I suppose."

Kovalic felt a tug on his sleeve and looked over to see Tapper glance meaningfully at the KO gun, then jerk his head towards the workroom. Then mime shooting the woman with it, just in case Kovalic had missed his drift.

It was an option, yes, but Kovalic wasn't sure about the odds of the woman getting a shot off before he did. Besides, it seemed like there might be more to learn from Page keeping her talking. He held up a palm in Tapper's direction and chose to ignore the older man's rolling eyes. At least the sergeant wasn't carrying any explosives, or this wouldn't have even been a conversation.

"You're proving to be more trouble than you're worth," said the woman. "Here I'd hoped you were committed to the cause."

"The cause was never my concern. It was the way in which you chose to carry it out."

"You're a fool for caring about them – they've certainly never cared about you," she scoffed. "Augur should have told you that much."

Augur? Kovalic's brow furrowed. The name didn't ring a bell, but something about the emphasis that the woman put on it told him that it was important. He filed it away for a moment when they weren't all standing around, guns drawn.

"Perhaps."

"Chip or not, you're a pain in my ass, and I'm better off without you." Her aim steadied again on Page's head.

Kovalic felt the grip of the KO gun pressing into his palms and he steeled himself to take the shot. He raised the weapon and was about to step out when overhead, a distant chime sounded.

Somebody else had entered the bookshop.

The whole tableau froze and, as one, they all raised their eyes to the ceiling, as if they could see through to the floor above.

The woman hesitated, unsure whether to keep her gun trained on Page, or swing it back towards the corridor she'd entered from.

Footsteps sounded overhead – more than one pair, moving in a rapid trot that belied it being a simple browsing customer – and Kovalic suddenly realized that he'd never heard the rumble of the secret entrance sliding closed again.

Shit. He glanced back at Tapper to see the sergeant had made the same connection. Brody, for his part, was still staring up at the ceiling, as if trying to do a particularly complicated math problem in his head. Kovalic waved them further down the corridor.

"What is this?" said the woman. "Your backup?"

For a moment, Kovalic entertained the insane idea that Page would tell her to hide in the niche with them and just barely managed to stifle a hysterical laugh.

"No," said Page. "I assume you swept for tails."

"This isn't my first operation."

The footsteps tramped closer and Kovalic pressed himself against the wall. Whoever was up there wasn't here to buy books and if they were armed then the room was about to turn into a shooting gallery, with Page in the middle.

Kovalic's sleeve buzzed and he froze, but it seemed like the woman was too distracted to notice. He glanced down and the smart fabric display glowed to life with a message: three words from an unknown source.

GET OUT NOW.

There was a murmur from overhead that echoed down the corridor and a moment later Kovalic heard the distinctive *clink-clink* of something metal tumbling down stairs.

Time to go.

Before the noise even finished, he'd stepped out of the niche, just in time to catch the woman's eyes widening as she saw him. But she too had heard the noise from the stairs, and her weapon was mid-swing in the other direction, back up the corridor; Kovalic had her dead to rights. He squeezed the trigger of the KO gun, the stun field rippling outwards, but she was already using the momentum from shifting her aim to overcompensate and throw herself to the floor.

Page, meanwhile, snatched up a wooden-handled hole puncher from the table, and hurled it with surprising accuracy towards the woman. It missed her head by mere inches as she fell and instead stuck, quivering, in a bookshelf on the opposite wall.

Then the concussion grenade went off.

A blinding light flashed from around the corner before Kovalic had time to shut his eyes and no sooner had it turned his vision to white then the concomitant explosion set his ears ringing. He staggered backwards against the wall and would have probably toppled over had not someone – Tapper, presumably – seized him by the arm and steadied him.

He shook his head to try and clear it, but that did little to dispel either the whine in his ears or his whited-out vision. But he was moving anyway, being chivvied further down the corridor from both in front and behind. He fumbled the KO gun, shoving it in his waistband; he wasn't going to be shooting anyone if he couldn't see.

He felt more than heard something whiz by him, a smattering of particles peppering off his jacket sleeve. The smell of hot metal and melted plastic. Live rounds were being shot in their direction, ricocheting off the containers on either side of them.

Blinking, his vision resolved into dark blobs and light blobs – not enough to navigate by quite yet. But he kicked out at some of the containers as they passed by, and was rewarded when the dark blob following him – Page? – seemed to continue his work, knocking them over and spilling their contents across the passage in an attempt to slow their pursuers.

And then Kovalic was being pulled upwards, stumbling over uneven steps as they emerged outside, the scent of the fresh, humid air of the Salaam day strong in his nose, compensating for his impaired senses. Arms seized his shoulders and he found himself staring into a blur that resolved into Tapper's face, way too close to his own. The sergeant's lips were forming words, and between the sight of them and the sound, resonating through his body and barely penetrating the cacophony in his ears, he could just make out the question.

CAN. YOU. RUN?

And all he could do was draw himself up and give a sharp nod. No, he couldn't see where the hell he was going or hear worth a damn, but give him an open path and someone to follow, and yes. Yes, he could damn well run.

Behind them, he heard a loud clank of metal and could vaguely make out Page slamming closed a bulkhead over the exit they'd just used, then sliding a bolt into place. His vision was starting to clear again, but something was still wrong. An errant spot of red light danced over Page's shirt, as though an afterimage from the explosion, but it was too small and too bright, and he was already moving towards the lieutenant even before his brain had realized what was about to happen.

He never even heard the shot.

# CHAPTER 23

For the second time in forty-eight hours, Addy had found herself stuck on a rooftop as hostile forces took aim at her friends. This time, she at least had one advantage: they didn't know she was here.

No less than a minute after her instincts had told her to take cover, a trooper had emerged onto the roof to assume a sniper position. It wasn't hard to conceal herself until they had set up their perch – in precisely the place that she herself had chosen, of course – then sneak back over and incapacitate him with his own KO gun, set to maximum power at point-blank range.

*I'm guessing he's going to leave that part out of the report,* she thought as she rolled him away from his rifle and settled down in his stead.

Standard law enforcement issue: Marks & Gray, short-range, variable ammunition. She pressed her eye to the scope and tapped the ammo selector then sucked in a breath through her teeth. *They've got this thing on live rounds? What the hell?* Most of the time, law enforcement was strictly required to deploy less-lethal weaponry, like shock-gel rounds or concussion weapons.

Then again, these people weren't really law enforcement,

were they? More of those CID goons who had 'special authorization' from the Commonwealth Executive in the aftermath of the Oluo Plaza bombing. It seemed intelligence agencies operating domestically wasn't the only norm that had been suspended.

*Well, I use what they give me.*

She peered through the scope at the scene in front of her: a few squads of similarly geared operatives were making their way down both ends of the street, enclosing the bookstore in a standard box pattern.

They weren't the only ones, either. Sitting back from the rifle, she checked the other rooftops near her position and picked out another sharpshooter silhouetted against the skyline, about half a block down. Their vantage gave them a view into the alley at the side of the shop and, as she watched, they lined up a shot.

*Shit. I don't have an angle on him.*

Addy pressed her eye back to the scope, swinging it towards the alley, where she could just see an open bulkhead and several familiar figures emerging: Tapper, ushering along Kovalic, who was carrying a sidearm and stumbling, followed by Brody. She felt an unconscious sigh of relief issue from her lungs as she saw that the pilot was unharmed. Behind him came the tall figure of Aaron Page, who was slamming the bulkhead closed and jamming something in the latch.

An iridescent light danced around the man's torso as the other sniper took aim. *Infrared targeting dot.* That meant it would only be visible to someone looking through a targeting scope – like Addy.

Her finger whispered over the trigger. The mission was to protect her team. That's what the general had told her, and it seemed clear that their association with Page had gotten them into hot water: there were multiple squads of troops trying to apprehend them, and the chances of them getting injured – or worse – were steadily rising as long as they tried to protect him. The simplest answer would be to just let the sniper take Page out.

*Or are you so willing to let them do it because that would mean* you *don't have to?*

*'I've read your jacket, specialist,'* the general had told her. But if he had, he'd know that for her entire time in the service, the war had been at a simmer. Yes, her unit had been deployed for security actions in half a dozen places, but most of it had amounted to little more than glorified guard duty.

For all the time she'd spent in uniform, she'd never once had cause to kill anyone. Shot them? Yes. Even before her time in the military, when she was growing up on the streets of this very city, she'd had to defend herself, and sometimes those strikes had even been preemptive. She'd certainly gotten in plenty of brawls in her youth and even during her military career, and god knew she'd come close to crossing that line – but she'd always pulled herself back.

And she wasn't sure she should cross it now, not when she hadn't expended every last alternative. The general, after all, had told her to trust her instincts, and right now her gut was telling her that if CID wanted Page dead so badly, that was good enough reason for her to keep him alive.

Her own targeting laser was already on, chasing the other sniper's, but with her decision made, she flipped it to a visible spectrum, seeing the dot turn bright red even in the light of the day. *I just hope it's enough.*

Kovalic's head perked up suddenly, but already Addy

knew he wouldn't be fast enough to warn Page. *Too much time deliberating.* There was no way the other sniper could miss the shot.

Unless his target wasn't there.

With no hesitation, Addy nudged her rifle to the right. She didn't have time to check windspeed or angle or gravity, but when it came to this kind of work, that had never stopped her before.

She squeezed the trigger.

# CHAPTER 24

Eli would have said all hell broke loose when they emerged from the bookshop, but it would be more accurate to say that all hell kept breaking loose. No sooner had Page slammed shut the hatch from which they'd emerged than Kovalic was barreling *backwards*, diving at him.

Something *zipped* through the air and Page flinched. A spot of red bloomed in his upper arm.

"Sniper!" shouted Tapper.

Eli just had time to register that the streets around them were surprisingly empty as the sergeant yanked him to the ground behind a shrub in a stone planter. The bulkhead had let them out in a cul-de-sac a few feet from the street where they'd gone into the bookshop.

Behind them, Kovalic and Page had slung their arms over each other's shoulders and taken cover behind a dumpster. The red wash on Page's sleeve had expanded, and Kovalic was blinking and fumbling with the cloth, trying to get a better look at the wound.

Eli peeked around the edge of the planter only to be rewarded with another round pinging a divot into the concrete. "We can't stay here!"

"No shit," said Tapper. "But we've only got a short-range knockout gun, one of us is bleeding, and another can hardly see a billboard right now."

Looking down the end of the street that he could see from his vantage, Eli noticed that the whole area had been vacated. While he was relieved to see that there weren't any civilians in harm's way, it was eerie and unsettling. *If this is Nova Front, how'd they clear it so fast? Call in another bomb threat?*

And if it wasn't Nova Front, who the hell was it?

Tapper, meanwhile, had produced a knife from somewhere – he probably had half a dozen in various places on his person, Eli rationalized – and was holding the blade around the corner of the planter, trying to use it as a makeshift mirror. After a moment he swore and pulled back.

"We've got more company. Looks like a couple armed squads of the same goons from the other night. They're cutting us off from the hovercar."

Eli's stomach fell. CID must have tracked Page here too, somehow. He'd have regretted pulling an all-nighter looking at books if his body weren't so flooded with adrenaline right now. "Can't we, you know, call their boss and at least tell them to stop shooting?"

"They shot Page already," Tapper pointed out. "Something tells me the talking part might be over."

*Great. So this is how it ends: curled up behind an evergreen bush?*

Another report came from overhead and Eli braced himself for the impact. There was a grunt from somewhere on the street, followed by some shouting. He exchanged a glance at Tapper, who leaned out with his knife again.

"One of the troops is down," he said, sounding puzzled.

Another *zip* and more shouting from the street, followed by what sounded like some hurried bootsteps.

"They're taking cover – someone's laying down suppressing fire. For *us*."

Kovalic leaned out from behind the dumpster. "Seems like it might be a good time for us to go."

"They're still between us and the hovercar."

Page appeared, a strip of his white shirt tied around his upper arm. He looked a little pale, but otherwise no worse for wear. "Leave that to me."

"Are you sure?" said Eli. "Seems like they could still shoot us from, you know, down the street."

"We're not going to get a better opportunity," said Kovalic. "On my mark."

"There's a hovercar across the street," said Page. "Straight on, about ten meters. Head for it and get ready to get in."

Eli blinked. "Is that your car?"

Page cocked his head to one side. "Not yet."

*Why do I even ask.*

"Go," said Kovalic.

They went. Eli peeled around the side of the planter, running as fast as he could. Sprinting had never really been his thing, but he had to admit that, if nothing else, his time with the SPT had been great for his cardiovascular health. *Running for your life is one way to keep in shape.*

Just as Page had said, there was a hovercar on the other side of ten meters of open pavement: a late-model silver four-door. Nothing fancy, just the kind of car that you saw by the dozens around town. Keeping his head down, Eli reached the door in record time, without a shot being fired in his direction. He risked a glance down the street and saw that the squad of troopers had taken cover behind cars and planters as they searched for the sniper above. *Oh, how the tables have turned.*

With a grin, he reached up and pulled the door handle.

Locked.

He glanced back over his shoulder to see the rest of the team zigzagging across the street. Page was tapping something furiously on his sleeve even as he ran.

There was a whine as the hovercar next to him whirred to life, followed by the click of the doors unlocking; Page, who hadn't slowed down a step, launched himself up, sliding over the hood of the car towards the passenger side.

"Move it!" shouted Kovalic, and Eli had never needed an order repeated less in his life.

# CHAPTER 25

The rifle bucked against Addy's shoulder. Through the scope she saw Page flinch, knocked back even as the sleeve of his jacket darkened with blood. A split second later, Kovalic had barreled him over, then pulled him behind a metal dumpster. Tapper and Brody ducked behind a shrub as the other sniper opened fire on them, chips of concrete flecking off the planter.

Addy didn't waste any time. She grabbed the rifle and hoofed it over to the parapet to the left of her, dropping down to settle the bipod on the edge. *No time for proper ranging.* With her eye back on the scope, she sighted the sniper on the next building, lining up their next shot. Flipping the ammo selector, she scrolled through and was glad to see that there were at least shock-gel rounds available.

From the weapon's magazine came the telltale click of the cartridges swapping. It took a few seconds, enough time for the sniper to fire off another round, but there was no time to check the situation below.

In the scope, the ammo selector blinked and then vanished, replaced with crosshairs. She eyeballed the windspeed and angle, then gave it her best guess and fired.

In training, they made you get hit with a shock-gel round,

just to know what it felt like – the kind of damage you were inflicting on someone else. What Addy remembered most was the split second of anticipatory horror as you heard the wet *smack* of the gel round hitting your body, felt the impact of its dispersal like somebody had socked you in the stomach, and knew beyond any doubt that it was about to hurt a lot more. The electrical capsules embedded within the gel fired off tens of thousands of volts, and while the low amperage prevented the damage from being severe, it was still incapacitating.

From this distance, she was too far away to hear the impact of the round, but she saw the sniper collapse into a heap on the roof. And that was going to have to do for the moment.

Swinging the rifle barrel down to the street, she saw the phalanx of troops heading toward the bookstore. *I can't stop all of them… but I can make them think twice*. Her mouth set in a grim smile as she fired off more shock-gel rounds at the leading edge of the formation. A few of the troops twitched and went down from her shots, sending ripples of surprise and dismay through their broken ranks as they tried to figure out why their own sniper had suddenly turned on them.

The tracker, still in her ear, started to beep more frequently as the distance between her and her quarry closed, and she was able to spare a glance down to see her team making a beeline for a hovercar. Kovalic and Page were holding each other up, but neither seemed seriously injured. And Brody was still miraculously untouched, unless you counted his hair being mussed up.

*Nine lives, nothing – he must have at least a dozen.*

Chaos had erupted in the street, and she heard a groan from a few feet away as the sharpshooter she'd incapacitated began to come to.

It was probably time to get off this roof. The beeps in her ear had slowed, spacing farther apart; she could only hope that meant the team had made it to the car and were now speeding away from the scene.

*I guess I can focus on saving myself, then.* First things first: don't leave anything behind that they can use to hurt you. She hit the ejector for the rifle's magazine and tossed the ammo cartridge off the roof. The KO gun she'd pulled off the sniper would be far more useful in a close-range combat situation anyway. And speaking of that sniper, a quick pat-down gave her a pair of plasticuffs that she used to tie their hands behind their back – though first she made sure to pull off their sleeve and relieve them of their earpiece. *The more I know about where they are, the better I can evade them.*

With that done, she stunned them one more time to buy herself a little more breathing room, reclaimed the tote bag containing her own sniper rifle, then headed for the stairs.

This time, at least, there was no backup waiting for her, and the building was only a few stories high, so it was the work of a minute to push her way through the exit at the bottom of the stairwell and step into the alley between it and the neighboring building.

She tucked the KO gun in the back of her waistband and covered it with her jacket. *Nothing to see here, just out for a casual mid-morning stroll… in the middle of a counterterrorism operation.*

Her hovercar was parked nearby, but based on the deployment patterns there were way too many of those CID troops between her and it, which meant she needed to improvise.

The good news was, she knew where she could find a vehicle – hopefully exactly where she'd left it.

# CHAPTER 26

Eli yanked the door open and dog-crawled into the driver's seat.

"Everybody strap in," said Eli as the vehicle's doors slammed all around him. He gunned the hovercar's motor and zipped out into the street.

"Christ, Brody," yelped Tapper from the rear, still fumbling with his seatbelt.

"Sorry, sarge, but it doesn't exactly seem like this is an 'obey all posted traffic laws' sort of situation. Now, where the hell am I going?"

The answer seemed to be straight into a barricade. He looked up just in time to see the crowd of troops posted a block down from the store, standing in front of a long narrow piece of equipment that stretched the width of the road, glowing faintly red. *Antirepulsor strip.* Drive over that, and the hovercar would fall to the ground like the two-ton chunk of steel it was – they'd be dead in the water.

"Right," said Page, who had pulled up the dashboard holoscreen and was consulting a local map.

Eli hauled the yoke to the right, and the hovercar fishtailed into a sharp turn down a side street, kicking up a cloud of dust in the faces of the troops at the barricade. A few haphazard shots pinged off the vehicle's exterior.

"They're going to have this whole area cordoned off," said Tapper, leaning up through the gap between the two front seats. "Getting out is going to be a trick."

Gritting his teeth, Eli slammed down the pedal, the acceleration pushing him back into the conforming gel seat; as an added bonus, Tapper was tossed back into his own.

"Right at the next intersection," said Page.

"You sure you know where you're going?"

"Positive."

*All right.* He swung the car into a right-hand turn down the next street, then glanced in the rearview camera to see a low-slung black vehicle accelerating from behind them, red and blue lightstrips undulating on its roof. "Soooo, I don't want to alarm anyone, but they're definitely behind us. Maybe thirty meters."

Out of the corner of his eye, he saw Page reach under the dashboard and yank out a fistful of wires.

Eli gaped in horror. "What the hell are you doing?"

But Page didn't respond, just started sorting through the various cables while keeping one eye on the map that was still floating in front of him.

Behind them, Kovalic lowered his window and fired off a shot with the KO gun, but even if they hadn't been moving too fast for the stun field to maintain cohesion, it would have splashed harmlessly over the frame of the pursuing vehicle.

"Can't you overload the power pack?" Eli asked, dividing his attention between the road and the rearview camera. "Like you did on the *Queen Amina*?" *Look at all the useful skills I've picked up, like turning a battery into a bomb.*

Kovalic shook his head. "The fuse time is highly variable.

Chances of hitting them are low – and it risks too much collateral damage."

"So maybe drive faster, Brody," said Tapper.

"I've got the pedal to the floor! This thing was engineered for cupholders and grocery capacity, not high-speed chases." He wove the car across both lanes, glad at least that the traffic had been cleared from the area, even if it made evading their pursuers more challenging.

"Right turn in forty meters," said Page, who had now disconnected several wires and was busy twisting them together. Eli heard the *zip* of a shock and the vehicle's dash display flickered for a moment, the whole car slowing and throwing them against their restraints, before it thrummed back to life. He floored the accelerator again and threw the car into the right-hand turn, dimly realizing that it was taking them back in the direction they'd come from.

Page reached out and pinched the map wider, then nodded to himself, satisfied, and connected a few more wires.

Behind them, a trooper had leaned out the window of the pursuing car, steadying himself in the window while struggling with a large device in both hands that resembled a grenade launcher.

Eli swallowed. "Uh, guys? What the hell is that?"

Tapper and Kovalic both craned their necks, and Eli heard the sergeant let loose a torrent of swears, some of which he wasn't even sure he understood. "That's a goddamn EMP rifle. He lands a shot with that and it's going to fry every piece of electronics in this car."

*So I guess the silver lining is that it* isn't *a grenade launcher.*

The trooper was still fumbling with the device, trying to get it lined up, giving Eli's piloting brain just enough time to take over. "You still got that KO gun?"

Kovalic lifted the weapon. "What are you thinking, lieutenant?"

"I'm thinking I hope you can see again. Hold on!" He turned the yoke hard to the right, then slammed the car's propulsion system into reverse and stomped the brakes. The car spun one hundred eighty degrees, its nose pointing in the direction of the pursuing vehicle, but just offset so that he could pull alongside it, leaving Kovalic pointing more or less directly at the trooper hanging out the window who, though his expression was unreadable through goggles and balaclava, still seemed nonetheless startled to be suddenly face-to-face with his target.

Kovalic put the KO gun out the window and fired. At that distance, he couldn't miss. The stun field splashed into the trooper, who went limp, his torso halfway out the window, and the EMP rifle slipped from his grasp and clattered to the street. The pursuing car veered away from them and Eli pulled the controls hard right, shifting back into forward drive, continuing all the way around the pursuer in a circle. He hit the accelerator again, and the car shot forward, narrowly slipping between the other vehicle and the sidewalk. Behind them, the pursuer hit the curb, and rattled to a stop.

"Ha!" crowed Tapper, and Eli felt the sergeant slap him hard on the shoulder. "I can't *believe* that worked, kid."

*Me neither*! He glanced over to see an unruffled Page give him a nod of respect before looking back at the map.

"Keep on straight through," said the lieutenant. "And get ready."

"For what?"

That question answered itself promptly as they bulleted down the street toward a line of barricades laid out in front of them. But that hadn't been what Page had been talking about, Eli realized – no, he'd meant *beyond* that, where the pale blue line of the Wolakota lay, just below an embankment. More out of instinct than anything, he let up on the accelerator pedal.

"Uh, Page?"

"Hold steady." He'd finished whatever he'd been doing with the dashboard wires, one of which now snaked into his sleeve.

Eli swallowed as the barricades grew larger in the windshield: large plasticrete slabs, shielding several more of the black-clad troopers, all of whom had serious looking weapons leveled in their direction and would probably not hesitate to open fire.

*There's a fine line between playing chicken and being fricasseed.* But Page had always come through when the chips were down, so Eli clenched his jaw and pressed the accelerator again; the hovercar jumped forward.

"The timing is going to be tricky," said Page.

"Ain't it always," muttered Tapper from the back seat.

Eli caught Kovalic's gaze in the rear-view mirror, but the major just nodded at him, as if saying 'do what you've got to do.' Hands white-knuckling the wheel, Eli willed his nerve not to give out, keeping his foot glued to the pedal as they approached the blockade.

"Page, if you're going to do something, now would be good."

"Just a little bit closer."

He was going to get his wish. Suddenly, something pinged off the front of the vehicle: a shot fired by the troops. Then another, and another. A shock-gel round slammed into the transparent aluminum windshield, cracks radiating outward like a spider-web. It held. Barely.

"*Page.*" The barricade and the troops were life-size now and a couple of them dove aside, clearly not willing to trust their lives to the madman behind the wheel.

"Hold on," said the lieutenant in his usual calm voice, as he touched a control on his sleeve.

There was a flare and a sharp high-pitched whine from beneath them as the repulsors fired with several times their normal strength. Eli sank into the gel seat, pressed down as though the hovercar were launching into orbit, even as his stomach seemed to remain far below him. The barricades and troops were gone as the vehicle sailed *over* all of them, maintaining its forward momentum, then, almost as suddenly, hurtled back downwards to reintroduce Eli to his gastrointestinal system.

Also, there was a river.

The hovercar didn't exactly hit it – the repulsors miraculously held and the water crested on every side as the antigravity field displaced it.

"Brody, *floor it*," said Page, with the most urgency Eli had ever seen him muster.

He didn't need to be told twice. His foot had let up on the pedal while they'd hung suspended in air, but he stamped on it once more and the hovercar skimmed across the surface of the water, staying just barely above it as they crossed the river and made for the embankment on the other side.

They coasted up the sloped stone bank there and clunked back down onto the street, water dripping off the vehicle and pooling below it as they caught their breath.

"Don't stop now," said Page, bringing up the map again. "That will buy us some time, but not much. We'll need to switch vehicles – I've got a spare stored here," he said, pointing at the map.

Eli nodded, still feeling his heart pounding against his ribcage as though it wanted to be let out, and he turned down the indicated street. The vehicle rattled and clanked as it went, and he could feel it sputtering. *Sorry, whoever's car this is. Hope your insurance is good.*

"Just one question," he said, when his brain had caught up. "How the hell did you know the repulsor coils wouldn't burn out?"

Page was tucking wires back under the dashboard and didn't look up. "I didn't. I guess we were... lucky."

Eli bit back a hysterical laugh and shook his head as they coasted down the street. *Of all the miracles I've seen today, the most improbable has got to be Aaron Page trusting in luck.*

# CHAPTER 27

The countryside sped by in a blur of greens and blues, darkening as the world around them faded to night. Kovalic stared out the back window, but the road was clear, as it had been for most of their journey.

A couple hours outside of Salaam, as they were, and the traffic had thinned to almost nothing. The land beyond the capital region was still largely rural, undeveloped, except for some of the large-scale industrial farms that provided the world with much of its food.

They'd swapped cars in the subterranean garage where Page had stowed his emergency getaway vehicle and emerged a block or two away, quietly making their way through the city streets in the most law-abiding of fashions, in stark contrast to their earlier hair-raising escapades. Brody, for his part, had seemed almost disappointed by the sedate pace, his adrenaline clearly still running high from earlier, but after half an hour with no further action, all of their energy levels had dropped and the pilot had been uncharacteristically willing to hand the vehicle over to the autodrive system.

Which had left them with the question of where to go. Salaam seemed an unsafe option at present, with no less than two major players gunning for them. They needed to get out of the city and regroup, hopefully out from under the watchful eyes of CID and Nova Front. Somewhere way, way off the radar.

And, as much as Kovalic had hated to admit it, he had just the place.

"Where the hell is Milo?" said Brody after Kovalic had punched in their destination. "I've never even heard of it."

"No reason you should have. It's a bit… off the beaten path."

The sandy-haired pilot whistled when he saw the travel time. "I'll say. Six *hours* off the beaten path. I didn't even know people lived out that far."

"Probably because you're a city boy," said Tapper, who was checking Page's wound and re-dressing it with the help of an emergency medkit they'd found under the seat. "There's some lakes out there with solid fishing. Cute little towns, too."

"Whatever you say, sarge." Brody scratched his head. "Shouldn't we be calling Addy? Letting her know where we're headed?"

Kovalic had given that some thought when he had a cycle to spare, and the conclusions weren't reassuring. He peeled off his sleeve. "We're still not sure how CID tracked Page to the bookstore. I'm worried our comms may be compromised." He ripped the smart fabric down the middle, and it sparked as it faded from life.

"But we ditched our old ones after they grabbed us," said Tapper, his brow furrowed as he pulled his own off, holding it up and peering at it as though he could see into its circuits. "How the hell would they get up on our new ones so fast?"

"That's exactly what's troubling me. For now, it's safer

for us *and* Sayers if we stay radio silent. Once we've gotten a moment to hunker down we'll figure out a secure way to get in touch with her."

With a cavalier shrug, Tapper ripped up his own sleeve, and Brody followed suit, albeit somewhat more resignedly. The pilot didn't like it, Kovalic could tell that much, but right now, he was less concerned about that than he was, oh, pretty much everything else that had transpired in the last several hours.

Much of the rest of the trip was made in silence, as Tapper and Page took the opportunity to get some much-needed shut-eye – like all good soldiers, they knew to take their kip where they could get it – and even Brody had relaxed, though he kept an eye on the road, just in case.

Kovalic, though, had found himself too wired to sleep immediately. His brain was turning over all the information they'd learned the past day, trying to figure out where the various pieces slotted into place. There were still too many gaps, though; the more he tried to construct a plausible narrative, the more he realized how much they still didn't know about Oluo Plaza, Nova Front's motives, and even what the hell CID's part was in it all. He rubbed his bleary eyes as he stared out at the darkened countryside, dotted with scrubby trees and uniform rows of crops. Automated harvester systems, their lights bright flares in the dark, crawled the fields as they collected and processed the haul. Every once in a while he thought he saw the dark shape of a person – a technician or even a farmer, perhaps – but they flashed by too quickly for him to be sure.

Something about the undulations of the landscape lulled him, and the next thing he knew, he was starting awake as the car slowed to a stop.

"I guess we're… here?" said Brody, peering through the windshield. "Wherever here is?"

It had gone full-on night while Kovalic had slept, the only light now coming from Nova's moon as it peeked through high, gauzy gray clouds. He blinked the grogginess out of his eyes, looking past Brody to see an unfriendly metal gate blocking the road.

"Gimme a second," he said, opening the door, and stepping out. The air was cooler here, somewhat less humid than the capital city, and the night breeze ruffled his hair.

The gate was secured with a keypad and a biometric lock; Kovalic pressed his thumb against the pad and it clicked open. With an effort, he pushed the gate, the recalcitrant hinge groaning. He waved at Brody and the pilot pulled the car through onto a road that was more gravel than pavement. Kovalic closed the gate after them, relocked it, and climbed back into the vehicle.

"You're going to have to do the last half mile on manual. The mapping system doesn't extend out here."

"I think I can handle that."

"And Brody? Take it slow – lots of nocturnal wildlife around here, and I'd be obliged if you didn't flatten any of it."

The pilot tipped him a mock salute, then pulled forward gently, following the ups and downs of the tree-lined road. As they continued, the foliage broke on the right side and Kovalic could make out the sparkle of moonlight on water.

"Beautiful," said Tapper, gazing out over the lake. "Bet there's all kinds of fish in there."

Kovalic grinned. If not exactly single-minded, the sergeant certainly had his pre-approved list of priorities. "You're welcome to find out."

After another few minutes, Kovalic instructed Brody to turn down a small drive, towards the lake. The headlights washed over a house: a simple two-story wood affair that stood on the shore, large windows facing out over the water. Brody pulled the car to a stop.

"Nice place," he said, hunching forward to look out the windshield. "Whose is it?"

"It's mine," said Kovalic. He opened the door and stepped out.

Another cool breeze washed over him and he couldn't help but smile at the smell of it: fresh and pure. A few meters away, waves lapped gently at the stony shore.

The other doors to the car opened and his team piled out.

"Yours, boss?" said Tapper. "You never said."

"Not much of a secret getaway if everybody's in on the secret."

"Isn't this risky?" said Brody, who had leaned on the hovercar's roof, chin in one hand. "Surely the first place they'll look is property associated with any of us."

Kovalic gave the younger man a tight smile. "That's why it's not in my name. I bought this place about five years ago, not long after we started the SPT. In part because I wanted something that was... separate from my life there. And I figured if I ever made it to retirement age, I'd like a place to call my own." Though he had never planned on retiring here alone, truth be told. But it was just the perfect size place for two people and one lazy but lovable dog. "Routed the purchase through a bunch of shell companies and dummy firms. They might be able to unravel it eventually, but it'll take time."

He felt a sharp gaze from Page's direction and looked over to find the man's dark eyes on him. "That was particularly clever of you, sir."

"I confess, the general helped me out with some of that; he's had considerably more experience with that kind of thing."

"Indeed," said Page, but his tone spoke volumes. Even through his usually stoic demeanor, Kovalic could feel the unease radiating off him like a physical vibration. The two of them still had a long talk in their future.

"Can't promise five-star accommodations," said Kovalic. "But the pantry's stocked, there's power and hot water, and should even be some clean spare clothes in there that'll make do for most of us. As long as everybody's comfortable seeing Lieutenant Brody in short pants." He jutted his chin at the tall, lanky pilot.

"Looking forward to crossing it off my bucket list," said Tapper.

"Sergeant, why don't you get the power on and see what you can find. Door code's 37521. Page and I will take care of the car."

Tapper gave a nod and dragooned a protesting Brody off towards the house.

There wasn't a garage proper, but the skyward trees created enough of a canopy to keep the vehicle from prying eyes. Most importantly the ones that were far, far overhead.

"The good news is that there's no permanent satellite tasked to this region," said Kovalic, following Page's glance at the heavens. "Not enough demand."

"Drones are the bigger concern," said Page. "But there's a lot of ground for them to cover if they didn't pick up our trail on the way out of the city."

"So your opinion is that we're secure."

"For now."

"Good." Kovalic lingered, sensing the younger man's hesitation. "Something on your mind, lieutenant?"

Even in the moonlight, he could see Page's lip twist slightly. "I don't think I have any right to that rank anymore, sir."

Kovalic rubbed his chin, then jerked his head towards the lake. "Walk with me a moment."

Behind the house, a narrow dock stretched out into the water, widening at the end into a large square with a bench bolted to it. Kovalic's boots thumped against the synthwood decking, and he felt the breeze pick up as he left the windbreak of the shore. He stood at the end, toes just at the edge, almost hanging out over the dark water.

"I don't get up here as often as I'd like," said Kovalic, taking a deep breath. The air held a hint of sweetness from the night-blooming flowers common to the area. "But when I do, I always make time to stand right here. There's a peacefulness to it." Something that was in short supply in his everyday life.

For a moment, they stood in silence, the only sounds the wind rustling in the trees and the rhythmic suspiration of the waves. Somewhere on the distant shore, a lone pair of headlights carved their way through the night.

"I have concerns."

"Join the club, lieutenant – and as far as I'm concerned, you not only still hold that rank, but you remain on active duty." He could hear Page shuffle slightly, sense his pent-up tension. "Even though you deliberately broke the protocol we established, NOMAD. We had a deal: you were supposed to remain in regular contact."

"I had reason to believe that those communication lines were no longer secure."

"And you couldn't find any other way to reach out? A man of your resourcefulness?" He turned back to face Page, who had taken up a parade rest stance. Out of instinct, no doubt, so deeply was his military training ingrained. "I find that difficult to believe."

"I made the best judgment I could at the time, given the facts on the ground."

"Not good enough, lieutenant. You've been out of pocket for the better part of a year. What you've been up to, I have no idea, and then you show up out of the blue at a terrorist bombing. Tell me what I'm supposed to think."

Page stiffened. "I was following a lead. And I'm ready to make my report now."

Report. Kovalic ran a hand through his hair. That had been the point of all of this, hadn't it? Only he had to admit that he wasn't sure he was ready to hear it. For the last nine months, he'd focused his sights on this moment, telling himself that all the strain of keeping Page's fate secret would be worth it in the end. Justified. And now that the moment was here, he found himself asking whether that was true, if this had all been worth it. Not to mention that whatever Page had uncovered might fundamentally change, well, everything.

"Very well, lieutenant. I'll hear your report. But not here, and not alone. I can't keep Brody and Tapper out of the loop on this anymore. They deserve to hear the whole truth, and they deserve to hear it directly from both of us."

# CHAPTER 28
*Bergfestung, Bayern – Nine months ago*

"No," Kovalic said at last. "There won't be a trial, lieutenant." He reached into his jacket and drew out the pistol, which he turned over slowly in both hands. "But I can't have someone on my team that I don't trust." Looking up, he forced himself to meet Page's eyes. But where he'd expected the man to be calculating some method of escape or some way to forestall the inevitable, he saw only hardened resolve. He shouldn't have been surprised, really.

"You were a good officer and I hate to lose you. I'm sorry, Aaron."

"Yeah," said Page slowly. "Me too, sir."

He sat there, cradling the pistol he'd pulled from his jacket. It was heavy in his hands – it had been years since he'd thought about the weight that came with a weapon, but right now he found he couldn't think of anything else.

After a moment, he turned the pistol over and offered it to Page, grip first. "Prove me wrong."

"Sir?"

"You seem to think the general has ulterior motives. It's a serious allegation, lieutenant, and you're going to need proof to back it up. Bank accounts and a mysterious code name aren't going to cut it. Get me hard evidence linking him with active attempts to undermine the Commonwealth and we can talk."

Page took the gun from him, automatically checking it over as *he did so: removing the magazine, reinserting it, working the slide, thumbing the safety off then on again, all as natural as breathing. "Understood. How long do I have?"*

*"My door's always open to you – but if you can't find anything inside of a year, maybe it's best if you just... disappear for good."*

*Page tucked the weapon into the small of his back. "What are you going to tell the general when I don't come back?"*

*"I'll tell him the truth. That you betrayed us to CID, and that I... dealt with it." Kovalic gave him a tight smile, but there was no joy in it.*

*The lieutenant's eyebrows went up, about as shocked an expression as Kovalic could remember seeing on the man's face. "And what about the rest of the team? They'll have questions."*

*"Let me worry about the team," said Kovalic, getting to his feet. He pulled a data chip from his pocket, and somehow it weighed no less than the sidearm he'd already handed over. "Full encrypted signaling and contact protocols under the code name NOMAD." He held it out to Page. "But once you take this, there's no turning back. You're on your own, for real – no backup, no safety net. Nobody can know you're still out there. Not Brody or Tapper, not Kester, not your family."*

*Page reached out and took the chip. "I understand. Sir."*

*"I'm just sorry that you didn't come to me, instead of going to Kester. Maybe we could have avoided this. I understand why you did what you did – even if I don't agree with it."*

*"Thank you, sir. And... I'm sorry."*

*"I won't wish you luck, lieutenant. If I'm being honest, I hope you don't find anything. But I trust your instincts. If anyone has to do the digging, I'm glad it's you. Take care of yourself." And with that, Kovalic turned and walked out of the park.*

# CHAPTER 29

Eli listened, slack-jawed, as Kovalic and Page recounted the events of nine months past, and it was only when they'd finished that he finally swallowed, feeling saliva once again flood his very dry mouth. "Christ," he said, his voice hoarse and cracked as though he hadn't spoken in weeks.

Tapper had been leaning against the wall that faced the lake, flanked by two large floor-to-ceiling windows propped open to let the night breeze in. He didn't say anything, just stood watching and waiting.

*For the next shoe to drop? They just poured a basket of footwear on our heads.*

"We're going to need to back up," said Eli, cradling his head in his hands. "You went after *the general*?"

Page glanced at Kovalic, who gave him a curt nod. "Yes. I've had concerns since my first operation with the Special Projects Team, but it wasn't until Deputy Director Kester reached out that they became anything more than vague unease."

"And you think, what, he's working for the Imperium? Why, because he's Illyrican?" Eli had deduced that particular tidbit a long time ago. He'd known plenty of members of the Imperium's upper classes when he'd been at the Illyrican Naval Academy and the accent was unmistakable.

"Because he was the former director of the Illyrican Intelligence Services."

Eli had just managed to reel in his jaw, but now it was like someone had released a winch. "He was *what*?" His head slowly turned to each of the other three men in turn, but there was no shock on the face of any of his teammates. *They all knew this.* "You're telling me that the guy we're taking orders from used to be *in charge* of the other side? How the hell did that happen?"

Kovalic's lips pressed together, his gray eyes even more steely than usual. "The general defected from the Illyrican Empire six years ago. The Commonwealth Executive deemed the intelligence he offered to be substantive enough to warrant special treatment, so they struck a deal: he'd work with the Commonwealth to help defeat the Imperium."

The inside of Eli's head was buzzing like he'd forgotten to turn down the squelch on his comms. "And why the hell would they trust him to help destroy the very regime he was part of?"

"Because his objective was peace. The general ran the numbers, played out the simulations, and every conclusion he reached involved massive loss of life, the galaxy in disarray, and Illyrica – his home – destroyed beyond repair." Kovalic's stare had gone fixed, and something clicked in Eli: the general wasn't the only one whose home was at stake. Earth had been occupied by the Imperium for two decades, and Eli knew Kovalic had been there, fighting, when it had fallen. "So he convinced the Executive to let him try to find a less destructive solution to ending the conflict."

"A peaceful solution," Eli muttered. *Jesus, I think I need a drink.* "Where do you keep the booze in this place, Kovalic?"

"I'd say I'm sorry we didn't read you in earlier, Brody," said Kovalic, "but it was cl–"

"Right, classified. Of course." It was a convenient catch-all excuse. "I wasn't kidding about that drink. Just in case you thought I was."

Tapper made a noise and pushed himself off the wall he'd been leaning against. From the kitchen, he somehow managed to produce a dusty bottle and four glasses. *How the hell did he have time to find the liquor already? I swear he didn't leave my sight.* But he might as well wonder how the man always seemed to know exactly where to acquire a veritable smorgasbord of deadly weapons, no matter what planet or space station they were on. It was a gift.

The sergeant poured, then handed the glasses around. Eli didn't wait – this wasn't a toasting occasion – and threw back a gulp of what turned out to be spiced rum. He made a face and put the glass down on a nearby table.

"Sorry," said Kovalic. "Nat likes the stuff." He took a measured sip himself, but didn't seem to care for it any more than Eli had.

"Speaking of the commander," wheezed Eli, still feeling the warmth in his throat. "She knows about all of this?"

"She knows who the general is, yes. And I read her in on Page right after our mission on the *Queen Amina*."

"Don't suppose that had anything to do with why she headed offworld first chance she got," said Tapper. Even Eli could tell it wasn't really a question.

Something very much like pain lanced through the major's face, lightning fast, but if there was one thing Simon Kovalic was a master of, it was keeping himself to himself. "Perhaps somewhat."

"So I was the only one totally out of the loop," said Eli. "Great."

"And Sayers," said Tapper. "I assume." He shot a glance at Kovalic.

"Specialist Sayers is not aware of the general's background, no."

"Oh good. She's going to *love* this." Eli's stomach turned – maybe from the rum – as he thought about Addy, all alone back in Salaam. "Speaking of which, now that we're safe and sound, how do we get in touch with her?"

"I'll put a message in one of our virtual dead drops tonight," said Kovalic. "She's probably already gone to ground, and, frankly, that's the safest place for her right now, what with Kester and his task force looking for us. We'll arrange a meet when the heat lets up."

Eli frowned. But he had to concede that Kovalic might be right on this one: more important for the moment that Addy keep a low profile than that they regroup.

"Sayers is a savvy operator," said Tapper, giving Eli a knowing look. "She knows how to stay under the radar."

Against his better judgment, Eli refilled his glass and took another, smaller sip. It tingled and burned on his tongue, but it was better than nothing. "So I guess we're all caught up now."

"Except," said Tapper, raising the hand holding his glass and pointing it at Page, "the boy wonder's been gone for nine months and now here he is. So the sixty-four million credit question is: was it all worth it? Did all that poking around actually find anything?"

A sideways glance from Page to Kovalic, who gave the lieutenant a nod and leaned back in his chair.

Page hadn't touched his drink, but he adjusted it on

the coaster in front of him, centering the glass. "I stayed on Bayern for a while after the team left. My cover at the Corporation had remained intact, and it gave me access to certain information that was useful in my investigations. One of those was, as I mentioned, the linking of certain bank accounts to General Adaj."

*Adaj.* In the year and a half that he'd been working with the Special Projects Team, Eli had never so much as known the general's name, much less heard it spoken aloud. Kovalic had always kept that information under wraps – just another in a long line of secrets – though, given what Eli had just been told, he thought he could understand why. *Not a lot of people would be willing to take orders from a former Illyrican spymaster.*

"Nothing unusual about that," said Tapper. "I've known plenty of spies who kept their dosh in numbered accounts on Bayern. It's practically the official operative retirement fund."

"Indeed. And the general does maintain a few accounts used as operational slush funds, as Major Kovalic can attest, in addition to some that seem to be purely reserves, with money coming in but little going out. However, one of the accounts that I uncovered was making regular deposits, laundered through several intermediaries, to a shell company registered out of Illyrica called Tanager Holdings. Tanager, in turn, showed a number of outgoing transactions – including in-person withdrawals."

"Makes sense," said Kovalic. "Money makes the galaxy go round; doubly so intelligence work."

"Perhaps, but it piqued my interest. So, after determining the pattern of withdrawals, I mapped out the most likely times and locations for the next in-person transfer. It took a few weeks of staking out those sites before I was able to confirm the identity of the courier, but once I tagged them, tracking their movements was relatively simple."

"Relatively simple" to Eli was heating up a container of soup or navigating Salaam's multitude of tram lines. *Only Page would use it to describe surveilling the courier of a former Illyrican spy chief.*

"And?" said Tapper.

Page's gaze, as calm as the surface of the lake outside, alit upon the sergeant. "And I followed that courier back to the Commonwealth, where they made contact with a man that I was able to identify as Ryou Garrido." His eyes swept across the room. "A member of the Nova First movement who I later established as one of the key players in the Novan Liberation Front."

Silence descended over the room like a weighted blanket as Page's words sank in. *Wait. Hold on a second.* Eli's mind ran back over the last several sentences, trying to make sure that he'd not only heard the words right, but that he'd correctly parsed their meaning.

"You're saying," he said slowly, "money came from the general's account and ended up in the hands of the people who bombed Oluo Plaza."

"Yes. That is precisely what I'm saying."

Kovalic shook his head. "There must be some mistake. You got the wrong courier. Or the account was hacked." But even as he was saying it, Eli could feel the doubt creeping in. Page was meticulous about these sorts of things; the chances of him getting it wrong seemed slim.

"I don't believe so. I performed a forensic evaluation via my cover identity and saw no indication of the system being compromised. I backtraced the funds and confirmed they came from the general's account. And I followed the courier on a second occasion and witnessed an identical exchange with Garrido."

There was a scraping sound as Kovalic pushed back his chair and stood, then paced over to the window. Outside, the moon was setting behind the hills across the lake, creating an illuminated pathway on the water that seemed to lead directly towards the house. "I can't believe it. Something about this feels wrong."

"No kidding," said Eli. "The guy you've – the guy we've *all* been working for has been funding terrorists."

Kovalic eyed Page. "Not to impugn your investigatory skills, lieutenant, but is it possible that you found exactly what you wanted to find? It was, after all, your contention that the general had ulterior motives."

"I'm not sure how that could be the case. If you're suggesting that somebody manufactured this evidence, how would they have known that I would be looking for it at all, much less where and when?"

It was a solid point, and it sat, rock-like, in the pit of Eli's stomach. *Goddamn wheels within wheels.* Somebody would need to be on top of things to put this all in motion. Well-connected in the intelligence community. With a grudge against the general, to boot.

"Well, one person springs immediately to mind," said Kovalic, clearly drawing a similar set of conclusions. "Your old friend Aidan Kester."

Tapper made a *tch* of disgust at the mention of the CID deputy director. "Seems a ballsy play for him. I always figured the man for an empty suit."

"Don't underestimate him. He's as ambitious as they come, and he's always believed the general was encroaching on his turf. Between that and the personal animosity Kester seems to have for him, there's motive enough to go around. With CID's operations department behind him, he certainly has the means and the opportunity as well."

Page's lips compressed and Eli could tell the lieutenant was far from sold. "Due respect, major, but now *you're* finding exactly what you want to find. We have no hard evidence of Deputy Director Kester's involvement. The simplest explanation is that this is exactly what it seems: General Adaj's defection was a ruse and he's been playing the long game, sabotaging the Commonwealth from within to the benefit of the Illyrican Empire."

The sergeant snorted. "Occam's Razor doesn't apply when it comes to espionage. You know that. Besides, we've been working for the general for years; if he was up to something, we would have found out."

"Would you have?" said Page. "We can all agree that, if nothing else, Adaj is a master strategist. This could have been his plan from the very beginning."

"The Commonwealth vetted him," said Kovalic. "Intensely, for almost a year."

"And I'm sure the assessment of the officer who actually handled his defection carried a substantial degree of weight in that vetting."

"I suppose. What are you getting at?"

Page cocked his head. "That officer was *you*, major, wasn't it?"

Now it was Kovalic's expression that had turned stony. "It was. So what?"

"I'm simply saying I can understand why you might take this whole matter personally. You told me about the general first approaching you, when you were stationed on Illyrica.

You said he'd done his research, that he knew who you were, your background. Maybe you don't want to admit that he fed you a line *designed* to appeal to you: a story about a man who was tired of the fight and just wanted to reclaim his home."

Eli squirmed in his seat, as an uneasy silence fell over the room. Kovalic's face hadn't so much as twitched, but Eli could sense the tension emanating from him.

"It's a fair point," said Kovalic finally, his tone grudging. "But," he raised a finger, "it cuts both ways. You said Kester came to you with his suspicions about the general."

A crack in the stoic demeanor: Page shifted slightly in his seat, but if he were anybody else, it would have been like he was just slapped. "Correct."

"And the idea to investigate the general's personal accounts. That came from Kester too, didn't it?"

"Yes, but–"

"And if suspicion were thrown on the general – and let's all agree that, given his position as a defector and an Illyrican, it wouldn't take much – Kester stands to gain. He'd have undisputed control over all Commonwealth intelligence operations."

"Maybe, but he would still have to answer to the head of CID," said Page, who then immediately snapped his mouth shut, eyes flicking back and forth as though calculating variables at immense speed.

"Director Özkul," said Kovalic, glancing at Tapper.

*Uhhh.* Eli was floundering. "Somebody want to fill me in?"

"The director was supposed to be at Oluo Plaza when the bombing happened," said Tapper. "Only there was a traffic jam and she didn't make it."

Eli rubbed his eyes. He'd almost forgotten about the Nova Front bombing in all the discussion of the high-stakes chess game. *But that's what started us down this whole road in the first place.*

"Dumb luck," said Kovalic.

Page cleared his throat. "Not quite."

Kovalic gave him a sharp look. "Explain."

"The traffic jam was deliberate, created expressly to prevent the director from being at Oluo Plaza when the bomb went off."

"Oh?" said Tapper. "And how the hell do you figure that?"

"Because I was the one who caused it."

# CHAPTER 30

Kovalic had already been running on fumes even before this whole day had started. First there had been the bombing, then he'd been grabbed by Kester's men, then stayed up all night to go through Page's belongings before heading to the bookstore. Had that just been this morning? It was one long blur in his memory.

And somehow, over the past half hour, he'd absorbed more information than he had in the last three days, and the hits just kept on coming. "*You* caused the traffic jam?"

"Yes, sir. Abandoning a vehicle in the middle of a busy highway is much easier than most people think."

Before Kovalic's muzzy brain could even formulate his next question, Tapper was picking up the thread. "How did you know about the bombing?"

"Ah. I think I've omitted part of my story. My apologies. I was told about the plans for the Oluo Plaza bombing by Nova Front. Specifically its leader, Kassandra."

Kovalic eyed the spiced rum, trying to decide if it was going to help his headache or only make it worse. Really, how much could it hurt at this point? He downed the remainder in one gulp, feeling the burn course its way down his throat. In a cocktail, it'd probably be fine – how

241

Nat drank this stuff straight, he still wasn't sure. "And Nova Front let you in on its plans because?"

"After I tracked the courier from Bayern and established the connection with Nova Front, it seemed that my best course of action was to attempt to infiltrate the organization, to determine what their agenda was."

"Oh," said Brody. "Sure. Of course. Only logical." His eyes rolled skyward.

"The woman in the basement of the bookstore," said Kovalic. "That was Kassandra, wasn't it?"

Page tilted his head. "Yes. Between my own background as a native Novan and my cover story as a spy whose uncaring government decided he was expendable, it was relatively easy to ingratiate myself with the organization."

Tapper had been midway through a sip of rum and the liquid clearly couldn't decide whether to go up or down, leaving him sputtering. "You call that a cover story? That's what actually happened."

"Stick as closely as possible to the truth," Brody muttered.

Using his own background explained Page's insistence that the rest of the team stay away from Nova Front: involving them could have compromised him and put the mission at risk. Not to mention his life, though Kovalic had no doubt that Page considered that only a secondary concern.

"Right," said Tapper, rolling his eyes. "Next you'll tell me that place with the secret basement where you were holed up was just a simple bookstore."

"Mostly," said Page. "The proprietor has also been known to dabble in creative reinterpretations of vintage manuscripts."

Brody stared at Tapper blankly.

"He's a forger," said the sergeant. "Black market sales?"

Page tilted his head to one side, a tacit acknowledgment. "Walter's a friend – and he owes me. I helped him deal with a particularly irate customer back when I was just out of the School."

"Back up," said Brody. "There's a big enough market for old books that people make fake ones?"

"Rich people, kid. As my old man used to say, they've got more dollars than sense."

Kovalic let the conversation wash over him; in his mind, he was replaying a different exchange – the one they'd overheard in the basement. Something had struck him at the time, but he'd forgotten it amongst the ensuing chaos. "Kassandra. She called you Aaron. You used your real name?"

A hint of regret flitted across Page's face. "I did. My ability to backstop a fake identity was somewhat limited in the field, so I used the resources I had available. Since my own story seemed to fit the part, that seemed like the easiest and most convincing option."

Convincing? Probably. Dangerous? Definitely. Burning your own identity was last resort stuff. It was nigh impossible for a covert operative to come back from that. For the first time, Kovalic found himself wondering exactly what Page's endgame was in this whole scenario: no matter how this wrapped up, what future was left to the man?

"Wait," said Brody. "So, you knew about the bomb and you didn't stop it?"

"I couldn't," said Page, shaking his head. "My status as an ex-covert operative already had Nova Front keeping a close eye on me – if I'd interfered directly with the bombing, I would have had a target painted on my back. So I did what I could to minimize the impact of the attack."

"Hence the traffic jam," said Tapper.

"Yes. I was concerned that were Director Özkul to be assassinated in the explosion, the disruption to the Commonwealth would have been severe, and the response much worse than it otherwise would have been."

Tapper exhaled, his eyes weary as they met Kovalic's. "I don't know how much worse it could be. As it is, we've got CID hunting us down on Commonwealth soil. Breaks just about every regulation in their charter. We're only a few steps away from martial law."

Kovalic cupped a hand over his eyes, staring into the blackness for a moment, and ignoring the corona afterimages from the lights. God, he was tired. And he felt like his brain was chasing itself in circles. He needed something to anchor to: some concrete point to start.

"Let's go back to the beginning," he said. "Why Oluo Plaza? Perhaps you can shed some light on why Nova Front wanted to target that particular location, lieutenant. General chaos and destruction?"

Page shook his head. "The bombing, as the plan was described to me, was not designed to result in mass casualties or damage; Kassandra knew that would be an easy way to lose the support of the populace she was trying to rally."

That earned him looks from around the room, including an especially skeptical one from Tapper. "Come on, kid. You don't set a bomb to *not* blow things up. Trust me."

"So Director Özkul wasn't the target?" said Kovalic.

"No, just a bonus objective."

Tapper whistled. "Hell of a bonus."

"I think that there was a personal component for Kassandra in targeting Director Özkul, but the main objective was what was *inside* Oluo Plaza. The explosion was merely a distraction to gain access to the site."

Ah, now the pieces were starting to come together. "The secret room we found behind ConComm's server room, then."

"Yes. According to Kassandra, it was a CID black site for a top-secret project codenamed AUGUR."

AUGUR. He'd heard Kassandra mention the name, back at Page's hideout beneath the bookstore, but it hadn't meant anything to him then, and that hadn't changed. He shot a look at Tapper, but the sergeant shrugged, clearly just as clueless as he was. CID had hundreds of projects, many of them above the clearances Kovalic, or even the general, possessed. And those were just the official ones. If CID was running an illegal operation within the Commonwealth – in the capital city, no less – then it was almost certainly off the books. Which explained the subsequent cover-up and the footprint he and Laurent had found. CID wouldn't want anybody to know what they had been up to.

Which led directly to Kovalic's next question. "And what exactly is Project AUGUR?"

"Kassandra called it 'more evidence that the Commonwealth has no respect for the Novan people.' Equipment had been installed to piggyback on ConComm's own servers and while I don't know the full extent of AUGUR's capabilities, it definitely allows one to override the local communication network in Salaam and broadcast to all local devices."

In Kovalic's mind, he saw the message splashed over every screen near Oluo Plaza, including the sleeve of everybody in close proximity: SIC SEMPER TYRANNIS. "Thus always to tyrants."

"Indeed. Kassandra chose the message and I configured it to go off as we left the scene."

"Wait, is *that* why you had the book?" Brody piped up suddenly, his expression puzzled. "*Integrated Communications Networks*? Were you trying to figure out what AUGUR was for?"

Page tilted his head to one side. "I was investigating it, yes, though that volume's contributions were negligible. It's an adequate, if basic, primer on communications networks, but not nearly recent – or, frankly, detailed – enough to address a system as sophisticated as ConComm's."

Brody threw his hands in the air. "What the hell was it for, then?"

"Kassandra insisted on extreme communications security, to an almost paranoid degree. She wouldn't send messages via the municipal network and insisted that we rely on one-time pads and physical dead drops. That book was the code key – mainly by virtue of the fact that I was able to find an identical pair."

One-time pads? Kovalic suppressed a wry smile: the classics never went out of style. All the technology that humans had developed and the only unbreakable communications methodology was hundreds of years old and required not expensive software or hardware but matching copies of paper books. It was an unorthodox move, but Kovalic had to admit it provoked in him a degree of grudging respect for Kassandra.

But the mirth ebbed at the larger implications of Page's story. Giving an intelligence agency the ability to override the communication network – and maybe more? Not something that left Kovalic with a warm fuzzy feeling. "Well, shit. So Nova Front bombs Oluo Plaza, gets access to this secret project on the communication network and then... profit?"

"The explosion was designed to let us enter the building posing as emergency responders, gain access to AUGUR via the ConComm server room, and set up the communications override hack," said Page. "She also downloaded critical information about the system from CID's servers onto a data chip."

"A data chip?" Kovalic raised an eyebrow. Kassandra had demanded a chip, at gunpoint, in her confrontation with Page in the basement of the bookstore. "Except she didn't end up with it – you did."

A slightly abashed expression appeared on Page's face, as though he couldn't stand the idea of not following through on a job, even if it was for a terrorist organization. "Given Kassandra's motives, I concluded keeping it out of her hands was a priority. I swapped out the one she used for a chip that I'd filled with garbage data."

Tapper whistled. "Gonna go out on a limb and suggest that she probably wasn't too happy about that."

"No," said Page. His lips thinned. "So much so that she decided to make me the face of the attack."

A bitter laugh issued from the sergeant. "Smart move. Now the authorities are looking for you instead of her. Say one thing for her, she's got misdirection down to a science."

Brody sat up. "But that's not fair – you didn't blow up that building."

"No. But I was there. And I could have stopped it. I made a choice, and I have to live with the consequences."

It still bothered Kovalic that CID hadn't poked a hole in the authenticity of the message. Mal was sharp, but if the tech could unravel it, then the intelligence agency's signals division ought to have figured it out too. At best, it was sloppiness from being pushed to provide an incomplete result too quickly; at worst, it was something more troublingly deliberate. Add to that a new fact – that a terrorist organization had more information about a top-secret intelligence program than he did – and the result wasn't particularly reassuring. "Where did Kassandra find out about AUGUR in the first place, anyway? Do you know her source?"

"No, though I have my suspicions."

Kovalic could do math too. Not only was Nova Front aware of a top secret intelligence program, but they were also well apprised of the CID director's movements. He rubbed a hand over his eyes; it felt like somebody had kicked a bunch of sand into them. "So, someone in the government – or, more likely, CID itself – is feeding information to Kassandra and Nova Front."

"That was my conclusion."

"Have to be highly placed, though," said Tapper. "The director's visit to Oluo Plaza wasn't widely known even within the agency."

"Indeed. And my understanding is that only a very few are cleared to know about AUGUR."

Tapper looked around. "We're all thinking it, right? Kester fits the profile to a T. Deputy director of operations sure seems like they'd be in a position to know about a super top-secret black site *and* about the director's schedule," he said, ticking off items on his fingers. "Plus, if Özkul *had* been killed, he'd certainly be in the running for CID director – especially if he knew exactly which perpetrators to round up because he was the one who fed them the intel in the first place. Plenty of motive."

Kovalic frowned. The pieces fit – snapped together like they were custom made for the purpose. Lord knew he had no love lost for the bureaucrat; he'd suspected that Kester had more ambition than sense ever since CID's Caledonia op, more than a year ago. The deputy director had personally overseen that mission, which had gone sideways *hard*, resulting in the death of a veteran operative. But, more damningly, Kester had swept it all under the rug; the general had proof of that, thanks to a report made by the operative before he'd died.

"Where's the chip now?" asked Kovalic.

"I've stowed it somewhere safe. Whatever it is, it's too important to fall into Nova Front's hands."

"We could turn it back over to CID," said Tapper. "Then at least *we'd* be shot of this problem."

While the sergeant might technically be right, Kovalic could see in the older man's face that even he wasn't sure that was the right course of action. And without knowing exactly what the implications of this AUGUR project were, Kovalic privately had to agree: the idea of putting something this significant back into play at CID – much less in the hands of someone as ambitious as Aidan Kester – didn't fill him with confidence.

Kovalic exhaled. "We need to stop Kassandra from whatever her next move is. I assume that she has one and she's not just doing this for kicks. What else can you tell us about her, lieutenant?"

Page's head tilted to one side as he thought. "She seems to be a study in contradictions. What I've seen of her plan seems focused, rational, and well thought out. But at the same time, it doesn't quite mesh with the behavior I've witnessed her demonstrate. That feels more rash and impulsive. It almost seems as if…"

"…she's executing someone else's agenda?" Kovalic

finished his thought. Perhaps Kester, or whoever Kassandra's source was, wasn't a pawn, but instead the one calling the shots.

"I have no information to confirm the hypothesis."

Scrupulously accurate, as always. But Kovalic knew Page well enough to see that the younger man had reached the same conclusion.

Opening his mouth to continue the conversation, Kovalic was interrupted by the sound of a ripsaw on a log, emanating from the couch. At some point, Brody's head had lolled back against the pillows and the pilot had passed out.

Tapper snorted. "More rum for me, I guess."

Kovalic chuckled and started to raise his own glass when there was a soft chime over the house system. He reached over to the end table and tapped a control to summon a holoscreen.

"Perimeter alert," he said, as the display sprang to life. "Looks like somebody's dropping by unannounced."

# CHAPTER 31

After she'd gotten clear of the bookstore's immediate vicinity, it took Addy about half an hour to reach a gravtrain stop that hadn't been shut down by the security action, and about as long to catch a train back to the garage where she and Brody had abandoned the hovercar after fleeing Page's detonated safe house... yesterday? Had it only been yesterday?

When she brought up the tracking program, the display showed the team well outside the city now, heading north at a rapid pace.

*What, are you guys going on vacation?*

On the one hand, she was a little annoyed that they'd left her behind without so much as a word; on the other, she'd been surreptitiously tracking them in the first place, so she couldn't exactly blame them for not looping her in. That left her two options: disappear somewhere into the city and lay low, or go after her team, wherever they were headed.

That choice made itself: she wasn't about to just sit on her hands when there was a fight on the way.

She made sure to double back multiple times before getting on the highway, at which point she engaged the auto-drive and let the adrenaline ebb away.

*What a fucking day.* All the emotions she'd pushed down suddenly rippled to the top of her mind and it took everything she had not to throw up in the passenger seat.

She'd almost killed a man. Shot him right through the chest. All because she'd been ordered to. While she might have been trained for just this eventuality, when it came right down to it, the idea of actually pulling the trigger was making her physically ill.

This whole operation was a mess, a fuck-up of epic proportions. Who the hell was she supposed to be trusting right now? Page, Nova Front, CID, even her own team – they all had their own agendas. How did you decide where to put your faith?

At some point, she dozed off from sheer exhaustion; she'd been going nearly flat out for the last forty-eight hours straight.

A gentle alarm from the car's internal sensors jolted her awake; she really shouldn't be sleeping, even with the car in auto-drive, but at least it prevented her from veering off the road.

Outside the window, the faint dark shapes of hills rolled by, illuminated by the rising moon. Blearily, she checked the car's display and saw that the tracker was stationary on the shore of a nearby lake.

Once she pulled off the highway, the local roads got her most of the way there before the mapping system basically threw up its hands and gave a big digital shrug, leaving her gliding to a stop in front of a heavy metal gate.

*Well, I didn't come this far to let a piece of metal stop me.*

From the car, she grabbed her Krennhauser rifle, currently collapsed into its components, and the KO gun she'd borrowed from the CID trooper on the rooftop. Locking the vehicle behind her, she popped in her earpiece and followed the tracker's chimes.

Gravel crunched beneath her feet as she made her way down the road. As the trees thinned, a sizable lake came into view, the reflection of moonlight off the water helping cut through the darkness.

After a few minutes, she saw a faint light poking through the trees and glimpsed a two-story wooden house. One window was brightly illuminated, though she couldn't see anybody inside from this vantage. All she could hear was the lapping of the waves against the shore, and the occasional *plop* of a fish having a nighttime snack.

She made it all the way onto the porch before she heard the soft footfall behind her. *Amazed I got as far as I did.* Turning slowly with hands raised, she found herself face-to-face with a KO gun.

"Sayers?" said Kovalic, stepping out of the shadows. "What the hell are you doing here?"

"Things back in the city were getting kind of hot. Seemed like a good time to get out of town. Sir."

Kovalic hesitated, and even in the dim light, she could see his eyes narrow. "You alone?"

*Always.* "Yes, sir."

With a nod, he lowered the gun. "Well, then, you'd better come inside and join the party."

# CHAPTER 32

Once Sayers was safely inside, Kovalic locked down the house and set the perimeter security to the highest alert. Hopefully she'd be the last unexpected guest, but you couldn't be too careful.

"Nice place," she said, after he'd offered her a seat at the table and poured her a glass of rum.

Tapper nudged Brody and he woke with a jolt, then seemed even more surprised to see Sayers sitting a few feet away, calmly sipping her liquor.

"Addy?" he said, rubbing his eyes. "I am awake, right? This isn't some weird stress dream, like the one where I'm naked in a starfighter cockpit?"

"Well," said Kovalic. "Looks like the gang's all here. I know we could use some sleep, but let's at least clear the decks before we do. Specialist, I'd like to start with you. Mind telling us how you found us? I assume that was you who sent me the warning text. And covered our exit up on the rooftop back in Salaam."

Sayers took another sip. "I did what I could." Her eyes darted to Page, his left bicep still wrapped in a field dressing. "Sorry about the arm, but I figured you'd prefer it to the chest."

The lieutenant's eyebrows went up in a rare display of surprise. "I'll live. Nice shot."

"Course, this doesn't answer the bigger question," said Tapper, crossing his arms. "How'd you know where to find us? At the bookstore *and* here?"

Sayers eyed the rest of the rum, then sighed and stood, walking over to Brody, who suddenly looked as though he were about to be an unwilling volunteer in a magic trick. "Page had already made contact with Lieutenant Brody twice – once at the café, and again when he saved him from the explosion at the safe house. So I made a gamble." She reached down behind Brody's ear and peeled something off; the pilot winced slightly and she held up her finger, where a small round patch was stuck. "Tracking dermal."

Brody, for his part, looked suitably chagrined, his face flushing red. "I thought that was a bandage!"

Sayers didn't make eye contact with him, just stepped back to the table and dropped the patch into the glass of rum, where it made a sad fizzing noise. "Seemed like it might be prudent to keep tabs on… you all."

But mainly Brody, Kovalic noted. He spared a glance at Tapper, but the sergeant's expression was closely guarded. Tracking their own team members seemed like a violation of not only protocol, but trust – that said, protocol had long gone out the exhaust port by now. Bigger fish, and all that. Nonetheless, it sat uneasy with Kovalic. After six months, he still had trouble reading Sayers, but he could tell she was holding something back.

"I can't say I like it," Kovalic said finally, "but we'll table this particular issue for the moment."

"Good, because me tracking you is the least of our problems." Raising her arm, Sayers flicked something off her sleeve and a holoscreen appeared in the middle of the room, a gleaming red border framing Page's face and angry text slapped across the lower third. "I think this is how those goons tracked you to the bookstore. No matter how careful you are, having thousands of eyeballs on high alert means somebody's bound to spot you at some point."

Kovalic held back a sigh. He should have known that Kester wouldn't be satisfied with keeping the manhunt for Page out of the public eye. Even with all the technology and resources the deputy director's task force had its disposal, sometimes there was just no substitute for a good old fashioned emergency alert.

"Great," said Tapper. "Only problem is they're all looking for the wrong person."

"Yeah?" said Sayers, waving the screen away.

Kovalic rubbed his mouth. "You've missed rather a lot. We'd better read you in."

The next ten minutes were spent running down a high-level summary of everything they'd put together: Page's role in the bombing and stealing the chip, Kassandra and her plans for Nova Front, and the CID cover-up of Oluo Plaza. As he laid it out, Kovalic was acutely aware that there were pieces missing all over the place: nothing seemed to quite fit together yet, and, until it did, their next move remained unclear.

Sayers absorbed it all, sitting at the table and listening intently as each member of the team added their own details. When they got to the part about Page's investigation into the general, and the reason behind his apparent death, Kovalic noticed something shifting in the specialist's demeanor, as though she were suddenly sitting on a bed of nails. But it didn't turn into outright shock until Kovalic mentioned the general's past.

"He's *Illyrican*?" Her eyes widened until they were moons.

"Former head of IIS," added Brody.

Sayers's mouth opened soundlessly, and she pressed her fingers to her temples, massaging them. "Holy shit. Kovalic, what the fuck?"

Four pairs of eyes turned on Kovalic with something less than the trust upon which he'd always prided himself. Even Tapper, who'd been aware of the general's history for as long as he had, seemed uncomfortable with the latest revelations – or, more to the point, the fact that they'd been kept from the rest of the team for so long.

"Look, I know this is unusual. Maybe it's not what any of you signed up for. But I'm asking you to trust me. I've put my faith in the general for six years, and I believe that we've done a lot of good in that time. It hasn't always been clear cut, but nothing in this business is. Without our intervention, the galaxy may very well have been at open war by now, with thousands of lives lost on both sides. I've been there. I've seen firsthand the havoc that kind of conflict wreaks, and I have no desire to revisit it. No matter what they might tell you, there are no winners in war." His cheek was rough against the tips of his fingers. "We'll figure out our next moves in the morning, but right now, I suggest we all get some rest. I'll set up rooms for everyone."

He rose and headed upstairs, leaving the rest of the team to have a moment without him. When he came back down, a few minutes later, they didn't say much beyond exhausted goodnights as they tramped off to bed.

Except for Sayers.

He found her sitting on the deck behind the house, staring out over the black expanse of the lake.

"So much water," she said, when he sat down in the chair

beside her. "There's lakes around Salaam, but not like this. Not ones where you can't see the other end." She waved a hand to the south where, miles away, the lake disappeared around the barely visible shape of a bluff and continued onward.

Kovalic smiled in the darkness. "I grew up near the ocean, so there's always been something about water that I just found calming. It has its own rhythm and it's unconcerned with yours. It just keeps going, no matter what. You're not going to stop it, or control it, no matter how much you try."

Sayers laughed, low and short. "I can see why that appeals to you."

They sat in silence for a moment, the splash of the waves like a clock ticking.

"There's something you should know," said Sayers at last. "The general came to me."

Kovalic had been keeping his unease at bay, making sure that the team was taken care of, that everything in the house was shipshape – just generally trying to keep himself steady so that they knew they could still rely on him. But at this, his stomach churned. The general had come to Sayers? Behind his back?

"Oh?" he said, forcing his voice to stay even-keeled, despite feeling anything but. "What did he want?"

Sayers turned towards him and, even in the dark, Kovalic could see the troubled glint in her eyes. "I think... I think he wanted me to kill Page."

He should have been tired after the day they'd had, but Sayers's revelations had hit Kovalic like a triple shot of espresso.

As Brody dozed peacefully on the master bedroom's daybed, muttering and shifting in his sleep, Kovalic stared at the ceiling, arms behind his head, turning over what Sayers had told him.

The general had always been a pragmatist. And it was hard to argue that he hadn't backed up his words with actions: leaving his entire life behind, helping the Commonwealth foil numerous Illyrican plots, providing much needed intelligence on the Imperium and what went on behind the crimson curtain. Everything Kovalic had done at the general's behest had been built on that pragmatic foundation: that neither of them was married to the ideals of a government but devoted to what was best for their worlds and the people in them.

But for all of that, the general had remained cagey, private. Played his cards so close to his chest that they were practically in an inside pocket. Kovalic had long accepted that it was simply Hasan al-Adaj's way: never give away more than you had to.

From that practical perspective, Kovalic could see why the general would have Sayers keep an eye on the team. All of them – himself especially – were definitely too close to Page to remain wholly objective. But, unlike the general, Kovalic wasn't convinced that connection was a vulnerability.

Asking Sayers to kill Page, even if he hadn't come right out and said it? That was a different matter, one that made his gut churn and clench like a plate of bad clams.

Of course, he'd kept Page's off-the-books investigation from the general, so it wasn't as though he'd been totally open and honest either. But he'd also felt confident that Page wouldn't turn up anything – more importantly, that there was nothing at all to turn up. The lieutenant's report about the general's Bayern connection, the bank accounts, the mysterious LOOKING GLASS project, the link to Nova Front; Kovalic had assumed it was all a misapprehension on Page's part, maybe enemy action, or possibly even a plain, old-fashioned mistake, even though he knew the lieutenant wasn't one to make careless errors.

But now, a tendril of doubt was curling through his mind, shuffling his thoughts into an order that was much harder to reconcile with what he'd thought to be the truth. It had forced him to ask a question that was shaking not only everything that he'd believed, but everything in which he'd asked his team to trust, for which he had put their very lives on the line.

What if Page was right?

Six years, he'd followed the general's lead. And if the man had been harboring some ulterior agenda the entire time, who knew what damage Kovalic might have unwittingly done at his bidding? Instead of keeping the peace, he might have just ended up with more blood on his hands.

Exhaustion dragged him to sleep eventually and when he started awake, it was to early-morning light glaring off the lake and streaming in through the window. Brody was still curled up in the daybed, dead to the world.

Even though he couldn't have gotten more than a few hours of sleep, Kovalic's brain was up and spinning already, chewing on all the developments of the last twenty-four hours, so he gave in and rolled himself out of bed, then padded downstairs.

He wasn't the only early riser: Tapper was already in the kitchen, pouring himself a fresh cup of coffee. The sergeant looked crisp and neat, shipshape as always, and without a word he poured a second cup for Kovalic.

Out on the deck, the hot coffee was a welcome antidote to the brisk chill of the morning air. Neither of them spoke for a while, enjoying the comfortable wordlessness of long-time camaraderie.

"I like this place," said the sergeant at last. "Case I didn't say so before. Seems like you could have been happy here."

"I'm hoping that possibility isn't in the past tense just yet."

"This life doesn't often give us a chance to walk away, boss. You know that as well as anybody. Most operatives end up dead or burned."

What did it say about their lives when being cut loose and living on the run was the *good* option? "We've beaten the odds before."

Tapper let out a long breath, shaking his head. "This is a tough one, not going to lie. Lotta people gunning for Page – and for us now. And not too many places to turn for help."

Kovalic grunted, took another sip of the coffee. He'd been running the pro-con ledger in his head and he had to admit that Tapper was right. Even if everything he feared about the general *wasn't* true, there was still enough of a risk that they had to leave him out of the loop from here on. Then there was CID. It offered the biggest counterweight to the general's influence, but Kester and the agency were clearly hip-deep in whatever was going on. And, given that the Executive had appointed the deputy director to head up the task force, the Bureau and local law enforcement were effectively just an extension of the intelligence agency at present. That left the team painfully short on allies.

"I don't like playing defense," said Kovalic, finally. "It's time for us to stop reacting."

"You're never going to see me object to going on the attack," said Tapper. "But we're not exactly flush with advantages right now."

"I don't know about that. We do have two things that everybody wants, which gives us leverage. First: access to that AUGUR data chip, whatever it contains."

"And second?"

Kovalic glanced over his shoulder into the house, where the rest of the team was just beginning to stir. He saw Sayers stumbling downstairs, rubbing her eyes, trailed by Brody, and then, finally, an impeccably put-together Aaron Page.

"We've got *him*."

# CHAPTER 33

Eli's brain didn't really fire up until he was halfway through the scrambled eggs that Kovalic had made, by which point, the rest of the team was deep into a discussion about their plan. *Ugh, it's like those dreams when you show up in class and there's a quiz you didn't study for. Also you forgot your pants. And your teeth are falling out.*

"Leverage is all well and good," Tapper was saying, "but who the hell are we negotiating with?"

"And for what?" said Addy.

Kovalic leaned back in his chair, cradling a mug of coffee. "Both Kassandra and – I think we can safely assume – CID want the chip. Maybe there's a way to make that work for us."

"Catch two birds with one trap?" said Eli.

"Is that actually a saying?" said Tapper.

"I just said it, didn't I?"

Kovalic ignored the two of them. "Page, you told Kassandra the data chip is in a secure location."

"Yes, sir. I can retrieve it at any time."

"Good. Start working up a plan to do so. Sayers, Tapper, run an inventory on our assets. There's a locker in the basement with some equipment in it. Code's 7582. Brody, we've got two hovercars. Make sure they're charged and ready to go."

Eli opened his mouth to make a snarky comment about not being good for anything beyond plugging things in, but Sayers and Tapper had immediately stood and headed downstairs, and Page was already consulting his sleeve, so it wasn't as if there was much of an audience. *Shame. I think we could have all used a little bit of levity.*

"What are you going to do?" he said to Kovalic.

Something about the expression on his boss's face suggested that, whatever it was, he'd rather eat nails. "I'm going to try and get us some help."


It was about a twenty-minute walk to where Addy had left her car by the gate. Eli punched the code Kovalic had given him into the keypad on the lock, swung the heavy metal bar open, drove through, then re-locked it behind him.

*Glorified chauffeur some days, I swear.* He entered Addy's door code – 7821, the same one she always used – and fired up the repulsors, driving the car slowly through the rustic scenery.

This wasn't quite what he'd had in mind when he'd joined the team nine months ago, much less when Kovalic had first made the offer half a year before that. He certainly hadn't expected that he'd be working for a man who had probably orchestrated at least some of the strategy behind the invasion and occupation of his homeworld of Caledonia, but here he was.

Hasan al-Adaj. The name rolled through his head, unfamiliar. Maybe he'd heard it whispered once or twice in his stint at the Illyrican Naval Academy, but it certainly hadn't stuck. Not that he'd been paying much attention to the Imperium's spymasters while he'd been trying to ace astronavigation and flight systems.

But despite all the terrible things Adaj must have done in his time running the Imperial spy agency, Eli couldn't dismiss the fact that his gut was telling him the general wasn't, at heart, a bad person.

*Based on, what, the handful of times you've talked to him? In about half of which he's coerced you into doing something?* Scheming, yes. Manipulative, yes. But one moment from their interactions stuck out in Eli's memory: nine months ago, when Adaj had asked him to go to Sevastapol, before the whole mess on Bayern. There had been a hitch in the general's voice, right before he'd said it was Kovalic's team that was in trouble. In that split second, Eli had sworn he'd seen something in those usually inscrutable blue eyes.

The general *cared* about Kovalic.

It wasn't like Eli had the inside track on the two men's relationship, but in the exchanges he'd witnessed, he couldn't help but detect a note of almost filial pride. Something he could only identify from its absence in his own life: Connor Brody had never been effusive toward either of his sons. Maybe his father had just buried it deep down under the piles of resentment and anger. Or maybe there had been a glint of it when Eli wasn't around to see it. Regardless, it certainly wasn't the prevailing memory he had of his father.

He pulled the car down to the cabin and parked it next to the one that Page had commandeered. There was a vehicle charger in the wall of the house with two plugs and he jacked both of them in.

When he looked up, he noticed Page standing out on the shore, holding an older looking rifle up to his shoulder, checking the sights before removing the magazine.

After the better part of a year, Eli had come to terms with the fact that people died in this line of work. Not that it was the first time he'd lost comrades, but Page's apparent death had somehow felt more personal than even his fighter squadron, gunned down during the invasion of Sabaea six years ago. At least part of that was all the time he'd spent wondering just how involved Kovalic had been in the lieutenant's demise.

*And it turned out those were all lies.*

Espionage, not a career for the straight shooter? Surprise, surprise. At least when he'd been in the military, the lies had been so bald-faced that everybody knew they were just propaganda. And the people who spun them weren't your friends, just your superiors, who were no doubt lied to by their superiors, and so on and so forth all the way to the emperor's gilded throne room.

The door to the deck slid open and Addy Sayers stepped out, holding a knockout gun in one hand. Even though she clearly wasn't expecting trouble, she still held it carefully, with respect, business end towards the deck and one finger alongside the trigger.

"Oh," she said. "Hi."

"Hey." He glanced over at the hovercar chargers, but they were still juicing up the vehicles, so he just leaned against the hood and tried to look casual. *Which is, in itself, the opposite of casual.*

"So, uh, must still be a little weird." Addy nodded at Page. "Seeing him walking around, I mean."

"Yeah," said Eli, crossing his arms. His right hand held his left elbow tighter than was strictly necessary. "Getting used to it. But weird."

Having apparently satisfied herself that the sidearm was as prepared as it could be, Addy tucked it in the small of her back. "This job is just full of surprises, I guess."

"I'll say. How are you doing?"

Addy's eyes narrowed. "Fine. Why do you ask?"

Eli gnawed the inside of his cheek. *Crossed the personal-work line, I guess.* "I'm just saying, it's been a crazy couple days. For all of us."

Her gaze stayed on him for a moment before the suspicion ebbed away. "Yeah, it has. Look… about before, with the tracker."

He flushed. "Don't worry about it."

"Brody, I didn't mean to–"

"Seriously. Don't worry about it. I know I'm not up to par when it comes to all the spy game stuff the rest of you get up to. I get it." There was a time that might have been performative; that he might have brushed something off, just going along to get along, but when he'd prodded deeper, he'd realized that in truth, it really hadn't bothered him. Addy was just trying to keep them all safe, and she had. Plus, the idea of being angry at her too was, frankly, exhausting. *Too much anger all around.* "I'm just glad you were there. We would have been in deep without you."

Addy shifted her weight between her feet, clearly uncomfortable. "Yeah. Look, Brody, it wasn't out of the goodness of my heart that I was there. I–"

But whatever she'd been about to say was interrupted as Tapper appeared through the same door with an armful of gear. "Good to see you're having a nice chat, but someone want to grab some of this crap?"

Timing was definitely not the sergeant's strong suit. Eli sprang over and lifted a rucksack from the top of the heap. "What the hell is in this?" he grunted, as he slung the bulky bag over his shoulder.

"We scrounged what we could," said Tapper. "But this is the boss's retirement home, not an armory."

Addy cleared her throat. "I'd better go check on… something else." And then she disappeared into the house without another word, leaving Eli alone.

"Damn it Brody, at least hold the door."

*Wait, no. Never alone.* With a sigh, Eli propped the door open, leaving Tapper to stumble his way towards the hovercar. He cast a last glance at the house, wondering what Addy had been about to tell him. She was struggling with something – that much he could tell – and he wanted to be there for her, but only when she was ready.

He raked a hand through his hair. *And I thought covert operations were hard.*

Tapper had shoved everything in the trunk of the hovercar, then slammed the trunk shut, wiping his hands off on his pants. "Come on, kid. Boss wants us to go for a drive."

"Drive?" Eli blinked and looked around. "Where to?"

The sergeant's weathered face broke into a grin. "To borrow a cup of sugar."

# CHAPTER 34

Kovalic took a deep breath and hit the Send button, feeling tension drain out of him as the message wended its way out into the ether. No guarantee it would reach its destination in time to be useful, but just in case things didn't go as planned, at least somebody would know exactly what had happened.

And when did things ever go as planned?

He logged out of the burner account he'd used, then securely wiped the terminal. CID forensics might be able to recover data off of it, but not before the heat-death of the universe caught up with them. Hopefully he wouldn't need that much time.

Outside of the window, the water of the lake rippled in the morning light. He'd always treated this place as his sanctuary, insulated it from the rest of his life so that he could have a peaceful refuge apart from all the intrigue and danger of his daily existence.

Bringing the team here had put that at risk – not from them: he trusted implicitly that they'd treat it with the same reverence. But he'd crashed his work life headlong into his private life, and the chances that the latter would walk away unscathed were rapidly diminishing.

Kester was going to be turning over every rock looking for

them. The CID presence at the bookshop told Kovalic that Page was at the top of the man's list – though whether it was because Kester really viewed him as a dangerous terrorist or because Page knew too much, well, the jury was still out.

There was a rap on his doorframe and he looked over his shoulder to find Tapper peering in at him. "We're about as ready as we're going to be, boss. You good?"

A sigh escaped from Kovalic's lips. Not the first time he'd had to let it all ride, but this time it felt personal. Then again, this whole thing had been personal from the get-go: a bombing on the planet where he lived, one of his own implicated, and now the suggestion that the general was somehow involved. Everything that he'd believed stable and solid in his life seemed to have crumbled in about forty-eight hours. But if he looked back, he could see the cracks had always been there. It was like the old saying about how you went bankrupt: first gradually, then all at once.

He slid his hands over the wood of the windowsill, warm from the sun beating down, then curled his fingers tightly around it. They'd been on their back foot since this whole thing had started. Time to turn the tables.

"Yeah. I'm good."

Downstairs, Sayers, Brody, and Page were arrayed quietly around the living room. As one, they looked up when he entered, and he gave them all a curt nod. "Everything set?"

"Transport's ready," said Brody.

"Not much in the way of weapons, but we're good," said Sayers, producing the KO gun Kovalic had liberated back in Salaam.

"Call's ready," said Page, holding up his sleeve. "I bounced it off two satellites and routed it through an encrypted proxy. Not foolproof, but it'll take time to trace."

"It'll do. Make the call."

Page tapped his sleeve, then flicked a holoscreen into existence over the coffee table, a line zig-zagged between several dots on a map of Nova, showing the circuitous routing he'd configured. After a few moments – longer than usual – it started to chime.

With a click, a voice came on the line. "Laurent."

"Inspector, it's Kaplan."

There was a pause and then the voice went soft, as if to avoid being overheard. "Kaplan. What the *fuck* is going on? I got a visit from the Deputy Director of CID, officially requisitioning my team to hunt down someone who looks very much like you. They said you shot your way out of a cordon in east Salaam yesterday, and they've been combing the entire city since. I hope you've got a hell of an explanation."

Page eyed his sleeve, then raised his index finger. One minute.

"Inspector, I don't have a lot of time so I'm going to need you to trust me. Something big is going on here: that room, at Oluo Plaza? It was a CID black site. Some highly classified project called AUGUR. I don't know what they were doing, and I don't think they wanted anybody else to know either. That's why the equipment was all removed after the bombing."

"I don't suppose you have any proof of this."

"I will. I've got an asset who was inside Nova Front."

Laurent sighed. "This wouldn't be the same ex-operative whose face CID's task force now has plastered on pretty much every screen in the world, would it?"

Kovalic exchanged a glance with Page, who barely blinked. "It's complicated. But you can't trust CID."

"Funny. They said the same thing about you." He paused. "Fine, if you've got evidence, come in. I'll guarantee your safety."

Page raised a fist.

"Only if it's just you."

Another pause. "I can do that. Tell me when and where."

"Chvatil Park. 4 o'clock this afternoon, by the fountain."

"Will do. Thank you, Inspector."

"Good lu–"

Page cut the line, but nobody exhaled; they all still looked as tense as if they were watching a gravball match gone into sudden death overtime.

"Clock's running, people," said Kovalic. "Let's move."


It was less than an hour before the rapid response team arrived, suggesting they'd taken a sub-orbital flyer out of Salaam. One team of black-suited troops cut through the gate lock on the gravel road, while another came across the lake on a wave-skimmer. With military efficiency, they filtered throughout the grounds, securing each entrance before breaching the doors and moving in.

All they found was an empty house.

Kovalic watched the raid unfold via his sleeve and tried not to wince as they knocked over one of the end tables in the living room. He was already going to need to repair the doorframe, assuming they ever let him back in again.

"Sorry about your place," said Tapper, buckled into the seat next to him.

"Me too." Kovalic flicked the screen away; he'd seen what he needed to. Anything else was just going to make him feel more dejected. "Brody, ETA?"

"About an hour out," said the pilot from the front seat.

It wasn't a sub-orbital, but the flyer that they'd 'borrowed' from one of Kovalic's neighbors still cut the travel time between the lake and the capital city down to a couple hours. Plenty of time for them to clear out before Kester's forces dropped in.

Most of Kovalic's neighbors on the lake were on the wealthier side, having built their homes high on the hillside, easily accessible only by flyers. No reason to spend the time and cost of creating and maintaining meandering gravel roads when you could just zip in by air.

Brody and Tapper had done recon earlier, so sneaking onto the property and hot-wiring the flyer had been relatively easy, especially with Page and Brody double-teaming it. Fitting five of them in the ship had been the most challenging part. Technically, it only had seats for four, but Tapper had wedged himself between Kovalic and Sayers, leaving the longer-limbed Page and Brody in the front seats.

"You sure you can fly this thing?" Kovalic had asked as Brody powered up the engines.

"Christ," said the pilot, as he consulted the holodash, then toggled a few switches. "Why do people ask me that every single time?"

"Brody."

"Do people keep asking you 'Oh, can you punch *that* guy?'"

"*Brody.*"

The repulsors started to thrum under their feet, and out the window Kovalic saw a pale, gaunt man appear on the nearby patio of the expansive estate, staring out at the flyer in an expression of puzzlement that was rapidly shifting to alarm.

"This is a little more weight than this thing's rated for, so you're all going to want to hold on. And try to stay still." And with that, the flyer lurched unsteadily into the air, leaving its gaping owner behind them.

"Maybe we should have left a note," said Tapper, following Kovalic's glance.

"Oh yes, rich people are famously forgiving as long as you leave a note," said Sayers.

Kovalic had cast a last look down at his house as Brody circled the area before laying in the course back towards the capital city.

"You sure they were listening?" asked Tapper.

"Page?"

The lieutenant didn't crane his neck, but he did give a short, sharp nod. "I know CID's capabilities and I made the trace hard enough that they'd have to work for it, but not so hard that even a first-year tech couldn't unravel it with a little effort."

And Page's assessment had borne out just under an hour later when the perimeter sensors at the house had tripped and Kovalic had pulled up the footage of the CID's troops ransacking his home.

The sergeant caught his eye. "Doesn't seem like we'll make it to the city in time for your meeting with the inspector."

Kovalic wasn't sure whether Kester had coerced Laurent into letting CID listen in or whether the agency had done it without the law enforcement officer's knowledge, but that had been part of the plan. Even if Kester had concluded that his people missing Kovalic had simply been unlucky, he almost certainly had the call readout, which meant he'd deploy troops at the meeting place.

So Inspector Laurent would have to wait. But at least it

would get Kester out of their hair for the moment. "We'll figure out a way to get in touch with the inspector after Page and I retrieve the data chip."

"And you're sure you don't want all hands on deck for that?" The sergeant had shifted into mother hen mode.

"Quiet is as quiet does, Tap. Besides, you and Brody have your work cut out for you elsewhere."

"Right," muttered Brody from the front seat. "Sticking our heads into the lion's mouth. Anybody you want us to say hi to when they throw us in front of the firing squad?"

Tapper rolled his eyes. "Stop being so dramatic, kid."

"Just saying, I would have been happy to go a gravtrain station with Page if anybody wants to trade. I could use a break."

They could all use a break, Kovalic reflected. The respite at the lake had been too short, leaving them all a bit frayed. This might not be a combat drop, but they still needed to be sharp. With Kester and Nova Front looking for Page – and now them – there was no margin for error.

Within the hour, they'd brought the flyer in to land at a private airfield outside the capital – the kind that didn't mind the occasional unscheduled flight with no transponder, as long as you had the money. Which, fortunately, they did, between Page's go-bag and the stash Kovalic had kept at the house.

Kovalic glanced around at his team as they packed up the little gear they'd amassed. Understaffed, under-equipped, up against insurmountable odds. Usually, that was standard operating procedure for them, but this time it wasn't so cut and dried. Even if they didn't know them personally, the people they were going up against were nominally their own.

"You've all got your assignments," said Kovalic. "Scheduled check in times have been established. Emergency dead drops and contact protocols are in place. Any last questions?"

Brody raised a hand. "Do we have a lawyer on retainer?"

Tapper grunted. "I don't think they let you have a lawyer when they throw you in a hole that deep and dark."

The sergeant wasn't wrong: at least when Kovalic had been an Illyrican prisoner of war, he'd had faith that his people would get him out eventually. This time, nobody would be coming to their rescue – because everybody they trusted would probably be locked up right next to them.

"Let's hope it doesn't come to that."

Walking out of the airfield, they went their separate ways: Page, Kovalic, and Sayers towards the nearest gravtrain stop, while Brody and Tapper hailed an autocab. Nods were exchanged all around, but few words. What could you say in a situation like this anyway?

Kovalic watched as the autocab pulled away, a trail of dust in its wake. He hoped it wouldn't be the last time he saw the two of them: the man who'd been at his side for more than two decades and the kid who he'd dragged into this life against his will. Both of them were anchored to him; he was responsible for the lives they were living now, and if something happened to them, it was on him.

But there was no other option. He had to trust them on this part of the job, or everything else would be pointless.

Looking up at Sayers and Page, he gave a tight smile. "All right. Let's do this."

# CHAPTER 35

They hit the Commonwealth Center gravtrain station right around the afternoon rush hour. That was good, Addy figured, because it meant plenty of cover amongst the bustling crowds making their way home, but it also made her job a lot harder.

*Too many people to watch*, she thought as she tried to keep her alertness at just the right level: low enough that she wasn't trying to analyze every single person she saw, but not so low that she missed the real threats, if they were there.

From her position on the stairway at one end of the main concourse, she had a good vantage point on the open gallery that made up the bulk of the station. Around the edges were kiosks selling everything from souvenirs to snacks and coffee. All the way at the other end of the concourse was the main entrance out into the city center, not far from the Commonwealth government's central administration buildings. And directly below her, through an arch leading down towards the gravtrain platforms, was the corridor lined with paid storage lockers.

She raised one hand to her ear, as though tucking an errant strand of hair behind it – more convincing since she'd let her hair grow out over the last few months – and spoke in a low voice. "You look clear from here."

In the concourse below, two figures drifted away from kiosks at opposite sides of the gallery and started strolling towards the archway. If she hadn't been looking for them, she doubted they would have stood out: just two more tired travelers.

And as good as Kovalic was at blending in, she grudgingly had to admit that Page was among the best she'd ever seen. When he started making his way towards the platform, she did a double take to make sure it was actually him: he'd nicked a coat and a hat from a chair at one of the terminal's cafés, and a shoulder bag when some unsuspecting commuter had put it down for a second. Somehow he'd changed his whole gait, too, moving with the slow, dreariness of a salaryman, barely looking up as he trudged his way home from the daily grind.

The quiet desperation almost seeped into Addy just from watching him. And all of this despite the fact that the man's face, attendant with large red warning signs, flashed on displays and holoscreens around the station roughly every two minutes.

*I can see why everybody talked him up. The man is* good. Brody had spoken about Page with the awe of someone discussing their favorite superhero; she'd largely tuned it out, chalking it up to the over-enthusiasm of an amateur. But she could see why Kovalic and Tapper had held the lieutenant in such high esteem, and, if she were being honest with herself, there was a tiny pang of jealousy in the back of her mind.

*Stay on mission, Addy.* With an effort, she drew her gaze back to the concourse, scanning over the crowd to see if anybody seemed too interested in their movements. Maybe that young guy in the hood and cap checking their sleeve?

But no, a moment later, he met up with a handful of others his age and they headed out to the street. Or that woman staring up at the departures and arrivals holoscreen? When she turned to head towards the platform, Addy saw she was holding the hand of a small child, trundling alongside her. *Hopefully CID's not starting them* that *young.*

Having found no obvious threats, she let her wariness slide into the background of her mind, which made plenty of room to allow the simmering anger she'd been holding onto to leak out around the edges.

She'd let herself be used. Again. The general, that Illyrican bastard, had sent her to do his dirty work. To kill Page, because he'd been a thorn in the man's side. And she'd come closer than she liked to carrying it through, putting a round in the man that would have done far more damage than a bloody arm, all because she'd been so eager to feel needed. To be a valued part of the team.

Why hadn't she pushed back more? Questioned the general's orders? Apparently Kovalic and Taylor's insistence over the past several months that she do things by the book had finally kicked in. *Just goes to show you that sometimes following orders is the most dangerous thing you can do.*

She resisted the urge to growl, settling instead for letting her hands tighten on the cold stone of the balustrade in front of her. She'd vowed to never let herself be a pawn again, but that was the trick, wasn't it? Pawns didn't choose to become knights or rooks. And the idea that you could get to the other end of the board and become a queen? That was an illusion, carefully constructed so that you wouldn't realize that the chances of you actually reaching that point, not to mention avoiding getting chewed up along the way, were infinitesimal.

In her mind she heard the silken voice of Ofeibia Xi, crime lord and arms dealer, whispering in her ear that she could have had it all. Been somebody important who chose their own path, instead of a cog in the machine. Xi had seen her value. *"Somebody who knows that sometimes rules get in the way of doing what's necessary."*

But almost as soon as the tendril of temptation had woven into her mind, it was gone again, her anger sapped with it. Xi had been using her too, and that dangled future had been nothing more than its own form of illusion.

So where did that leave her, in all of this? How was she supposed to get out of just being a weapon pointed at other people?

*Take control*, her mind whispered.

Once Page and Kovalic retrieved the chip from the locker where Page had stowed it, they'd finally have options. She wasn't sure exactly what Kovalic's next move would be: delivering it to the Commonwealth Executive might be enough for them to prove what CID had been up to with Project AUGUR. Taking it to Inspector Laurent or the press would likewise all but guarantee the same, though acting as whistleblowers wouldn't necessarily bode well for their own futures. But she had to admit that part of her would take far greater satisfaction in simply destroying the chip – grinding it under her boot heel like a scuttling pest.

If only they could be certain that that would be the end of AUGUR.

*You've got to look at the bigger picture, Addy.* AUGUR was an overreach, a betrayal of the populace and the powers they'd given to the Commonwealth and its agencies to ostensibly keep them safe. If it were exposed, the resulting chaos might take down the government.

Her stomach roiled at that. She had no love for the entity that was the Commonwealth government; they'd never done anything for her. She'd raised herself on the streets after her parents had died, despite their vaunted social safety net. If it hadn't been for Boyland taking matters into his own hands, she'd probably have been dead or in prison by now.

In the end, though, it didn't really matter: it still wasn't her call to make.

Noise spiked out of the pleasant susurration of the background as a loud clattering came from behind her, yanking her out of her reverie. She whirled, one hand already on the KO gun at her back, but managed to restrain herself from drawing it in the middle of this crowded public venue.

A young man sat splayed out at the bottom of the stairs, the ones that led up to the skyway stretching across the street to the nearby shopping center. He looked dazed, and a crowd of people had gathered around in concern, asking him if he were all right.

*Must have slipped.*

Something flared, white hot, in her mind: her heart ramping up, her breathing coming faster, vision widening. This wasn't right. The man was climbing back to his feet, waving off offers of help, and giving a generally apologetic smile to everyone around him, assuring them that he was okay, that it had just been a little tumble.

And then his eyes flicked to her.

*Shit. Shit shit shit.* She spun back towards the concourse, raising her sleeve, but she hadn't even managed to trigger her comm when she felt something hard and blunt poke her in the side.

"If I were you," said a pleasant conversational voice, "I would put your arm down. Unless you've been really looking forward to have your liver regrown in a vat."

# CHAPTER 36

Eli tugged at his top again, trying to pull it down to fit over his mid-section. *Midriff-baring isn't exactly the style I'm going for.*

"Stop fidgeting," said Tapper out of the side of his mouth. "You'll draw too much attention."

"It's not my fault that you nicked me the clothing of the shortest person on the planet."

"Look, it was the largest one I could find at the base laundry. Maybe if you'd kept your own handy."

"Oh, right, because I have so much call to wear an official Commonwealth Naval uniform."

In truth, Eli had never donned the outfit before. His own had been delivered after the Bayern mission, sent over as a matter of course following his tarmac commission in the military, but since then had been hanging, undisturbed, in a vacuum-sealed garment bag in his closet.

*Probably still has that new uniform smell.*

Tapper's, on the other hand, seemed to fit him like a second skin. Something about putting on the uniform had straightened his spine and put a gleam in his eye that took in every other uniformed officer they passed and sized them up. As if he were deciding whether to poke one in the chest and demand that they drop and give him twenty.

Unsurprisingly, people were giving them a wide berth.

There was no shortage of uniformed personnel to blend in with as they strode up to the security checkpoint. One gate slid aside to admit them to the screening area, putting Eli in mind of an airlock. At least they didn't get vented into space if something didn't check out.

*Instead we just get surrounded by people with guns.*

Inside a small booth, a pair of soldiers wearing the fatigues of Commonwealth marines eyeballed them as they waved their sleeves over the reader, though Tapper's master sergeant tabs and chest full of ribbons had already elicited a certain amount of deference.

"Morning, lads," said Tapper cheerfully.

"Master Sergeant," said one of the men, consulting a holoscreen. "Looks like you've been offworld for a while. Welcome home."

"No place like it."

Eli tried not to swallow as he watched the soldiers' eyes flick over their records. Well, *someone*'s records, anyway. There'd been no doubt that Kester would be on the lookout for the whole team by this point, so, with a little help from Page, they'd used some dummy ID files and slapped their own photos, biometrics, and service information on top of them.

"Doesn't exactly fill me with confidence about our security," Eli had said, watching the ease with which Page had edited the files.

"Forward planning," Page had said. "I placed these dummy files in the system years ago. You never know when they could come in handy. If there's one thing you can trust, it's that a large organization isn't going to be diligent about purging old data."

Still, Eli shifted from foot to foot, awaiting the alarms that he felt sure were about to go off. He tried to smile pleasantly at the guards through the window, but their stoic faces gave nothing away. This wasn't his first time hiding behind an alias, but he'd never tried it on their own people before. The thought made his stomach churn.

When the light above the gate blinked green and the guards waved them through, he almost passed out from relief.

Tapper saluted the men, who returned the gesture. Eli hastily complied, catching himself just in time from using the standard palm-out Illyrican salute, leaving him with a raggedy one that he was sure had Tapper muttering under his breath.

"Jesus, Brody," he said as they fell into step again. "That was the *easy* part." They strode through the courtyard beyond the security checkpoint to the huge, low-slung plasticrete and glass building in front of them. Out front, a trio of flags whipped in the breeze, but it was the seal, set in the concrete, that sent a trickle of sweat down Eli's temple as they walked over it.

The Commonwealth Intelligence Directorate.

*Hopefully it's the last place they'll expect us to be.* And hopefully not the last place they would ever be.

Tapper nudged him from behind, and Eli realized he'd been frozen, staring down at the seal like a gawking tourist. "Come on, *lieutenant.* Can't stand around all day."

After the security outside, the interior of CID headquarters was anticlimactic: it looked like any other office building in which Eli had set foot. A slightly higher preponderance of people in uniform, to be sure, but otherwise, it was the same sort of bustling crowd full of people talking in small groups or staring at their sleeves as they made their way to lifts or traversed the helical staircase that rose through the center of the atrium. Everybody was on their way somewhere, and the easiest way to blend in was to follow that example.

"You know where we're going?"

"Roughly," said Tapper, not breaking his stride. "Been here enough times I should be able to find it." He'd made a beeline for the lifts, wending his way through the daily hustle and bustle.

Eli couldn't quite banish the sensation that everybody was looking at him, that there was a bright flashing sign reading IMPOSTOR hanging over his head. He pushed down the urge to straighten his uniform again, even though the collar felt uncomfortably tight, like his head was swelling.

But the lift arrived without incident and Tapper punched the button for the third sub-basement. Eli blinked as he looked over the panel, noting that there were fully *five* subterranean levels in the complex. *That is a whole lot of underground storage. What are they keeping down there – aliens?*

The panel requested Tapper's authorization and he waved his sleeve over the reader, which blinked green. Their stated cover was retrieving archival files for a high muckety-muck over at Special Operations Command, via the secure terminals in CID's basement. It was a fairly routine sort of courier mission, Kovalic had assured them: many sensitive files weren't available outside of the CID network, and access was strictly controlled.

More to the point, it would get them in the building with few questions asked.

The sub-basement lobby where the lift let them out was quiet and low traffic. Unlike the main gate, there were no actual guards here: just a kiosk next to a heavy set of blast-proof doors. In the corners of the room, two security cameras stared unblinkingly at the doors and kiosk, while two others were pointed at the lift entrance.

*So, uh, just act natural I guess.* He followed Tapper's lead as the sergeant walked to the kiosk and held his sleeve up to the authentication panel. After a moment, a holoscreen sprang to life, displaying a map of the archives; a dotted line showed the path to follow to reach the specified terminal, and then with a *clank* and the sound of machinery, the heavy blast doors slid open to admit them.

A series of lights clicked on, revealing long lines of shelving units, stretching off as far as Eli could see. He let out a low whistle as the doors hissed closed behind them, sealing the room again.

Most of the shelves contained servers, blinking away behind sound-dampening plexisteel cabinet doors; they kept the noise level to a dull roar that would have been deafening otherwise. But, beyond them, Eli could see that some of the shelves weren't full of hardware but instead what looked like small metal boxes. When he got closer, he saw each was labeled with a barcode and a small display showing an ID number. He peered at one and started to reach out for it.

An iron grip seized his wrist and he looked over to find Tapper shaking his head. "We're not authorized for those. So unless you want to bring the entire CID protective services division down on our heads, let's stick to the plan."

Eli withdrew his hand, massaging the wrist. "Sorry. What's in them?"

"Records."

"Like, data chips?"

"Hard copy."

"*Hard copy*? Like *paper*?"

Tapper shrugged as he continued down the aisle. "Lot harder to hack into something that's not on a network. When you've got as many dirty secrets as CID does, you want to be careful about who's got access to them."

"When you've got that many dirty secrets, why keep *records* of them?"

"Sometimes it's to cover your own ass. Sometimes it's to hold someone else's over the fire. And sometimes there's just a little bit of you that's proud of that thing that you can't tell anybody else you ever did. Intelligence officers are a strange breed, kid."

That, in Eli's opinon, was putting it mildly.

Tapper glanced at his sleeve, then turned right down another aisle, lined again with servers. About halfway down, there was a small transparent booth, inside of which was a single seat in front of a terminal. With a wave of Tapper's sleeve, the door popped open, and they both stepped inside.

Behind them, the door again hissed shut, then the clear plexisteel walls suddenly went opaque, as though they were sealed in a small box.

*Or coffin.* Eli tried not to imagine the booth flooding with some sort of toxic gas when they hit the wrong key.

The sergeant seemed unbothered that they were in a possible death trap and held his sleeve up to the terminal. A holoscreen sprung into existence above it, welcoming Master Sergeant Talbot and Lieutenant Boothroyd.

"Boothroyd?" said Eli. "Really?"

"What about it?"

"Just… sounds like a made-up name."

Tapper leveled him with a steely glare. "Served with him back in the wars. He died at Earthfall."

"Oh. Sorry."

"He *was* kind of an asshole. But at least something good will come of him."

The welcome screen disappeared, replaced with a search query box. Tapper cracked his knuckles. "All right. Now we see who's paying attention." He slowly typed in AUGUR, his finger hovering over the search icon.

Eli's mouth was dry suddenly and he glanced around the booth again, looking for vents. Or cameras. Or anything to suggest that this might be the last place he set foot in his life. *I definitely didn't expect to die in a tiny box deep in the bowels of an intelligence agency.*

Tapper pressed the search icon, then leaned back in the chair and crossed his arms, waiting as the terminal did its thing, combing through the no doubt millions of documents held in this facility.

*This might take a wh –*

"Nothing," said Tapper. "Not a single hit."

Eli frowned. "What's that mean?"

The sergeant grunted. "It means that this is the kind of project that's too classified to even be in the *normal* classified archives. They're not just going to leave it lying around for anybody to find."

"So, what, that's it? We just slink back out of here, tail between our legs?"

Tapper raised his hands. "Unless you've got a better idea."

There had to be something else that would get them the information they needed. Something that proved what CID had been up to with AUGUR. Whatever it was, Kassandra knew it. She'd been a step ahead of them the whole way. Maybe, like Kovalic thought, she had a mole feeding her information.

*Or maybe she didn't need one.* "Hold on, let me try something."

"Be my guest," said Tapper, vacating the chair, and giving an expansive sweep of his arm.

Eli sat down and carefully typed in 'KASSANDRA' then hit the search icon.

A few results blinked in, but at the top of the list was what appeared to be a dossier. "Looks like CID knows more than they let on." He tapped on the document, and then heard Tapper suck in a breath.

"That's not just an intelligence report, kid. That's a service record."

"What?"

The sergeant jabbed a finger at the line at the top, which blared DECOMISSIONED. "According to this, Kassandra was a code name used by a former CID operations officer, Alys Costa. Looks like she went off the grid about a year ago, but before that she'd been working as a mercenary."

Everything wobbled like somebody had knocked Eli's ship into a tailspin. He fought valiantly to get back on course. "Wait. We're saying Kassandra – the leader of Nova Front, the person who just blew up a building in the Commonwealth capital city – was a *CID operative*?"

The sergeant rubbed a hand over the gray bristles on his chin, as though attempting to cover up the grimace on his face. "Sure looks like it. Not the first time I've heard of someone going rogue, but that is a hell of way to make some waves. According to this, she was in the Activities branch until she left, about six years ago." He scrolled through the data, then shook his head. "Shit, Sevastapol, Haran, even Hanif space. Looks like Costa was a serious operator – I'm surprised we never crossed paths."

Eli glanced nervously at the walls around them. No armed guards had descended yet, and the booth hadn't been flooded with incapacitating gas, so it seemed like they were still safe – at least for the moment. "Maybe have a nostalgia trip on your own time?"

Tapper rolled his eyes. "Calm down, kid. Here, look: her last mission was in 2412. Details are redacted, but she left the service just a few months later."

*This fills in some gaps at least.* Eli found himself studying the picture on the file: a woman of indeterminate age, with dark hair shorn into a fade on one side, and reaching to the top of her ear on the other. Her eyes were almost as dark as the hair – in the image, the pupil and iris seemed to blend into each other – and gave her a thousand-yard stare that bored right through the screen and into Eli. "So the reason she's been two steps ahead of us is because she was on the inside. She must have already known about AUGUR."

"Could be," said Tapper. "Sure would help if they hadn't blacked out all the juicy bits." He waved a hand at the numerous redacted marks that made the file look more like a zebra than anything else.

"Don't suppose you've got a way to *un*redact it?"

"Well, maybe. Gimme a second." The sergeant motioned Eli to get out of the chair, and he scrambled upwards all too happily.

Tapper stretched his fingers and started tapping in commands. "A pal in Signals showed me this one. In these older files, there used to be a loophole, if they were sloppy when they put the data in. You just select the whole document, copy, and voilà–"

With a *blatt*, an angry warning appeared on the screen, red letters next to an exclamation point: "CLASSIFIED. C6

AUTHORIZATION REQUIRED. THIS REQUEST HAS BEEN LOGGED."

"Uh," said Eli. "That doesn't look good. How worried should we be?"

"Let's say medium."

"Time to go?"

"Time to go."

Relief flooded through him when the booth's door gave under his hand and the walls flipped back to transparent. As quickly as they could, they retraced their steps through the aisles of archived documents and servers, making their way back to the blast doors. But those opened too, and no guns were being pointed at them as they stepped back into the antechamber. The lift likewise arrived without incident, and they rode back to the main floor.

Eli's pulse settled back into a normal rhythm once they were in the elevator, and he glanced over at Tapper, who was leaning against the wall, seemingly without a care in the world. "Not exactly mission success, sarge. We were supposed to find out the details on AUGUR, and we're not any closer. What now?"

"Take the win where we can, kid – we tell the boss what we found about Kassandra. First, though, we make ourselves scarce."

The elevator chimed as it reached the lobby, and the door slid aside. Eli stepped out, shading his eyes against the bright afternoon light after the dim surroundings of the archives, so it took a moment before he saw the two officers in dark suits waiting for them. Both had their hands on the butts of knockout guns holstered at their waists.

Eli's stomach flipped like he was doing a high-G maneuver, and beside him he could feel Tapper go calm. *Never a good sign.* Some people got tense before a fight, but Tapper just settled into the rhythm of a professional.

"Master Sergeant Talbot. Lieutenant Boothroyd," said one, a woman with a dark blue headscarf that matched her suit. "A word, please."

"Sorry," said Tapper, "This will have to wait. We've been recalled by our CO for a high-priority situation." He took a step forward.

The woman held out her free hand, palm towards them, and smoothly moved to intercept Tapper. "I'm afraid I must insist. We received a notification that you attempted unauthorized access of archive files. I'll have to ask you both to come with us."

Eli could feel the sweat beading on his temple, threatening to make a downhill run along his jawline. "Officer, I think this is all some misunderstanding. As the sergeant said, we're on an assignment, and we've been ordered to report back immediately."

The woman hesitated, glancing at her partner, who gave a minute shrug. "I'll need to speak to your CO, then. What's their name?"

A throat cleared from behind the security guards, followed by a familiar voice. "That would be me. And I assure you, I will be taking care of this matter personally."

# CHAPTER 37

Everything always went smoothly until it didn't. At Sayers's signal, Kovalic and Page had regrouped to head to the lockers under the arch. There was just enough crowd to blend in, but not so much that they were constantly underfoot as they approached the long rows of metal boxes lining the corridor.

Page took the lead, Kovalic hanging back a few feet as the lieutenant stepped up to one of the lockers and pressed his sleeve against the reader panel. With a click, the door popped open, and Page reached in and upwards, then, with a ripping of tape, pulled out a data chip stuck to the top of the inside of the compartment.

In the same moment, Kovalic's instincts flared, and he started to turn, only to find a man already standing behind him, hand in a jacket pocket. It wasn't the only thing in that pocket either, judging by the bulge pointed in his direction.

Even if Kovalic had had a weapon, there wouldn't have been time for him to draw it, much less use it effectively in the crowded civilian thoroughfare, but he doubted that their assailants would have the same compunctions. And even as the plural floated through his mind, he knew it was accurate: this wasn't a solo foray.

He glanced over his shoulder to see a figure approaching

Page, hood drawn. As they drew closer, they pulled it back to reveal the same woman who'd accosted Page in the basement of the bookstore.

Kassandra.

They'd been waiting for them down here, that much was clear. Not a peep from Sayers up top, and no indication that they'd been tailed.

"You forgot that you're not the only one trained in fieldwork, Aaron," said the woman. "Got a sensitive package? Dead drop it somewhere public and easily accessible. Only so many places that you could have gone from Oluo Plaza that morning, and this was by far the most likely. All I needed to know was which locker. Thank you for making it easy." She held out a hand; her other was, like her compatriot's, nestled in her jacket pocket, grasping a weapon.

Page spared a glance at Kovalic, blandly questioning.

He sized up the situation: Kassandra and her partner were no dummies. They both stood a few feet off of their targets. Make a move? They'd get shot – stunned, hopefully – before they even closed the distance. Alert Sayers? Stunned before he reached his sleeve. Talk their way out? They were painfully short on leverage. Kassandra didn't seem like she was looking for clemency, even if they were in a position to offer it.

"Don't try my patience," said Kassandra, hand still outstretched. "You know me well enough to know that this," she raised her hand in the jacket pocket, "isn't a bluff. I'm giving you a chance to hand it over and walk away, but if I need to, I'll just take it off you."

Kovalic's jaw clenched. Over a barrel. Not a position he liked bargaining from. "Give it to her."

Kassandra's eyes flicked to him, then back to Page,

widening slightly. "Taking orders again, is it?" The gaze sharpened again. "Or was it always that way? Were you still a pawn, even as you assured me of your loyalty to the cause?"

Page said nothing, hand curled lightly around the data chip; his expression was inscrutable as ever, no sign of remorse or regret, nor of righteous conviction. "I did what I had to do."

"That makes two of us. The chip. Now."

For a moment, Page did nothing. If Kovalic could have peered inside the man's head, he knew he would have seen the analysis in progress: each and every path – even more than the few that Kovalic had considered – thoroughly assessed and discarded, until the only decision left was the Hobson's choice Kassandra had left them with.

Page tossed the data chip to her in an underhand lob. She snagged it in mid-air and smiled at them, a cold, heartless smirk of satisfaction. "You're on the wrong side of this. Both of you. The Commonwealth doesn't care about you, just like it doesn't care about any of its citizens. It's all part of the same machine that grinds down everybody in the galaxy, grist for the endless mills of war and destruction. The same battles have raged for millennia on Earth, and they're still going here and now. You're part of that, whether you know it or not, and you might think it's better to be doing the grinding than to be fed into the machine, but guess what? You're *not* the ones doing the grinding." Her fingers wrapped around the chip. "And I'm going to prove that – with this."

"How exactly?" said Kovalic. "AUGUR's gone. Even with that chip, you've got nothing."

She cocked her head to one side. "You really don't know

anything, do you? Fancy yourself the center of the web, but you're just a fly who can't see the spider creeping up behind them."

"And who's the spider in this scenario? You?"

"I'm not some monologuing villain from a holo vid. Stay tuned and you'll see, just like everybody else." She'd started slowly backing away, towards a turn in the corridor, and Kovalic could sense the man with the gun behind him following suit. He tensed – they might have a split-second opportunity when their assailants were forced to disengage; even if they couldn't overtake them, maybe they could at least see where they went, pick up their trail later.

But before he could spring into action, a loud series of bangs echoed from the concourse above, the sound ricocheting through the tunnel, followed by screams. People around them looked up in alarm, and then began to move as one mass, pushing towards the platform.

Kovalic and Page were ensnared in the crowd; just over the top of the roiling mass, he could see the man who'd held the gun on him disappear down the tunnel. Catching him was out of the question: the frenzied mob buffeted Kovalic this way and that, as though he were in one of the antique pinball machines he'd played as a kid.

With an effort, he managed to thread his way through the crowd to meet up with Page. But Kassandra had disappeared as well, probably letting herself get carried off into the throngs before making her escape.

Which meant she – and the chip – were in the wind.

# CHAPTER 38

Addy froze mid-motion, all her muscles going tense. The gun – and she was beyond certain that's what it was – was jabbed into her mid-section, and there was little chance she could wrest it away from her attacker before they got a shot off.

And any shot at this range wasn't going to be pretty.

*God* damn *it. You dropped the ball, Addy. So wrapped up in your own thoughts, you lost focus on the job. Rule* one. Not that recriminations were particularly helpful right now.

Swallowing, Addy lowered her arm. "So. How's this going to go?"

"It's going to go just fine," said the voice. It was a man, hovering just outside of her peripheral vision. Not the same one that had feigned falling down the stairs, she thought – he'd just been the diversion. "I'm here to keep you from interfering in a little transaction taking place downstairs. Once that's done, I'm going to walk away, you're going to walk away, and we're never going to see each other again."

*You clearly haven't met my boss if you think he's going to take that lying down.* She couldn't quite stifle a chuckle, though a jab from the barrel of the gun cut it off abruptly.

"Something funny?"

"Just looking forward to the situation being reversed."

She could hear the smile in his voice. "You're quite the optimist."

"First time anybody's said that."

"Well, good luck. Maybe if you hadn't decided to join an oppressive regime, this could have gone differently."

"Oh, please," said Addy. "I'm Novan born and raised. Doesn't mean I have to run around blowing things up."

"Sometimes action is the only way to make yourself heard."

"Keep telling yourself that. It'll sound great coming from inside a cell."

There was a pause and, for the briefest of moments, Addy wondered if she'd found a crack in his armor. But then the pressure of the gun in her torso eased.

"Looks like we're done here. It's been a pleasure."

"Really? What makes you think I'm not going to come right after you?"

"You're going to be a little busy." Then the weapon was no longer in her side.

*I don't like the sound of –*

"Look out!" shouted the same voice, now filled with alarm. "She's got a gun!" Followed by a rapid series of shots overhead.

*Oh no.*

A cacophony of screams erupted around the terminal, people scattering every which way. Addy turned, trying in vain to catch a glimpse of the man, but everybody was rippling away from her as though she were the epicenter of an explosion.

*Time to go.*

She dashed down the stairs to the concourse, then

hooked around underneath into the tunnel where the lockers were. The panic from upstairs had spread down here too and she was caught up in a throng of people heading for the theoretical safety of the platform – as though they wouldn't be penned in, were it a real emergency. A handful of security guards were trying to maintain order, push their way back up toward the concourse, but they were practically swimming upstream.

It was hard to get a glimpse over the sea of people and Addy was about to try and raise the rest of the team on her sleeve when a hand grasped her arm.

Instinctively, she turned and tried to break the lock, only to find herself face to face with Kovalic. They stood, buffeted like trees in a windstorm, as the crowd flowed around them. Distantly, Addy thought she could hear the approaching sound of sirens.

"What the hell happened?" Addy had to shout to make herself heard over the crowd.

"Kassandra," said Kovalic, and Addy could almost see his teeth grinding. "She got the drop on us. And now she has the chip."

# CHAPTER 39

A string of curses, each more colorful than the last, issued from Sayers – even some of the passing crowd eyed her in surprise as they tried to flee. Kovalic couldn't blame her; he had some choice words for himself for going into this situation underprepared. He'd underestimated Kassandra, hadn't thought through all the angles, and this whole op had gone belly up.

Sayers was peering around, looking for any sign of their quarry. "Any idea where she went?"

Kovalic shook his head. "Long gone by now."

"Shit. We should move too. Security will be looking for us."

"Oh?"

Sayers's mouth twitched. "They framed me for firing those shots. It won't hold up, but I don't want to spend the time explaining myself, do you?"

Especially because the civilian security officers would no doubt hold onto them until someone else arrived. And Kovalic was betting that someone else would be Aidan Kester, who he really did not want to explain himself to anytime soon. "I think that's a hell of a plan, specialist. Lead the way."

It took ten minutes to extricate themselves from the station without running afoul of security, but they managed to sneak out of a maintenance entrance before it was sealed off. Most of the rapid response teams had headed for the concourse, which gave them just enough time to make their way onto city streets ahead of the cordon. Flashing blue-and-red police drones were already in the air, but they hadn't expanded their search radius quite yet.

"So, now what?" said Sayers, once they were a few blocks away from the station and the sirens had started to fade. "We lost our only leverage, the authorities are probably looking for *all* of us by now, and we still have no idea what Kassandra and her people have in store."

"Except they're not done yet," said Kovalic. "She made that much clear. Page, any insight?"

The tall, slender man grimaced in thought. "Kassandra didn't particularly like to share: she only told us what we needed to know. For all of that, though, she's remained single-minded in her pursuit. So whatever she has planned, it seems likely that it will be cut from the same cloth as her earlier actions."

"Another attack on CID?" said Sayers. "She certainly seems to have it out for them."

Page cocked his head to one side. "There's no reason for Nova Front to carry out another attack – that just risks losing what little public sympathy they may have garnered. And the attack on Oluo Plaza was a means to an end: to obtain that chip. She must have a use for it."

"You also said that it seemed personal. Like she wanted revenge for something. There are worse ways to hurt someone than blowing up their stuff."

Plenty of worse ways, Kovalic reflected. Losing an

installation like the one at Oluo Plaza might be a blow to CID, but in the grand scheme of things it was a setback of material and money, not something to shake the agency's entire foundations. No, that would require something far more severe.

The work of an intelligence agency was always tenuous: by nature, what they did was distasteful, even if it was practical. People didn't like to think about what those covert agencies were doing in their name, preferring instead to remain in willful, blissful ignorance.

Unless those actions were dragged, kicking and screaming, into the sunlight, and the people were forced to confront it. And to make a choice.

"No," said Kovalic slowly. "Attacking them directly doesn't help her – it just reinforces that she's a terrorist. Far, far worse would be to have what CID does in the shadows be thrust into the cold light of day. That would be a lot harder to ignore."

Page voiced his unspoken thought, as though reading his mind. "You think she's going to *expose* AUGUR."

Kovalic nodded. "Any crackpot can claim that the government is spying on them, but that chip might give Kassandra what they all lack: hard evidence. If she can find a way to disseminate that evidence, then she can get the people on her side. And with the people on her side…"

"She can bring down CID," said Sayers.

"Or," said Page, "the government that enabled them."

…*your treachery will be revealed for all to see.* Kassandra had told them, had put the threat in Page's mouth; they just hadn't understood what she meant. Well, CID and the Commonwealth Executive probably had – that would explain why Kester had been so determined to track down

Nova Front, and why the government had seemingly given its intelligence agencies free rein: who was more invested than the very people whose existence was at threat? And how else could you keep it compartmentalized?

"Well, in that case, how do we stop her?" said Sayers.

"Do we?" Page interjected softly. "AUGUR is a crime against the citizens of Nova and the Commonwealth. CID shouldn't be allowed to have that much power – nobody should. The people who made that decision need to be held to account."

"You're talking about sitting back and helping a *terrorist*. She blew up a goddamn building," said Sayers. "Kovalic, come on. We can't let her get away with this – who the hell knows what she'd decide to do next?"

They'd slowed to a stop, several blocks away from the gravtrain station, the distant sounds of sirens still wafting on the air. Above them, holoscreens hovered, broadcasting ads or the latest news reports, including the note about an incident at the station they'd just left.

Both of his officers had turned to him – Sayers angry, Page as calm and unruffled as ever – waiting for him to make a judgment call, to decide what their course of action was going to be.

Kovalic rubbed at his bleary eyes. "You're both right. We need to stop Kassandra from doing more damage *and* we need to hold CID's feet to the fire. But right now, Nova Front is the bigger priority. They're still out there, and they've proved that they're not above causing harm if it furthers their agenda. So we find out where Kassandra's going to strike next, and we stop her. Then we've got her *and* we've got the proof of what CID has been up to and we figure out the best way to use it."

Splitting the baby? Maybe. It depended on how well they pulled this next part off. And a part of him couldn't help but note that if CID ended up taking the fall here, it could leave a power vacuum in the Commonwealth's intelligence apparatus. And the last man standing, the one whose integrity would seem beyond reproach because he'd never been involved in the scandal, would be none other than Hasan al-Adaj.

Had that been the general's plan all along? Use Nova Front to expose CID and eliminate his chief rival? Kovalic's instincts still told him he was missing something, but he couldn't dismiss it out of hand either. If ideas alone could create ulcers then this one was boring through his stomach right now. But they had bigger problems to deal with.

"Page, I need you to put yourself in Kassandra's shoes. If she's going to find a way to expose the Commonwealth government, how would she do it?"

"She'd find the biggest platform she could," said Page. "Like the area hack I carried out at Oluo Plaza, only on a much, much larger scale."

"So, what you're saying is she needs something a lot like... AUGUR," said Sayers slowly.

Page's eyes glimmered as he picked up Sayers's line of thought. "You can't deploy AUGUR just anywhere: it was specifically set up at Oluo Plaza because it could directly link into ConComm's backbone servers for Salaam. If she's going bigger, then she'd need a location with *worldwide* communications access."

Kovalic found his eyes drawn to one of the giant holoscreens, where the news coverage had moved on from the station incident. It was now showing a piece about the imminent switchover of Nova's communication infrastructure to the orbiting Station Zero, perched at the top of the carbon nanotube space elevator cable that stretched all the way beyond the atmosphere.

"I think I know where that might be," he said. "Anybody got an idea about how to get to space?"

# CHAPTER 40

Eli wasn't sure whether to gape in wide-eyed amazement or start laughing uncontrollably as the security personnel turned to face the officer who'd accosted them.

"I've been waiting for an hour for you to report and *you will stand at attention while I'm talking to you,*" snapped Commander Natalie Taylor, as she stepped between them, her eyes flashing in what was hopefully a simulacrum of cold fury.

"Commander," said the woman, who was clearly the braver of the two, "we received a report that your officers attempted to access a restricted file."

Taylor sighed and pressed thumb and forefinger to her temples. "Of course they did. Look, I asked them to retrieve an archival data store for analysis at NICOM and they probably forgot they were supposed to clear it with the deputy director first." She arched a slender eyebrow at them, and Eli found his mouth going dry despite his best efforts.

"Uh... sorry, uh, commander. I–"

"I'm not interested in your excuses, lieutenant. I suppose I'll have to go up to see Deputy Director Kester myself."

"He may be off campus," started the other security officer

gamely, earning a glare from his partner, who was still trying to maintain a degree of authority in the situation.

"May I see your credentials, commander?" she asked Taylor.

The commander's attention shifted like the wind and Eli could see the security officer's erstwhile confidence shiver like a tall tree. "Oh, of course," she said, in a saccharine sweet tone that Eli was glad to not be on the receiving end of. "Let me just call up Admiral Chatterjee, Officer…" She made a show of glancing down at the ID tag on the woman's uniform, "Wecker, is it? I'm sure she would be delighted to take time out of her busy schedule to confirm my orders for you."

Basically, it had all gone downhill for the security officer since the word 'admiral,' and by the time Taylor had gotten to the end of her sentence, Officer Wecker was standing far too straight, trying to avoid even the least bit of impropriety. "That won't be necessary, commander. I apologize for the inconvenience." She drove an elbow into her slouching compatriot, who muttered 'very sorry' while trying not to look as though he was about to throw up.

"Good. Now, if that's all resolved to your *satisfaction*, I will be taking my officers to the fourteenth floor." And with that, Taylor snapped her fingers in Eli and Tapper's direction and walked toward the lift, which had stood empty since their arrival, as though waiting for them.

The two security officers watched them go and, just before the doors slid closed, Tapper tossed them a salute, one corner of his mouth curled up in a barely restrained grin.

Eli let out a breath almost in unison with the doors whooshing closed. "Holy shit, that was close."

"Nice timing, Commander," said Tapper. "Where did you come from?"

Taylor rolled her eyes, leaning back against the wall of the lift. "Simon contacted me this morning to say you might need a hand, and fortunately, I'd just gotten back in system from Centauri."

"Well, we appreciate the assis–"

"What the *hell* do you two think you're doing, trying to access restricted files at CID headquarters? Whose brilliant plan was this?"

Tapper and Eli exchanged a glance. "The boss's."

"Absolutely," said Eli.

"Not ours."

"Nope. We just go where we're told."

"Well," said Taylor, glancing at the steadily rising numbers on the lift display, "I suppose I should be glad you didn't just blow up the building."

"That was the backup plan," said Tapper.

"After we evacuated it!" Eli added.

The commander looked like she was going to object, but then waved it aside. "We don't have time. Get me up to speed."

They had just enough time to fill her in on the bare details they'd uncovered about Kassandra when the lift doors slid open into a lobby far more posh than the one below. Wood paneling with honeyed tones lined the walls, while the lush carpet absorbed their footfalls no less effectively than a high-end baffle. Dotted throughout the room were several small tables, many of which held exquisite vases or other works of sculpture. Light streamed in from large glass windows on either side of them, dousing the whole room in a pleasant, almost homey feel that was a long way from the cold, utilitarian air of the conference room they'd been assigned at Yamanaka Base. *You'd think spies wouldn't want something quite this open*. But it probably got boring when you were stuck in a windowless room all the time.

"Okay, I'm calling an audible," Taylor said as they stepped out. "We need more details, but that's going to require someone with deputy director clearance or higher."

"Uhhh, and you think Kester's going to help us?" said Eli, following in her wake.

"He's not," Taylor said quietly, as they crossed the waiting room towards a large desk. Behind it sat a thin blonde man, working on a holo terminal, and a frosted glass door with 'Deputy Director of Operations' on the nameplate. "Which is why you're going to distract his assistant while I hack into the terminal in his office. I need two minutes."

Eli shot a glance at Tapper who shrugged as if to say 'we're just here to follow orders.' *Can't blame her – we didn't exactly put our best foot forward. Unless you count sticking it in our mouth.* Any objection he may have had died in his throat.

Taylor strode up to the desk, her best military bearing on display, towering over the young man. To his credit, he didn't let himself immediately get distracted, finishing what he was doing on the holoscreen before dismissing it, folding his hands, and fixing Taylor with a polite if insincere smile.

"Good afternoon…" His eyes sought out her rank tabs. "Commander. May I help you?"

"I'm here to see Deputy Director Kester."

"I see. And do you have an appointment?" The much too pleasant tone suggested he already knew the answer.

"I do not. But this is a matter of urgent importance."

"I'm sure." False sympathy flooded his voice – the man was probably great at funerals – but he didn't seem to be in danger of budging. "Unfortunately, Director Kester is unavailable at the moment. Perhaps you'd care to leave a message?"

Tapper had drifted away from the desk and was peering closely at the detail work on one of the vases: white, with a geometric blue and green design that spiraled outward on the side, almost dizzying in nature.

*Oh well, here goes nothing.*

"What are you doing, sergeant?" said Eli, striding over towards him. "Be careful with that."

"I am being careful, *sir*." Tapper drew himself up. "I wouldn't touch an antique like this."

Out of the corner of Eli's eye, he could see the expression on the assistant's face go fixed, gaze darting to them, even as Taylor continued to press him.

"This isn't something I can leave a message about, mister... what's your name?"

"Uh, Lawson, ma'am." His attention was ping-ponging back and forth between the officer in his face and Tapper and Eli hovering near the vase.

"Antique? Come on," Eli scoffed. "There's no way they put something this valuable out in the middle of a waiting room. That's preposterous."

"I'm telling you, sir. I've been to the Royal Museum on Haran, and this," Tapper jabbed a finger perilously close the vase, "is clearly from the early Isak period."

Eli fancied he could hear the assistant sweating from across the room.

"Uh, if you'll excuse me, commander, I just need to–" He'd already pushed back his chair and stood, as though gravity was drawing him towards the two men arguing about the vase.

"Mr Lawson, this is a matter of national security."

"I understand that, ma'am, but as I said, Director Kester is not in."

"I can wait."

Lawson wrung his hands. "Very well, just give me one moment." And then he was zipping around the desk like a fighter launched from a carrier, making a beeline towards Eli and Tapper.

*Almost there, just need to take it up one small notch...* "Sergeant, I'm telling you, this thing is a replica, you can tell by the texture of the material–" And Eli reached out to touch the vase.

There was a wordless cry as Lawson hurled himself towards them, trying to intercept Eli's finger before it made contact. Behind him, Eli just had time to see Taylor slip through the door behind the aide's desk, and mentally he started the clock.

Tapper reached forward, as if to help steady the table on which the vase stood, and somehow, despite it being perfectly stable already, the vase started wobbling in widening concentric circles.

Eyes wide, Lawson dove and seized the vase with both hands before it could tip all the way over, letting out an audible squeak of relief, slightly tinged with horror as he realized that he was actually now touching the vase himself.

"If you would kindly step back, gentlemen," he managed in a strangled voice. Gently, ever so gently, he settled the vase back on its table, then stepped back with the delicacy of someone withdrawing from the presence of royalty.

"Settle a bet for me, mate. Tell my lieutenant over there that this thing's the genuine article."

"Yes, it is. It was a gift from the Harani ambassador to the former director of CID," said Lawson.

"No kidding," said Eli, leaning in close to peer at it while Lawson apparently restrained the urge to seize him by the scruff of the neck. "How much would you say something like this goes for?"

"My understanding is that it is immensely valuable." Lawson hovered closer, not quite willing to drag him away from the table, despite his inclinations. "And almost certainly irreplaceable. Might I have you gentlemen take a seat while I assist the commander?" He started to turn back towards the desk.

But Taylor still wasn't out, which meant Lawson's attention had to stay on them. Two minutes, the commander had said, and it couldn't have been more than one. So all they needed was to keep him busy just a little longer. *Ugh, reaching pretty deep here.*

"Say, we haven't met before, have we?" said Eli.

Lawson drew himself up, frowning. "I don't believe we have. Perhaps you have me confused with someone else."

"Nah, I don't think so. Talbot, back me up here."

The sergeant was holding his chin in one hand, eyes narrowed in speculation. "He does look familiar, but can't quite…" He snapped his fingers suddenly. "You know what? He's the spitting image of that guy in the vids."

Eli stepped backed from Lawson, giving him an appraising look of his own. He raised his hands, as if framing the assistant in a camera. "Oh *yeah*. The guy we just saw the other week in the… which one was it? The one that took place during the war?"

"Right, right. Handsome devil. People ever tell you that? That you look like wossisname?"

"Well, that is, I mean, nobody's ever *said* anything, but I suppose I've always thought…" Lawson's cheeks had turned a rather pleased shade of pink as he looked down at the carpet.

"That look! That's the one. Damn, it's uncanny, LT. Maybe he could have a career in the vids too."

"I should think so. As a body double at least."

"Do you really think so?" Lawson's head wagged between the two of them. "I mean, as a kid I always wanted to, but then I had to find a real job…" As soon as he said the word, he perked up, straightening his spine as he remembered precisely where he was and what he was supposed to be doing. He took a step back, as though moving out of range of whatever flattery they had been plying him with, and cleared his throat. "Anyway, very kind, thank you, but I'm afraid I've left the commander waiting."

He started to turn back around and Eli's heart leapt into his throat. *Oh crap, oh crap…*

"Personally, I don't see the resemblance." Commander Taylor's voice dripped with sarcasm. "But don't mind me, I'm just dealing with matters of urgent Commonwealth security here."

Relief washed over Eli as he saw her leaning against the edge of Lawson's desk, arms crossed over her chest and wearing a dubious expression that he knew all too well.

Lawson flamed scarlet as he stepped back around the desk. "My apologies, commander. Now, did you want to leave a message?"

Taylor's lips thinned into a line. "You know what? I don't have all day. I'll find Deputy Director Kester and relay the message myself. Thanks for all your *help*." And with that, she turned on her heel and stalked back towards the lift; as she passed, Eli and Tapper fell into her wake like ice particles trailing a comet.

The lift door slid closed behind them and the car sank back towards the lobby.

Eli faced forward, then shot a look towards Taylor. "Hope that was enough time, commander."

She smiled. "And then some. CID really needs to stop allowing fingerprint authentication, given that people's offices are just *brimming* with their fingerprints. It's a spy's dream come true."

"Did you get what we needed?"

The smile curled into a frown. "Even with Kester's access I couldn't find anything about AUGUR. But I did manage to fill in some blanks on Alys Costa's last mission before she left CID."

*So this wasn't a total loss.* Eli glanced over at Tapper, but the sergeant appeared lost in thought, staring up at the lights in the lift car. "Sarge?"

Tapper shook his head, looking quizzical. "You know, funny thing is, I feel like I *did* know him from somewhere."

There was a chime from the direction of Taylor, and she raised her sleeve to answer it. "Simon? Yes, I've got our wayward pair, and we're on our way…" Her eyebrows climbed for the sky. "I'm sorry, you need to get *where*?"

# CHAPTER 41

The vehicle that pulled up next to them was an unusual one: it had a large boxy chassis that looked almost more suited for military usage than, say, tooling around the city streets.

*Good thing, too,* thought Addy as she, Kovalic, and Page piled in, since otherwise the three of them wouldn't have fit alongside Brody, Tapper, and Commander Taylor. The blond woman cast a look over her shoulder at Addy, and gave her a tight but genuine smile – and by now Addy could tell the difference, having spent a lot of time under the other woman's scrutiny – before her eyes softened at Kovalic's appearance.

"Looks like we've got a full boat," said the commander, once they'd found seats, and she'd pulled away from the curb. "It's good to see you, Lieutenant Page, though I wish it were under different circumstances."

"The feeling is mutual, commander."

"Status report, Simon?"

"Kassandra has the data chip. We think her plan is to expose AUGUR's existence to the entire Commonwealth."

"A more expansive version of the local area hack I performed at Oluo Plaza," said Page. If he felt any remorse about having assisted a terrorist organization, it wasn't immediately obvious.

*Jesus, how does anybody get a read on that guy?*

"I thought you said space," said Brody. "Where the hell does space come into it?"

"She'll want to get her message out as broadly as possible," said Kovalic, "which means planetwide. With the upcoming communications interconnect, Station Zero is the logical choice."

"Boy, do I not like where this is going."

Kovalic leaned forward, resting his hands on the front seats. "Nat, we need to get up there."

"Or," she pointed out, not taking her eyes off the road, "I could just alert the naval security detachment onboard and *they* can take care of Kassandra. Honestly, Simon, you don't have to do all of this yourself."

"Station Zero runs on a skeleton crew," said Page. "The naval security detachment is only one team, and if I know Kassandra, she's prepared for them. Moreover, even if she is neutralized by the Commonwealth military, the data chip ends up..."

"...right back in CID's hands," finished Tapper.

*Square one.* Only worse, because if Station Zero could be used as a platform to enable AUGUR throughout not just the capital city but the entirety of Nova, who knew what purposes CID could turn it to? Kassandra and her Novan Liberation Front started to sound a whole lot less like paranoid terrorists when the government really was abusing its citizenry's trust.

"We can't let that happen," she heard herself saying, before she'd even consciously formulated the words.

"What about the CID archives?" said Kovalic, eyeing Brody and Tapper. "Anything useful?"

Tapper exchanged a glance with Brody as he touched a

few controls on his sleeve. "You're going to love this, boss. Our friend Kassandra is actually a decommissioned CID operative: Alys Costa." A holo projection of a CID dossier appeared, hovering in the backseat.

Addy's mouth went dryer than the plains of Nova's desert moon. "That's the woman I fought at the safe house." *Finally, some of these goddamn puzzle pieces start fitting together.*

"Her last op six years ago, before being cut loose by CID, was codenamed PYTHIA. We don't know exactly what it entailed, but I can tell you who signed off on it: Kester's predecessor as deputy director of operations – who's since moved into swankier digs."

Kovalic's gray eyes lit up. "Françoise Özkul."

"One and the same."

"That helps clear up the personal angle, at least. Whatever happened on PYTHIA, it seems like it left a bad taste in Kassandra's mouth. No surprise her old boss was on her hit list."

Addy huffed a laugh. "Can't entirely blame her. I've had a few COs that I'd have liked to kick out an airlock." Five pairs of eyes swiveled towards her, including Taylor's in the rearview mirror. "Present company excluded, of course."

"But why use her CID code name as her nom de guerre?" Brody piped up, his brow furrowing. "Seems kind of obvious."

Kovalic's mouth twisted into a knot. "I think it was a warning. She *wanted* Özkul to know she was coming."

"Anyway," said Tapper, "we think this might explain how Kassandra knew to target AUGUR in the first place. She must have been read in on it at some point during her tenure."

"Could be," said Kovalic. But Addy could see the lingering

doubt in his eyes – something still wasn't adding up, apparently. Whatever it was, he pushed through it, focusing back in on the rest of the team. "This doesn't change the plan. We still need to find a ship and get to Station Zero as soon as we can."

In the front seat, Taylor exhaled, then nodded as if coming to a decision. "I can get you a ship. If we're lucky, we might beat Costa and her team to the punch – they probably need to find a way up the tether, which might take them a while."

"Oh good," said Tapper. "Trusting to luck. That always goes *great*."

To Addy's utter lack of surprise, Taylor delivered exactly on her promise. Less than half an hour later, they'd been waved past a gate guard at the headquarters of Naval Intelligence Command and onto the tarmac, where they found a small transport waiting for them. The commander had made some calls en route and the ship was already fueled and prepped.

*Just one problem.*

"Only four seats," said Tapper, surveying the group. "We drawing straws?"

"Brody, Sayers, Page, you're with me," said Kovalic. "Nat, Tap, we may need you to run interference on the ground for us."

Tapper tipped him a salute. "Have a fun outing with the kids. Don't let them eat too much sugar – you know how they get."

"And Simon?" Taylor added, touching his arm. "Try to come back in one piece."

Addy climbed the rear ramp into the transport while they said their goodbyes, taking the seat behind the pilot's. Brody was already flipping switches and checking readouts; sitting directly behind him meant it was the one place he couldn't really make eye contact with her. *Oh yes, this seems like an ideal permanent situation. When this is over, we really need to sit down and talk.*

It probably said something about her that the idea of flying to a space station in order to confront a hostile terrorist organization seemed more appealing.

She buckled herself into the five-point harness, pulling on the straps to test them. A holster with a KO gun had been left on her seat and she clipped it to her waistband. She'd have preferred something with a little more kick, but live ammo and a space station was a bad mix.

A moment later, Kovalic and Page joined them, the major taking the co-pilot seat with Page behind him. Craning his neck to make sure everybody was onboard, Brody sealed the cockpit and Addy felt the repulsors hum to life beneath her.

"Commander Taylor arranged for us to be cleared all the way to Station Zero," said Brody. "So I hope none of you need to make a rest stop, because this trip is going to be an express." And with that, the ship rose from the ground and turned skyward.

"All available speed, lieutenant," said Kovalic, tugging his own restraints.

Addy didn't need to see Brody's face to imagine the grin on it. *Oh no.* Instinctively, she grasped the edges of the seat and braced herself and she was not disappointed when the ship shot forward and what felt like all her internal organs were pressed against the rear of her ribcage.

Dimly she thought she could hear the pilot cackling as the ground disappeared far below them, quickly transmuting into a mottled brown quilt. Within moments they were enveloped in a cloud layer and, almost as quickly, had punched through it, rising into the rich blue tapestry of the sky.

Addy sucked in a lungful of air as the pressure on her chest relaxed and the ship leveled out. *I never thought I'd miss flying civilian.*

"On course," Brody reported. "ETA to Station Zero is one-five minutes."

Kovalic had brought up a holoscreen depicting a schematic of the wheel-shaped station, and the tether that connected its hub back down to the planet's surface. The cable itself was only around a dozen centimeters at its widest point, with a cross-section measured in micrometers. Composed of miles of carbon nanothreads, the ribbon was carefully woven by an advanced process that made the material strong enough to maintain structural integrity, but flexible enough to deal with the reality of being connected to the planet below. That meant dealing with the attendant issues of weather, rotation, and gravity – all those things that you didn't really have to worry about in space. But, for all that trouble, it made moving bulky and heavy cargo into space easier and cheaper than loading up freighters, especially for the host of communications satellites that ConComm was deploying.

The tether was just visible in the distance now, a silver shimmering line that might easily have been mistaken for a trick of the eye, stretching directly through the horizon and up endlessly into the sky. Thankfully, the ship's HUD showed a hazy, bright green outline around the tether, providing a wide berth for the pilot to avoid colliding with the strand.

The elevator itself was a boxy affair the size of a small

freighter, big enough to contain not only several dozen cargo containers, but also a personnel compartment. A series of mechanical rollers atop and below the elevator clamped around the ribbon, providing the mechanism by which it climbed from the surface to the station. From this far away, the car was nothing more than a blip on the horizon, red and green lights flashing like those on an aircraft.

"That's the 15.35, right on schedule," said Kovalic, consulting the schematic in front of him. "Technical parts and resupply, according to the manifest."

"And probably more than a few things that aren't on the manifest," said Page, leaning forward.

Addy shook her head. "Why don't we just contact the station and tell them to lock down the elevator before it reaches them? Then we can scoop up Costa and her team at our leisure."

"Or send it back down," suggested Brody. "Arrest them at the bottom."

"The elevator's automated," said Page. "Station control could override, but Costa would know something's up."

And what Page didn't say was that Kassandra clearly wasn't the type to go into such a situation unprepared. Addy's mind flashed back to her fight with the woman on the rooftop, and the ensuing explosion at the safehouse; the heart-stopping moment when she'd thought Brody might have still been inside. *She knows she'll be trapped on the elevator car, and she'll be ready for it.*

"So, are we going to beat it there?" Kovalic asked.

"I'm at max velocity," said Brody. "We'll be leaving the atmosphere in a few moments – when we lose the drag, we should be able to up the speed." He glanced at the schematic on Kovalic's holoscreen, on which the elevator car rose steadily towards the station. "But it's going to be damn close."

Addy's mouth set in a grim line and she found herself reaching down to press the reassuring weight of the weapon at her side. *Looks like it's going to be a fight after all. Fine by me.* It had been a frustrating few days, and she could already feel her pulse amping up at the idea of a rematch with Kassandra.

A shimmy rippled through the ship as it left the bonds of Nova's atmosphere, the ride smoothing out as the blue of sky shifted to the black of space, punctuated by the pinpricks of stars. And, hanging in the distance, the wheel-and-spokes design of Station Zero. It had been built in an era before artificial gravity generators had been commonplace on stations, instead relying on the older method of harnessing centripetal force from a rotating wheel. But converting it to the space elevator counterweight had meant retrofitting the whole thing, including installing gravity generators in the previously weightless hub.

The silvery filament of the tether glimmered starkly against the pitch black backdrop of space, as though the station were a yo-yo attached to the globe beneath. Lights flashed along the perimeter, signaling the various docking ports.

"Station Zero Control, this is NICOM Transport... uh..." Brody scanned the console, "NI32-8. Requesting permission to dock."

Static filtered over the channel. Brody frowned and toggled the com again. "Repeat, NI32-8. Do you have a berth for us?"

After a moment, there was another sputter of static, and then a voice – surprisingly tense – punched through. "NI32-

8, abort docking. No berths available at this time. Reverse course."

Kovalic gave Brody a sharp look, but the pilot was already pulling up a holodisplay, even as he throttled down, bringing the ship to a stop. "Uh, so that's a lie. I'm reading literally *one* emergency shuttle currently docked and there are three more ports that could easily accommodate us."

Addy frowned. "Did the elevator arrive already? Could Costa have taken control?"

"I don't think so," said Kovalic, pointing to the schematic in front of him. "They're still two minutes out." He rubbed his chin, then nodded to Brody. "Can you get me a tightbeam signal to the station?"

*Tightbeam?* The point-to-point comm system was generally a backup, since it only worked via line-of-sight – though, admittedly, in space, line-of-sight could go a long way. Usually it was only employed in situations where you wanted to cut through jamming or avoid interception.

"Can a dolphin jump through a – uh, yes, yes I can," said Brody at a glare from the major. "Opening tightbeam channel."

"Station Zero Control, this is Major Kaplan of Naval Intelligence Command." The fake credentials rolled right off his tongue without a hitch. "Status report."

The same voice came on the line, but this time it sounded almost relieved. "Major, thank god. The operations crew on the elevator has been compromised and I'm told there's an explosive device on the car – if we send them back down, hold the car, or allow anybody else to dock, they'll detonate it. They also said they're monitoring all broadcast radio signals to and from the station. We would have tried to tightbeam the nearest Commonwealth Naval vessel, but, uh, we weren't sure how risky it would be." Tension had flooded their voice again.

Addy had never regretted being right quite this much. *Well, shit.*

Kovalic exchanged a look with the rest of the crew. "Copy that, Control. How many security personnel do you have onboard?"

"Just one fireteam – three marines. But the hijackers are demanding they all be present in the cargo terminal, visibly disarmed, when the elevator arrives."

"Understood. Standby, Control."

There was a strangled quality to the voice, as though they'd tried to swallow and cough at the same. "Uhhh, standing by."

Kovalic muted the comm. "So, we've got an unknown number of hostiles, armed with an explosive, aboard a vulnerable target. I'm taking suggestions."

"Maybe they're bluffing…" Brody started, before trailing off, and Addy knew he too was remembering the explosion at the safe house.

Page picked up on it as well. "Costa was well-trained in explosives, and she was a former CID operative. She knows the playbook."

"Then we throw out the playbook," said Kovalic. "Because letting them have unfettered control of the station isn't an option. And neither is blowing up the tether."

Addy glanced at the station in the distance. She could just see the elevator car with the naked eye now, lights flashing on the box's corners as it ground slowly but inexorably towards the cargo terminal where the tether attached to the center of the station. From the display on Kovalic's console, it was only a few moments out. She fidgeted in her seat, then checked the charge on her knockout gun again; the illuminated bars on the back still showed green, as they had the first three times she'd looked.

*Enough sitting around.* "So," she said. "If we can't dock the ship, I guess we're going for a walk."

# CHAPTER 42

Kovalic locked the vacsuit's gloves into place and hefted his helmet. Beside him, Page and Sayers were doing the same, all of them crowded into the transport's cramped rear compartment. The bulky suits were unwieldy but at least they looked to have been well maintained; moreover, they were military issue, which meant that they were designed to accommodate soldiers carrying weapons, a thought that brought Kovalic some relief as he strapped a sidearm to his thigh.

"So," he said, looking back and forth between his operatives. "Page and I will make for the operations center to locate the AUGUR terminal and intercept Costa before she takes control of the system. Sayers, your top priority is to find and disarm the explosive onboard the elevator. We can't be sure how Costa's team is deployed, so prepare for some resistance."

The woman shifted uncomfortably, her mouth set in a thin line. Kovalic knew she wanted another shot at Costa, and while he had no doubt that she'd be more than capable of taking the ex-CID operative down, he only had so many personnel to go around.

"Major," came Brody's voice, filtered through the

intercom. "I've got Commander Taylor on tightbeam for you. I've given her an overview, best I can. Signal's a little spotty because of the atmosphere, but patching her through."

Nat's voice, choppy and degraded, filtered over the ship's intercom. "Si... n. Copy?"

"We've got you. We're prepping for EVA now. I need you to run interference on the ground."

"Underst... d. Can't let... command know. May... spatch another team."

"Just what we need," Sayers muttered. "A shootout on a space station. That's likely to get us all killed."

Kovalic ignored the commentary, though privately he didn't disagree. Still, he'd put the three of them up against even an elite Commonwealth Navy special ops team if it came down to it. Anyway, they were already here; the rest was moot. By the time another team arrived, it ought to be over.

One way or another.

"Copy that. Is Tapper there?"

There was a pause, then the sergeant's gravelly tones came through. "Here, boss. ...'s up?"

"Tap, I'm sending Sayers to disarm the explosive. I may need you to walk her through it." He cocked an eye in her direction; she looked ready to object, then seemed to think better of it, and gave him a curt nod. After the last several months of operating on the team, she'd recognized her limits. Suppressing your pride was a key part of the job – always be ready to admit what you didn't know, because pretending you did could get a lot of people killed.

"...py that."

"Good. Standby. Brody, you got us in position?"

"Maneuvering now," said the pilot over the intercom. "I'll

maintain the tightbeam relay to the surface as best I can, but once you're onboard the station we'll be out of contact. You'll need to signal me when the explosives are secured."

Hardly ideal. They might be able to patch into the station's internal comm system once they were there but it depended how closely Costa and her team were keeping an eye on things. If Nova Front gained control of the operations center first, then this was going to be a hell of an upward climb.

"Roger that," said Kovalic. He picked up the vacsuit helmet and pulled it on, twisting the locking collar to seal. The suit's environmental systems kicked on, the internal air supply hissing to life. Next to him, Sayers and Page donned their own suits, each giving him a thumbs up once they'd established everything was working properly.

Kovalic toggled the suit comm with his chin. "Okay, Brody. We're locked. Pop this can."

"Depressurizing now."

The compartment's lighting turned a deep dark red, and Kovalic could hear the sound of the air being pumped out of the compartment and then, as the last of it was evacuated, nothing. A green light flashed and the rear hatch opened into the dark of space.

Kovalic had spent plenty of time in vacuum during his service in the Commonwealth marines, and though there hadn't been as much call for it in recent operations his training came flooding back as he stepped into the void: pick a point to orient yourself; remember to breathe; stay focused.

Brody had spun the transport, orienting the ship's rear airlock towards the station, just a few kilometers away. Kovalic kept his eyes on the structure as he floated out of the ship, summoning the heads-up display to keep him apprised of the distance to his target. The relative position of his teammates were two small blips aft and to either side of him, the transport a larger dot behind them. His breath was loud in his ears but he did his best to ignore it, instead toggling the tightbeam comm system to loop in the rest of the team.

"Transport, this is One." No time for clever code names on this op, so good old-fashioned numbers it was. "We're clear. Passing mark one."

"Roger that, One. Moving to station-keeping. Good luck."

Kovalic watched the blip signifying the transport drift away; hopefully they'd executed this quickly enough that it looked like the transport had merely turned around once it had been informed that docking was unavailable. He wasn't sure how Costa was monitoring the ship traffic, but three people in vacsuits ought to be small enough to avoid detection.

"Two, Three, head to your marks."

There were double-clicks of acknowledgement from Sayers and Page over the comm channels as they engaged their reaction control systems, small jets of gas propelling them towards their destinations.

Working the thumbstick in his right glove, he directed the thrusters to push him towards the hub of the wheel, where the operations center was located. The blips on his heads-up display diverged; Page kept with him as Sayers jetted towards the cargo terminal at the bottom of the hub, where the tether connected.

He didn't love the idea of sending Sayers in without any backup at all, especially without knowing if the explosive had been left guarded, but he suspected that Costa would be the more difficult of the two targets, and Page was the only one of them who had any idea how she thought, what she might do. Maybe he should have sent him with Sayers to neutralize the bomb first, but what was done was done. No point in second-guessing it now.

The station got bigger in a hurry, expanding to fill the view through Kovalic's helmet. Not the largest structure he'd been this close to in space – an Illyrican dreadnought was still probably two or three times the size of it, and the massive bulk of Jericho Station was more like twenty – but something about the way it hung over the glowing orb of the planet Nova made it seem even larger, whether it was optical illusion or even just a frame of reference.

The station's hub was a spherical structure about the size of a low-rise office building, around fifty meters in diameter; the outer ring stretched another fifteen meters in either direction, connected by half a dozen long cylindrical spokes just thick enough for a couple people to pass through abreast. Small truck-sized habitat pods were dotted around the outer rim, interspersed with the occasional lab, technical facility, or docking port. On Jericho Station, people lived, worked, ate, socialized, and so on; Station Zero, by comparison, had no permanent population: just a rotating complement of around twenty military, technical, and scientific personnel. Habitable as Nova was, there was little point in building a massive space station overhead, at least for the moment. Moving cargo up and down the tether had its advantages, but the abundance of shuttles and transports with orbital capability had limited the space elevator to specific uses, including as a launching platform for satellites.

He was just a few hundred meters away from the hub when his heads-up display located the beacons for the personnel airlocks. There were two on opposite sides of the central sphere, both designed for maintenance via EVA, though they were not immediately adjacent to the ops center, on the station's top level. He toggled the tightbeam to Page.

"We don't know exactly where Costa's team is, but I'm thinking a pincer move is our best option to catch them unaware. They won't have a good sense of our numbers."

"Agreed," said Page. "I'm guessing her squad is small... no more than half a dozen. Getting even that many up the tether was probably a challenge."

Three on six – still not great odds. But if Sayers could disarm the bomb, that could free up the station's military detachment to help level the playing field. On the HUD, he could see her blip approaching the elevator car hanging below the hub and he subconsciously found himself muttering one of the prayers his mother had been so fond of.

As he and Page closed on the hub, they split down the middle, Kovalic heading left to one airlock while Page took the right side.

"Ingress in two minutes on my mark... mark." Kovalic heard Page's acknowledgement as the suits synced their mission clocks. With the hub in between them, they'd be out of tightbeam contact – they could have bounced it back to the transport, but they'd lose contact as soon as they were inside anyway, so better to stick to a schedule.

As long as they could, anyway. These ops had a way of not going to plan.

Reaching the airlock was easy enough, and though it was nominally secured with a keypad, Kovalic knew how these things worked: nobody wanted to be stuck outside in an emergency or, more to the point, nobody wanted to be responsible for someone *else* getting stuck outside. Plus, hostile forces trying to sneak onto the station from cold space were not exactly a daily occurrence high above the Commonwealth's capital planet.

He tried 0000, 1234, and 1111 and, on the third try, the light blinked green and the outer hatch irised open, allowing him to float into the airlock proper. A glance at his mission clock showed that he'd just about nailed the two minute mark, which hopefully meant that Page was on schedule on the other side. If anything, Page was probably savvy enough to crack the lock without even having to resort to random guessing.

Once inside, he clicked his gravboots' heels together and felt the inverse repulsors glom onto the decking. At a touch, the outer airlock door closed and the small compartment began to cycle the air back in. He kept his helmet and vacsuit on – just on the off chance that Costa and her crew had already taken ops and decided to override and shoot him back out into space.

But the cycle finished uneventfully and he was able to open the inside door; no security code here, because once you were already in, hey, who cared? Drawing the KO gun from its holster, he pressed himself against one wall and checked both directions in the corridor that ran around the station's circumference. Clear.

With the airlock door closed and sealed behind him, he hastily pulled off the helmet and stripped out of the vacsuit. Great against the harsh environment of space, not so great if you wanted to move fast enough to avoid getting shot. He clicked off his gravboots before removing them; the hub's artificial gravity would at least make navigating it a bit easier.

Raising his sleeve, he brought up the schematics of the station that he'd loaded while on the shuttle. The airlocks were on the middle level of the hub, with the ops center two levels up and the cargo area two levels below. Ladders bridged the levels at roughly ninety-degree intervals around the station's circumference, and the airlock he'd entered from sat halfway between two of them, about a twenty-meter walk in either direction.

From the schematic, it looked as though the one to his left might be the better option, providing at least a modicum of cover when entering the ops center. Halfway there, he passed a terminal and attempted to connect his sleeve to the station's network, only to find that it had been largely shut down, leaving only essential systems like gravity and life support running. Internal communications were definitely disabled, probably at Costa's demand. Kovalic had hoped to piggyback on the network to stay in touch with Page, but it looked like they were on their own for the moment.

Upon reaching the ladder, he peeked both down and upward, covering the openings with his sidearm until he was confident that nobody was about to spring from either direction. Keeping the KO gun in his right hand, he awkwardly climbed up to the next level of the station, poking his head through to survey the compartment.

The level below the ops center appeared to mainly be for systems maintenance, with banks of servers lining the walls, as well as panels for environmental control: heating, plumbing, ventilation. Equipment whirred away at a frankly raucous level, despite the soundproofing foam that had been secured to the walls.

At least they probably wouldn't hear him coming.

He took the next level of ladder slower than before,

creeping upward towards the operations center. Fortunately, no hatches blocked his way – like the spokes that led to the station's outer ring, the station's control room could be sealed, but only in an emergency depressurization scenario. Plus, again, nobody worried overly about security when you were tens of thousands of kilometers above the surface of what, up until this week anyway, was the safest planet in the Commonwealth. Naive? Maybe. But Kovalic couldn't blame them for not planning for every single eventuality, especially the unlikely ones like 'terrorists threaten to blow up your space elevator in order to seize control of your station.'

As his head rose into the ops center, he took in the scene: the large circular room was ringed with displays showing a variety of camera feeds, onboard conditions, and other information about the station. Sitting against one wall, hands on their heads, sat four people in light blue jumpsuits, each emblazoned with the insignia of the Commonwealth's civilian space agency.

Nearby stood a pale man with dark hair, who was hard at work on one of the terminals, a pistol sitting on a console just within his reach. Next to him was a woman with dark brown skin and a purple crop cut; she had a sidearm tucked in her waistband and her eyes on the crew.

And standing over the Commonwealth personnel, carrying a pistol loosely in one hand as she surveyed the displays before her, was the same woman he'd seen beneath the bookshop, easily recognizable even from an out-of-date dossier picture.

Alys Costa.

# CHAPTER 43

Addy glided towards the elevator car, gently applying the thrusters on her suit while trying not to throw up in her helmet. She'd fixed her gaze on the container, now at the top of the long silver strand; her heads-up display helpfully marked the personnel access hatch on its side.

She was very pointedly not looking down at the globe below her.

*If I don't look down, I won't think about falling.* Logically, she knew she wasn't really in danger of falling onto the planet from space, but her brain wasn't really trucking with logic right now. All she knew was that it *looked* like it was down, and that was good enough for her brain to trigger all those reflexes that fired up when you were about to tumble off a cliff.

*The hatch. Look at the hatch.*

Her breathing sounded loud in her ears but she forced herself to focus on the rectangle on the side of the elevator car, and how it was getting closer and closer with each second, until finally it was just a few feet away and she could use her thrusters to bring her to a stop.

That had been the easy part.

Somewhere in this 40-meter long container was an

explosive device that might rip apart this entire station, not to mention severing a multi-thousand kilometer long strand of highly tensile material. And she had to find it and disarm it before everything went to shit.

*Just another day at the office.*

First problem: the hatch was locked. She toggled the tightbeam transmitter and locked on to the transport's signal.

"Four, it's Two – you copy?"

"Five by five, Four." Brody sounded like he was standing next to her, so much so that she almost jumped at his voice.

"I need to bypass the outer airlock security. Any ideas from the ground?" She hoped Taylor had a trick up her sleeve; Tapper would probably just suggest blowing it up.

"Oh, oh! I know this one. There should be a manual release under the maintenance panel to the right. Standard procedure for any space-capable vehicle. But it's only functional in an emergency, so you'll need to kill the power to the hatch first."

"Copy that. Wait one."

She nudged herself closer to the door and saw the panel Brody was talking about: a small square plate adjacent to the hatch. She pulled the panel open and flipped on her helmet light to reveal a mess of wiring next to a heavy metal handle.

"Four, there are a whole bunch of cables. Which one cuts the power?"

"It should be the thick red one."

Addy sorted through the cables: thick black, thin red, medium silver... no thick red. If she could have pinched the bridge of her nose through her helmet, she would have, but instead she just gave a heavy sigh.

"No matches, Four." She ran down what they had.

"This is why wiring should always be standard," Brody muttered across the channel. "Hold on, I'm checking schematics."

"Oh sure, I'll just hang out." In hard vacuum, floating next to a space elevator car that contained a bomb. *Just real casual-like.*

She blinked up the mission clock that Kovalic had synced with them, its numbers counting upward at what seemed like an inordinately fast rate. "Any joy, Four? We're running out of time here."

"I'm looking! You try searching for 'manual airlock release power cable.' There's like two thousand results here."

Addy pushed down a growl. This whole mission held up because years ago some electrician had used the wrong color wire. Impatience bubbled up in her chest, pressing outward like it wanted to escape. *I have to get in there.*

"Shit, I'm not finding anything here…" said Brody. "Wait… maybe purple? Is there a purple – or, like, mauve?"

Time was still ticking away on the mission clock and here they were playing 'guess the color.' The impatience finally boiled over. *It's got to be* one *of these. Screw it.* She seized all the cables in her gloved fist and yanked as hard as she could.

There was a spark from the wiring, quickly extinguished by the vacuum and she paused, still holding the cables, but nothing else seemed to happen. Letting out a breath, she reached over and grasped the release lever.

It didn't budge.

"Two, you still with me?" Brody's voice came over comms, a rare note of worry injected in his tone. "Status?"

"Working the problem," said Addy, through gritted teeth as she added her other hand to the mix. But either the door was still power-locked shut or she'd shorted out some other system by mistake. They'd deemed it likely that Costa had left at least some of her team to oversee the bomb, and Addy had been counting on a stealthy insertion to handle them. Now, for all she knew, she'd just rung the doorbell.

Not that it would matter if she couldn't get the damn thing open.

She planted both feet on the side of the elevator car and clicked her heels to activate her gravboots, feeling the *zip* as they adhered to the hull. And then she leaned back and, with all of her might, pulled on the release until it slowly gave way and slid down. Beside her, the airlock door cracked open, just wide enough for her to wedge her gloves in and slide the two halves of the door apart, her muscles straining at the effort. *This is what you're supposed to do in an* emergency? *Would anybody still be alive by the time they'd finished?*

Relief flooded through her. "Door open, Four. I'm heading in. I'll be out of tightbeam range."

"Copy that, Two. Good hunting."

The airlock was dark as she floated in, all the light strips inactive. Where the wall panels should be displaying status information, or providing her with an interface to operate the airlock mechanism, there were just black slabs of inert glass. She reached out and tapped one's surface, but it didn't respond. Nothing in the entire airlock seemed to be operating at all, almost like...

*Oh, shit.* Pulling out all those wires hadn't just killed the power to the airlock door, but to the whole compartment. Which meant not only no lighting, but no way to cycle the air and trigger the inner door – no way for her to get into the car without depressurizing the whole thing.

She stared daggers at the sealed interior door, as though it were somehow responsible for her plight. At least being inside the compartment meant that she was out of tightbeam contact with the transport, and didn't have to tell Brody that she'd blown the whole operation right out the airlock.

Blown right out.

Slowly, a grin crept across Addy's face. *Now we're talking.*

Reversing course, she propelled herself back out the airlock compartment to the exterior entrance, hanging off a gantry while she reestablished contact with Brody.

"Four, this is Two. I got the outer airlock open, but there's no power."

"Uhhh, how exactly did–"

"Let's not waste air assigning blame. The point is I've got an idea but it's, uh, kind of risky. And…" Here she drew a deep breath, pushing down every instinct, honed over two decades of living off her own wits, trusting nobody's counsel but her own, "…I can't do it alone."

Brody's voice came back in a heartbeat, devoid of any and all hesitation. "Copy that, Two. I've got your back. Tell me what you need."

There was something ineffable about his tone, a warmth that suffused her, causing an almost tingling sensation in her chest. The mission on the *Queen Amina* had shown that she wasn't alone in her work, that she could count on the rest of the team, but it was different somehow with Brody – it ran deeper. And while there was an undercurrent of terror at the idea of someone unconditionally supporting her, it was… pleasant, too.

The part of her that had kept her alive all these years rebelled at that, warning her of betrayal or disappointment, but she drowned it out. It had sustained her this long, yes, but maybe, just maybe, it had outlived its usefulness, and was now focused on keeping itself relevant, to the exclusion of what she actually *needed*. She felt it shrink at that revelation, like a scuttling creature with a spotlight on it, and in that moment, she pushed through to the other side.

"All right, then," said Addy. "Here's exactly what I need you to do."

# CHAPTER 44

Kovalic ducked back down the ladder, out of view of the hostiles in the ops center. He certainly hoped Page was mirroring his movements over on the other side, but he hadn't been able to see him from his vantage point at the top.

Having climbed down, he made his way across the maintenance room, and, to his relief, met Page at about the midpoint.

"Three hostiles."

The lieutenant nodded. "All armed, and spread out far enough that we can't guarantee we'll hit them all, even with two well-timed knockout shots."

"And any of them could potentially trigger the explosives in the elevator car," said Kovalic, rubbing a hand across his mouth. Not odds he would have taken on his best day. "Ideally, we'd have Sayers disarm the bomb before making a move on Costa and her team."

"We don't have a lot of time," said Page, glancing up at the ceiling. "Costa isn't going to sit around and wait for us to neutralize her only advantage. It's only a matter of minutes before she's got AUGUR up and running."

"What if we cut power to the comm array? Then she won't be able to connect to AUGUR."

Page shook his head. "Too obvious. She'll know we're here, and she might blow the bomb."

"So we need to slow her down... but in such a way that she doesn't realize we're slowing her down." Kovalic's eyes drifted to the racks of servers around them, blinking and whirring away merrily. Keeping a station running took a significant amount of resources, and when something went wrong – as it invariably did – you fixed it right away, because if you didn't, the results were generally not good. Space wasn't a particularly hospitable place to be. "Can we overload one of these servers? Or disrupt some of the environmental systems? Make it look like a routine breakdown?"

Page cocked his head in thought. "I might be able to cause a small oxygen leak – they'd have to fix that. It might not raise suspicions, but it's still risky."

"I don't know that we have an option that *isn't* risky on the table." Kovalic nodded. "Do it."

It turned out causing an oxygen leak on a space station was frighteningly easy. Page spent a couple moments at the environmental controls before regrouping with Kovalic behind one of the server banks, just outside of view from the ladders descending from the ops center.

"It'll take a moment to kick in." Page glanced at his sleeve. "The station crew might be smart enough to realize that this kind of thing doesn't happen without some help, so maybe they'll play along."

"I just hope you didn't make it too subt–"

A loud klaxon blared overhead, almost forcing Kovalic's eyes crosswise, and red lights started to flash on the corners of the room, even as several of the servers began a cacophony of beeping. Through the ceiling, Kovalic could hear the sudden thump of boots and dimly, even over the noise from the alarm, the sound of people yelling at each other.

Too subtle wasn't going to be a problem.

Out of the corner of one eye, Kovalic saw movement near the top of the ladder he'd climbed up earlier. He tightened his grip on the KO gun and risked a peek around the server rack.

One of Costa's crew – the pale man with dark hair – had apparently been dispatched to deal with the oxygen leak, leaving Costa and her other compatriot in the ops center, probably to watch the station staff. The man seemed to know what he was doing, making a beeline for the same console that Page had tinkered with earlier; he probably had some sort of engineering training.

Kovalic held up one finger towards Page and pointed towards the console. They could just shoot him with the knockout gun and hope that the noise wasn't heard upstairs, but Kovalic was content to play this one a little more carefully when the whole station was at stake.

So he stepped out from behind the rack, pistol held loosely at his side, and leaned against the console. "Hello there."

The pale man started and looked up, his face flushed. "Who the hell are you?" His eyes went to the gun at Kovalic's side and then, uncertainly, started to reach for the weapon holstered in his waistband.

But he never made it. A forearm snaked around his neck, putting him in an adroit headlock. He struggled against the grip, his mouth opening and closing, but after a moment, his eyes rolled back into his head, and he slackened.

Page let the man down gently and checked his pulse. He gave Kovalic a quick nod to signal that he'd live. "One down." Producing a pair of plasticuffs, he secured the man's arms through one of the server racks. "That leaves Costa and one other. And something tells me the same trick isn't going to work twice." He reached over to the console and undid whatever he'd done to cause the alarm, returning the room to a blissful state of, if not silence, then at least as quiet as the background noise of a space station got.

Kovalic checked his sleeve: it had been ten minutes since they'd first breached the station. It might have taken Sayers a minute or two longer to gain access to the elevator car than for them to make it to the operations center, but she ought to be inside by now. The question was how long it would take her to neutralize however many people had been left with the bomb and then defuse it. But the clock was ticking down on Costa's plan, and they couldn't just sit around waiting.

"You've spent time with her – how serious do you think she is?"

Casting a look up at the ceiling, Page let out a breath. "Serious enough. She didn't hesitate to blow up Oluo Plaza or my safe house, and she would have had no compunction about killing the director of CID had I not caused that traffic jam."

"Two on two is probably as good as we're going to get," said Kovalic, glancing up at the ladders. "We go in hard and fast, incapacitate them before either has a chance to set off the explosives. Make it thirty seconds to get back to the ladders, and another thirty to get into position." He set the timer on his sleeve.

The lieutenant's curt nod was all business as they both checked the charges on their pistols and confirmed their chronometers were synced. But, as was par for the course, he didn't ask any further questions, just waited until Kovalic was ready. The same quiet competence the man had always exhibited – probably what he had missed the most during Page's absence from the team.

"Well," said Kovalic. What else was there to say? "I hope this works."

"Yes, sir."

And with that, they moved to either side of the room and climbed up the ladders towards the operations center.

When Kovalic peeked over the lip, he saw that the situation hadn't changed much. Costa was still standing over her hostages, staring speculatively at one of the holo displays, pistol gripped in one hand; on her other side, closer to Page's ladder, her remaining lackey had moved over to take up the console vacated by the man they'd knocked out downstairs. Looked like they hadn't gotten curious about his late return quite yet.

But the positioning meant it was up to Kovalic to take down Costa. He aimed his KO gun as his chronometer continued to count down from ten seconds. They only had one shot at this, he'd better not –

A furtive moment caught his attention from out of the corner of one eye, and he looked over just in time to see one of the station personnel, wide-eyed, give a quick shake of the head as their glance darted towards Costa.

Frowning, he followed their line of sight, but he could only see the woman's back – whatever the hostage was trying to point out wasn't visible from his vantage. His finger grazed the trigger; surely it could wait until after they'd incapacitated the two Nova Front members.

But even as the countdown clock hit three, his gut told him that was the wrong call – they'd miscalculated, missed something. His eyes went to the other side of the room, but there was no way to signal Page to stop.

And so, as the countdown clock hit zero and the heat shimmer of a stun field zipped across the other side of the room, Kovalic threw his own weapon onto the deck in front of him and raised his hands.

"Costa! We surrender."

# CHAPTER 45

On the face of it, Addy's plan sounded insane. But the closer Eli looked, the more he became convinced that it really *was* one-hundred percent insane.

"You sure about this?" He'd powered down most of the transport's systems, but not before matching velocity with Station Zero so that he'd never be more than a minute or two away if he had to get there in a hurry. Before him was Terra Nova, hanging amongst the tapestry of stars; he thought he might be able to see the sprawl of Salaam from orbit, but it would have been easier at night with the city's streets illuminated in a golden grid.

"If you have something better, I'm open to suggestions." Even over the tightbeam connection, Eli could hear the frustration in Addy's voice. But somehow he knew it wasn't directed at him so much as the situation. He'd gotten surprisingly good at reading her. *Well, I thought I had, anyway.*

"Can't say I do," said Eli, reaching over to flip a bank of switches. Power flooded back into the transport's systems and there was the crescendo of a hum as the engines came back online. "You want me to relay this to Commander Taylor?"

"She might try to talk me out of it… and, honestly, I worry she might be right."

*Doubt? That's a new one.*

"Hey," said Eli, leaning closer to the transmitter, as though he could shrink the distance between them. "There's no easy choice here. Trust your instincts."

For a moment, the only response over the channel was dead air. "Thanks, Brody," she said finally. "I appreciate it."

"Besides, I've definitely seen way worse plans than this succeed."

A laugh escaped, quickly smothered. "I'll take that as a vote of support. Let me know when you're ready."

Eli fired up the thrusters, bringing the ship's nose around to face the station and the elevator car. The HUD overlay on the canopy isolated Addy's position, illuminating her with an onscreen blip; at this distance, she floated so close to the car as to be indistinguishable from it. He started in on the calculations: how long it would take to close with her position, how fast he could do what she'd asked. A vector guide appeared on the overlay in dashed amber lines leading towards the intercept point.

*I'm not even sure whether I should hope this works or not.* He lined up the transport's course with the elevator car and his hand hovered over the throttle. The speed would need to be precise if there were any chance that this would actually work. "In position, Two. On your mark."

"Copy that. Three... two... one... *mark.*"

Eli shoved the throttle to its two-thirds point. Any slower and he wouldn't reach his destination in time; any faster and he wouldn't be able to slow down. The ship accelerated forward, the elevator car growing larger in the canopy by the second.

Cutting the throttle to zero, Eli kept his hands on the thrusters as the ship kept coasting forward from its inertia.

He hit the controls for the front left and rear right thrusters, precisely spinning the ship on its z-axis until he'd turned one hundred eighty degrees, the transport's rear hatch now facing the elevator car. But, thanks to the momentum from the initial thrust, the ship kept moving on its same path, just backwards.

He checked the rearview display, watching the elevator car get closer, and keeping an eye on the access hatch; Addy's beacon had disappeared from view, back inside the airlock compartment.

*Here goes nothing.* It had been years since Eli had attempted a manual docking; usually he was content to let the automatic systems onboard handle it, given the precision maneuvering required, but what he was about to do was way out of its parameters.

So manual it was. Which meant he had to kill his speed at the exact right moment to line the ship up with the docking port on the elevator car. Eyes on the speed and distance displays, his hand danced over the thruster joystick; the temptation to glance over at Addy's beacon was strong, but he couldn't check on her at the same time – he trusted her to do her job, just as she was trusting him to do his.

As if summoned by his thoughts, her voice came over the speakers. "Standby Four, overriding inner airlock door… now."

Eli hit the rear thrusters, pushing the ship to a stop so that it just about lined up with the airlock port on the elevator car, leaving only a slight gap between the two – which meant no docking seal. He tapped the control for the hatch on the rear compartment, which he'd already depressurized, and the door slid open to the vacuum of space.

*The next part is no fun.* On their mission aboard the *Queen*

*Amina*, he'd been thrown off into space – in a wormhole no less! – and if the experience hadn't quite reinvigorated his fear of flying, it had at least given him a healthy respect for being *inside* a ship.

Still, it came with its own challenges. The moment Addy cracked open the inner door on the elevator car, all the air came pouring out, knocking the ship this way and that. Valiantly, Eli wrestled with the thrusters, one eye on the holo display as he tried to keep the transport's rear hatch lined up with the elevator's airlock. The superimposed guides flickered to yellow and red as the ship juddered and wavered, and an alarm flared, reminding him that he had not properly initiated the docking procedure.

*Yeah, yeah, I know!*

He was just starting to revise his opinion of this plan to 'unwise' when the first object shot from the hatch on the elevator car and into the rear compartment of the transport, bouncing around the interior as though it were at a gravball match.

"One in the pocket!" But without a clear view on Addy's beacon, he wasn't sure if she could hear him.

There were probably only another thirty seconds before the air had been entirely evacuated from the container. The real problem was that they didn't know exactly how many targets were in the elevator car, much less how close they might be to the airlock. But the car was essentially one big room, and anything they could do to even the odds in Addy's favor – including simply depressurizing it – couldn't hurt.

A second object careened into the elevator car's airlock, just visible on Eli's rear-facing camera. This one seemed to snag on the edge, gripping tightly to the inner rim of the interior airlock door, but now Eli could make out Addy's beacon as she wrestled it loose, sending it flying into the transport; he felt the muted thump through the deckplate.

"Ten seconds left on the clock, Four!" said Addy. "I think that's all we're going to get."

Already, Eli could feel the ship starting to settle down as the air evacuating from the elevator car tailed off. "Copy that. Readying for docking."

He flipped on the docking guides and gently moved the ship backward towards the open outer hatch. It still fought him slightly as the last remaining vestiges of air tried to escape. You probably weren't supposed to dock with two open airlocks if there was still air coming out of one of them, but it wasn't going to be first inadvisable decision he'd made in the last five minutes.

The hatch wobbled in the rearview display, but Eli gently tapped at the thruster controls as the ship glided backwards, until all four guides showed green and he could slap the button to engage the docking collar. With a metallic clank the seal locked into place, securing the transport to the elevator car, and Eli let out a deep breath that he hadn't even realized had been building in his lungs.

"Two, this is Four. Docking collar secure." He tapped another control and the outer hatch on the transport's rear compartment slid shut, the pumps starting to cycle air back in. The elevator car's systems should be able to re-establish atmosphere there as well, though Eli wasn't sure that they'd been designed for precisely this eventuality.

With the ship securely docked, Eli spun in his chair and got up to walk over to the hatch that led into the rear compartment, where a red spinning icon still read 'Pressurizing.' After a moment it blinked green and the door slid open.

On the floor lay two pitiful looking figures, a woman and a man, groaning and looking a bit worse for the wear, their faces gone puffy from even the brief exposure to the vacuum. There wasn't any more acknowledgment of Eli's appearance than a slight rolling of the eyes that might have just been from the pain.

"Afternoon," said Eli cheerily. "Welcome aboard. Let me just make sure you're comfortable for the flight." He produced two pairs of plasticuffs and dragged each of them over to jump seats on the opposite sides of the compartment, securing their wrists to stanchions on the wall, making sure to relieve them of their sleeves first. A quick pat down showed that whatever weapons they had been armed with had been lost somewhere along the way, but he did relieve one of them of a foldable utility knife that could have been a problem.

"Sit back and relax," he said as he headed into the cockpit. "You're not going anywhere for a while." The door slid closed behind him and he retook the pilot's seat.

"Two, we're secure over here." He peered at the rearview display and saw Addy raise a hand with a thumbs up in response.

"Roger that, Four. I'm heading in to find the explosive device." She hesitated. "We're going to lose communications when I go through that door. Brody, I just wanted to say... well, that is, I–"

Eli couldn't help but smile. Amazing how self-assured they could all be at the things they were good at and yet utter rubbish at the rest of life. "Save it, Two. We'll talk later."

"Yeah. Right. See you on the other side." Her beacon blipped out as she passed through the inner door into the elevator car and Eli was left alone in the cockpit, silent except for the hum of the transport's systems.

*And Addy? Good luck.*

# CHAPTER 46

The thud of her compatriot falling to the deck and Kovalic's simultaneous shout had Alys Costa whirling on him, her pistol held in a marksman's stance. The gaping barrel was aimed unwaveringly at Kovalic's head, poking through the floor.

Her eyes widened in recognition. "You again."

As she'd turned, Kovalic spotted what the station personnel had been trying to alert him to, and his heart sank: a piece of smart fabric wrapped around Costa's index finger – the one that wasn't resting on the pistol's trigger.

A pulse sensor.

He'd seen this before, the medtech device repurposed as a dead man's switch. If Costa's heart rate dropped below a certain level – say, were she rendered unconscious by a shot from a KO gun – then it would register on her sleeve which would, in turn, send a signal elsewhere.

In this case, presumably to the bomb in the elevator car below.

At a beckoning wave from Costa's pistol, he slowly climbed up into the room, then raised his hands again. On the opposite side of the room, Page, who had clearly heard Kovalic signal his own surrender, had innately followed his lead, earning an over-the-shoulder scowl from his former associate.

Costa shook her head. "I should have expected you'd get out of the gravtrain station before the authorities showed up."

She gestured Page over with her pistol, then picked up a pair of plasticuffs from her downed colleague and quickly manacled Page's right wrist to Kovalic's left, but not before looping it through a metal handhold on the wall.

An ideal situation it wasn't, but without knowing whether or not Sayers had been able to disarm the bomb, they didn't really have any other options. Press the advantage, and Costa might detonate manually – even if they subdued her. They needed to find a way to keep her conscious, but unable to trigger the explosion.

Costa pursed her lips and cast a glance at the ladder he'd climbed up. "I assume you're the reason Garrido hasn't come back yet."

Kovalic offered a half-hearted shrug in return.

With a shake of her head, she turned to one of the consoles: on it, a countdown clock was ticking down, text proclaiming 'Time to Communications Interconnect.' "Not that it matters. We're almost done here."

Five minutes and thirty-seven seconds. That was all the time Kovalic had to stave off a disaster that could bring the Commonwealth to its knees.

"Look," he said. Their only play at this point was to keep Costa talking, buy Sayers all the time they could. And if there was one thing he knew about someone in Costa's position it was that they *loved* a chance to prove to their opponents that they alone had the inside track. "I understand what you're doing – *why* you're doing it."

"Spare me. You'll say anything at this point to convince me to back down, and it's not happening."

"Costa, I've been part of the Commonwealth since its founding. I *do* understand. It's far from perfect. *I'm* far from perfect. I've had to live with the things that I've done, the ones that I'm not proud of, in the name of the greater good."

Spinning around, Costa jabbed at him with her index finger, the same one with the pulse sensor on it. "The greater *good*," she scoffed. "That's what they tell you. But whose good is it, really? The people at the top, all they want is to keep this war going. Forever, maybe. Because as long as it does, they have the power. And that's what they crave. Everything they've done – the things they made *me* do – those weren't for the greater good. They were all so those self-serving, corrupt bureaucrats could hold on to their power. If not for them, we could have had peace a long time ago."

Kovalic put up his hands, at least as best he could with one wrist still shackled to Page. "That's all I've been dedicating my life to for the last twenty years. Keeping the peace."

"Then you're a fool. I saw what happened when the Illyricans put peace on the table. The Commonwealth couldn't let it happen."

He risked a glance to his left, but Page's expression was bland even by Page standards – he didn't seem to have any more idea what she was talking about than Kovalic did. "What do you mean?"

"You wouldn't know, of course. The cover-up was seamless. Six years ago, right after the disappearance of the Imperium's Fifth Fleet at Sabaea, the Illyricans sent an envoy to hold backchannel talks with the Commonwealth Foreign Office. Just an exploratory meeting, nothing more. Improving relations, that sort of thing. But an early version of the AUGUR program caught wind of it – that's why CID designed it in the first place, you know, to keep an eye on the diplomats in the Foreign Office. Their own goddamned side."

A sensation pressed against the inside of Kovalic's head, like an idea waiting to burst free. "AUGUR... it's more than just a broadcast override, isn't it?"

Costa stared at him for a moment, then threw back her head and laughed, sharp and loud. "It's far, far more than that. AUGUR was designed to *intercept* communications. It started with the diplomats, but then they worked out a deal with the higher-ups at ConComm and got access to Oluo Plaza..." She waved a hand at the countdown timer behind her.

Kovalic's spine tingled, and he felt all the hairs on the back of his neck stand up. "ConComm's data hub in Salaam. That means AUGUR had a backdoor into all communication in the capital city..."

Page got there at the same time. "So, once the interconnect to Station Zero is complete, it can read the communications of *anyone* in the entire Commonwealth."

The spider in the middle of the web. No wonder Costa had been so insistent on an antiquated method like one-time pads – sometimes paranoia was just good operational security.

She tilted her head to one side. "Now you're seeing the big picture. But not just anyone in the Commonwealth – any communications traffic that passes *through* the Commonwealth."

"But all those messages are encrypted."

"True," said Costa. "But who provides the encryption service?"

"ConComm," said Page slowly, his eyes scanning rapidly

back and forth, as though he were reading from a screen. "Their algorithm is built into every sleeve and terminal. Messages are encrypted on their way to the server and from the server outbound, but in the middle, ConComm could theoretically read the contents. And if they can…"

"…then AUGUR can," finished Kovalic. They'd had it drilled into them time and time again during his service in special operations and later at the School: don't trust any message you haven't encrypted yourself. And even then, be careful how you phrase any critical information. But most people didn't bother with those kinds of precautions.

"They said all of this was to keep us 'safe'," said Costa, her voice taking on a mocking tone. "AUGUR was the perfect way to get one up on the Illyricans, keep informed about what they were up to without having to use valuable human assets. That was the line I heard, anyway."

Instinctively, Kovalic went to rub at his forehead, before being reminded that his hand was cuffed to Page's. Lakshmi must have known of, or at least suspected, AUGUR's existence – she'd dropped a big fat hint in his lap at their meeting. "But the Illyricans don't use the Commonweath's communications systems. All their important traffic is passed via diplomatic pouch." It was slower, using couriers to hand deliver messages, but far more secure.

Especially if you suspected that the other side was reading all your mail.

"The Imperium learned that lesson the hard way," said Costa. "When the CID brass learned that the diplomats were even considering normalizing relations with the Imperium, oh no, they couldn't stand for that – if the war came to an end, there goes all their precious funding, their relevance, their power base. So they arranged for the talks, which were being held in a secret neutral location, to be attacked by 'pirates'." Her fingers twitched, forming quotes around that last word.

It was the kind of conspiracy theory you might hear someone ranting about on vids circulated through the shady part of the net, but Kovalic's stomach had already begun to sink as he saw where this was going. "But *you* know the truth. Because you were there. That was Operation PYTHIA."

There was a firmness to Costa's jaw that hadn't been there a moment ago, and some degree of calm descended over her. For a moment, Kovalic could see past the paranoia and the bluster to the person who must have made such a good operative. "My Activities team was dispatched to play the part of the pirates, yes. Our orders were... discriminating. Make sure to leave some of them alive, to go back and vouch for the fact that Imperium and Commonwealth were both attacked, that it wasn't a ploy by one side or the other, but also to make sure that the key players in such an attempt wouldn't be around to try again. Plus, it didn't hurt to sow a little distrust and fear in the bargain."

Her brow darkened. "Of course, once I'd done their dirty work, they turned around and kicked me out. But they made damn sure to remind me that they had the evidence of what *I'd* done and if I ever tried to breathe a word of it to anybody, they'd have me strung up for treason. If they didn't just have me killed."

A wave of nausea rolled over Kovalic. Much as he wanted to instinctively disbelieve what Costa was saying, he'd spent too long in the shadowy parts of his own government to argue that they weren't capable of something like this. He could feel Page's gaze on him, waiting to see if he'd put up a feeble defense that would be self-delusion at best. They both knew what they themselves had done in the name of the Commonwealth, and it hadn't always been pretty.

But sabotaging peace talks... it still hit him in the solar plexus. He'd been laboring all this time to keep the war cold, to prevent more people from dying. To know that an end had been within their grasp, only to be snatched away? It burrowed into him like a tick.

He shook his head. There must have been something else at play here, some detail he'd missed. But even as he spun the idea around from every angle, he couldn't figure out what it might be. It was a betrayal, plain and simple. Not just of him, and every other person who had sworn an oath to defend the Commonwealth, but of the average citizen caught in the middle of an endless war. Because of those actions, the vicious cycle of hostility and mistrust would just continue.

Unless they could find a way to break it.

Drawing a deep breath, he locked his gaze on Costa. "Alys, you still have a choice. Do the right thing. Come forward. They want to put you on trial, you can testify to who gave the orders. They're the ones who committed treason – not you. We can bring those responsible down."

Costa stared at him as though he'd suddenly grown gills. "Are you really that naive? You think they'd let me get that far? That I'd even survive to a trial? Or, even if I did, that *anything would change*? They've gotten away with *murder*. Time and time again. And the public doesn't respond to stories in the media, or even evidence in a trial. No, the only way to convince the masses to act is through fear." She nodded to herself, quick and sharp, solidifying her rationale once again. "So fear is what they'll get."

For a moment, the only sound was the rhythmic beeping from the operations terminals. On the wall, the countdown clock continued its downward trend. A minute and a half left.

"You're going to expose it all," said Page, who had been quietly sitting by and, if Kovalic knew the man at all, processing everything that had been said. "Everything that AUGUR has ever intercepted. Every piece of communication that it's logged: government, business, personal. Show the people what their government has been up to in the name of their security."

Even cuffed to the wall, Page's explanation of Costa's plan was matter-of-fact as ever, as though he were explaining how to bake a cake. The horror was starting to dawn on Kovalic, but if Page was aghast, it wasn't puncturing that layer of armor in which he'd wrapped himself.

Costa tilted her head to one side, eyeing him like a bug under a magnifying glass on a hot day. "You're as astute as I first thought, Aaron. Not particularly loyal, but astute."

"It'll be chaos." Chaos that could very well destabilize the Commonwealth, tipping the balance of galactic power towards the Illyricans, who Kovalic was sure wouldn't hesitate to use such an opening to their advantage.

"It'll be *freedom*. Transparency. Something that the government has never been willing to offer. No. More. Secrets."

"And what do you get out of it?"

A smile spread across Costa's face, and her eyes glimmered with satisfaction. "I get to watch all of them – the people who ruined my life – *burn*."

# CHAPTER 47

Red emergency lighting doused the inside of the elevator car in blood tones as Addy entered. With the inner airlock door sealed behind her, everything was dead silent; the pumps had not yet started to replace the atmosphere that had vented into space. She toggled the flashlight attached to her helmet, the small pool of illumination following her gaze.

*Well,* this *feels like I'm in a horror vid.* She gripped the KO gun tightly in both gloved hands as she peeled her gravboot off the deck, feeling the momentary drift as momentum propelled it upwards before she pushed it back down. *No artificial gravity in here either.*

The elevator car was claustrophobic, filled to the brim with three-high stacks of shipping containers, creating a warren of paths and eight-meter high walls that she had to slowly navigate.

And somewhere in here there was a bomb.

It was too much to hope that the evacuation of air and the gravity being off signaled that the bomb had already been rendered inert. From what she remembered from the meager space-based explosives training the military had given her, the lack of oxygen would prevent the bomb from creating a massive fireball and resulting shockwave, but the shrapnel would still probably do enough damage to leave the container – and maybe the station above – in tatters.

*So I'm still on the clock.*

She crept down the narrow chasm between the two stacks of containers, reaching a T-shaped junction at the end. One direction seemed to dead-end after a few meters, hitting the outer wall of the car; the other led towards the compartment's center before splitting off into another junction.

As she walked, she looked up and down, her helmet light playing over the makeshift walls, looking for any telltale sign that one of the shipping crates had been tampered with. *It could be in literally* any *of these.* Her heart sank – how the hell was she going to find one container among hundreds?

She brought up the mission clock she'd synchronized with Page and Kovalic before they'd split up. The plan with Brody and the transport had cost her time: it had been more than fifteen minutes since they'd deployed to the station, which probably meant that the other element was waiting on her. Hopefully the decompression had removed any resistance that Costa might have left behind – they'd gotten rid of two of her people, at least, though one had required a little... nudging on Addy's part.

Quickening her pace, she clomped to the next junction, then stopped to consider the three options that diverged from there. A bead of sweat trickled down the side of her head and she unconsciously lifted a hand to wipe it away before remembering she was wearing a helmet.

*Think, Addy. Think. How do you find a bomb in a haystack?* What had Boyland always said about looking for clues? *Look for what's wrong. What's out of place. What's* not *there.* The old cop had always loved a good Zen koan.

But he was also usually right.

Addy cast her eyes around the junction, the flashlight beam rippling over the corrugated metal sides of the containers, looking for something, anything, that didn't fit. Several of them were stamped with ConComm's shaded circle logo – probably satellites due to be launched into the company's orbital network – but the bulk of what was transported by space elevator wasn't ultimately bound for the station; that was simply a convenient transfer point for docking freighters. Which meant that it was generally loaded in a logical fashion, with the freighter-bound cargo towards the outside and the local cargo nearer the center, where the docking port for the station was.

What she needed was a manifest. There ought to be a terminal in here somewhere. She picked the center-most passage, since it seemed to be the one most likely to lead towards the middle of the elevator car, near the docking port to the station. With another glance at her mission clock, endlessly counting up, she double-timed it.

A few moments later, she emerged into a wide open space amongst the maze of cargo containers. In its midst stood a large yellow-and-black industrial crane, a circular inverse repulsor the size of a small hovercar dangling from its arm. Relief surged in Addy as she caught sight of a terminal next to the base of the crane. Its screen was blank. *Probably powered down like the rest of the container.*

Addy laboriously clanked towards it, already running through her plan. There should be a manifest on the terminal, but she'd probably need to route emergency power to it first. Then she could cross-check the containers and see when they had been loaded on, working backw –

The tackle took her by surprise, a figure barreling into her mid-section with enough force to overwhelm her gravboots' lock and send her cartwheeling into the air, limbs flailing in all directions. The knockout gun flew from her grip, spinning off into the darkness above her.

She just glimpsed the space-suited figure before a blow caught the side of her helmet, ringing her head like a bell and knocking her flashlight out of commission. The room descended back into the eerie red glow of emergency lighting as Addy tumbled head-over-heels towards the top of the compartment.

*Shit!* The walls and ceilings flashed by in a blur as she spun, trying not to lose her lunch. Clearly they hadn't accounted for all of Costa's crew. Either this one had had time to get into a vacsuit before the air had been evacuated, or they'd been a lot better prepared than their buddies.

*Gotta stop spinning before I throw up in my helmet.*

Bringing the suit's reaction control system online, she fired a burst on her leg thrusters, aligning her back with the ceiling of the compartment, which gave her an unobstructed bird's-eye view of the space.

Unfortunately, by disabling her flashlight the assailant had given themselves a lot more places to hide. The dim red lighting made it hard to discern details, especially from seven meters up, and there were more than enough shadows cloaking large swaths of the room from her view. Despite being military issue, her vacsuit was still a basic model, not equipped with night vision or thermal. *Not exactly meant for covert insertions.*

Her brain rapidly sped through what she knew and came to the conclusion that though the attack might have been opportunistic, it also meant that she'd probably been close to the bomb. That made sense: it would be centrally located in the elevator car, someplace that it'd be easy to control access, with good sightlines, even in the dark.

Giving up the search for the person who'd tackled her, she checked the compartment again, looking for that sign of something out of place. She had a good view of all the crates and containers from up here, arranged in their labyrinthine pattern winding out from the center, where the crane sat below the large doors that opened into the cargo hold of Station Zero. Almost directly below it was a second matching set of doors, used to offload cargo to waiting freighters.

But nothing immediately caught her eye. Just rows and rows of cargo boxes, all of them tinged red in the light, their doors sealed tight against the vacuum.

Except one. It took a second for her brain to process what her eyes were seeing, but near the center of the compartment there was a single container with a door that was slightly ajar. Not much, but just enough that the angle stood out amongst all the other straight edges.

*Someone went in… or someone came out.* Either way, it was the best lead she had.

Of course, her assailant had the advantage here: they already knew exactly where the bomb was. Which meant she was probably walking into a trap. She craned her neck, surveying the compartment as thoroughly as she could, given the limited visibility of her helmet, but her weapon had disappeared into the shadows, and every second she spent looking for it was time she didn't have to defuse the bomb. *Priorities.*

Gritting her teeth, she used her thrusters to orient herself towards the open container she'd spotted, then flexed her legs and pushed off the ceiling as hard as she could, sending her sailing down towards it.

Just before she hit head on, she reached out and grabbed the top edge of the container, and swung her legs down to clamp the gravboots onto the outside of the open door.

Her breath, loud in the helmet, was the only sound in her ears as she slowly walked her way down the container and back to the deck. Turning her back towards the container door, she checked her surroundings, but her assailant was nowhere to be seen. *Fine. I don't have all goddamned day to wait around for you.*

She pulled the container door all the way open and peered inside. For a moment, she worried that she wouldn't be able to see anything, that the interior would be shrouded in darkness.

Turned out that was the least of her worries. At the back of the container sat a crate about the size of a small dresser; a glowing screen on the side facing her illuminated the inside of the container in a pale white light. Her relief was short-lived: splashed across its screen was merely the word 'ARMED.'

*Okay, well, at least I found the bomb. Good job, Addy. Now what?* It certainly didn't look like there was a big off switch anywhere. And the sum total of everything she'd learned about explosive ordinance disposal was 'fall back to a safe distance and call in the bomb squad.' Which wasn't exactly an option.

Or was it? Her mind was just starting to formulate a plan when some deeper part of her hind brain suddenly started screaming at her. Maybe it was a slight shadow looming over her shoulder or a vibration in the deck plates, but without a second conscious thought, she jammed the thruster controls on her suit and sent herself flying backwards, directly into the vacsuited figure that had crept up behind her.

The impact knocked both her and the assailant off their feet, and they careened back into the open compartment in a tangle of clumsy limbs. Addy writhed, trying to grapple her opponent, but with their joints insulated in suits and a helmet protecting their head, she couldn't get purchase. Her arms and legs felt clumsy in the vacsuit and the zero g, all her usual leverage and techniques useless, reducing her to scrabbling ineffectually at her opponent. Her hand-to-hand trainer would have shaken her head and tsked at the inelegance, but, well, maybe she should have emphasized how to more effectively fight in zero g.

With a thump, they smacked into another container, rebounding off the side to float in mid-air. The assailant's gloved hands pawed at Addy's helmet; in panic, she realized they were trying to pull it off. Her pulse ratcheted up as she punched them in the side, but she couldn't deliver enough force to cause any real damage.

*Shit shit shit.* She jammed down on the control for the forward thrusters and both of them shot forward until they slammed into a container. The assailant took the brunt of the impact, crumpling as they were smushed between Addy and the metal surface.

Addy's breath heaved raggedly as she fumbled with her thrusters, trying to regain stability so she could get her gravboots secured to the deck. Her assailant wasn't moving, just spinning slowly. She reached out with a hand and cautiously poked them and they drifted back towards the container, gently rotating until Addy could peer through the helmet. It was still tough to see in the dim light, but she could just make out a woman with curly red hair cut tight around her face. It seemed like she was still alive, but it was hard to tell.

Just to be on the safe side, Addy pushed her assailant against the container and reached over to trigger the woman's gravboots, locking them into place; if the woman came to, she could override them, but it would at least buy Addy a few moments, and it wasn't like she had any other way to secure her.

That done, she turned her attention back to the container with the bomb, and her heart sank anew. There was no way she was going to be able to disarm it, and Costa's crony had already eaten up precious time.

She bit her lower lip, worrying it between her teeth. *If I can't defuse it, the next best thing is to get it off the car. But how?* Moving it in zero g wouldn't be too hard, but she needed to get it away from the station, fast… and there was a risk of it exploding at any point along the way.

Her eyes scanned the room again, jumping to the inverse repulsor on the end of the crane and the hatch in the floor below it. Well, it was designed for moving cargo, so that certainly seemed like the quickest way to get it out of the elevator car.

Finding the hatch controls only took a few moments; with the power still on emergency standby, she had to use the manual override to crank it open – fortunately, easier from inside than it had been to pop the exterior airlock. Plus, with the atmosphere already vented, she didn't have to wait for the decompression cycle.

As the large port opened to space, she found herself instinctively drawing a deep breath. The mottled green and blue hemisphere of Nova came into view below her, gleaming with the reflected light of the sun. Stretching far beneath them, all the way down to the surface, was the meter-wide silver ribbon of the tether.

*Well, that's going to be a problem.* She could get the bomb out the hatch and into space, but she'd need to get it pretty far away before it wasn't a threat to the station *or* the tether. If she just pushed it, it would coast along all right from the force, but it would still take a while before it was safely out of range. What she really needed was something to push it *harder*.

The idea came to her in an instant, like a lightning bolt shattering an otherwise blue sky, and she almost belted out a laugh.

*I think I finally know how Brody feels when he gets one of those terrible plans.*

# CHAPTER 48

The timer on the holo display hit two minutes, counting down to the activation of the communications interconnect – but also, unbeknownst to anybody on the ground, the potential downfall of the Commonwealth government. Kovalic stifled a bitter laugh. Just like in a physical fight, Costa was redirecting her opponent's energy against themselves. And here he was, literally handcuffed to the wall, forced to watch it happen.

So when Page's fingers started tapping on the gantry, his first thought was that anxiety had finally cracked through the man's usually stolid veneer. But after a few moments, he realized the pattern was too regular.

More to the point, Page wasn't one to do anything idly.

Captive code. All Commonwealth military personnel were taught a non-verbal communication method, allowing them to converse surreptitiously in the eventuality that they were captured by the Illyricans – or even if they simply believed themselves under surveillance. At root, it was basically Morse code, but with a few special patterns to convey concepts that you might need in a hurry, such as the rippling of fingers that Page was doing right now, which Kovalic – assuming he wasn't too rusty – knew meant 'get ready.'

He tensed, but avoided turning his attention to Page. It seemed the lieutenant had a plan, but with no way to let Kovalic in on it, that meant he was just going to have it to play it by ear.

"…and we'll make sure that those bastards get what's coming to them," Costa was saying.

"Alys."

Her eyes turned towards Page and what elicited a shiver from Kovalic was that they weren't the wide, glassy eyes of madness, but instead cold, calculating ruthlessness. "Yes, Aaron? You have something to add?"

"I acknowledge your argument, that there is something inherently broken in the system, but is this kind of destruction really the only way to fix it? There must be an alternative." He sounded, if not quite sympathetic, then at least pragmatic in his acquiescence.

Costa wasn't convinced. She stalked towards him. "If a stray dog bites you, you don't stop to *discuss* matters with it. You take action. Swiftly, incontrovertibly." The gap between them closed, until she was almost in his face. "You should understand that."

Page ducked his head. "I do."

When he moved, it was with such suddenness that Kovalic barely had time to react. Still holding the bar to which they'd been secured, Page kicked out his legs and scissored Costa around the waist, holding her locked tight.

Kovalic scrambled towards her as best he could while still restrained by the cuffs, reaching for the hand with the pulse trigger. His fingers wrapped around her wrist, preventing her from reaching her sleeve on the opposing arm.

But that other arm was still free and she used it to punch Kovalic in the temple. His head spun, lights flashing in his vision, but he pushed through the pain, clinging to her wrist.

"Get off," she snarled, trying to wrench her hand away.

Even in his muddled state he held on as tight as he could. If she couldn't reach the sleeve, she couldn't manually detonate the bomb and if she was still alive then the dead man's switch wouldn't trigger either.

The real problem was how long they could hold on.

Over her wriggling shoulder, Kovalic could still see the display, where the interconnect timer continued counting down – just one minute and ten seconds remaining.

Time wasn't on their side. Even if they managed to hold her here, Costa could just wait them out until all that communications traffic was disseminated throughout the Commonwealth. She'd still win.

Unless they blew the station.

A leaden feeling descended into the pit of his stomach. He'd had to make hard choices before: when the Commonwealth was still at open war with the Illyricans, he'd sent soldiers to their deaths on Mars and in space. And in his intelligence career he'd done things he wasn't proud of, even to those purportedly on his side of the conflict. In the back of his mind, he'd known that someday he might end up in a situation where there was no way to accomplish an objective *and* survive.

He'd just hoped it wouldn't be today.

Over Costa's struggling, he locked eyes with Page, and he could see that the younger man had run the same calculation, come to the same conclusion. Maybe simply incapacitating her wouldn't blow the bomb – they didn't know, but they had to take a chance if they were going to stop the interconnect. If the station did explode, there would be casualties, but it might at least stop the entire Commonwealth government from collapsing, leaving the rest of the galaxy undefended from the Illyricans' opportunism.

It wasn't a choice that Kovalic wanted to have to make, but he didn't see any other options. Somewhere below, Sayers was presumably trying her best to disarm the explosive, but for all they knew, she'd been stopped by the rest of Costa's team before she'd had the chance. He hoped Brody, in the transport, might at least be beyond the radius of the explosion. Down on the surface, Tapper and Nat – the two people he was closest to in life – would mourn him, but at least they would have each other to share in their grief, and he trusted they would understand the choice he'd had to make.

He swallowed, his throat dry. "It's been an honor serving with you, Aaron."

The man ducked his head. "Major." And he used his legs to pull Costa closer, then dropped the lock and looped an arm around Costa's neck, holding her back against him as she flailed. Kovalic kept the arm with the pulse trigger immobilized, even as she strained against him, trying in vain to reach her sleeve. The struggling became more frenzied as unconsciousness approached.

As he held her arm, Kovalic awkwardly jammed his chin into the comm transmit button on his own sleeve, broadcasting over the team's channel – no point in radio silence anymore. "Two, if you're going to do something, now would be the time!"

Costa's struggling ebbed, then faded entirely as she passed out, slumping to the deck. Kovalic closed his eyes and waited for oblivion.

# CHAPTER 49

Eli's fingers drummed across the console of the transport. There was absolutely nothing for him to do but sit and wait, twiddling his thumbs and hoping that Addy would dispatch the explosive, Kovalic and Page would deal with Costa, and they could all fly back down to Nova and crack open a bottle of whisky. *Preferably expensive. And not on my tab.*

But until then, he had nothing to do but stare out at the stars, glancing up at the station floating above him, arms wrapped around himself as though they could warm him in the vacuum of space.

"– our, this is Two, do you copy? Repeat: Four, do you copy?"

He scrambled for the transmitter at the sound of Addy's voice. "Two, this is Four. Got you loud and clear. Did you accomplish objective... uh... A? One?" His brain felt like it had been shaken and stirred. "I mean, how's it going?"

"Shut up and listen, Brody. I've got the bomb, but I need your help."

"Cool. Yes. What do you need?"

"I need you to hit it with the transport."

Eli opened his mouth. "You need me to what now?"

"I can lower it out the hatch in the bottom of the elevator car, but I can't get it far enough away from the station in time."

"So you want me to hit it. With the ship that I'm in. Is this a good time to mention that it's *a bomb*?"

"I know it's a fucking bomb, Eli. Just do it."

But even before she'd started the sentence, Eli was already buckling in and bringing up the transport's engines. "I'm going, I'm going!" He yanked the disengage lever and felt the ship jostle as it disconnected the docking collar from the elevator car.

Gently, he used the thrusters to rotate the ship around so the nose was pointing towards the car's underside. Below, the silver cable of the tether stretched down towards the planet. The strand was wider here at the station than below, maybe ten centimeters across – thicker too, though that was measured in microns imperceptible to the human eye. Something to do with supporting the weight of the tether itself, he vaguely remembered from a long ago physics class.

As he maneuvered the ship beneath the car, he could see the gaping maw of the hatch and, just at the edge of it, a ping from Addy's beacon. She'd had to lean out of the hatch to use the tightbeam receiver, but as Eli watched the heads-up display, she disappeared from view again.

He reversed thrust, holding the ship steady as he waited for Addy's next move. *Is this what all* my *plans sound like?* Kind of explained why Kovalic always seemed to have a pained expression on his face. Maybe he owed the major an apology – if they managed to get out of this alive, anyway.

A container appeared at the hatch, lowering slowly through the opening, attached to a large disc on the end of a crane. The arm telescoped outwards, lowering the container until it hung ten meters or so below the edge of the elevator car. After a moment, the disc on the top disengaged and pulled up out of view, leaving the container floating right below the car.

Addy's beacon popped up at the edge of the hatch again. "All right, Four. You're up."

"Roger that. I just wanted to tell you how much I admire the sheer insanity of this idea. Just in case it literally blows up in our face."

"I learned from the best. Also you."

Eli snorted, but didn't bother to transmit that particular sentiment over the tightbeam channel as he engaged the forward thrusters. "Here goes nothing."

He locked in the container's signature on the HUD, setting his course straight for it, but kept the thrusters at minimum. If he rammed the thing with too much force, it might set the explosive off. He just needed a gentle, consistent push; inertia would do the rest of the job.

With a gentle *thud* through the ship's frame, the nose made contact with the container. Eli kept applying thrust, making minute adjustments to keep the container centered so it wouldn't bounce off to one side or another. It was a little like dribbling a soccer ball, something that he'd never been too good at as a kid. Then again, they'd never let him use a spaceship – maybe he would have fared better.

The station started to shrink in the rearview display as he pushed the container further into open space. There were plenty of satellites and debris in Nova's orbit and he tried as best as he could to steer the container onto a course that took it away from the planet. Fortunately, ship traffic into and out of Nova seemed to be low right now, so he didn't have to worry about hitting a flight path. Just had to get this clear before…

There was a crackling over the team's radio channel – not tightbeam – and with surprise he heard Kovalic's voice filter through the cockpit's speakers. "Two, if you're going to do something, now would be the time!"

*That doesn't sound good.*

With one last burst, Eli pushed the container forward then immediately fired the front thrusters; the ship slowed to a stop, then started moving backwards. The force from the forward thrusters gave the container a last little bit of push and he watched it tumble end over end into space, growing smaller by the second.

Then the cockpit viewport automatically dimmed as a brilliant flash of light emanated from the spot where the container had been just a moment ago and a brand new sparkling debris field appeared like a celebratory firework.

*No time to flip the ship.* The engines would provide more power, but the time it would take him to rotate was too long. Instead, he just hit a long sustained burst on the forward thrusters, sending him careening – still backwards – towards the station, and hopefully out of the range of any of the shrapnel from the bomb's explosion. The particles would keep moving, but the good news was that there was a lot of room in space, and most of it wasn't taken up by people, ships, or space stations. Through the plexisteel cockpit, he could already see the sparkling fading back into the blackness of space as quickly as it had come.

Eli heaved a sigh of relief and felt the tension ebb out of him, like he'd turned into a wet noodle. He toggled the comm channel for the team. "This is Four. Package neutralized. Please tell me we can go home now."

# CHAPTER 50

Kovalic rubbed at the raw spot on his wrist where the plasticuff had bit into it. Even between that and the still slightly rubbery feeling in his head where Costa had hit him, he'd had worse after a late night out.

The station hadn't exploded around them but he still hadn't been able to relax until he heard Brody's voice over the comm channel, confirming the bomb was out of play. Then he and Page had jointly been able to apply enough leverage to snap the plasticuffs off the bar through which they'd been threaded.

Relieving Costa of her pulse trigger, sleeve, and sidearm, Kovalic had used one of her other pairs of cuffs to secure her arms behind her back, propping her up – still unconscious – against the bulkhead. Page, meanwhile, had darted to the console, halting the communications interconnect with just seconds remaining on the clock and shutting down the wide-area hack that had been prepared to broadcast all of the decrypted communications.

Uncharacteristically, the man hesitated before he removed the data chip, his hands hovering over the console. "There's one thing that's still bothering me. How did Costa know that CID had deployed AUGUR up here?"

"You heard her. The operation she worked on was connected to AUGUR. Even if she wasn't in the loop, I have no doubt she was smart enough to read between the lines and figure out there was only one way CID could have gotten that intel."

The lieutenant shook his head. "That might explain why she was aware of the existence of AUGUR. Maybe she even got wind of the test site at Oluo Plaza. But expanding the project to Station Zero wasn't planned until well after Costa had been cashiered from CID."

Kovalic felt the knot in his stomach, which had started to unwind, clench again. Page was right: she'd known too much, been too far ahead of them the whole way. "Then there *is* a mole."

The lieutenant's expression was carefully neutral. "Somebody's clearly been funding Nova Front. It wouldn't be too much of a stretch to say they provided Costa with the necessary intel as well. Especially if they were in a position to know about the Commonwealth's secret projects."

Kovalic didn't have to ask exactly who Page thought that was. "You're short on proof, lieutenant."

"We could just look it up."

"Look it up?"

"If the general really is working to overthrow the Commonwealth, the evidence could be in here." He nodded at the AUGUR system, which was still finishing up its decryption of the massive volume of communications traffic. "This might be our only chance to find out for sure."

All those communications – the intelligence that could be gleaned from them. It wasn't hard to see why CID had been tempted: think of all the threats you could anticipate if you could simply look up the person planning them and read all of their mail, listen to their comm calls, see the pictures they were sending. You could save a lot of lives. Maybe even, in the long term, win the war.

But at what cost? What would you have to give up? In practical terms, it would take only one bad apple – one overreach, one person who decided to set aside morality for even a moment. Even that was overlooking the very inception of the system in the first place; it didn't matter what they *did* with it. AUGUR's very existence was a breach of the contract between the government and its people, the one that said 'this far and no further.' That they'd gotten away with building it in the first place chipped away at Kovalic's soul: he'd broken the rules on this operation, had breached that same social contract, because he'd told himself that it was for the greater good. But in truth it had been at the behest of the general's questionable motives – motives that, for this very moment, might lay open like a book before him.

He reached for the console, hand hovering over it as though he were about to draw lots. And then, with a sharp nod of his head, he plucked the data chip from its slot on the terminal. The AUGUR system whirred for a moment, a spinning wheel appearing on the screen as the decryption progress bar froze, just a small chunk from completion.

"I served with a man once, back before the SPT," said Kovalic turning the chip over in his hands. "While he was on deployment, he became convinced that his wife was fooling around with one of his buddies. So when she was out one day, he logged into her terminal and checked all her messages. And you know what he found? Nothing. Not so much as a hint of impropriety. They got divorced a year later.

"Because once you *start* looking, it's over. The damage

is done. You figure the die is cast, you've already broken trust, so it doesn't really matter whether you do it once or a thousand times. And every time you cross the line, it gets a little easier to cross. It just becomes a thing you do.

"Back on Bayern, I told you that I check the general every step of the way. So if he has misled me, the team, or the Commonwealth, then that's on me. And I'll be the one to set it right. But not like this." Kovalic held up the AUGUR chip. "Because I do believe in what we've been doing. I've broken a lot of rules in the pursuit of something larger, but everybody's got to draw the line for themselves somewhere. I'm drawing it here."

For a moment, Page said nothing. Then he gave a curt nod. "I hope you're right, major. What are you going to do with the chip?"

Kovalic's fingers tightened around it. "Costa had the right idea," he said, glancing over at where the woman lay unconscious, hands cuffed behind her back to a gantry. "Sunlight is the best disinfectant and there needs to be a reckoning for the people who did this *and* the people who allowed it to happen on their watch. She just went about it the wrong way."

Page stepped over to the terminal, where the wheel continued to spin idly, waiting to complete a job it would never finish. "Without the chip, the system's useless. But I can wipe it anyway; it'll take them time to set it up again. But the pieces will still be here, if they want to try."

"The horse is out of the barn and three pastures over by now," said Kovalic. "We can't un-invent the technology, much as we might want to. We're going to have to place some measure of trust in the people who come next not to repeat the mistakes of their predecessors."

Tapping a few commands on the terminal, Page stared thoughtfully at the display as it briefly went black and then, a moment later, scrolled through a wall of text. Stepping away from the machine, he turned to Kovalic. "Done. I've wiped and rebooted the system, though I'm sure there are backups somewhere. But that's all we can do for the moment."

Kovalic opened his mouth to respond, but before he could do so, his comm chimed in his ear and Nat's voice came through. "Simon? Are you there?"

"I'm here."

Tension ebbed from her voice. "Oh, good. We detected the explosion, but I'm glad to see the station didn't fall out of the sky. Everything all right?"

"Station Zero is secure. Sayers neutralized the bomb, and we have Alys Costa in custody."

"Copy that. You also have a platoon of Commonwealth marines en route. ETA about fifteen minutes." The warning in her voice was unspoken.

Kovalic exchanged a look with Page. "Roger that. Just tying up some loose ends. We'll see you soon."

"Looking forward to it. Ground out."

Page had moved over to a different terminal and, at a few taps, a holo display popped up, showing the incoming ships and their estimated arrival.

Kovalic spared a glance at Costa, but she was still out. Much as he'd like to press her on where she'd gotten her information, whether she knew where her funding had come from, there wasn't time to do that *and* get back to the transport before the marines arrived. Which meant that he had little choice but to let the chips fall where they may.

"Seems like this would probably be a good time for you to leave," said Page.

Kovalic hesitated. "You're not coming back." Some part of him had already known that would be the way it played out. What was left for Page back on Nova anymore?

The younger man shook his head. "I can't. I'm blown in the Commonwealth. Real or not, that was my face all over the news, branded as a domestic terrorist. I think my career in covert ops is over." He held up a hand, forestalling a protestation from Kovalic. "But it's more than that. That line you don't want to cross? I crossed it a long time ago. I know you believe in what you're doing and I hope you're right, but my trust in the general? That's not coming back. And I can't say I trust Kester either."

"So what am I supposed to tell them about you? They're going to ask, and I don't think they're going to buy it if I tell them you died *again*."

"You'll think of something, sir. You always do."

"At least come back to the transport with me. We'll get you offworld."

"It's best for both of us if we go our separate ways. Costa disabled all the security systems before we came onboard, so there's no record we were ever here. The less you know about where I'm headed, the more plausible deniability you have."

"Page, we're on a space station." Kovalic gesticulated at their surroundings. "Hard vacuum in every direction. Where the hell are you going to go?"

All he got in return was the faint hint of a smile playing about the younger man's lips. "I'll think of something too. I learned from the best." The smile faded, and once again, Page was all business. "You should get moving."

Reluctantly, Kovalic headed for the ladder, but as he

swung around and started descending, he paused, his head just above the deck. "Don't be a stranger this time, Aaron. Stay in touch. If you need anything, let me know and we'll be there. All of us."

"I appreciate it, major." He drew himself up to his full height, and issued a clean, crisp salute that could have been right off a parade ground. "Give my best to the rest of the team. Tell them I appreciate everything they've done for me. And Kovalic?"

"Yeah?"

"Check the NOMAD drop – I left you everything you need."

"Will do. Be careful out there." Kovalic's return salute was a bit more ragged; he tipped two fingers at the man, then slid down the ladder's outer rails before Page could see his eyes turning glassy. Not the first person under his command that he'd lost, but he couldn't lie: this one had punched him in the gut, knocked the wind right out of him. On Bayern, he'd made a choice to let Page go dark because he honestly didn't think that the man would find anything and, having thus satisfied his curiosity, he'd return to the fold. It had never really occurred to him that it had just been the beginning of a long goodbye.

Retracing his steps through the empty station, he found the path to the cargo bay and followed the red line on the wall until he reached the entrance. He drew himself up before entering, set his spine and rubbed his face. There'd be a place and a time to deal with Page's departure, but it wasn't here and it wasn't now. Right now, there was still work to do, starting with getting off the station.

He toggled his comm. "Two, Four, this is One. Rendezvous for exfil. Time to get off this merry-go-round."

* * *

Brody had already docked at one of the cargo bay's free ports, even as the marine ships continued their approach. With Kovalic's help, Sayers quickly offloaded their two prisoners from the rear compartment, dropping them off not far from the container into which the station's security detachment had been deposited. Between them and Costa, the marines would have plenty of sweeping up to do.

Within five minutes, they were disengaging from the station and heading home. Nat must have done some finagling to clear their presence with Naval Command, because the marines did nothing to intercept their ship as they passed within a few hundred klicks of each other. Kovalic cast a last look back at the station in the rearview display, wondering how Page was planning on making himself scarce, but if there's one thing the man had always been good at, it was disappearing.

Their return trip was probably the least eventful Kovalic had ever experienced with Brody in the pilot's chair and less than twenty minutes later they were touching back down at the same NICOM tarmac from which they'd left – hell, had it only been a few hours ago? The adrenaline had already wound down, and without the restraints to prop him up, he probably would have been a puddle on the deck. Sayers and Brody seemed about the same; the short trip back had passed in uncharacteristic silence.

When the exit ramp from the rear of the transport lowered to the ground, two familiar figures stood waiting for them.

"Can't say I'm sorry I missed this one," said Tapper, arms crossed over his chest. "You know how I hate space."

"Welcome back." Nat took them in at a glance. "Only three of you?"

"Just three," said Kovalic. "No casualties."

"I see."

"Well," said Brody, scratching his head. "I'm done in. I could use a hot shower and about twelve hours of sleep. Uh, Addy, you want to split an autocab? That is, if you're going my direction. Now-ish."

Sayers rolled her eyes, then clapped the pilot on the shoulder. "C'mon, Brody. Let's go home."

The pilot flushed and probably would have started sputtering further, but Sayers dragged him away before he could dig himself any deeper into that particular hole.

Tapper and Nat fell into step on either side of Kovalic as he headed towards the nearest outbuilding.

"He's not coming back, is he?" said Tapper, craning his neck up at the blue of the sky.

"Nope."

"Damn shame. But can't say I'm surprised, after everything he went through. You think we'll see him again?"

"I wouldn't bet against it. After all, he's already come back from the dead once. I think one more miracle makes him a saint." And if anybody could pull off another miracle, he'd be willing to bet his last credit that it would be Aaron Page.

# CHAPTER 51

The general was still in residence in his official digs at the Commonwealth Executive building the following day, a fact that Kovalic knew would rankle his boss. Even with Costa and her compatriots under arrest and Nova Front nominally defanged, the security level remained high. Kovalic had to pass three separate checkpoints before making it to the outer chamber of the general's office.

Rance looked up as he came in, brushing a lock of her chestnut hair out of her eyes. "Good morning, major. You can go right in; he's expecting you."

Usually, he'd have greeted her with a smile and some chitchat, but this morning he couldn't quite muster the energy; he saw puzzlement in Rance's face as he passed, but she quickly directed her attention back to her terminal. Probably not the first unhappy person she'd seen come through today.

The general was standing with his back to the door when Kovalic entered, looking out the third-floor window at the boxy buildings of the rest of the Executive compound while leaning heavily on his walking stick. Not nearly as spectacular a view as some of the man's myriad other offices, but at least he had a window. He looked over his shoulder, smiling, as Kovalic came in.

"Ah, Simon, come in. Can I offer you tea? Coffee? Alas, that is the extent of what passes for hospitality in this bastion of officialdom." He gestured to the seat across from his desk as he sank into the chair behind it, the creaks of old age supplanted with the faint whirring of machinery from the artificial legs that long pre-dated his association with Kovalic.

"No, thank you, sir." Kovalic stayed standing, earning his second puzzled look of the morning – and the day was young yet. He'd promised to meet Nat for lunch after his meeting; apparently her trip offworld had been… eventful.

"Quite some news this morning," said the general. "Both CID Director Özkul and Deputy Director for Intelligence Bryce handed in their resignations to the Executive upon the revelation of a secret program for spying on the communications of Commonwealth citizens."

Kovalic chewed his lip. There was a name conspicuously absent from that list, and he didn't like what it portended. "But not Deputy Director Kester?"

"From what I hear, it was Kester himself who leveraged Alys Costa's confession to demand their resignations. As they apparently devised AUGUR six years ago, at which time Kester was still a lowly desk officer, he claims to have had no knowledge of the program." The general's expression was almost impressed.

Of course, Kester would have figured out how to play this to his advantage. A sour tang flooded Kovalic's mouth. "We still suspect Kester may have been the one who supplied Costa with the information about AUGUR, not to mention Director Özkul's schedule."

The general put out his hands, palms up. "Without any evidence, I'm afraid there's little more for us to do, and

Costa certainly isn't implicating him. The consensus seems to be that she and Nova Front were operating on their own behalf, nobody else's."

And somehow Kester came out smelling like roses. At the very least, that made him an opportunist – at the worst, a traitor.

One other fact had not escaped Kovalic's attention. "I can't help but noting we're discussing resignations and not arrests. Operation PYTHIA alone was a clear act of treason against the Commonwealth."

"Ah. Yes." The general pursed his lips. "I agree, but as you prevented Alys Costa's plan from coming to fruition, the full details on both AUGUR and PYTHIA have effectively been kept under wraps. Whatever evidence there may be is still buried somewhere deep in CID's archives and the Executive is not inclined to start digging and embroil itself in a scandal – after all," and here his eyebrows raised in a significant look, "elections are coming up."

Weren't they always. Kovalic's lip twitched as he wondered how many of the same people who didn't want to dig up the embarrassing incidents of the past had been instrumental in putting those very events into motion. Costa may have taken things too far, but she'd been right about one thing: the powerful rarely faced the consequences.

"Regardless, congratulations are in order for neutralizing Nova Front *and* disabling Project AUGUR. You stopped what could have been a significant disaster for the Commonwealth."

Kovalic found his right hand clenching around the data chip he held there. "It was a team effort."

"I'm sure it was. And they performed admirably, as always." The general swiped his fingers across his desktop, glancing at them in disinterest, as if checking for dust. "I noticed your report contained no mention of Lieutenant Page."

"No, sir. We have no evidence that Aaron Page was involved at all. The message from Nova Front was established to be a fake – which CID should have known, but I believe that they found it as useful as the Front did to distract us from the real threats, namely AUGUR and the involvement of CID's own ex-operative, Alys Costa. Plenty of cover-ups to go around on this one." That might have been a little bit too on the nose, but Kovalic managed to keep a straight face.

The general's eyes glittered. "You're telling me, what, that Lieutenant Page wasn't even on Nova?"

Kovalic met his gaze evenly. "How could he be? He's been dead for nine months. There's no video footage of him connected to any of the attacks, and, as far as I'm aware, nobody has come forward with any concrete evidence of his presence at all." Costa may have disabled the security feeds on Station Zero for her own purposes, but it had proved an unintended side benefit for Page to disappear. However he'd pulled it off.

"I see." A note of disappointment had crept into the general's voice. "Very well. I will trust your judgment on this."

"I wish you'd done so all along. But I can understand why that may not have been in your best interests."

The puzzlement on the general's face had shifted gears into cold calculation. "Do enlighten me, major."

Kovalic fidgeted with the data chip, turning it over in his hand. "We've worked together for a long time, sir, and though I know you haven't chosen to share everything with me, I've always trusted that our work has been towards the mutual goal of ensuring that the conflict between the Commonwealth and the Imperium did not descend into open war. We've both experienced the horrors of that firsthand, and you convinced me that if we're ever to see our respective homeworlds free again, this was the only way. I never had reason to question that... until now." With that, he tossed the data chip onto the desk, where it slid to a stop in front of the general.

He made no move to pick up the chip, merely glancing down at it, then back up to Kovalic. "Am I supposed to know what that is?"

"That's evidence from a trusted source about the disposition of funds from secret bank accounts you've maintained on Bayern."

For the first time, something flickered in the general's eyes, as though Kovalic had punched through the veneer that the man had always maintained, that last bit of noblesse oblige that the former marquis had held tight, even with his title stripped away. There was a little bit of guilt in there and some sadness as well, but shot through with a streak of defiance. "I see. You've been checking up on me."

"As they say: trust, but verify."

"And what has your 'verification' uncovered? The existence of personal bank accounts? Very well, I admit to that. My decision to defect was not taken lightly or quickly. In the years before I left the Imperium, I had already been quietly diverting funds to Bayern to ensure that I would still have access after my departure. And to forestall your next question, no, I did not report those assets to the Commonwealth upon my defection. I wished to maintain my own resources not subject to the Commonwealth's authority, just in case our arrangement did not... pan out."

"I don't care that you kept the accounts. I care that you used them to actively fund terrorism against the Commonwealth. That all of this – everything we've *built* together – has been one long grand design in service of your beloved Imperium."

The general looked as though Kovalic had just slapped him and followed it up with a challenge to a duel. "What are you talking about? I most certainly did not. Those accounts are for personal use only."

Kovalic leaned forward, looming over the general as though he were a defendant on the stand, and jabbed a finger at the data chip. "Withdrawals from those accounts of yours were laundered through a series of other shell corporations and eventually to a courier, who handed that money directly to the Novan Liberation Front."

Shock had overtaken every other emotion in the general's eyes as he looked down at the chip and then back up at Kovalic. "That's impossible. There must be some mistake."

"No mistake, sir." Page had left all the files from his research into the general in the NOMAD dead drop as promised, and Kovalic had reviewed the evidence early into the morning, attempting to poke a hole in the story, to no avail. "They were routed through an Illyrican-registered shell corporation, Tanager Holdings, but all the transfer information is right there."

At the name of the company, all of the blood drained from the general's face. For the slightest of moments, Kovalic thought perhaps the man had suffered some sort of medical calamity rather than just being caught out in a deception.

"Oh dear," said the general softly, looking down at the chip. He raised a hand and pressed it to his mouth, before his eyes came up again to Kovalic. "I fear, Simon, that I have made a terrible mistake. I am so very sorry."

"Sorry? You're *sorry*? You sold me on all of this. Told me that we would retake our *homes*." Kovalic's vision blurred and he found himself gripping the edge of the general's desk. "You used me. I *trusted* you, and now you admit that it was all bullshit?"

A sad smile crossed the general's face, and suddenly he looked much, much older than Kovalic had ever remembered seeing him. "I admit that I have been... outplayed. Our mystery adversary, the one we theorized pulling strings behind the scenes as far back as the Bayern operation, appears to have taken advantage of a particular blindspot that I have indulged. I have been terribly naive, which is truly a horrific thing for a man of my age and position to admit to."

"What are you talking about?" The tables turned, Kovalic found himself utterly baffled by the general's words.

"Tanager Holdings, Simon."

"Yes?"

"Do you know what a tanager is?"

"Should I?"

"It's a type of bird. Closely related to the *cardinal*."

Kovalic's jaw hung open slightly as he started to assemble the same pieces that he realized the general had put together only moments before. But he barely had time to process those thoughts before he was interrupted by a commotion from outside the office.

"– can't go in," said Rance's voice, loud but muffled through the door. "He's in a meeting."

But the door slid open regardless and in strode a pale man, impeccably dressed in a fine gray suit, his hair carefully slicked and parted.

"Good morning, Adaj. Ah, Kovalic, you're here too. Saves me the trouble of having you tracked down."

"Deputy Director Kester," said the general, quickly regaining his composure with nothing more than a raised eyebrow. "This is a little forward of you. As you can see, I'm meeting with the major here at the moment, but I'll be happy to talk to you after we've concluded."

Kester straightened, brushing an invisible speck from his lapel. "It's *Acting Director*, actually; the Commonwealth Executive has just confirmed my interim appointment to head up CID in the wake of Director Özkul's resignation."

"Congratulations," said the general drily, "though I'm not sure that announcement merits storming into my office."

A sliver of irritation crossed Kester's face, but it was quickly wiped away with a broad brush of smug. "Not in and of itself, no. But as I now report directly to the Commonwealth Executive, it gave me the opportunity to broach some concerns. Especially in light of the overreach of power demonstrated by my predecessor's involvement in Project AUGUR."

"I really don't see–"

"New evidence has come to light," Kester continued, "suggesting that this attack may have been orchestrated by another party. Somebody who provided not just aid to the terrorists who carried out these horrific assaults, but also specific intelligence about the locations of these CID facilities."

"Very interesting," said the general. "I am happy to help in any way I can. Now, again, if you'll excuse me."

Kester snapped his fingers and a second man appeared at the door. His suit wasn't as chic as the acting director's, and he tugged at the collar of his shirt as he entered, clearly uncomfortable. Kovalic's heart sank at the sight, as he saw exactly how this was about to play out.

"Inspector Laurent, Commonwealth Security Bureau," said the man, in his deep voice, holding up his credentials.

"Now," said Kester, "even my current temporary dispensation to operate domestically has limits, but Inspector Laurent here has been seconded to my task force, and I think you'll find that he has all the authority needed."

But the general's eyes had turned towards Kovalic. "Simon," he said, a note of reproach entering his voice.

Kovalic just shook his head. "It wasn't me." He'd wanted to wait until his suspicions had been confirmed before involving the authorities – it was his hope that, upon confronting him, the general would admit to any involvement with Nova Front and turn himself in. If nothing else, it would have given him a chance to get some direct answers before the official questioning took over. Who exactly was CARDINAL? What was the general's connection with the LOOKING GLASS project Page had mentioned? How much damage had Kovalic done just by following the man's orders?

Either way, everything they'd accomplished together would still be put under the harshest of microscopes, but perhaps the ill effects could have been mitigated by the general's confession.

But not like this.

Kester seemed, if anything, bemused at the exchange. "Don't worry too much, Adaj. Major Kovalic has his own problems to see to."

Kovalic looked up sharply. "What?"

Laurent cleared his throat, seemingly wishing he were anywhere but here, and gave a reluctant but dutiful grimace. "Hasan al-Adaj. Simon Kovalic. I'm arresting you both for suspicion of treason against the Commonwealth of Independent Systems."

For the second time in as many minutes, Kovalic's mouth dropped open in shock; he saw the same expression mirrored on the general's face. The ground seemed to shift under his feet, and he found himself sitting down hard on the edge of the general's desk.

"You'll remain under detention in this office for the moment," said Laurent, "pending your transfer to a prison facility to await trial."

The general cleared his throat. "I see. If I may say one thing?"

Laurent glanced back at Kester, who smiled, pleased with himself. "The inspector will advise you to wait for your attorney, but if you wish to confess, by all means."

Leaning back in his chair, the general folded his hands on his stomach and, in that moment, Kovalic could see the steel re-emerge as the mantle of aristocracy draped around the Marquis al-Adaj once again. "ESCHATON."

Kester blinked and looked at Laurent, who seemed just as puzzled.

Kovalic's stomach hit free fall, but the general had pointedly avoided looking at him, leaving the choice in his hands: to trust the man that he'd spent the last six years following or to sever their connection at this very moment and leave him – both of them, perhaps – high and dry. The latter was tempting, given everything he'd just learned, but one thought pierced through the anger and frustration: with a word, the general had reminded him that this wasn't just about the two of them. The rest of his team was still out there and, if their predicament was any indication, probably in imminent danger from Kester and his machinations.

"Right," said Kester, barreling through the perplexing statement. "Now, Inspector–"

"ESCHATON," Kovalic echoed.

Both the acting director and policeman gave him a baffled look, which quickly morphed into one of horror as Kovalic's sleeve gave a strangled electronic wail, then went dark. It was followed by a similar sound from the terminal on the general's desk, a plume of smoke curling up from it as its insides turned to slag.

Kester closed the distance to Kovalic and grabbed his shirt front, attempting to haul him forward before realizing that he didn't quite have the balance and strength to do so, leaving him standing on tip toes in Kovalic's face. "What the hell did you just do, major?"

Kovalic grinned. "Don't worry, Kester. This will be far from your last disappointment." Hopefully, the message would reach the rest of the Special Projects Team before Kester's goons rolled them up too. And as long as they were still free, then Kovalic, the general, and the Commonwealth still had a fighting chance.

# ACKNOWLEDGMENTS

It's been a heck of a couple years. I started writing this book in May 2020, just a couple weeks after *The Aleph Extraction* came out, and only two months into what has turned into a two-year-and-counting global pandemic. It's the first book I wrote almost entirely in the confines of my own home rather than out gallivanting in local coffee shops, which will never not be weird.

As ever, an undertaking like a novel isn't a solo work, and I've benefitted immensely from the help of a plethora of truly fantastic individuals, all of whom I will now try to name without omission.

Thanks to all the folks at Angry Robot who continue to invest in this series, including Eleanor Teasdale, Gemma Creffield, and Ailsa Stuart. Special thanks to my editor, Simon Spanton, for his keen insights and enthusiasm, and copyeditor, Rob Lowry, for making sure I got all the commas in the right places. And Tom Shone knocked it out of the park with the cover design.

My most heartfelt appreciation to my agent Joshua Bilmes, who is forthright in his insistence that he will read anything with Eli Brody and Simon Kovalic in it, as well as the rest of Team JABberwocky.

Every author has their tried-and-true stable of beta readers, and I'm no exception: Antony Johnston, Jason Snell, and Brian Lyngaas all read and offered their advice on early versions of this. Gene Gordon provided much needed scientific consultation, though as ever, any errors are mine and mine alone (probably because I didn't listen to him!).

I've always relied on the support of several online communities, but they've become even more valuable over the last few years. Whenever I felt like I was stumbling, I always knew I could turn to my friends for perspective or a (virtual) hug. So big thanks to the folks at Relay FM, The Incomparable, and the Fancy Cats. A special shout-out to my writerly pals Adam Rakunas and Eric Scott Fischl, who can always be counted upon to put up with my griping, especially about creative endeavors. Stay fresh, cheesebags.

Deepest love to my parents, Harold Moren and Sally Beecher, whose support is unending and whom I only wish I could have seen more frequently in the last couple years, as well as the whole Beecher/Kane/Moren clan, who are simply The Best™.

Finally, this all would have been utterly, totally impossible without the help and steadfast support of my wife, Kat. Not only did she read an early version of this book and provide an unflinching and much needed critique, but she's perpetually my biggest fan and champion. Embarrassing as it is for a writer to say, there aren't words enough for me to express how much I appreciate her for everything she does (and you all don't know the half of it). Love you.

# ABOUT THE AUTHOR

DAN MOREN is the author of the Galactic Cold War series of novels, as well as a freelance writer and prolific podcaster. A former senior editor at *Macworld*, his work has also appeared in the *Boston Globe*, *Popular Science*, *Fast Company*, and many others. He co-hosts tech podcasts Clockwise and The Rebound, writes and hosts nerdy quiz show Inconceivable!, and is a regular panelist on the award-winning podcast The Incomparable. Dan lives with his wife in Somerville, Massachusetts, where he is never far from a set of polyhedral dice.

ANGRY ROBOT

We are Angry Robot

angryrobotbooks.com

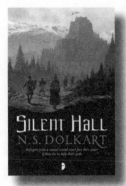
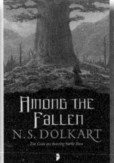

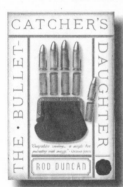